Praise for K

"The story is an unvarnished chronicle of a young woman doing what
she must to protect herself and her daughter."

—Historical Novel Society

"*Gerta*'s main strength is its lyrical language, translated exquisitely from
the original Czech into English by Véronique Firkusny. The nimble
text elevates the narrative and evokes deep emotions, while succinct
descriptions capture Gerta's—and her country's—pitiable condition."

—Washington Independent Review of Books

"Tučková has tackled one [of] the most difficult chapters in European
history, one that has been influencing the relationship between two
nations for decades. It's a tale of prejudice, of exclusion and collective
shame. *Gerta* is both a disturbing novel and a wonderful piece of
literature that could easily become a classic."

—*The Constant Reader*

"I think [*Gerta*] is beautiful and relevant. One of its basic themes is the expulsion of the German population from Czechoslovakia after the Second World War, but as a whole the novel carries a much broader theme that seems crucial to me today—that the mutual problems between people and nations will not be solved simply by an acknowledgment, and not even by an apology. An apology is just the beginning. We can admit our own guilt, take it on ourselves, but an even more difficult and important step, which is not spoken of so much and for which there are no laws or entitlements, is forgiveness—whether toward others or toward ourselves. For me, *Gerta* is a book about forgiveness."

—Alice Nellis, director of the Czech TV adaptation of
Gerta (English translation by Véronique Firkusny)

"A great book . . . Immediately after reading, [*Gerta*] is unforgettable . . . Although she certainly did not plan for it, Kateřina Tučková wrote a novel that should be required reading."

—Jan Hübsch, *Lidovky*

"The central story of Gerta Schnirch can be captured in one word, the clichéd adjective *strong*. Its strength lies particularly in its vivid depiction of frightful experiences immediately after World War II, experiences resembling terrible nightmares. To achieve this, the author does not need cheap effects or explicit, detailed, or shocking descriptions."

—Petr Hrtánek, iLiteratura

"The author describes, with a great writing talent and empathy for human suffering, Gerta's life from the moment she stood at her mother's grave in 1942 . . . We have read of various anabases, but few are as dreadful as the one depicted with deep pity by Kateřina Tučková. And so forcefully described as if she were Gerta, experiencing it all firsthand."

—Milena Nyklová, *Knižní novinky*

"[*Gerta*] masterfully fulfills one of the potential and important functions of literature. It is a means of self-reflection for a particular community, which is the Czech nation in this case."

—Pavel Janoušek, *Host*

THE
LAST
GODDESS

ALSO BY KATEŘINA TUČKOVÁ

Gerta

THE LAST GODDESS

A Novel

KATEŘINA TUČKOVÁ

TRANSLATED BY ANDREW OAKLAND

AMAZON **CROSSING**

Text copyright © 2012 by Kateřina Tučková
Translation copyright © 2022 by Andrew Oakland

Previously published as *Žitkovské bohyně* by © Host — vydavatelství, s.r.o. in the Czech Republic in 2012. Translated from Czech by Andrew Oakland. First published in English by Amazon Crossing in 2022.

Published by Amazon Crossing, Seattle

www.apub.com

Amazon, the Amazon logo, and Amazon Crossing are trademarks of Amazon.com, Inc., or its affiliates.

ISBN-13: 9781542036382 (hardcover)
ISBN-10: 1542036380 (hardcover)

ISBN-13: 9781542036375 (paperback)
ISBN-10: 1542036372 (paperback)

Cover design by Kimberly Glyder

Printed in the United States of America

First edition

THE
LAST
GODDESS

*I*t's not easy to see inside. Dora gets up on tiptoes and rests her nose against the glass. Now she can see beyond the curtain that hangs from the middle of the window. Among the lush heads of the geraniums that at other times nod into the open and today are inexplicably imprisoned behind the panes, it is dark. But it's almost always dark in there. Only on bright days does the light get through the little windows.

She turns to get a view of the path that leads up to their cottage. Surmena just about manages to shuffle along; she's struggled with her legs for many years, and Jakoubek makes it even harder for her. Dora knows how heavy he is because she can barely carry him herself anymore.

She turns back to the window. It seems to her that she can see legs. From behind the oven, some legs are peeping out, just from the knees down. She is sure those are feet, shod in black boots that are high and heavy.

"I can see legs! Daddy's home!" Dora shouts back to Surmena. "I told you he'd be home!"

"Wait. Move out of the way."

At last Surmena has caught up with her, and she pushes Dora aside without first putting Jakoubek down. Shielding her eyes with her hand, Surmena presses her face against the highest pane.

"So he is. The scoundrel." She straightens up, pitches Jakoubek into the crook of her elbow, and says, "Come on, then." As Surmena turns away, the girl hears her mutter, "He won't want to cross me, the drunk."

Dora strides along the crude-plastered walls in the wake of Surmena's skirts. Her feet squelch in the slushy ground. She tries to hop into Surmena's footprints, but she can't make the distance between them. The gate creaks open, and she, too, darts through it. Without closing it behind her, she runs past Surmena to the front door. The broad satchel on her back rocks, and above it, two small brushlike braids—each held now in only a single ribbon—bob up and down. She stops before the threshold and, with wide-open eyes and mouth, turns back to Surmena. There is a chopping block next to the door, but the ax that usually sticks out of it is missing. The bloated bodies of the cat and her kittens must have been lying there for several hours.

"It's Mitzi," Dora says in surprise. "Our Mitzi. And her kittens. She didn't even have time to show them to us!"

The cat's body has swelled into the shape of a balloon, and the bloody gash on its neck is teeming with flies. Dora could fit the kittens' bodies in the palm of her hand. Tiny and bloated to roundness; if she tipped her hand, they'd fall out and roll down the hill, all the way to Hrozenkov.

Surmena is choking with rage. "That drunk! That rotter! He'll pay for this!" She takes the girl roughly by the shoulder, turns her away from the bloody scene, and pushes her toward the door, inside, into the small entrance hall.

"Wipe your shoes so that you don't make a mess," Surmena tells her crossly. But there is no need: Dora is standing where she should, scuffing her feet slowly across the mat. She turns to catch another glimpse of Mitzi.

"Look away; it'll give you nightmares!" Surmena commands, and Dora darts through the hall. At the door to the room, she crashes into Surmena. The never-ending split second of her last small step sends her between Surmena's flank and the doorframe and ends with her gaze fixed to the wooden floor. Lying next to Dad's legs is Mum, with her skirt rolled up over her thighs and around her—all around her—a pool of dark, dried blood. Silence. And the three of them in the doorway like statues.

"Out! Out!" Surmena's high voice goes through Dora like a sharp knife, yanks her up, and dashes her head against the doorjamb. She runs out, staggers; it's a wonder she doesn't fall. Behind her she hears Jakoubek's terrified wails and Surmena's screams that have stuck on a single word: "Out! Out!" And she runs, past Mitzi and her kittens, along the picket fence, through the gate, past the cottages, down a path waterlogged with summer rain, on and on. To Surmena's. Where she stops, opens and closes the gate in a well-mannered way, and slowly approaches the bench on the mound, as she always does. Dora sits down, fixes her gaze on the hill opposite, and waits. She sees Surmena, hobbling down the path she has just taken, bent under Jakoubek's weight but moving fast, faster than she has ever seen her. Then she can hear her brother's wails and Surmena's rasping breath.

Surmena lands awkwardly on the bench. With one hand on Jakoubek's head and the other on Dora's shoulder, she comforts them.

"It's all right; it's all right," she says.

Dora doesn't believe her.

By now the sun has gone down, and dark is stealing over the mountains. They sit on the bench, and Jakoubek's crying slowly quiets, now and then bubbling up in a small, torn sob. After a while all Dora can hear is his regular breathing and the rattle of his snot. Surmena's breathing is calm now, but the arm that embraces Dora's shoulders—which are still girded by the straps of her satchel—is trembling. On these shoulder straps are the big red reflectors she wanted. Flat pieces of plastic that reflect the light when it shines on them, just like the kids down in Hrozenkov have. She and her mum went all the way to Uherský Brod to get the bag. That was last summer.

On the slope opposite, it is dark already above their cottage. Night has come from behind the hill in a slow, unstoppable stream, as though someone in Bojkovice poured it out.

"You'll stay with me," Surmena says then.

And soon she is on top of the kitchen range, and Surmena is wrapping her in blankets and tanned sheepskins, in a warmth that is all around her, the steamed poppy seeds she has eaten deep inside her tummy. Dora hears her say, "There's nothing to be afraid of. Together we can manage. You'll be my *andzjel*. And you'll be fine. You'll see."

Part I

Surmena

For a long time, Dora thought that all their troubles began with that event—as they stood on the threshold of the Koprvazy cottage, staring at the bodies of her parents. But it wasn't the case at all. Dora was not so stupid that she failed to read in the excited faces of the villagers that it had begun long, long ago, further back than her short memory could reach. She was not taken in by their doleful expressions and the words they spoke: "What a terrible misfortune!" or "Why should this happen to you, of all people?"

She was not fooled because she was part of the whole; she felt and breathed with them. Try as they might to spare her, what they whispered behind her back reached her ears in no time. "It fits together perfectly," they said. "It had to happen like this. And if not like this, then a little differently, but just as unhappily." Because her mother, too, was a goddess, and no goddess's lot is an easy one.

But once Dora overheard that in more than three hundred years, no one who knew the secret of goddessing had ever been put to the ax, she understood that this went beyond all known limits.

So why my mother? she asked herself over and over again. She never got an answer. No one wanted to speak of it. Whenever she broached the subject, they turned away in horror as though she had blasphemed at the place of some holy relic. Surmena, too, was silent on the matter.

A few months later, she came to a conclusion: she had no choice but to pack the incident down somewhere deep inside. She slammed the door shut and determined never, ever to reopen it. No matter when it might have started, no matter how it ended up.

Besides, she had a lot to do. She had to learn to be an angel, and her grief was slowly, gradually washed away in a flood of new and exciting events. She was an andzjel!

Before that she had only heard about them. Good angels who led the needy to the goddesses and did quite well out of it. But she had never met one, even though many times she had lingered on the hillsides, where she could see the approach to Surmena's, to Irma's, and to Kateřina Hodulíková's.

"Show me your andzjel, Auntie. Who's your andzjel?" she would want to know whenever her mother took them that way.

Surmena would give the impression she had never heard of any angels, and her mother, Irena, would laugh and say, "I'm a goddess, too, you know, but have you ever seen one anywhere near me?"

But her mother was a different kind of goddess, an unusual one. She didn't do much goddessing. So the angels never brought anyone to her.

And then the secret burst, all by itself. It opened up like an overripe pod and discharged all its contents at once. She did more than find out who the goddesses' angels were—she became one herself.

Her world changed from the bottom up. Gone were the long afternoons, each the same as any other; hours of boredom in which life's blurred contours bled into one another were a thing of the past. From the moment she became an angel, never again did she sit listlessly on the bench in front of the remote mountain cottage. Her time became a part of the time of many people, and her role among them was an important one. She performed it with pride, mindful of her responsibility to a mysterious tradition that came from a past so distant that no one from Žítková or Kopanice knew how far back it went. Everyone just nodded respectfully. "Goddessing is ancient. Goddesses and andzjelé have been here from time immemorial."

From time immemorial, it was always so. Dora knew this very well, but what she didn't know until she became an angel was that goddesses and their art were a rarity. They weren't found anywhere else. When she was small, she had thought that being a goddess was an existence like any other; she thought that women divided themselves into aunties who worked at the post office or the co-op store, milkmaids and feeders at the farmers' cooperative, and those who made their living as goddesses. To her, a goddess was as natural an occupation as any other. It never crossed her mind that perhaps this wasn't the case elsewhere.

Only once she was an angel and realized the great distances people traveled for advice or a cure from a goddess did she understand that these women were unique. This made her keener still; she stuck closely to all that Surmena urged her to do in her role as an angel.

"When the bus arrives, always be standing close to the stop. Attract no one's attention, and just wait until someone addresses you. If they ask the way to a goddess, ask them if they're so foolish that they believe in goddesses. Wait until you hear their answer. If they're embarrassed, bring them. If they're too sure of themselves, better make yourself scarce: no good will come of them. And watch out for couples. Remember that people often come here with troubles they face alone and that need no witnesses."

All this Surmena would repeat often, and Dora always kept it in mind. She looked on carefully as the afternoon buses from Brod disgorged their passengers. If she saw an embarrassed stranger looking this way and that, she would cross their path and wait for their question: "Do you know where the goddesses live, young lady?"

The people were many kinds of ordinary and odd, but practically all of them looked forlorn and worried. From time to time came the couples Surmena had warned her about. Commonly a man and a woman, both young and healthy and looking not at all as though they had much to worry about. By appearances, Dora never would have said they needed the help of a goddess. There is a particular couple she still remembers today, one she encountered in the early days of her angelling.

This pair hung around the stop long after the bus had left, as strangers did who had made up their minds to seek out a goddess but didn't know how to find one. Dora took a good look at them. The woman was dressed for the outdoors, which, on a working day, set her apart. Her male companion passed comments to her from the side of his mouth; whenever he did this, she would jerk her shoulders straight. The man was wearing a hat and a long coat and behaved as though he had nothing to do with the woman. To Dora, they looked suspicious, and she was about to turn and leave, but then she saw the man give a nod of instruction to the woman; the woman approached her.

"Do you know where the goddesses live, young lady?" asked the woman in an oily tone.

For a few moments, Dora stood there in silence. Then she gave a hesitant nod and pointed to the top of the Kykula hill.

"Right up there, in the woods. Follow the blue signs and you'll come to a wayside cross. From there, you'll see a solitary cottage. That's where the goddess lives."

The woman offered eager thanks before reaching into her pocket for a crown coin, which she pressed into Dora's hand. Then she turned briskly and headed off in the direction Dora had indicated. The man trailed several yards behind. Dora watched them disappear around a bend in the path that led to the foothills of the Carpathian wilderness.

She still wonders today if the couple spent the night in the middle of woods so deep that nothing got through them but a blue-signed path, which led to a wayside cross and then lost itself. Perhaps they managed to get back to the village. In any case, the last bus to Brod left at a quarter past four, and there was no way they could have caught that.

But not all strangers were so suspicious. Quite the contrary—most were people who truly needed what Surmena knew. In time, Dora learned to recognize them at first sight. A glum-looking elderly lady with a bag was a certainty; she came because of the children, mostly. A young woman loitering in embarrassment around the timetable board was another sure thing—she'd come to hear about love. Then there were the people who looked sick. Dora was happy to lead these to Surmena because she knew she would help them and put a special light in their expression—the light of hope.

Dora would be at the bus stop, and they would ask her to lead them to a goddess. She would take them by the hand and guide them uphill, past the cemetery, over the Černá pasture, through the woods to the parting of the ways, from where they could see Surmena's cottage on the Bedová. And all the while, she was angelling as Surmena had taught her, asking searching questions while giving the impression that she was making light conversation.

"Did you have a long journey?"

"Aren't you tired after your journey? Surmena will make you some plantain tea. How good it'll make you feel."

"Why so sad? Is there something bothering you? Your body or your spirit?"

She lost count of the number of times she and Surmena had practiced this—a system of clever questions, their dispersion in time, and the seeming carelessness with which they were posed. Then it was as though Dora was chatting to them all by herself, all the way, right to the top of the Žítková pastures. And the higher they climbed, the more intimate and open the conversation became; their long-repressed worries issued forth, sometimes slowly, sometimes in a rush, but with the consciousness that relief was imminent, that they were about to set down the boulder of their tribulations at the threshold of a cottage, at the feet of a woman who, it was said, could help, whatever the trouble. On that climb, they would reveal to Dora—a child unknown and strange to them who would disappear from their lives a few moments later—what troubled them, and at the end of the way, where the path forked in the direction of two of the pastures of Kopanice, Koprvazy and Bedová, and where they said their goodbyes, Dora knew all there was to know about them and was ready to tell it to Surmena. After that it was a ten-minute dash through the woods to Surmena's cottage, which she would reach by the back way before the visitor, who was sent on a winding path across the meadow.

"Come on in!" Surmena would be welcoming the visitor before they could open the gate in the fence. "Come on in. There's nothing to fear. I can help you, whatever the trouble is. Your aching back or all that bother with the lost money. You're quite a scatterbrain, aren't you? But never mind—perhaps you've seen the worst of it. So come on in! You and me, we'll figure out how to put it right."

Every last visitor was overcome by a religious awe for this woman: as soon as she saw them, she was able to read all their troubles without their having to speak them. Meekly, they would enter the dark room where time had stopped in the middle of the previous century, where Surmena would hastily set things up: a pot on the range to melt the wax, a bowl of cold water on the table.

"This is what helps them most," she would say with a kindly chuckle, after a visitor had gone, when Dora asked if they were cheating people.

"If they've decided to come all the way out here, to see some old woman they don't even know, having believed some old wives' tale, then by now, they must be in a right pickle. Maybe I'm their last hope. When they come here, they're full of fear and doubt, but it's the hope that leads them on. And for your information, it's more often people whose difficulties are of the spirit, not of the body. They can be better helped if we don't bother them with needless questions about whether or not I'm able to help them . . . Can you imagine how relieved they must feel when they realize even before they're through the door that I have special powers? And what we spare ourselves with those who are wary of spilling the beans about the trouble they're in? They say that faith is a healer. They have faith that I will help them, and so it comes true. Do you understand now? It's not cheating; it's cleverness, and it helps them."

Dora accepted this without further questions, just as she accepted Surmena's command: "But you must never speak of this to anyone. You must never tell anyone but me what people say to you on the way here, even that they speak to you at all. It's a secret that must stay between the two of us. Do you understand?"

Dora nodded.

"If word of it got out, the help wouldn't work anymore, you see. Understood?"

Dora nodded again.

"Most important of all, you must forget as quickly as you can everything the people tell you. Do this for your own good. Otherwise, what bothers them will start to bother you. Do you promise?"

Dora promised because at that time, she would not have refused Surmena a single thing.

Surmena took them in when she was eight and Jakoubek four. Dora is sure she never considered any other way of doing things. In those days Surmena was not so old that she couldn't manage them, and her heart was too broad for her to behave otherwise. Besides, she didn't have children of her own, and Dora sometimes thought that in the end, they came to her as a blessing. Certainly it would have been worse for her to face old age alone.

In 1966, when they came to her, she was well over fifty. But already something about her made her an old woman. Perhaps it was the hair rolled up in a scarf, which she wore even though she had never been married, or the network of fine wrinkles that crisscrossed her cheeks in improbable, singular routes, or her bearing, as if the body was trying to hide within itself. She walked with her shoulders hunched and her chest hollow—you couldn't even really call it walking; it was more a kind of sparrow's scamper, where the leg buckled slightly at every step, making it look like a skip. She said this was a memento of the war. Forced to run and hide in the woods, she'd had a fall so bad that she was beyond even her own help. "A healer known far and wide, and she limps," people would say afterward. But how could she give her own dislocated joint a violent tug and a sharp twist, thus setting it back in its right place? She had done what she could, allowed the other women to help her, made a splint for the leg out of branches, and waited. Six days in the woods until the front moved on.

Later, Dora several times witnessed Surmena performing a similar operation. She would stand astride the injured person and bend forward to grasp their thigh or calf, depending on which joint was dislocated, all the time clenching the patient's ankle in her armpit. With all her strength, Surmena would throw, yank, and turn the leg while the person screamed so that Dora thought he or she was dying. Then silence. The joint was back in place, and the pain was gone. When Dora asked Surmena where she had learned this, Surmena made a strange face at the memory. Apparently, it was the only thing she hadn't learned from her mother, the goddess Justýna Ruchárka. She had learned it thanks to the gravedigger at Hrozenkov, who was in direct contact with people. Dead people. Of all the goddesses at Žítková, he had chosen her because she lived alone, but for her younger sister, Irena. So one evening he brought the crates to Surmena there, at her home. She said she heard in the distance the rattle of bones in the three wooden crates piled on the cart; he was coming straight from the cemetery, to set them down right there in the front room. He had an idea that she might learn how each of the bones fit together. He wouldn't be dissuaded: the county needed it. Now more than ever, with a war on the horizon. At first Surmena was horrified. For three days the three crates stood in her room. Closed, just as the gravedigger had set them down. She and Irena slept in the attic so as not to be in the same room with them. But the gravedigger came every evening to see how Surmena was getting on. On the third day he ran out of patience, prized off the lids, handled the bones—which were blanched and spotted with soil—and proceeded to arrange them. Surmena said she thought she would faint at first. But she couldn't hold herself back. She relieved the bumbling gravedigger by taking the bones from his hands and set about the assembly work herself, drawing on what she already knew of the human body. She rooted around in the crates for as long as it took, with no thought of tiredness, testing the fit of one bone against another until the work was done. She said that the three beaux who appeared in the front room were the very three for whose sake she had never married. Thanks to them, her fame spread further, and people came to her from the Moravian and the Slovakian side, even after it got around that she had a crooked leg and would never again stand straight.

In Dora's memory she was always hobbling and huddled. But her character was untouched—she was hard and uncompromising with herself and performed all physical tasks without demur, even when her deficiencies proved an impediment. And this was how she treated others, too, including them, the children.

Today Dora was grateful to Surmena for this loving lack of consideration, for showing her no pity, for allowing her no respite from the catastrophe. Surmena behaved as though nothing had happened; the very next day, she pressed her to work and go to school. But those first afternoons, she and Jakoubek collected Dora from school and led her up to the Bedová; it was as if she knew that inquisitive onlookers would gather around her in a fan, shout bold questions at her, and worse still, pity her. This was the only concession Surmena made in the hard weeks following the event that changed Dora's life so abruptly and dramatically.

Dora Idesová

$\mathcal{D}$ora was at lunch with her colleague Lenka Pavlíková.

"Listen," said Lenka. "That Surmena of yours. Have you ever looked for her on the lists?"

Dora shook her head. She didn't see why she should. Lists of servants of the regime had been in circulation for some time. It had been nine years since the revolution of 1989. Why would she take an interest in them now?

"I don't see what it could have to do with your research. But I've noticed her name there. Just the name. A few lines below my uncle's—I couldn't miss it. I thought you might like to know."

Dora realized her heart was pounding. Surmena on the lists? Why, for God's sake?

She climbed the two floors back to her office as if in a daze.

Till then she thought she'd searched through everything, that not a single source had escaped her, that in all the years she'd devoted to discovering the truth about what happened to Surmena and, ultimately, the other goddesses, she'd left no stone unturned.

And the effort it had cost her! The dozens of hours spent in the research rooms of dusty archives. Mile after mile trudging the tracks of the White Carpathians, weighed down by a rucksack containing gifts for contemporary witnesses, plus a heavy tape recorder and long-corded microphone that they refused to speak into. She'd spent months—years—gathering all that now surrounded her, carefully cataloguing, photographing, backing up, compiling, and labeling the folders and thick ring binders in the shelves that lined the walls of her office. Every day she came to it with awe, as if to a shrine. Until a few moments ago, she'd thought that those steel shelves stored everything she could possibly find out about it.

But perhaps she'd been wrong.

Dora paced the narrow space of her study. The new information refused to sink in. Lenka couldn't have looked properly. Surely she was mistaken. How could Surmena have been on the lists? She sat down at her computer and went to the website of the municipal library, where she ordered a copy of the Cibulka list of agents and collaborators of the secret police. On her way home from work that evening, she would stop off at the library and check it.

Until then she had several hours to get through, and their slow passage would torture her. For a while she tried to get on with what she'd been doing that morning, to complete the work she'd set for herself, but her efforts were in vain. She couldn't concentrate, and she made mistakes. In the end she realized she was sitting at her desk with her hands in her lap, her gaze wandering from the computer screen to the books and folders on the shelves; she was doing nothing productive. This would be a wasted day. With a sigh, she reached for a book whose spine her gaze had failed to register moments earlier. It was a hardback volume bound in black cloth that bore the gold-embossed title *The Goddesses of Žítková*. And below the title, her own name. The first product of years of effort, her dissertation. She wanted something to remain of the goddesses.

Today Dora had reservations about its content. Yet it was this very work she had to thank for her job here, the shadowy corridors and cramped offices of the Institute of Ethnography and Folklore of the Academy of Sciences, a job she had held since the late 1980s. It was thanks to her dissertation that her application to stay in Brno, and thus close to Jakoubek, had been accepted; otherwise, she'd have been given a job in a regional museum somewhere. And she'd been allowed to stay on here after the revolution, when the institute was shaken to its foundations, perhaps because her research was uncontroversial and her character so unforceful that in the shallow waters of Czech ethnology, she would never be a threat to her seniors, past or present. In terms of numbers of articles, conference papers, and citations, her output was just about right. As for career advancement, she was entirely without ambition. She was consumed by her own affairs, which had little bearing on topics popular with predatory types. She stood exactly where others wished her to stand—beyond the field of battle. Closed up in her office, an environment unchanged for years, she worked on what was hers. Writing another work that would complete what she had started with her dissertation.

But now all that was at an end. She could go no further until she knew what was hidden in the archives of the Ministry of the Interior, where information was kept on those who had collaborated with the State Security Police. Snitches, informers, spies.

That evening she found Surmena's name on the Cibulka list. Her head swimming, she closed the book and sat still until she was able to carry herself to the exit. This unreal, impossible finding paralyzed her. That night she fell asleep just before dawn.

The next day she applied to the Ministry for the opening of a lustration procedure on behalf of Terézie Surmenová (1910–1979) of the Bedová hill, house no. 28, Žítková village, Uherské Hradiště County. The application was preceded by several phone calls. It was sealed with official confirmation from the registry of the local authority in Žítková that Dora and Surmena were related.

Several days later Dora contacted the Ministry to ask whether her application and documents had been accepted. "You will receive our statement within three months," came the answer.

There was nothing she could do but wait. Patiently, day after day, week after week—for three whole months.

While she was waiting, she reviewed the material she had gathered over the years and checked her results and conclusions. In her mind she mapped streams of events touching on the lives of the goddesses, from their sources in the distant past until they washed up at the feet of many people she had known. And she exercised an ability to remember as if she herself were party to events. She closed her eyes, freed herself of her surroundings, and found herself in goddess country, in Žítková, in the cottage with Jakoubek or Surmena. It was perhaps thanks only to these thoughts, which came whenever she summoned them, that she had survived the long years of forced separation from Jakoubek and Surmena—each of them in a different part of Moravia, each of them alone. In the hostel in Uherské Hradiště and then in Brno, these thoughts kept her from going crazy. Even now they gave her strength. Whenever she found a shard of historical information for the mosaic of the family of the goddesses of Žítková, the thoughts were at once fuller and more colorful. This information might concern a goddess tried for witchcraft or one pursued by the court in Uherské Hradiště just a few decades ago. Through the documents she found, it was as though she knew them as intimately as Surmena. But did she really know them?

From the moment it was confirmed that Surmena had been involved with the secret police, Dora was tormented by doubt, accompanied by a nervousness that increased as the three-month deadline approached. Her desire to know the result was welded to her fear of what it would be.

On the final day of the three-month period, her patience gave out. She called the archive.

She heard indifference in the voice of the official. "Lustration is still in progress. You are on a waiting list."

Dora was taken aback. How could it be that they still had no news for her? Could Surmena's file have been lost? Or perhaps they didn't want to hand it over. She started to panic. As days became weeks, the tension within her built to what felt like a bursting point.

Then one morning the silence of her office was violated by the telephone's crude ring.

The voice on the other end of the line was reserved. "We have a file for you. Terézie Surmenová, 1910 to 1979. Not a collaborator but a subject of surveillance. When should we expect your visit?"

Archive: Day One

S everal weeks later—having been informed by letter that a copy of the file on the subject of a lustration procedure was ready for her perusal—Dora was sitting at a gleaming-new varnished desk in the reading room of the State Security Police archives in Pardubice, before her a large pink A4 folder with "SURMENOVÁ, TERÉZIE" printed on its front.

The folder was surprisingly bulky—Dora reckoned its thickness at about three inches. Obviously it would take her hours and hours to read. She flicked through it. Forms completed on a typewriter, official documents filled with text, plus newspaper clippings and handwritten notes.

Her throat was tight. Although she was glad to learn that Surmena had not been an informant for the State Security Police, she was afraid that Surmena's life would open up to her in a previously unsuspected form and that the pain wrought by their brutal separation would return.

Her hands unsteady, she opened the well-thumbed folder and picked up a faded sheet of carbon paper:

1
from the District Department of Public Safety in Uherský Brod
case no. ČVS VB-3814/01-1953
to the Local Council of the National Committee in Žítková

re: SURMENOVÁ, Terézie: Request for report on reputation

Hereby I request a report on the reputation of Terézie Surmenová, born 7/24/10, resident at house no. 28 in Žítková, that shall state details of her class origin, her attitudes and activities during the war, her past and present political affiliations, her participation in public life, her relation to the systems of the people's democracy, and to work, her family life, and qualities of her person and character.

This report should be submitted in duplicate to the DDPS in Uherský Brod within eight days.

Labor be honored!

Supervisor: Dvořák
9/17/53

2

**from the Local Council of the National Committee in Žítková
case no. ČVS VB-3814/01-1953
to the District Department of Public Safety in Uherský Brod**

re: SURMENOVÁ, Terézie: Report on reputation

Terézie Surmenová (b. 7/24/10; unmarried) comes from a family of smallholders. She was not a member of the party before the war, nor has she been since 1945. She has no political affiliation. No positive evaluation can be made regarding her relation to the systems of the people's democracy or work for the collective at the United Farmers' Cooperative, to which she refuses use of her 1.6 ha field. Although she is not a participant in public life, she cannot be regarded as inactive: she has relations with many citizens who seek her out for her alleged abilities as a healer, a state of affairs that applied before the war and continues to apply now. This aspect of her reputation is condemned by local comrades as deliberate deception of the gullible and unprogressive among the citizenry of Czechoslovakia. For this reason—and as she profits systematically at the expense of society by income derived from her activities as a healer and the illegal trading of herbs—it is my duty to report that the subject is of bad character.

Nor is the subject's family life of a respectable nature. It is known that she kept the company of Jan Ruchár (b. 1/17/1884; resident at house no. 98 in Žítková), who was a cousin of her mother's, and that their unmarried union produced two children, both of whom died shortly after their births in 1939 and 1942. She meets her quotas.

Labor be honored!

LCNC Secretary: Lipták
9/25/53

Dora put down the typescript. She was shocked.

Surmena had never mentioned having children. Although she had visited the cemetery regularly to tend the graves of deceased relatives, she had paid no attention to those of her children. And what about this business with Ruchár?

Still incredulous, Dora read the report again before turning her attention to the facing page. On her next visit to Žítková, she would ask Baglárka all about it. If anyone knew more, it was Baglárka.

But it wasn't because of her illegitimate children that the authorities became interested in Surmena. The problem was apparently Surmena's goddessing. The next document was a call from the District Department of Public Safety in Uherský Brod requesting detailed information on Surmena's activities.

"Please state the names of citizens who visit Surmenová, should their identities be known, and purposes for which they employ her activities."

From the raft of pages that confronted Dora, it was now clear that Secretary Lipták did not keep the authorities waiting long. Within a week a report of several pages was on its way to Brod, followed in subsequent weeks by supplements and specifics as requested and then copies of the minutes of several meetings of the National Committee in Žítková, in which committee members were eager to express their opposition to the behavior of citizen Surmenová, with statements such as *"This outrage must be brought to an end!"* and *"Such activities scar the face of the community!"* and *"We must prevent unauthorized enterprise in our midst!"*

But it was not until the end of the following year that Surmena was first summoned to the police station.

Nothing.

Of course there was nothing. What could they possibly have had on her?

With a sense of gratification, Dora put down the document revealing that the investigation had been abandoned.

Under this was a collection of letters stuffed into a transparent plastic envelope. She handled the yellowed papers with care. Some of them were written in a small, childlike hand on the inside of flattened-out packaging that had held sugar or flour.

Gossip, fabrication, and slander. Dora leafed through the letters in disbelief.

The poisoning of the pets of neighbors against whom she held a grudge. The preparation of intoxicating drinks that deprived the imbiber of his or her own will. The undermining of the morale of village youngsters. The letters were written by a Mrs. Ruchárová. To write denunciations based on such desperate nonsense, she must have been mad with jealousy, Dora thought. The problem was, among the absurdities, the meandering lines contained snippets of important information. Names of Surmena's visitors. Who wanted what from her, and what they gave her for it.

Had she waited on the path from the Bedová in order to question Surmena's visitors, who, ignorant of her intentions and consumed with relief, babbled their confessions?

With disgust, Dora tucked these products of oafishness back into their envelope. Her mood dark, she flicked through several more reports from the National Committee in Žítková until her attention was arrested by a letter addressed to the Public Prosecutor's Office in Uherské Hradiště.

23
from the Department of Health, District National Committee, Uherský Brod
case no. Health 277/1955
to the County Public Prosecutor's Office in Uherské Hradiště

re: request for investigation of illegal medical practice of Terézie Surmenová

The Dept. of Health of the DNC in Uherský Brod has been alerted to the fact that citizen TERÉZIE SURMENOVÁ of Žítková operates an unqualified medical practice for financial gain. We have learned from patients and been able to observe for ourselves that there have recently arisen a number of cases of the "correction" of dislocated limbs, with the concomitant danger that the above-named citizen may cause harm to the sick by her inexpert advice or intervention. We justify our concern on the basis of the following cases:

ÚBĚHLÍKOVÁ, JANA: b. 6/27/53, daughter of a driver's mate, resident at house no. 43 in Zlechov—dislocated hip.

ČERNOCHOVÁ, JARMILA: b. 11/19/54, daughter of a vehicle body repair operative, resident at house no. 12 in Polechovice—dislocated hip.

TOUŽIMSKÁ, RENATA: b. 12/3/50, daughter of a teacher, resident at house no. 86 in Strážnice—dislocated wrist.

All these cases were subject to the appropriate initial professional treatment. It was later discovered, however, that the parents failed to present their children for follow-up examinations; instead they visited Surmenová, who performed some kind of manual treatment on the children for financial gain. Her assurances to the parents that her actions were successful caused harm to the children by delaying the legitimate care of the attending doctors. Such delay necessitates double the treatment, with the associated expense being borne by the state.

I recommend that the public prosecutor investigate the activities of citizen Surmenová and render impossible her further attempts at medical practice. It is necessary to take such action because medical treatment is available to all citizens of our people's democratic republic through professional organs of state health administration in the highest possible quality and free of charge; there is no need for the sick to seek out the help of laypersons and to pay exorbitant sums for this help.

Head of Dept. of Health of the DNC: K. Lešný, MD
4/27/55

24

**from the County Public Prosecutor's Office in Uherské Hradiště
case no. Health 277/1955
to the District Department of Public Safety in Uherský Brod**

re: SURMENOVÁ, Terézie: unauthorized operation of medical
practice—investigation

> We are sending a request from the Dept. of Health
> of the DNC in Uherský Brod for the conducting of an
> investigation. This investigation should concentrate on
> the establishing of circumstances for the determination
> of whether the facts of the behavior of the above-
> named citizen constitute a criminal offense under
> Article 221/1 or Article 222/1 of the Criminal Code.
>
> Please send a report on the results of the inves-
> tigation to this Public Prosecutor's Office within one
> month of receipt of this notification.
>
> Chief Clerk, County Public Prosecutor's Office: Maňák,
> JD
> 5/9/55

25

**from the District Department of Public Safety in Uherský Brod
case no. Health 277/1955
to the County Public Prosecutor's Office in Uherské Hradiště**

re: SURMENOVÁ, Terézie: unauthorized operation of medical
practice—report

> Pursuant to your request of May 9, 1955, we submit the
> following report.

In the cases named by the Dept. of Health of the DNC in Uherský Brod, our investigation has shown that the mother of JANA ÚBĚHLÍKOVÁ (Jiřina Úběhlíková, b. 2/12/30, resident at house no. 43 in Zlechov) paid no visit to Surmenová. Regarding her daughter's dislocated hip, Jiřina Úběhlíková states that this is now perfectly healthy, as demonstrated by the fact that the now two-year-old girl stands and walks in a manner befitting her age. Asked why, after the initial difficulties, she failed to pay subsequent visits to the attending physician in Uherský Brod, Jiřina Úběhlíková stated that the child's hip healed of its own accord, so she did not consider such an action to be necessary.

Also the mother of JARMILA ČERNOCHOVÁ Jr. (Jarmila Černochová, b. 8/12/29, resident at house no. 12 in Polechovice) denied having visited Surmenová and claimed that her daughter was well.

Ludmila Toužimská (b. 2/13/25, resident at house no. 86 in Strážnice), the mother of RENATA TOUŽIMSKÁ who suffered a dislocated wrist, attended an interview at our invitation and stated:

"The day after my daughter's accident I attended Dr. Hříb at the district health center in Uherské Hradiště. The child had cried the whole night, and her wrist was swollen. Dr. Hříb told me that the injury was slight and sent me home without having treated it. As the child continued to cry, on the third day I went to Surmenová, whom I'd heard was a well-known healer. She moved my daughter's wrist about, rubbed an ointment into it, and bandaged it. The child felt so much better that she was no longer crying. The wrist remained like this for a week. We changed the bandage and applied the ointment Surmenová had given us only once. The child's wrist healed. Now she can move it normally."

Asked whether Surmenová demanded money, Ludmila Toužimská replied in the negative, although she stated that she took eggs and lard as a gift. For a check-up examination, we sent Ludmila Toužimská and the child to Dr. Dufek at the department of orthopedics of the local District Institute for National Health. After the examination, Dr. Dufek told us:

"The child had probably suffered no more than a sprain of the left wrist. The nature of this minor injury means that the pain disappears spontaneously and the function returns within a few days. This was obviously the conclusion reached by the attending physician in that he considered the bandaging of the wrist to be unnecessary. The fact that the patient's state corrected itself shows that the doctor's diagnosis was the right one. I believe that stabilization occurred of its own accord and would have done so without Surmenová's ministrations."

Further, Dr. Dufek proposed the prevention of Surmenová's activities, which by their inexpert nature serve to confuse the public and complicate the performance of the duties of qualified physicians.

An investigation was also carried out by Chief Inspector Vařejka and Inspector Kladka at the subject's place of residence, an action that began at 9:15 a.m. on 5/19/55 at the National Committee office in Žítková in the presence of Comrade Loubal (chairman) and Comrade Lipták (secretary).

They described Surmenová's activities as dishonest and deceitful, as embezzlement of systems of the

people's democracy through theft of the public property of the Forestry Authority of Uherský Brod (the
subject misuses the nation's natural wealth), and as the
performing of treatments on gullible citizens for financial reward. Asked to name a specific case, Comrades
Lipták and Loubal answered that they knew of none,
although they referred the investigators to Comrades
Ruchárová and Hodoušková, older citizens and close
neighbors of Surmenová's who could be expected to
have a grasp of the situation.

At house no. 98 in Žítková, the investigators
found Comrade Ruchár, who did not confirm the allegations of the chairman and secretary of the National
Committee and stated only that many people visited
Surmenová whom he did not know. He knew nothing
of any treatments or financial rewards. Nor did the testimony of Comrade Hodoušková, resident at house no.
46 in Žítková, confirm the allegations, although the in-
terviewee did state that the subject of the investigation
could cure ailments in livestock, ward off storms, and
see into the future. Comrade Hodoušková's testimony
is not to be trusted: she seems to be a very religious old
woman prone to fantastical ideas and to have a skewed
view of modern life in a Socialist republic.

At 12:45 a.m. an attempt was made to question
the subject, who was found not to be at home. (She
returned only at 4:00 p.m.) Investigation suspended.

On 5/25/55 a new, successful attempt was made
to find the subject at home. Asked whether she knew
the above-named children, she replied that she did
not. Asked whether she operated an illegal medical practice, she replied that she did not but that she

gave advice if she was able; as an example she cited gargling with slivovitz as a cure for a sore throat. She denied that strangers came to her for treatment. She denied deriving financial gain from her activities. She denied that she stole national property from the forest. In her home, comprising one room and one entrance hall, a sizeable quantity of dried herbs was found, otherwise nothing remarkable. The subject was warned of the possible consequences of illicit activities.

Operation ended on 5/25/55 at 4:53 p.m.

Total expenses: 202 Czechoslovak crowns

Conclusion: The investigation has established reason to suspect the subject Surmenová of operating an unauthorized medical practice, notwithstanding the fact that she denies this. Uniformed authorities did not succeed in establishing the scope and extent of her services nor whether she gains by them financially. Due to the nature of the task, these authorities believe that Surmenová's activities should be subjected to deeper inquiry, which will succeed only if it is performed undercover. To this end the District Department of Public Safety in Uherské Hradiště, to which the results of the investigation were submitted, has been informed. Officer Švanc of the Third Division, who conducted an earlier investigation of the subject, has taken charge of the case. It is to Officer Švanc that questions concerning the further conduct of the case should be addressed.

Supervisor: Rudimský
5/29/55

The mention of a slivovitz gargle made Dora smile. But the smile froze as she read on. In the middle of 1955, Surmena was declared an enemy of the state, and her case was placed on the agenda of the State Security Police.

There followed in rapid succession dozens of terse official reports. On entrusting of the case to Officer Švanc of the Third Division of the State Security Police in Uherské Hradiště. On approval of procedure. On delegation of the investigation to Inspector Kladka, who, having conducted the initial inquiry in the field, was apprised of the situation. On adoption of the case by operatives of the State Security Police in Uherské Hradiště and assigning of the code name INTERPRETER. And so on.

The eager beaver had been promoted, Dora thought as she carefully returned the documents to their file. Then she turned to the next report.

42

to the District Department of State Security in Uherské Hradiště, Third Division
FAO Officer Švanc
Processed by: code name/file: INTERPRETER/15701
Type of cooperation: operative worker
Registered state security authority: Uherské Hradiště

Report: investigation of Terézie Surmenová

Due to the fact that the investigation of the subject has been unsuccessful hitherto for reasons of reluctance on the part of the citizens addressed to speak with Public Security authorities, it has been necessary to conduct the inquiry undercover. In fulfillment of our orders, Sergeant Novotná and I went on 9/18/55 to the village of Žítková, our apparent purpose a hiking trip. Sergeant Novotná was under instructions to make operational contact with Surmenová on the pretext of asking for help and thus determine the form her activities take, whereas I was instructed to make contact with local citizens with the purpose of obtaining additional information.

It was found that Surmenová has a good reputation in her place of residence, where she lives a quiet life. Since 1944, when her relationship with Jan Ruchár (resident with his lawful wife at a house nearby on the slope of the Černá hill) ended, she has lived alone. Her parents having died before the war, of her siblings, she maintains contact only with her younger sister, Irena. Surmenová is reported to leave her home rarely—to church once a week and to shop in Starý Hrozenkov. She has strong religious convictions; from random conversations in the local tavern, it transpires that she is unprogressive in other ways, too (she does not trust doctors, officials, and authorities, and she lives in one room where, in winter, she keeps her livestock), and she has a hostile attitude to the Socialist order.

Asked whether she has any contact with the public, she answered that she has a lot but none beyond her home (none of her fellow citizens know of contacts she may have abroad). Informants testified that Surmenová receives numerous visitors to her home. The landlord of the local New School Tavern testified that these often drop in at the tavern and ask him for directions and that sometimes they come after they have visited Surmenová. He testified that many of these are women who have their fortunes told and citizens seeking help with illness.

The citizens present were civil in their attitude. One citizen reported that Surmenová cured his father's tuberculosis; further testimony was given that a woman whose name and place of residence are unknown made repeated visits to Surmenová and was cured of her epilepsy. Further testimony was given that with the help of herbs, Surmenová practices a great variety of "charms" and that she is able to mend broken bones; as regards fortune-telling, however, she has no great experience, unlike the ones known as "Chupatá" and "Leonora"; with theft, "the Krasňačka from Hudáky" reportedly gives the best help. Asked about the level of fees for such services, more than one citizen answered, "Each according to his own."

The continuing inquiry in low-lying parts of Žítková, at house no. 17 at Koprvazy and house no. 44 at Rovné, confirmed the above findings. To the question of whether Surmenová helps cure ulcers, the answer was received that she does; it is enough to go to her. The daughter of the owner of house no. 44 offered to assist with directions, whereupon the owner of the house indicated that I should go with her, as Surmenová would then give her something too.

Investigation of Surmenová's home established that the subject lives in meager circumstances. She showed herself to be mistrustful of strangers, and we had to request admission to her home, which she granted only after careful presentation of our trouble: Sergeant Novotná complained of insomnia and headaches. Eventually Surmenová went to the stove, heated some wax, and poured this into a bowl of water, a task she performed while mumbling to herself unintelligibly. Then she pretended for a long time to see something in the bowl. Having induced Sergeant Novotná to take off her blouse, she ran her hands along Sergeant Novotná's spine and felt her neck. Then she became angry and ordered Sergeant Novotná out of her home. As we were leaving, she told Sergeant Novotná that had she not lied, she would have helped her, not with her headaches but with conceiving, with which she was having difficulties. Asked whether Sergeant Novotná was in her debt, she replied, "I wouldn't take anything from her anyway."

Operation ended on 9/18/55 at 4:40 p.m.

Total expenses: 148 Czechoslovak crowns

Conclusion: The investigation has proved that the subject engages in unauthorized treatments for which she receives unspecified remuneration. It has been proved that she is the perpetrator of fraudulent acts and thus exploits the ignorance of local and nonlocal citizens. Surmenová's activities are a danger not only to these gullible citizens but also to society as a whole, as by her negative attitude to the Socialist order and her appreciable influence on a network of clients, she undermines the position of our Socialist republic. Due to a lack of evidence and witnesses willing to testify, however, it is not possible to establish the facts of the case and bring charges under Article 221/1 of the Criminal Code. I recommend that Surmenová remain under surveillance, as I believe it to be only a matter of time before her activities give rise to criminal prosecution.

Note: I propose the removal of Sergeant Novotná from the case. In the course of the operation, she has not demonstrated sufficient capacity for fieldwork. (Her emotions failed her immediately after the visit to the home of the subject.)

The swine, thought Dora with bitterness as she reached the end of the interpreter's account and flicked through the documents that followed.

It was obvious at first glance that his proposal to continue surveillance had been accepted with all the trimmings. Next came a series of summaries written at regular monthly intervals. They were keeping a steady eye on Surmena, waiting for her to make a mistake. And while they waited, the snare was laid around their cottages, winding down into Žítková, along the path to the bus stop at Hrozenkov and from there directly to Hradiště. It was enough to wait patiently and then to tug on the line.

In the meantime, their life together unraveled.

54
**from the Local Council of the National Committee in Žítková
case no. 7-Nc 103/66
to the District Court in Uherské Hradiště**

re: the personal and financial circumstances of Terézie Surmenová in relation to the minors Dora Idesová and Jakub Ides

Terézie Surmenová is a close relative of the minors Dora Idesová (b. 10/30/58) and Jakub Ides (b. 2/16/61): as the sister of the late Irena Idesová (née Surmenová), she is their aunt. It is known that their mutual relations are good. The minor Dora and the minor Jakub are now in Surmenová's care. Dora Idesová attends daily the nine-class primary school in Starý Hrozenkov; Jakub Ides is at home with Surmenová, who is in receipt of a disability pension from the state. It is both well known and obvious to the layman that Jakub Ides is insufficiently developed both mentally and physically. It seems that he will not be capable of compulsory school attendance and will continue to require full-time care. Surmenová is able to provide this.

On the other hand, it is obvious from Surmenová's attitude of indifference to the Socialist order of the Czechoslovak republic that she cannot be considered capable of ensuring a fully progressive upbringing for the children in her care. The solution to this would seem to be regular inspection and overseeing of developments by the office for social services.

As to Surmenová's financial circumstances, it can be stated that she receives a disability pension of 740 Czechoslovak crowns, owns two head of cattle, and partly manages a field of 1.6 ha. It is also known that she engages in healing activities, from which she allegedly derives a high income; thus, there is no cause for apprehension concerning her ability to provide for the Ides siblings.

Of Surmenová's healing practices we informed the district Public Security authorities, whose investigations were subsequently suspended owing to a lack of evidence. In this case we therefore find no further obstacles to the continued charging of the above-named minors to the care of Terézie Surmenová.

Head of LCNC Dept. for Internal Affairs: Srp
7/20/66

Dora flicked through a number of other documents with statements regarding her and her brother being under Surmena's care. The Local Council of the National Committee memo was followed by letters from the District Public Prosecutor's Office and the District Public Security Departments in Uherský Brod and Uherské Hradiště, all testifying to Surmena's irreproachability, and then a testimonial from Dora's class teacher on behalf of the school and a statement from the office for social services. In the context of these earlier accounts and reports, Dora could hardly believe that their move to their new home had proceeded so smoothly.

But still, they had kept a beady eye on Surmena.

Dora skimmed through a number of documents that described their life together up to that point. Typewritten data on the wonderful years she had spent with Surmena flashed by; some of the events recorded she remembered well, others hardly at all.

There was the story of a girl who spent the summer holidays with them. For years she and her name had gone missing in Dora's memory, but now she remembered her as suddenly as if she had been produced by a snap of the fingers from the conjuror whose tricks she used to watch on the East German TV show *Ein Kessel Buntes*. Květa Mazovská, that was the name of the sad girl whose case was discussed in several more reports.

At first Surmena told Dora that she should pay no attention to Květa until the girl wanted to be noticed. So Dora just looked on, wondering how Surmena could put up with her, at how infinite her patience was. The girl could manage nothing—she was afraid of cows, so she couldn't even be sent to the pasture, nor did she do much in the garden or the field. The whole of the first month, she hung about the house or up on the hillside, or she just slept. She spoke to no one. That was it. She had no interest in life, Surmena said. When Baglárka was at their place, Dora overheard Surmena saying that she'd tried to do herself in. A suicide? If Baglárka had been startled, Dora had been astounded.

A suicide in the house! After that she couldn't take her eyes off the girl; whenever she went for a walk, Dora crept along behind her, captivated by every step she took. But after a week, she tired of this—truly the girl did and experienced absolutely nothing. She was like a sleeping doll.

It was the middle of August when Surmena finally had her fill and put her foot down. The girl's quiet time was over. Surmena pursued and nagged her wherever she went until Květa sat down next to the cows and tried to milk them, until she crouched to the earth and weeded the garden, until she went out at five in the morning and returned with a basket on her back filled with grass, legs reddened by the cold of the dew. By now her cheeks had red in them, too, and suddenly she was laughing. Dora was astonished and mystified by the two sudden transformations that produced an angry Surmena and a Květa with a zest for life.

Surmena answered Dora's hesitant question thus: *"She's drunk enough Saint John's wort. What the girl has to do now is learn how to live. And work will teach her that."*

There was certainly something in this. When Květa left them in early September, she was happier and rounder. She returned for a week or so in each of the next two summers, then came only for brief visits with her husband, and after that she sent a photograph of herself holding a baby in a swaddling blanket. Surmena put this photograph on display on the cup shelf, occasionally looking at it with a tender expression.

But there was nothing tender about the reports on the desk in front of Dora now. That summer, she, Surmena, and Květa, who came from a troubled Ostrava family, had been under day-to-day surveillance, for weeks that became months and then years. And they had snooped on people who came to visit them, some of whom were described in detail, with some of whom they spoke, and on some of whom they sent reports to their places of residence.

The stream of reports was seemingly endless. They became more and more alike, their clichés repeated a hundred times, so boring that Dora began to skim—until she came to a document with frequent mentions of her own name. It appeared that their attention was now focused on her, Dora, because there was nothing of much interest going on with Surmena. They exposed her as an angel and tried to figure out how much she was earning by her subversive activities. The estimate was hundreds of Czechoslovak crowns. Dora felt laughter bubble up inside her. The occasional crown that came her way burned such a hole in her pocket that she ran to the co-op shop down in the village and spent it on ice cream or chocolate. It was far more common that she was given an apple taken from a rucksack, just so that she wasn't left empty-handed.

Hundreds, then, was it? Dora smiled. But then she turned the page and was startled. The document now in front of her she knew well; although she hadn't seen it for years, she'd never forgotten it. Her vision clouded. She leaned back in her chair and felt springs of perspiration at her forehead and temples. This was the document that had destroyed the lives they had built for themselves on the wreckage of the past.

Little White Snake

It was a Friday in early summer 1974. The document arrived in a sealed envelope with an official stamp. The day, on which things occurred that would eat away at her for years to come, was engraved in her memory.

Perhaps it had all been her fault.

Perhaps she had crushed their life of contentment with the sole of her shoe.

But who could have guessed what the little white snake was harboring?

Perhaps it had hatched inside the cottage; perhaps Jakoubek had brought it in; perhaps it had lived for years in their walls, as Surmena claimed. And yes, perhaps it really was completely harmless. But what she saw was the reptile's long, thin body clutched in Jakoubek's clumsy hands, first one, then the other, followed by his unknowing eyes. He was delighting in the snake's every twitch as it tried to free itself.

In such a situation, who wouldn't have panicked? And Dora had never seen a snake like this, with shiny, scaly skin.

She grabbed at it, and Jakoubek gasped in horror. Then the snake's head cracked under her shoe.

Then his wails.

He was fine. Just frightened, then angry. He turned his anger on her. She held on to him—in those days, she still could—as his hands tried to lock themselves around the snake. Soon all that was left of it was a trampled, bloody mess on the stone floor.

Their screams summoned Surmena. It was not the first time she had adjudicated their disputes, but now her face was white. In a fit of weakness, she rested a palm against the wall to stop herself from falling.

"You killed a little white snake?"

A little white snake? Dora had crushed underfoot a horrible creature that Jakoubek had ferreted out God knows where; she had no idea what it was. So yes, she had killed a little white snake.

"Then God help us," said Surmena, sliding down onto the wooden bench.

Dora stood awkwardly in front of her. Jakoubek was crawling about the floor, still in shock. Dora demanded an explanation.

It was many minutes before Surmena spoke. "The little white snake is the protector of the home. A terrible fate awaits those who kill it."

She couldn't have said anything worse. With these words something rose up in Dora that had been growing over the last few months, weeks, and days. A disgust with all the nonsensical rules to which Surmena and the people of the Žítková hillside were bound.

Another superstition? More tidings of bad luck? Another folly to give them the shakes, like crossing yourself to fend off the grave after an owl had hooted in the woods.

Weren't there enough threats and things to avoid as it was, without adding fear of a dead snake?

From now on Dora would refuse to share these ridiculous superstitions. Surmena and others like her were still refusing to accept the new—twentieth—century. But there were no doomsayers abroad in the hills, no squealing ladies to tempt you from the path, no black cats bringing bad luck.

This was the second time Dora and Surmena had clashed on such matters. After the first, it was clear that Dora would strike out on her own.

The first clash had happened not long before. For Dora its effects were permanent; she recalled it in tandem with the memory of her powerlessness in the face of what happened. To all of them—her, Jakoubek, and Surmena.

It all came about because of what she brought back to the Bedová from school. That day an anger that had long been bubbling up inside burst free and engulfed her classmates, the new comrade teacher, and finally Surmena, whose fault it actually was. It was because of Surmena that they were different. It was because of Surmena that they were talked of as weirdos who turned to God rather than the local health center, in the hope that prayers were the cure. It was because of Surmena that they grubbed about in the earth for herbs for their decoctions, as if they were living a hundred years in the past.

"Not just for yourself, but for all the other unfortunate people who are fooled by these silly, outdated beliefs and so risk their health. It's unforgivable!"

These words of contempt had been delivered by the new comrade teacher, who wore her hair in a topknot and modern glasses whose arms tapered to a point. For emphasis she fished in her handbag for a bottle of pills, which she shook in Dora's face before embarking on a lecture on the wonders of modern medicine, as though it were news to everyone, not least to Dora, that patients with aches and pains should go on Wednesdays to the health center in Hrozenkov to be attended by a traveling physician from Hradiště, whereas those with broken bones should go to the hospital in Hradiště—not to a cottage on the Bedová hill to be attended by a folk healer.

But what was Dora to do when Surmena continued to insist that every day after school, she should go to the bus stop to see if anyone there was looking for a goddess? And in spite of her increasing shame, Dora would lead these people up to Žítková. There were plenty of such people, and they even came on Wednesdays when they could have seen the physician at the health center instead.

But this was not all that made the Surmenová family different from those down in Hrozenkov. Over time Dora noticed many more things. That each passing year set their cottage deeper in the ground; this was in stark contrast to the detached houses and new apartment blocks on the square at Hrozenkov, where her classmates lived. She became aware of the difference between her own clothing—the skirts, coarse blouses, stockings, and peasant shoes Surmena dressed her in—and the leisurewear of her peers. And she noticed that of the hill dwellers who attended Mass every Sunday at the church in Hrozenkov, there remained only a few who wore the traditional local dress. Many more among the congregation wore new pumps or well-maintained suits with creases in the trousers. There had been a time when it was impossible to see the altar from the back of the church because of the colorful headscarves and red embroidered caps; now Dora's view was obscured by hair puffed out in permanent waves.

These differences could not be overlooked. And many people did not wish for them to be overlooked. Spruced-up sons and dolled-up daughters treated her with condescension, sneered at her, and called her names. Dora the fraud. Dora the angel. Would she, too, turn into a witch one day? Wherever she went she was accompanied by children's guffaws, the swishing of switches, stones propelled from boys' hands. And then the loneliness. She would climb to the Bedová alone, leaving behind the newer Hrozenkov with its new apartments, the new road that took one car after another to Trenčín, the people of a new world so distant from theirs, where Surmena's word was law, and the law knew but two domains—church and nature.

"Why do you invite those people, Auntie?" asked Dora, home again and unhappy after the scene with the teacher.

Surmena was surprised by the question. "I don't invite anyone. They come on their own."

"Why don't they see the doctor at the center on Wednesdays?"

"The doctor can't help them."

"Why not? Can't he give them pills to make them better?"

Surmena's tone was patient. "Pills aren't good for everything, Dora."

"Your chants are?"

"For many things they are much better than prescriptions."

"But that's how things are done here. Everyone goes to the doctor. Those who don't are laughed at for having been taken for a fool."

"Taken for a fool? By whom?"

Dora stopped. She didn't want to say. "The frauds of Žítková," she faltered.

Surmena flinched as if struck. "You think that I'm a fraud?" There was pain in her voice.

Dora lowered her eyes. "Of course not. It's just that's not how things are done today. People go to doctors."

"And what if the doctors haven't learned at school all there is to know?"

Dora was taken aback. "Why wouldn't they have? Isn't that what books are for? If someone's a doctor, then they must know everything. That's obvious."

Surmena smiled, but bitterly. She hobbled across the room to fetch a tin cup from the dresser. Then she reached to the shelf above the window for one of the bottles of spirits that stood there in a long line. Donations from visitors to the hills. A clear liquid bubbled at the bottom of the cup.

"Just because someone's a doctor doesn't mean that he knows everything! In my experience, neither the best nor the worst of them knows even the most basic thing—that sickness of the body is also sickness of the mind. That was the first thing my mother taught me, and the doctors haven't worked it out yet. So how can they know everything better than I do? Or Irma does? Or Kateřina? Well?"

"But they prescribe pills, and pills help!"

"Pills? And who sees what's in them? Little flat white tablets made in a factory to chase away the pain. I wouldn't let one pass my lips, even at the bidding of a priest. Forgive me, Lord, for what I'm saying! How can a doctor in his smelly white office, where the nurse is hurrying you out almost as soon as you've sat down, be expected to find out what your trouble is? What help can he give when even God is afraid to hang around?"

"But they don't need God's help. They're doctors!"

Surmena sighed. "What have people been telling you, my girl? Have you forgotten that faith is the most important thing of all? God is everywhere, even with those doctors. But all the saints be with those who go to them for advice and help instead of trusting in God! No wonder they go back there so often."

Surmena shook her head in agitation and then took a long drink.

"But it's not like that, Auntie! God doesn't treat the sick. Unlike doctors, he can't write prescriptions!"

"Don't talk like that! God is a healer, but of a different kind. Through faith that you will give up your sickness, you rid yourself of it. We know how faith works. We know exactly where it works and how it works on different people. We've known this for centuries. How do you think people were healed before pills existed? By herbs! And by faith in their properties."

"But, Auntie! This is a new age."

"A new age in which herbs have lost their power? I don't want to hear about it."

Dora had been close to tears. She'd managed to express hardly anything of what she was feeling. She spent the rest of the afternoon at the top of the hill. The tears finally came when evening reached their field and she saw the flickering lights of televisions in the windows of the Hrozenkov valley. In the world to which she would never belong, the life of the day was yielding to the life of the night.

The white snake turned up several weeks later. Dora could take no more. The moment Surmena slid down onto the wooden bench by the front door of the cottage, Dora hardened her heart against all the follies Surmena had made her accept. She would believe in them no longer.

But it wasn't long after this that an out-of-breath postwoman made her way across their field and pulled that letter from her flat leather satchel.

The letter stood on the table, propped up against a jam jar filled with meadow flowers, for the rest of Friday, all of Saturday, and all of Sunday, its angle unchanged as the level of water in the jar got lower and lower as the flowers drank their fill. It was not until Sunday evening that Dora asked Surmena if she was going to open it. Surmena shook her head.

"It's got an official stamp on it," Dora objected.

Surmena limped about the room, preparing the supper plates, setting water to boil on the stove, spooning chicory coffee into mugs.

"If it's got an official stamp on it, it's important. Why don't you look at it?"

Surmena shrugged, then grumbled as she added wood to the fire. "It's not as if I've got nothing better to do. Who's going to settle the livestock? Who'll tidy away the supper things?"

After she went out, Dora tore open the envelope. Her eyes rushed over the lines. From the other side of the table, Jakoubek looked on with curiosity.

She remembered herself struggling for breath when Surmena returned.

"Read it," she pleaded softly and tentatively, holding out the letter.

Surmena made as if she had not seen the gesture. Without speaking, she returned to the stove, where the water had begun to boil.

"You can't just leave it!"

Jakoubek cringed at the urgency in Dora's voice.

Surmena looked at her with cold indifference.

"What are we going to do?" said Dora, placing the letter, which bore her sweaty fingerprints along one edge, in Surmena's hand.

Surmena did not even look at it before putting it down on the hot stone of the oven, her eyes fixed on Dora until she turned them sullenly away.

Dora knew how stubborn Surmena was. But until that moment— when the knowledge came to her in a flash—she had been unaware that Surmena was unable to read.

Embarrassed, she picked up the letter and read it aloud.

**from the District Public Security Department in Uherský Brod
CSSR Criminal Police Service
to Surmenová, Terézie
house no. 28, Žítková, Uherský Brod district**

<u>Summons</u>

> On suspicion of the perpetration of a criminal act of bodily harm by negligence as a result of the performing of unqualified healing practices and fraud pursuant to Articles 224/1 and 250 of the Criminal Code, you are summoned to appear during office hours on

> 6/17/74

> at the District Public Security Department in Uherský Brod to provide an explanation concerning the unlawful performance of the termination of a pregnancy, resulting in the death of Anna Pelčáková. You will present this summons and proof of identity.

Note

Should the subject of the summons be unable to present an explanation in person, she is obliged to submit an adequate excuse pursuant to Art. 66 of Act 141/1961 Coll. Failure to respect this order without submission of an adequate excuse may result in a disciplinary fine of up to 500 Czechoslovak crowns (pursuant to Art. 66, Para. 1 of the Criminal Code).

Signature: Novák (commanding officer)
6/11/74

When Dora finished reading, Surmena showed no reaction. Jakoubek started to sob, not because he had understood the letter's contents but because of the horror in Dora's reading voice. In the end Jakoubek's cries scared even Surmena. She served them buckwheat groats, her hands shaking. They ate their supper in silence. After this they prayed together: first the Paternoster, then a prayer for Surmena. Then they went to bed as usual.

When they woke the next morning, there was a jug of fresh milk on the table and a chicken boiling in a pan on the stove. Dora saw its claws and head hanging from the fence in the front garden, bound together with the herb known as "come-back-again." The one that you should never pick because if you did, you would die within a year. The one that is tied to a dog's tail so that the dog pulls it from the ground when it breaks into a run. *"Does the dog die then?"* Dora had once asked; Surmena had shrugged in reply. That strange bundle of come-back-again and chicken parts was supposed to protect Surmena and bring her back, cleansed of blame and immaculate. To make absolutely sure of her safe return, several times on that last day, the three of them went together to the threshold of the cottage and raised threatening fingers in the direction of Uherský Brod while chanting, *"Shoo you fears / Shoo you lies / Shoo like crows / Fly to all sides / I'm the grain of gold inside / I'll be home by suppertime!"*

Surmena took the bundle of claws and come-back-again with her. It didn't help.

It was as though the reading room had suddenly turned cold. Dora was in a chilled sweat, goose bumps on her arms. That awful memory of the moment another chapter in her life had closed, when Surmena's red embroidered headscarf had disappeared beyond the bend in the path that led from their field. Forever.

Dora got up from the desk and went out into the dim hallway. It was a while before she was able to seat herself back at the desk; then for a while longer, she just sat there, wrapped in her sweater, her gaze wandering the map of the marble linoleum. Knowing what to expect, she contemplated the rest of the file with dread.

75
from the District Public Prosecutor's Office in Uherské Hradiště to the State Social Services Office in Brno

<u>re: removal of minors Dora Idesová and Jakub Ides from the care of a person who represents a threat to the social order</u>

On 6/17/74 the District Public Prosecutor's Office in Uherské Hradiště was informed of the taking into custody of suspect Terézie Surmenová, b. 7/24/10, charged with the criminal act of bodily harm resulting in death, being a danger to the public, and being a fraud.

Terézie Surmenová is currently the guardian of the minors Dora Idesová and Jakub Ides, who were entrusted to her care on 11/17/66 and with whom she resides in one household at house no. 28, village Žítková, district Uherský Brod.

Proposal of an interim measure

On 6/17/74 the district public prosecutor in Uherské Hradiště proposes an interim measure pursuant to Article 76 of the CPR and charges the State Social Services Office in Brno under Article 76 of Act 99/1963 Coll. of the CPR to perform the removal of the below-named children from the care of a person who represents a threat to the public by immediately detaining said children at their place of residence prior to their removal to regional care institutions as follows:

1. IDESOVÁ, Dora (minor), b. 10/30/58—Children's Residential Care Institution in Uherské Hradiště

2. IDES, Jakub (minor), b. 2/16/61—Social Care Institution for Mentally Handicapped Children in Brno-Černovice, Brno-Chrlice site

You should submit a report on the detention of the children and their delivery into care.
Richard Angel, JD, District Public Prosecutor
6/17/74

79
from the State Social Services Office in Brno
to the District Public Prosecutor's Office in Uherské Hradiště
FAO Richard Angel, JD

re: report on the delivery of minors Dora Idesová and Jakub Ides into institutional care

I hereby report that the minors Dora IDESOVÁ (b. 10/30/58) and Jakub IDES (b. 2/16/61), residents at house no. 28 in Žítková, Uherský Brod district, were detained on 6/18/74 at their place of residence prior to their removal to institutions charged with their care.

Note: The delivery of the children into institutions of care was not accomplished without complications. Due to a situation of tension provoked by Dora Idesová, mentally and physically handicapped Jakub Ides suffered shock and a resultant seizure that was calmed only with the help of medication applied at the District Health Center in Uherský Brod, after which he was transferred to the Social Care Institution for Mentally Handicapped Children in Brno-Chrlice. Dora Idesová consistently refused to obey instructions issued by Public Security authorities; her delivery into the care of the Children's Residential Care Institution in Uherské Hradiště was accompanied by aggressive behavior and attacks on the authorities and caregivers in attendance.

On account of the situation, we recommend that she be kept apart from her fellow residents for a period of several months, with even short-term contact denied to her. Further, we recommend that Dora Idesová be subjected without delay to examination by a psychologist, upon the basis of which a suitable program of education and care will be determined.

For further information, representatives of the above-named care institutions should be contacted directly.

Alžběta Fuchsová, PhD

6/19/74

82

from the District Department of State Security in Uherské Hradiště, Third Division
to the Children's Residential Care Institution in Uherské Hradiště

> On 6/18/74 the Children's Residential Care Institution in Uherské Hradiště admitted Dora Idesová, b. 10/30/58, resident at house no. 28, Žítková, Uherský Brod district. On account of her upbringing in the family of a person representing a threat to the social order and public of the Czechoslovak Socialist Republic, please report without delay any strange or hostile actions on her part. For her further education, proceed with special reference to the matter of her relation to our Socialist society and her ideological principles. Submit regular reports on results. Until further notice.
>
> Officer: J. Švanc, ext. 708
>
> 6/29/74

A communication compressed into a few terse sentences of official language, as if from another world that ran parallel with her own. A world in which compassion did not exist, allowing people to produce automated official reports or statements filled with rumorous falsehoods of the kind her caregivers had regularly sent off about her.

These documents took Dora back into her life of that time, a life saturated with stormy emotions. She felt helpless and abandoned. Her eyes filled with tears.

A young archive staff member with golden fluff under his nose looked at her with curiosity before pinching his mouth into the shape of a small, hard heart. In the few years since the opening of the State Security Police files, he had seen many people reach into a pocket or a handbag for a handkerchief in an attempt to hide a momentary weakness.

Dora could still remember every last, tiny detail of that day in June 1974. She couldn't have forgotten it even if she'd wanted to. Now and then it all came back to her in dreams she couldn't rid herself of, so she relived the awful moments over and over. Again they had her, again they were holding her, again she saw Jakoubek struggle with them as they pulled him away.

On the day Surmena left, all they did was wait. Noon passed, the afternoon dragged by, evening approached, darkness fell. Surmena didn't return, either in the night or the following morning. Dora didn't go to school. She and Jakoubek spent the whole morning sitting in front of the cottage.

Only after this did figures appear on the path below. Two women and two men, making their way up to the cottage.

Dora watched the approach. She was afraid. The foursome rested several times on the steep ascent; during one such stop, she made out that one of them was wearing a police uniform. She grabbed Jakoubek's elbow and they dashed into the cottage, where they sat on the bench by the window, holding hands. Jakoubek was anxious, and Dora tried to assure him that there was nothing the matter; perhaps the people were not even coming to them. But a few moments later, they stepped into the cottage and spread themselves about the room, without having asked. The policeman remained standing at the door but looked about with curiosity. The second man sat at the table and pulled a folder from a brown leather bag. For a while the women paced the small space; then the taller of the two went out into the garden and walked around the house in the direction of the sheds.

Suddenly the smaller woman turned to Dora. "Where do you sleep?"

Dora indicated the oven and a narrow wooden bed next to the table.

"I suppose that's where Mrs. Surmenová sleeps. You sleep up there? With your brother?"

Dora nodded.

The woman turned and took a good look about, resting a particularly meaningful glance on the bottles of spirits lined up on the shelf. Then she stood over the man who was filling in columns on forms that had spilled out of his folder and were spread all over the table. Jakoubek's head was buried in Dora's lap, and his arms were around her waist. She could feel him trembling.

"How can I help you?" Dora asked awkwardly. "My aunt is not at home today."

The woman glanced at her and nodded. "Your mother, Irena Idesová, died in 1966, did she not? Your father is serving a custodial sentence. Mrs. Surmenová—who is currently in custody—is your only relative, is she not? Or do you have any other relatives in Žítková?"

Dora was confused and frightened.

"In custody? In prison?"

"I will ask you again. Do you have any other relatives in Žítková?"

Dora nodded reluctantly. "The Baglárs . . . She's our godmother, and . . ."

"Write it down. We'll let them know."

"Is Auntie in prison? What for? What's happened?"

No one paid any heed to Dora's repeated questions.

Jakoubek's trembling was intensifying.

The tall, bony woman came back and made her report. "Out the back there's a cow in calf, fifteen or so hens, a cock, and a flock of ducks. To be taken down to the farmers' cooperative as soon as possible."

Dora gasped. Surely they weren't going to take the animals when Auntie wasn't there.

"Where is my aunt Mrs. Surmenová?" she repeated, this time angrily.

"Where's Auntie? Where's Auntie?" His head still in her lap, terrified Jakoubek was parroting the question.

No reaction; it was as though they were not there.

In the end Dora could take no more of their haughty indifference. "Can you please tell us where our aunt Mrs. Surmenová is?" she shouted.

The women winced and scowled. The one who had come back from inspecting the yard pointed an index finger at her so that it almost touched her forehead and hissed, "She's upsetting him, don't you see? She's upsetting him. There's something wrong with that boy . . . Take him away from her, please . . . Calm him down . . ."

The skin of her cheeks and neck was so taut it looked fit to burst. Her goggle eyes and gaping mouth made her look like Death, Dora realized in the moment before she decided to throw herself at the woman. She wanted to scare her, but most of all she wanted to suppress the sobs that were welling up in her chest. But her sudden movement threw Jakoubek to the floor. He shook and twitched as the first spasms overwhelmed him.

After that, the rest of the day passed as though it were a single minute. Jakoubek went into a seizure and twisted and squirmed at their feet. They wouldn't let her try to calm him, but in any case, she wasn't sure she could manage him without Surmena. He continued to writhe until the man at the table raised his eyes from his forms for the first time, grabbed Jakoubek, and ran off with him across the field, down toward Hrozenkov. Having moments earlier been in the act of compiling an inventory of their property, the other woman hurried along the meadow path, her arms filled with forms. Dora wanted to go after them, but the stern, imperious policeman took a firm hold of her arm. Although she pleaded and screamed, they wouldn't let her go. They carried Jakoubek off, just like that—to some center, to a social care institution, so they said; it'd be better for him there because Surmena wasn't coming back. And what would happen to *her*? She'd be put in a home and watched over by caregivers. In a few years she'd come of age. And Surmena? It was all over for Surmena—Surmena was a murderer, a fraud, and an agent of the petty bourgeoisie. Surmena was undermining the authority of the republic. In the eyes of society, Surmena had failed. And that was the end of things for many years.

Pardubice Nocturne

The wrought-iron door of the archive building clicked shut at ten minutes past five. Dora busied herself with Surmena's file until the very last minute; the archivist practically had to push her from the reading room. Out on the street, she didn't know what to do with herself. Her head was still among the bureaucratic documents.

The square beyond the building was bathed in the last rays of a warm autumn day. Slowly she walked through these to the park in the middle of the square and a bench beneath a spreading lime. She was thinking about how she had gone through barely a third of Surmena's file, reaching no further than the moment of their separation. The time until the next morning and the resumption of her work—a whole evening and night of idleness—seemed infinite to her.

She considered taking the almost three-hour journey to Brno and traveling back to Pardubice in the early morning, but that was pointless, she knew. She would stay.

She turned her face to the sun and closed her eyes. She was tired. The intense effort involved in trying to burn into her brain every word imprinted on the carbon paper had made her eyes sting; the pressure at her temples was so great that it was as though her head was in a vise. Her stomach was tight—from hunger or nerves, perhaps both.

For twenty years, she counted, they had stuck to Surmena, until in the end, they got her for abortion. What total nonsense!

Dora was certain that no such thing had ever been performed at their place; Surmena would never have been a party to it. She shook her head in disgust before rising with a sigh. She needed to find a hotel, have dinner, and lie down. Sort out all the new information in her mind. And sort the notes in the blue notebook that for several years now had been held together with a thick rubber band because of the loose pages, clippings, and notes on scraps of paper it contained. In her hotel room, she would take from the desk drawer a clean white sheet of notepaper and jot down dates and events to form a new map of Surmena's life. As presented by the spies.

She walked slowly through the park and into a street that led to a square with a plague column at its center. Disturbed by the hustle and bustle of the city, she turned on her heel and went back to the narrow side streets.

The sign for the Champion Hotel showed a prancing horse. The place appeared big enough to provide her with enough privacy for the next two nights. She had dinner brought to her room.

She spread out on the bed and ate in comfort, meanwhile turning the pages of her notebook. She had made the first notes in the mid-1980s, when, very slowly, she was setting out on the trail of the goddesses of Žítková.

The notebook was an essential complement to her dissertation. It contained records of cases that the limited range of her dissertation could not contain, plus amendments, clarifications, detailed observations, brief transcripts of the testimony of contemporaries. And a list of questions that she had not been able to address. To these she was now adding others of which earlier she'd had no inkling.

She finished her meal and put the tray of dishes under her bed. Then she reached for her dissertation. This black bound volume was heavy, at first sight arousing much more respect than the crumpled, grubby school exercise book crammed full of loose scraps of paper. How appearances could deceive!

She straightened the pillow at her back and turned to the introductory chapter.

Introduction: The spiritual culture of Moravské Kopanice and the goddesses of Žítková

The issue of the existence of the so-called goddesses of Žítková has not yet been the subject of a complex academic work. Nevertheless it is a phenomenon worthy of the attention of modern Socialist science, not least because it provides us with a picture of an unknown segment of folk culture in Moravia.

Much has been written about Moravské Kopanice, its material culture, and the extraordinary abundance of folklore that manifests itself primarily in the unorthodox exuberance of its embroidery. Works include several dissertations from the Faculties of Arts of the J. E. Purkyně University in Brno and Charles University in Prague. Among the most significant contributions is *The Material Culture of Moravské Kopanice* by Josef Jančář (1958).

The nonmaterial traditions of Kopanice and the highly specific manifestation of the spiritual culture of the region have not, however, attracted serious scholarly inquiry.

My study, which is based on research conducted in the first half of the 1980s, seeks to address this lack. It focuses in particular on the issue of an endemic spiritual culture whose bearers are the goddesses of Žítková; it studies the lives of individual members of a family in a historical context and gives a number of examples of how their activities reflected the time in which they lived.

Ethical and legal aspects and the credibility and effectiveness of their activities do not fall within the remit of my study, which attempts to capture and describe disappearing practices of an almost-extinct phenomenon. I believe that this issue warrants careful consideration from the point of view of ethnography based on scientific materialism.

Had she written it today, it would be different, she thought as she arranged her pillow so that she could lie on her side. She might have written it differently even then. But she hadn't. She had often wondered whether she'd betrayed her own intentions and whether what she had written had done harm to society or to someone in particular. Now, years later, as she read her work again, nothing and no one came to mind, but still, she had a pang of conscience. The phrases *"attention of modern Socialist science"* and *"based on scientific materialism"* made her cringe; she regretted the fact that she had abandoned her original intention to rehabilitate Surmena and her work. She had wanted to dedicate the dissertation to Surmena. That had not been acceptable, of course: in the academic literature of the postwar period, Surmena and her kind were considered obscurantists who disseminated a misguided worldview, *"which will inevitably retreat as science gradually clarifies phenomena once deemed inexplicable and diseases once thought incurable. The extinction of superstition and the magical practices connected with it is a historical necessity,"* the university textbooks of normalization stated.

Although Dora had once thought Surmena's superstitiousness ridiculous, and although she had rebelled against it as a child, she did not want it to be trivialized. The goddesses had not produced cures out of simple superstition! She had intended to cite Surmena's practices in order to demonstrate the provable healing effects of "goddessing." She had wanted to capture the hitherto uncharted breadth of the goddesses' knowledge, from their familiarity with nature and the human body to abilities that not even she, a firsthand witness, could explain. She had wanted to speculate on the extent of the supernatural. She had intended to devote a chapter to the results of her consultations with experts, including a psychologist, a neurologist, and a pharmacologist. She had wanted to highlight the unrepeatable nature and historical uniqueness of the goddesses. She had managed only the latter.

At the beginning of the year in which she would write her dissertation, she had been to see Assoc. Prof. Lindner, her supervisor. Swamped by the upholstery of the low chair he had placed her in, she communicated her research intentions, causing him to study her in silence for a long time. When she could bear his gaze no longer, she lowered her eyes. She looked up again when she heard a sigh as he raised his arms above his head, followed by the crack of the joints of his interlocked fingers.

"Write these down," he said sternly. "Prokofiev: *Science and Religion*, 1952. Nahodil and Robek: *Folk Superstitions in the Czech Lands*, 1959. Ryazantsev: *Sushchestvuyet li sudba?*, 1959. Bílek: *Mediums, Telepaths and Clairvoyants Deprived of Magic*, 1961. Prokop: *Medical Science against Superstition and Charlatanism*, 1984.

"And finally you might brush up on the mission of your chosen discipline. I recommend 'The Political and Ideological Function of Ethnography,' an essay by Hana Hynková. I should point out that it was published relatively recently, and our department respects and is guided by its opinions. I advocate"—here he gave an amused snort—"that you do not allow yourself to be carried away by the conclusions of those dubious conferences on psychotronics that are popping up all over the place, nor by thoughts of the supernatural abilities of certain individuals. Ethnography is a factual, descriptive discipline that should record important aspects of folk culture, ideally with regard to benefits it may afford for the addressing of current challenges. Certainly you should not allow yourself to be influenced by fashionable pseudoscientific trends. I am aware, of course, of those international meetings in Bratislava that flirt with the supernatural, in which certain Soviet laboratories are involved. But as a possible topic for a dissertation, I would say that it is too fresh. Besides, I cannot imagine how you would wish to classify your dissertation within the framework of the recommended scientific challenges with which our institution, as others, must work."

Nor could Dora. When, a little later, she reread the list of preferred research categories that might embrace her dissertation, she had to admit that it did not belong in "The Culture and Way of Life of the Czech Working Class," "The Folk Culture of the National Revival," or "A Bibliography of Czech and Slavic Ethnography." Before her consultation with Lindner, she had thought "The Way of Life of the Socialist Village" was a possibility, but now she doubted it.

"I recommend strongly that you limit the topic of the goddesses of Žítková to the gathering of historical and ethnographic material," Lindner continued. "Were you to concentrate your study on the pre-twentieth-century period, we might be able to accept it in the 'Ethnography of the Slavs' category."

For several weeks Dora went through the literature assigned to her, hoping that somewhere in it, she would find a connection with her topic of choice. At the semester's end, she closed the last of the recommended books in disappointment. It ended with a quote from Diderot: *Do you believe that a man can live without superstition? As long as he is ignorant and faint-hearted, he cannot.* With this, Prof. Lubomír Hobek, CSc, triumphantly concluded his condemnation of folk beliefs and magic, in so doing underscoring the right culture, which was nationalist in form and Socialist in content.

In spite of her past reservations about superstition, Dora considered this judgment a cruel one. It was as though everyone wanted to pour out the baby with the bathwater; what, after all, was folk culture without its peculiarities? Even if they were unprogressive.

Dora thought of those monstrous folk festivals that served to showcase the Socialist culture of the provinces, of the folk-inspired jamborees in concrete Houses of Culture that stuck out like sore thumbs on once-quaint village squares, all to remind the population of the advantages of living in a workers' paradise—and she shuddered. This was the result of the academic theses and aesthetic imagination of the likes of Prof. Lubomír Hobek, CSc.

She either had to reject Lindner's requirements or take a strictly descriptive approach that was limited to the charting of the question in history. She had chosen the second course. And since that time, she had felt guilty. By her hesitant and hypocritical efforts to put on a friendly face for the regime, she had broken faith with Surmena and her legacy. But what else could she have done? Consign herself to a life behind the deli counter in a shop assistant's apron while she looked forward to stolen moments with Jakoubek on weekend afternoons, if her shifts allowed? She chose to take evening classes at the university in an attempt to link her future with a subject that fascinated her: the goddesses of Žítková.

Feeling tired and bitter, she skipped a few paragraphs. Her heavy-lidded eyes scanned the last few lines of the first chapter:

> I have succeeded in tracing the topic of my research back to the first half of the seventeenth century, although it can be assumed that the tradition by which the bearers of knowledge in question passed this knowledge on is older still. As to its origin, however, we can only speculate.
>
> It is a proven fact that the phenomenon was current into the second half of the twentieth century. At the present time the autochthonous form of the tradition is in the phase of demise.

Due to the historical focus of the research and the availability of written and archive materials, I decided that my work should address the period between 1630, when the first reference to the activities of the goddesses of Žítková was made in the *Blood Book of the Town of Bojkovice*, and 1925, when the period in which they were principally active came to an end.

Kateřina Shánělka

*D*ora saw her as if she was standing right there in front of her. Tall and graceful, but gaunt. The skin of her once-firm, strong arms hung limp, and her legs were buckled. Her once-luxuriant dark curls had been shorn, and all that remained were bristles; her gabbling mouth was missing most of its teeth. Dora didn't understand her, couldn't even hear her. But she didn't need to: she knew what she wanted to tell her; she knew her case down to the smallest detail.

Shánělka should have gone home to Žítková, where her mother was still living; now she regretted that moment long ago when she had made the wrong decision. Or she should have moved to Brod to be with her sister Kůna. She shouldn't have stayed in the house, especially a house in a town where she didn't know anyone properly, not even the family of dear departed Michal, who had taken her away from Kopanice. Everyone turned their back on her; no one had a word to say on her behalf. So they were hardly about to testify in her favor. There weren't six honorable souls among them. They didn't know her here, and they were afraid of her because it was said she could do strange things. No one minded these things if they were good for them—quite the opposite, in fact. She would get someone's cow to recover, or find a lost thing. She was able to treat illnesses, and everyone came to her for herbs. That suited them well enough.

But after Fucimanka spat at her, no one had a word to say to her. Anča just managed to tell her what they were saying about her, but by then it was too late; they had come for her.

Dora saw how Shánělka's tyrannized face was tormented by a tic that curled her lips into a painful sneer. This was for the town's bailiffs, who had rummaged through the house, looking for stolen wafers and/or human bones, finding nothing. They were fools. What need would she have of such things? They found nothing but herbs, and lots of them, which she dried in the attic and sorted into cloth pouches that hung from the rafters. Everyone had at least some herbs at home, so why should they show such an interest in hers? But their interest was real. They swept the herbs into a sheet. When they came for her, they threw this sheet onto the cart along with her. They didn't want so much as the sole of her shoe to touch the ground of Bojkovice. This was how witches were taken.

She was incarcerated at Světlov. In the castle cellars, where they shoved murderers, thieves, and poor women accused of infanticide. In a dungeon about as long as her outstretched arms. But she couldn't stretch her arms because they were tight against her body, held in manacles attached to a chain that was nailed to the wall under the skylight. For days, she sat there. No one told her what to expect. No one said anything to her. From time to time a jailer shoved a bowl of water and a piece of bread into the cell. At first she slept, but later her eyes wouldn't close. Day merged with night and morning never came, or she never recognized it when it did.

Then they dragged her out. Once out in the fresh air, she realized how much her cell stank and how she herself stank, in her pissed-in skirt, to whose inside and upper edges remnants of her feces clung.

"Is it true that you burned human excrement for your cows so that the milk of the person concerned would run from their teats?" Dora heard.

"Is it true that this was the excrement of Adamcová, and that it was taken from the cesspit by your girl on your instruction after Adamcová had performed her natural evacuation? Is it true that you prepared a witch's ointment for Fucimanová, which should cause her to conceive but by which you deprived her husband, old Fuciman, of his virility?"

Shánělka shook her head. Were they crazy? What good was human shit to her? How could it possibly benefit her cows? And as for Fucimanka, she was unable to conceive because her husband had long ago lost control of his tool, which was perfectly understandable—he was almost eighty, and what ointment could help an eighty-year-old man?

"No!" Shánělka protested, reaching out a trembling hand to Dora, beseeching her for help. But no help was forthcoming: Dora was rooted to the spot. All she could do was watch as Shánělka was dragged to the dam at the pond, where she would be subjected to the first Hungarian test—ordeal by water.

When Shánělka was tossed into the pond in her three skirts, it was as clear as day that she wouldn't sink. Bubbles of air caused the cloth to swell, keeping her afloat while she thrashed around frantically. She couldn't swim. Before she could sink into the calm, stagnant water, however, there was a fierce tug at the rope around her abdomen. Startled, she looked toward the men on the dam. Through a curtain of wet hair, she saw their furious faces and the wild motions of their hands. "The water has not taken her! She's floating. The water takes only the pure!"

Then Dora saw her lying naked on a table, her hands tied behind her head, her ankles locked in cold metal, her legs far apart. Five men—among them the executioner—were standing between her thighs and bending over her. All of them were staring where Shánělka had forbidden even her late husband to look, and their fingers were everywhere, including places she touched only when bathing herself after her monthly bleeding.

Because she wanted to thrash about, they had strapped her to the table at the waist and below the breasts. Because she had cried out, they had placed a scarf over her mouth and tied it around her head. Before they threw a sack over her head, Dora glimpsed the streaming tears of her helplessness.

"Here! Here! *Signum diabolicum*! It's here!"

By the time of the tribunal, her tears had dried. She sat slumped on a wooden bench, her body lifeless and her head apparently emptied by the examination and refusing to cooperate. Dora saw that Shánělka could now do little more than stare at the freak show that was going on around her. Certainly she was incapable of answering the endlessly repetitious questions put to her by the quartet of Bojkovice worthies, with the magistrate and the provost of the Dominican friary in Brod at their head. Had she told a girl to gather herbs in her nakedness and then to bathe in them in order to make herself more beautiful? Had she told her to go on Walpurgis Night to Saint Peter's stones, where she should commune with the devil at his infernal mass? Had she . . . ?

Shánělka shook her weary head. "No."

So they showed her the torture chamber. The thumbscrew. The boot. The rack, and how it stretched. She felt faint. She turned pleading eyes on Dora. What on earth should she say? That she was the devil's mistress? But what kind of nonsense was that? How could she ever have become involved in such things? And what would her mother have to say about it? Her sister Kůna? The family of her dear departed husband?

"No!"

So they crushed her big toes in the thumbscrew, even though she wept and begged for mercy. The bare floor of the torture chamber greedily absorbed the beads of blood that trickled from her feet.

"Why did you give Fucimanka that ointment?" Dora heard for the hundredth time.

"Because she wanted it," Shánělka answered. "So that her husband would give her the child she so much desired."

"And what magic was in that ointment? Who gave you the recipe?"

"There's no magic in it. It's herbs; that's all. Herbs you can gather in any forest and in every meadow, which you boil up with lard and then rub in to give men back their male strength. No one gave me the recipe; everyone knows it who knows anything about herbs. Ask any midwife or field doctor!"

"What kind of midwife? What kind of field doctor?"

Shánělka was choking back tears, but instead of giving an answer, she lowered her eyes and shook her head.

"For the manufacturing of your ointment, did you use the corpses of children? How many women did you rid of unwanted pregnancy? Were your nails so long that they could pierce the amniotic sac?"

"Do not fear. This court is just and does not crave your blood. Confess and you shall be forgiven."

Dora saw that Shánělka was confused. But what could she have been thinking when she confessed and then withdrew her confession? She could have spared herself the boot and the lighted candles. There were suppurating burn wounds to the sides of her breasts; the blisters burst, and her blouse was soaked with pus. She couldn't take any more, so she signed what they pushed in front of her. Of her own free will, everything important to her, everything she wanted to live and die for; she signed it without duress because on the day her signature was made, she was not subjected to torture. They held her under the arms, and because she couldn't write, they guided her trembling hand across the white sheet of paper, on which she left a brown trail of drying blood from her crushed thumbs.

"If a man abide not in me, he is cast forth as a branch, and is withered; and men gather them, and cast them into the fire, and they are burned." As she heard these words, Dora saw Shánělka look at her in surprise, suddenly fearful, terrified, as from the mouth of the magistrate, these words, the words of their Lord Jesus Christ, against whom she had never offended, could only mean the very worst. As this occurred to

her in all its force, she twitched several times; her bony face was lit by the horror in her wide eyes. She opened her toothless mouth, and the silence of the room in which Dora was sleeping was rent by a dreadful, inhuman scream.

When Dora woke up, it was still dark. She had fallen asleep on top of her dissertation, which she now pushed out from under her. She switched on and was dazzled by the cold light. As she picked her way to the bathroom, the strangeness of the room took her by surprise.

Again the dream about Kateřina Shánělka's trial. She'd had the dream countless times since discovering, in the *Blood Book of the Town of Bojkovice* records, Shánělka's tragic story, which had ended in her execution for *crimen magiae*. She had then established that it was Kateřina Shánělka who was the first in the long line of goddesses. Try as she might, however, Dora hadn't been able to reach any further into the past. She'd been faced with a desolate, timeless space, and there was not a single thread for her to pick up. For the period before the Thirty Years' War, parish books were incomplete; this was a time before registries and land records, which might have provided her with a lead. It was a dead end.

But even with nowhere to look, Dora was still tormented by a sense of unfinished business. Her intuition told her that Shánělka could hardly have been the first in a mysterious tradition passed down for many generations from mother to daughter. As there was no other course available to her, she addressed the threads that tied Shánělka to her sister Kůna and their cousin Kateřina Mrázka, who, five years later, escaped from the same tribunal by the skin of her teeth, leaving the place of execution to Zuzka Ouřednička, who had instigated the court proceedings against her. And these ties led to other witch trials in Bojkovice, in one of which Kateřina Divoká, Kůna's granddaughter, did indeed meet the headsman from Uherský Brod, who traveled to

Bojkovice in performance of his profession; the magistrate granted her clemency, but only insofar as she met her end not on a bonfire but under a sword's sharp blade.

If she closed her eyes and concentrated hard, Dora could hear the swish of the headsman's weapon as it cut through air in which there was no other sound, even though the square in front of the Bojkovice town hall was filled to bursting. Followed by groans and wails from Kateřina Divoká: the executioner's first swing was inaccurate and had to be repeated. The sweat that pricked Dora's forehead was as cold as the beads on the brow of the executioner; from under his red hood, it trickled from his temples and stung his eyes. But perhaps his eyes were welling with tears, not sweat: it was no everyday occurrence to separate from its body the head of someone he had known since she was in diapers.

Dora shook her head to rid it of these thoughts. She leaned against the washbasin and blinked at her mirror image, noticing the bruise that a corner of the hard cover of the dissertation had left on her cheek—on pale, dry skin that looked much older than it actually was. Only her thick, light-brown, shoulder-length hair did her any favors. Although she was past forty, there was not a speck of gray in it. But what of it? There was no one to appreciate its absence, was there?

She turned on the tap, cooled her face with cold water, and felt the blood flood back into her cheeks. She took a glass from the shelf, filled it with water, and drank. She didn't feel like going back to sleep.

She returned to the bed, stretched out on it, and opened the black volume. Having found the chapter about Kateřina Shánělka and Kateřina Divoká, she turned the pages slowly until she reached the pictorial supplement.

Contemporary engravings with scenes of interrogation with the use of instruments of torture. The thumbscrew. The boot. The rack. Lighted candles. A contemporary engraving of a witch anointing herself with a magical unguent. Plus a photocopy of the record of the trial of Kateřina Divoká in 1667 in the curling cursive script of the Late Gothic.

Confession and judgment of Kateřina Divoká, issued in the town of Bojkovice on the eleventh day of the sixth month of the year of Our Lord 1667

Since Kateřina Divoká is accused of fellowship with the devil and of consorting with him in the performance of sorcery, she was subjected to interrogation by pain and confessed the following:

1. That after midnight she would go to the churchyard, there to cut off the members of unbaptized children for their subsequent use in various potions for the detriment of her neighbors. This was corroborated by Jur, a cooper in Luhačovice, who saw her one night when he passed this way on his return from the tavern.

2. That she forced strange potions on young virgins for the infatuation of men, who would then pursue them as though deprived of their wits. This was corroborated by Markéta, daughter of a draper and esteemed councilor of Bojkovice, who refused to be involved in Divoká's amatory intrigues.

3. That strange things occur in her cottage; that there is a pot placed upside down on the table with herbs underneath it and a bowl on top of it into which she strained something through Talaš's tunic, which she had earlier stolen from the fence. Allegedly this was performed under some kind of invocation reminiscent of a prayer to the devil, which served as love sorcery to Divoká's benefit, rendering Talaš

unable to prevent himself from going to her against his will. This was corroborated by Marie Křestnička, a neighbor of Divoká's, who saw it all.

4. That Divoká offered to honorable Bojkovice women various intrigues, for instance, to escort Marie Křestnička's husband from this world (which the latter denies she would have wanted), by her charms to produce a child for Rozina Kudlička (refused), to heal Anna Rokytačka's physical ailment (refused).

As the aforesaid Divoká has, following torture by lighted candles, confessed to transgressing God's Commandments with evil intent and stated that she wishes to die for this, such is the verdict that is passed on her. Although by the strict letter of the law she should be burned at the stake to serve as a warning to others, by the grace of the law she will be punished by the sword and buried in the earth. By decree on the eleventh day of the sixth month of the year of Our Lord 1667.

Magistrate of the town of Bojkovice

Dora skipped a few pages, until she came to the following.

Letter regarding the performance of the task of the master executioner

Dear esteemed, wise, and prudent lords, let us be well favored! In accordance with the lessons of supreme law, we ordered a judgment to be discharged on Kateřina Divoká of infamous memory by the sword of the master executioner. The master executioner did not act as it behooves a master executioner to act, and he did not perform his task properly; he was compelled to complete the act of severance by a second blow. As he has answered for this in all humility before the law, I ask that your lordships deign to treat him mercifully and pardon his transgression. As to the person under judicial consideration, she was taken to the place of execution and there advised by the magistrate to come to her senses in her last moments by repenting before God and man. Divoká denied everything for which she was about to be executed, stating that she never did anybody any wrong, although if her guilt consisted in her knowledge of herbs and in using their power to help sick local people and their sick children, then she was guilty indeed; she was not guilty, however, of sorcery in her own home or of enchanting a local man and inducing madness in him. The convicted woman appealed for justice to be done, not through the honorable court but through the master executioner, to whom she was known; for this reason, his blow was imprecise. It is necessary to remark that although the execution of Divoká was at first accepted by the people, on the same day word began to spread that she was a martyr who had fallen victim to slander while the deeds by which it was alleged she had many times saved the lives of local children had been forgotten. We wish to thank you for lending the services of master executioner J. M., who is satisfied with the fee he has received from us as is appropriate to his humble profession.

On this thirteenth day of the sixth month of the year of Our Lord 1667, we remain your lordships' obedient legal servants and magistrate of the town of Bojkovice.

Beyond the window of Dora's hotel room, daylight had arrived. The sound of traffic on the road outside was slowly scaring away the shadows of the night and Dora's imaginings on the ends of the two women. In Dora's mind the faces of Kateřina Shánělka and Kateřina Divoká dissolved and then disappeared.

With her gaze now fixed on the new day, Dora snapped the black book shut. It was time to get up and return to Surmena's case.

Archive: Day Two

She got to the reading room on the stroke of eight. She rang the bell twice before a voice came through the speaker at the door.

"Archive. Can I help you?" The receptionist's words were almost drowned out by the sound of his chewing.

Dora dipped her head to the level of the microphone. "I'm going to the reading room."

The door clicked.

She hurried up the spiral staircase to the second floor, hung up her coat in a locker, wrote her name in the visitors' book, and received a folder from the greasy fingers of the archivist, who had just gulped down his breakfast.

Soon she was in her chair in the corner of the room, leafing through the file to the place where she had finished the day before.

95
from the District Department of State Security in Uherské Hradiště, Third Division
FAO operative worker INTERPRETER

Case: SURMENOVÁ, TERÉZIE—Instructions

> The above-named citizen represents a known risk to public safety. For a period of at least twenty years, she

has practiced deception on CSSR citizens, theft of public property, and subversion of the Socialist order. It has been concluded that these activities and her present behavior are outcomes of mental illness. For this reason Surmenová will be placed under observation at the State Psychiatric Hospital in Kroměříž, where the staff will be instructed to subject her to special attention. In the public interest, her contact with persons from outside the hospital, including members of her family, will be restricted.

Please apprise me without delay and through the relevant secret collaborator of any of her activities, utterances, or other circumstances of her hospitalization.

Officer: J. Švanc

6/17/74

Dora was astonished. As a first note of the time following Surmena's departure, she'd been expecting to find a form accounting for her being taken into custody, a record of her questioning, or the court hearing. There was no sign of any of these. Dora went a few pages back in the file and then a few pages forward. No, there was nothing she had missed: Surmena had not even been questioned. Was the file incomplete? The serial numbers on the pages suggested not. This was strange. Dora turned to the next document.

96
State Psychiatric Hospital in Kroměříž; Psychiatric Dept. 5A
Mental health record: SURMENOVÁ, Terézie
Attending physician: Dr. Ivan Kalousek

Family anamnesis: Paranoia in mother's family line (patient manifests same type of delusions as suffered by her mother and grandmother). Alcoholic father.

Personal anamnesis: Has experienced no serious illness; surgeries—0; in 1945 suffered a fractured left fibula, walks with a limp due to permanent damage to ligaments.

Abuse of addictive substances: Patient comes from region where consumption of spirits is common, resulting in her alcoholism. Nonsmoker.

Social anamnesis: Single, childless. From family of smallholders, poor social conditions, no emphasis placed on inclusion in collective. Strong faith in God (self-declared Roman Catholic) and low intellect have apparently deformed her character. Patient declares that she has never entered into marriage. Lives with her nephew and her niece, who have been entrusted to her care.

Occupational anamnesis: Primary education in-complete. Worked on her own smallholding until 1974. Has received disability pension since 1952.

Attitude to the Socialist order: Negative.

State on admission: On 6/17/74 patient was de-livered to the hospital by authorities of Public Security because during questioning and subsequent custodial interrogation, she demonstrated aggressive behavior and threatened said authorities, and her utterances made it clear that she was suffering from delusions. Authorities of Public Security reported manifestations of paranoid behavior and that their detainee had sev-eral times urinated in a public space at the station. On admission, patient was conspicuously unkempt;

demonstrations of her unstable emotions included anger, uncontrolled verbal production and racing thoughts, and anxiety made manifest in her squatting in the corner and refusing to communicate. Several times caught praying—unhealthy fixation on religious belief. Chaotic behavior.

Psychopathological analysis: Psychotic disorder with paranoid delusions and systematized bizarre visions diagnosed. She is convinced she can treat sickness using herbs she claims to have at home and to heal broken bones by touch. Also convinced she can see the future and influence the weather. She has a fixed idea that she is under surveillance by authorities of Public Security, who wish to harm her by taking away her foster children, causing her to lose her court case and resulting in her imprisonment. Convinced of conspiracy against her. Not aware of any of her crimes. Preventive therapy initiated due to suspicion of illness of psychotic character.

Medication: 6/18/74: On admission to hospital 2 amp. Plegomazin applied IM for tranquilization. Plegomazin (3 × 6 mg) again applied IM on 6/20/74. Patient uncooperative when medicated; refuses to take oral medication. Neuroleptic haloperidol (3 × 6 mg) applied IM; dose increased to 3 × 8 mg on 6/24/74. Reaction negative; hence on 7/1/74 medication changed to chlorpromazine (3 × 8 mg). As of 7/7/74 patient's state unchanged: delusions persist, remains uncooperative. Patient has begun to show depressive symptomatology. Patient refuses food and does not communicate.

107

to the District Department of State Security in Uherské Hradiště, Third Division
FAO Officer Švanc
Processed by: code name/file: INTERPRETER/15701
Type of cooperation: operative worker
Registered state security authority: Uherské Hradiště

Record of meeting with s.c. "BOLETUS"

On July 19, 1974, a meeting took place at the "Peace" services on Highway 47 (in the direction of Křenovice) with a secret collaborator with the code name "BOLETUS." Having been contacted at his place of work, the above-named arrived at the appointed time. For the course of the conversation, his behavior was normal; he showed no signs of nervousness and spoke fluently.

The beginning of the meeting addressed his family circumstances and his position at work, from which it transpired that his family circumstances are satisfactory (his is a regular marriage, and he has one child); in the workplace, however, he claims to be troubled and frustrated by a matter with a coworker.

At this point he was informed that following a review of his character, background, and civic stance, he had been identified as a responsible citizen to whom we, one of the most important organs of our state, could turn with confidence. BOLETUS responded to this information only to say that he was gladdened by it. Further, he was told that cooperation performed to our mutual satisfaction would surely contribute to the resolving of his difficulties in the workplace. BOLETUS responded to this news with considerable enthusiasm. He went on to say that Dr. Danuše Rezková, deputy to the consultant Assoc. Prof. Formánek, was plainly inadequate in her role, to which she had been appointed only thanks to her close contacts, which BOLETUS thought unprofessional.

Further, he was told that this interview concerned not only the establishing of mutually beneficial cooperation; it would also instruct him in matters of national security. He was told that among the patients at his place of work was a person who was hostile to the regime—a subversive element of the petty bourgeoisie whose illegal medical practice made her rich at the expense of dozens of unenlightened citizens, to some of whom she had caused harm. When the "Surmena" case was explained to him, BOLETUS knew exactly which case was meant: he is Surmenová's attending physician. Given the seriousness of the information he had just been given, he promised to review the patient's treatment.

Further, the question was put to him of whether he could help us complete our survey of developments at the State Psychiatric Hospital in Kroměříž, especially among its junior staff. BOLETUS answered this by saying that if what we asked of him was within his power to communicate, he would do so. All he wished to know was the direction this information should take. He was told that this would be discussed in detail at the next meeting, as would be the matter of his position at work.

The meeting was closed with the assurance that we would remain in friendly contact and that I would get in touch with him in the near future in the same way as before.

Conclusion: BOLETUS seems to be a suitable candidate for secret collaboration. He is motivated by his own aim, which is in accord with our intentions.

Operation ended on 7/19/74 at 6:05 p.m.

Total expenses: 247 Czechoslovak crowns

APPENDIX I

On the subject of himself, the s.c. informed us that he was born on 3/17/44 to a working-class family and that both his parents work, his father as a maintenance operative for municipal technical services, his mother as a bookkeeper for the same employer. His parents are not politically active. He is an only child. After primary school he completed his secondary education at the Secondary Comprehensive School in Kroměříž; in 1969 he graduated from the Faculty of Medicine of the J. E. Purkyně University in Brno. He performed his basic military service in Prachatice. He is married to Eva, née Burdová, currently on maternity leave. His son's name is Ivan. His hobby is volleyball.

It was established that the s.c. attended the Pioneers and was active in the Socialist Youth Association, where he played volleyball for the Kroměříž juniors; from 1959 to 1961 he was leader of this team. Found to be an active and Socialist-minded member. While a university student, he was active on the student committee, proving his enlightened attitude, demonstrating understanding of the dangers of counterrevolution, and expressing his agreement with the entry of friendly armies in August 1968. A member of CP CSSR since 1972.

In 1972 an unsuccessful candidate for the position of deputy to the consultant of Psychiatric Department 5A of the State Psychiatric Hospital in Kroměříž.

Is politically mature and has a good general understanding of social issues.

111

to the District Department of State Security in Uherské Hradiště, Third Division
FAO Officer Švanc
PROGRESS REPORT ON CASE: Surmenová, Terézie
Submitted by: s.c. "BOLETUS"

At your request I am sending supplementary information on the condition of the patient Terézie Surmenová. The patient is hospitalized with a diagnosis of a psychotic disorder with delusions (paraphrenia), which is currently in partial remission. The patient is still subject to affective disorders and disorders of perception and thought. She is confused and believes herself to have a daughter, claiming: "My daughter's name is Dora"; the record shows that the two children she bore in 1939 and 1942 are deceased. Mistrustful, uncooperative.

Throughout August the patient's reaction to medication was negative; the patient is pharmaco-resistant. Thus in September her symptoms indicated electroconvulsive therapy: application of 6 el. shocks 2× weekly, under general anesthesia. After first session of ECT, condition good, patient calm.

In November symptoms of illness reappeared: recognition of own difficulties low, aggression and hostility; unintelligible mumbling of prayer-like utterances later established to be a kind of incantation, by constant, breathless repetition of which patient exhausted herself till the moment of falling asleep. Further series of ECT indicated for alleviation of difficulties. In reconvalescence, yielded to depressive symptomology.

Since January 1975 increasing irritability accompanied by symptoms of persecutory delusion—patient has convinced collective of nurses and doctors of her persecution by CSSR public authorities. She names comrades from the Regional Court and National Committee of CP CSSR, e.g., M. Zelenka and I. Jirák, who she claims made use of her services.

Difficulties alleviated by medication with sedative effect, with various reactions. Owing to patient's condition since last ECT, I propose discontinuation of this treatment.

112
District Department of State Security in Uherské Hradiště, Third Division
FAO operative worker INTERPRETER

Case: SURMENOVÁ, TERÉZIE—Instructions

I repeat with emphasis that the Terézie Surmenová case concerns a person who represents a threat to the Socialist order of the people's democracy and whose activities are systematically injurious to citizens of Czechoslovakia; this is why she was admitted for medical treatment. It is plain that her condition is worsening, as testified by her lies and shameless accusations against irreproachable persons serving our Socialist order and CP CSSR; this slander represents a criminal act of subversion against the republic. Since the perpetrator is a mentally disturbed individual, it is our belief that the patient's attitude should be normalized not by criminal proceedings but by the application of more effective methods of treatment than medication alone. Convey this information to our secret collaborator at the State Psychiatric Hospital in Kroměříž; also advise him that the patient should continue to be denied visitors, through whom she would continue to spread misguided opinions damaging to civic morale.

Officer: J. Švanc

3/2/75

116
to the District Department of State Security in Uherské Hradiště, Third Division
FAO Officer Švanc
PROGRESS REPORT ON CASE: Surmenová, Terézie
Submitted by: s.c. "BOLETUS"

A rigorous examination conducted at your recommendation has established that the illness of patient Surmenová is proceeding progressively. Previous therapy has been deemed ineffective; hence, renewal of electroconvulsive therapy is indicated—a series of 8 el. shocks 2× weekly.

Dora closed her eyes in pain, imagining Surmena's convulsing body gripped in an unnatural shape, her hands clenched into fists; she imagined the straps that held her to the bed, her head in the hands of a warden to prevent the charge-pumping electrodes from slipping from her temples. Ten seconds, twenty seconds, thirty seconds . . .

Her heart pounding, Dora leaned against the chair back and struggled to catch her breath.

A few minutes earlier, she had thought that Surmena was a victim of circumstance, in which the principal roles had been played by biased police and obtuse officials of the regime who dismissed whatever they were unable to process and so had dropped Surmena, like a hot potato, into the arms of the physicians. As contributory factors she had considered Surmena's failure to deal with the demands of her situation and later her disturbed mental health; no one was immune, after all.

Now Dora took an entirely different view of things. Now she was prepared to listen to a voice that had been at the back of her mind since the day before. Suddenly this voice seemed paranoid no longer. What once she had seen as a series of accidents, now she saw as a carefully planned course of action aimed at getting rid of Surmena. But why? Why?

Dora stumbled out of the reading room.

By the time she returned from the toilet, the man in the glass cubicle was concerned. She had been in there for over an hour.

121
to the District Department of State Security in Uherské Hradiště, Third Division
FAO Officer Švanc
PROGRESS REPORT ON CASE: Surmenová, Terézie
Submitted by: s.c. "BOLETUS"

At your request I am submitting information on the current state of the patient Terézie Surmenová. As of 7/12/75 it can be stated of the course of the patient's stay at Women's Department 5A of the State Psychiatric Hospital in Kroměříž that it is proceeding in a manner common to patients with a diagnosis such as hers.

On admission, Surmenová was placed in a ten-bed room with women aged between twenty-seven and sixty-nine years whose diagnoses coincide to a large extent with hers (psychotic delusions, in some cases schizophrenia). Patients are monitored constantly by a service performed by specialist nurses; this service is supervised by a team of doctors led by the department's consultant, comrade assoc. prof. Dr. Formánek, CSc. Although Surmenová is on an open ward to which relatives of patients have access every Sunday afternoon, visitors are led to rooms only after their presence has been approved by the ward sister, who is apprised of the consultant's decision that Surmenová should be denied visitors. So far no one has attempted to visit Surmenová.

Relationships among patients are generally good. Surmenová tends to be withdrawn; of her own free will she does not seek personal contact with any of the women on the ward. When personal contact occurs, there is a tendency among the women, including those older than Surmenová, to treat Surmenová as an authority. This state of affairs was exemplified by an incident that occurred on 3/21/75, following a conflict on the ward concerning the approaching Eastertide, as on public holidays some patients are permitted to return temporarily to their homes. The disturbance took place in room 17, where Surmenová stays. It culminated in a brawl between two patients, Růžena Drmolová and Irena Kučerová, in which other patients became involved and in the course of which the latter-named suffered lacerations to the forehead and left temple caused by the beating of her head against an iron bedstead and bruises to the neck as a result of strangulation. Subsequently, Kučerová suffered a severe epileptic seizure with convulsions. Having succeeded in forcing entry to the room (patients had been blocking the door), the nurses on duty found the stricken Kučerová with her head in Surmenová's lap. Surmenová was holding Kučerová around the head and chest, thereby subduing the convulsions that were tossing her body about in the narrow space and might easily have caused her injury. The back of Surmenová's hand was wedged between Kučerová's teeth, causing a painful wound but preventing Kučerová from biting her tongue. By an unspecified "invocation" uttered in a loud voice, Surmenová then acted upon the other patients, causing them to scatter to all corners of the room, where they were discovered by the orderlies. Of undoubted fascination are the facts that that very morning, Surmenová had undergone the last in a series of three electric shock treatments, and at an inspection conducted approx. half an hour before the incident, she had been lying in a state of reduced perception verging on apathy. Most patients in such a condition are incapable even of verbal communication, let alone walking or demanding physical activity. We are unable to explain the mobilization of energy by which Surmenová rose from her bed, held down 168-pound

Kučerová as she writhed in convulsions, and dispersed a group of eight women in an atmosphere of neurotic delirium; no one in our collective of doctors and nurses has ever seen the like. Following the intervention of the nurses and orderlies, Surmenová fell back into a state of apathy consistent with a post-electroconvulsion state. Nevertheless, since this incident the respect she commands among her fellow patients borders on religious awe. To our great displeasure, this attitude is shared by some of the nurses, although they have received instruction on pathological reactions in the course of electric shock treatment and should view the incident from the perspective of modern medicine.

I am now obliged to submit a further report concerning the frame of mind of certain staff at the State Psychiatric Hospital in Kroměříž.

Despite the fact that Surmenová tries to remain aloof from the collective, she has become a person much sought after, not only by her fellow patients but also by comrade nurses of 5A and other departments. This has happened because the word has been spread (probably by some psychiatric patients) that Surmenová has special abilities. As proof of these abilities, the circumstances behind the departure from Dept. 5A of comrade registered nurse K. Jirková are cited. Although it was known that Comrade Jirková had long had difficulty conceiving, she fell pregnant and was granted sick leave from her high-risk workplace. Comrade nurse Ludmila Kopáčová commented that as a result of Surmenová's advice—that Comrade Jirková apply hot compresses, perform certain physical exercises, and take a certain mixture of herbs—she had managed to fall pregnant at age thirty-nine.

As further proof of these abilities, it is reported about the workplace that Surmenová allegedly foresaw the health problems of comrade nurse Trnková, who is now on sick leave with chronic kidney disease, which is in the final stages and requires regular dialysis. It is alleged that in March, Surmenová urged her not to add salt to her food and not to eat eggs and meat, but to eat buckwheat, garlic, and onion.

It transpired from consultations with Comrade Trnková's attending physician and with Comrade Trnková herself, conducted in her own interests by comrade ward sister Ledvíková, that in the past month Comrade Trnková exhibited growing and progressive renal insufficiency until a point was reached where her kidneys were working at less than 30 percent, although two months earlier—i.e., in March—this condition could have been prevented by a balanced diet. I consider it pertinent to add that in such cases, the diet should limit, above all, the intake of salt and protein. This incident, too, has earned Surmenová the uncritical admiration of staff in 5A and other departments.

I believe it would be appropriate to take action against such irrational behavior by instructing those nurses who have succumbed most to Surmenová's influence on the quality of Socialist medicine and the proper, modern approach to charlatans and quacks. Further, I propose that they be warned that failure to reevaluate their obliging treatment of the patient will result in their immediate transfer to another workplace. By such a measure, we would remove the possibility of the circulation of misguided reports among the patients and staff of Dept. 5A, the latest of which concerns the state of the building and climate-related processes.

It is generally known that owing to their great age, many of the buildings of the State Psychiatric Hospital have, for a long time, fallen short of the common standard in terms of their technical state. As for the building of Dept. 5A, the hospital's administrators are aware that it leaks and that the capacity of the antiquated boiler is insufficient for its heating needs. For this reason, at the beginning of 1975 an application was placed for a new boiler manufactured by Bertsch; in the coming months, it is planned that a new boiler room will be built for this, together with a storage tank for mazut.

In the winter of 1974/1975, the weather in the Kroměříž region was unusually harsh, resulting in the cracking of a long-unchanged central heating pipe (due to freezing temperatures in January and February) and numerous visible changes to the state of the building (a March gale carried away part of the roof; heavy rainfall in April and May soaked the building, as a result of which we continue to battle with mold on the walls of patients' rooms).

It is perhaps logical that these minor mishaps should befall only the pavilion of Dept. 5A, as it is one of the oldest and least maintained of the pavilions that comprise the State Psychiatric Hospital in Kroměříž. Unfortunately, however, this fact has provided a breeding ground for the proliferation of other fantastical ideas connected with Surmenová, whom patients believe to be able to manipulate the weather, bringing these unusual climatic phenomena on the Kroměříž region in defiance of the fact that she is detained in the psychiatric hospital. Because of the increased unrest that the spreading of these rumors has caused, I arranged for Surmenová to share a room with five patients in the later stages of dementia, where she is sufficiently isolated. She reacted badly to her removal from room 17, where she had been until that point: she was aggressive and threatening toward me, the attending physician. Her behavior frightened not only the patients but also the nurses on duty, who reported to me that she said the following: "The Lord God will not forgive you this. You take years from your own child, just as you take years from me."

Due to the patient's increased aggression toward those around her and the worsening of her illness, I have decided to apply a fourth series of electroconvulsive therapy, which I expect to bring the patient greater tranquility and allow her to be more considerate of her illness and surroundings.

A Shared Inheritance

Dora trudged from the archive building as if in a daze. She had dozens of questions, most of them for Dr. Kalousek, who had concealed himself behind the inventive alias BOLETUS.

Only yesterday she had remembered him with deep gratitude.

So convincing had he been in his attitude of empathy that she had given him all the information he had asked for, without hesitation. He had explained to her the procedure for Surmena's treatment; his deep, soothing voice had been the only one that had managed to calm her anxieties. For her, their telephone conversations had been like absolution after confession.

That day she had finally found out the truth, and this knowledge was devastating. She was overwhelmed by guilt for having failed to see through him. How stupid she had been! Not even four years at the hostel had been able to teach her to be more cautious and suspicious. She had swallowed his stories hook, line, and sinker.

But who could really have known? Who could have guessed that the doctor responsible for Surmena's treatment, a man who had promised to do everything in his power to promote human health, was merely pretending to treat this woman who had hitherto been a stranger to him, and that on top of all this, he had the nerve to make telephone calls that would keep Dora and her doubts at a safe distance?

Dora was disgusted, and she could feel herself shaking.

On reaching her hotel, she headed straight for the bar. She needed something for her nerves and couldn't imagine being all alone just then in the silence of her room.

She chose a secluded table in the corner; she didn't want to attract attention. It wasn't even six yet, and she was wary of questioning looks from people who spotted a woman drinking alone. By the time the waiter brought her drink, her laptop and dissertation were open in front of her.

All things considered, her dissertation was pretty comprehensive. In the course of her studies, Dora had gathered a great many materials; her work contained all she had managed to dig up in the archives of 1980s Czechoslovakia. It had taken an impossibly long time for her requests to pass through the hands of officials seated in the bowels of the enormous Archive of Moravia building. Most requests had been approved; the regime would cite witch trials and disputes between women and village priests as examples of the insidious and destructive power of a church that, for years, had "prevailed in its exploitative struggle against the oppressed classes."

It was only after the revolution that she realized how many of her requests had not been approved. Suddenly databases were listing magazines published in the years of the First Republic, which she had supposed lost forever (they contained work by ethnographers of "right-wing, bourgeois government" whose conclusions were "contaminated by capitalism") and scientific journals that librarians and archivists had claimed to be lost or stolen. Parish records reappeared; in previous times Dora had been told that church dignitaries had destroyed these rather than hand them over to the archives. And the foreign publications coming into the Institute of Ethnography's library were no longer misappropriated or deposited for good before researchers could get to them.

The accessibility of recently released sources and the new age, in which no one forced researchers to compromise their plans and use hypocritical diction, opened a path to Dora's original aim. The volume whose writing she was about to embark on would become her key professional achievement. And it would rehabilitate the goddesses. All of them, but above all, Surmena. As soon as she had read to the end of Surmena's file, she would devote herself to the rewriting of her dissertation and the addition of several new chapters. She could hardly wait to get started.

With a glass of clear liquid at her elbow, Dora opened the black hardback cover and turned to the first chapter.

Had the situation permitted, she would have opened her dissertation with a description of the place. Everyone said that it was peculiar, which was why it produced peculiar individuals. Perhaps the people of Kopanice said this about themselves because apart from this sense of their exceptionality, they had nothing. They were small, gnarled people, underfed because their soil was poor, health broken from a young age not only by hard work but also by strong homemade brandy. They had an abiding, unbreakable faith without being able to respect that faith's moral values. Outside their own territory, they were known as thugs and thieves; they were ridiculed as would-be fraudsters whose efforts to deceive were easily detected. There was a connection here with education: for the people of Kopanice, it had no value—school was a waste of time that could be put to better use by working in the fields or other means of making a living.

Fifty years after the abolition of labor without pay, they were still working on the estate of the counts of Světlov. In Kopanice no one could read or write, so why would they take newspapers? Hence the news had not reached them that labor without pay had been abolished. The situation was rectified only by the intervention of a horrified lawyer called Večeřa, a pioneer of tourism, lover of the virgin nature of the White Carpathians, and author of an article titled "Modern-Day Serfs" that appeared in the magazine *Independence*. Having apprised the surprised villagers, at the end of 1896 Večeřa paid a visit to Minister-President Badeni in Vienna in order to get the situation changed. But what did the unauthorized sweat and toil of two generations of villagers have to do with him? Nothing. Perhaps he was incited by his incredulity at the fact of such deep unconsciousness and ignorance resulting in slavery in civilized Moravia at the end of the nineteenth century. But these failings would remain for many years to come. Even in the 1950s, when the Communists were boasting that they had eradicated illiteracy, at least a third of Kopanice inhabitants couldn't read this news.

In any case, the people of Kopanice held on to the notion that they were exceptional because they lived in an exceptional setting. Dora would have liked to begin here in the writing of her dissertation. But of course, it was nonsense to open an academic work with an essay on a mountainous landscape whose slopes were covered with forests of Carpathian beech and oak, their trunks too broad to put one's arms around, where the hillsides were dotted with narrow tilled fields and squat little cottages and meadows that, in summer, were aglitter with rare orchids and anemones. An academic work cannot begin with a description of a fresh summer day in the mountains that gives way in a moment to winds and storms that swathe the ridges in dark, impenetrable clouds, nor with one of a hard winter when the hills are whipped with snowy gusts more reminiscent of Siberia than southern Moravia. The pages of such a work cannot describe the huge round moon and the shreds of night sky between the tips of the serried hills, nor can it observe that on a cloudless night, the hillside paths are seen almost as clearly as in daytime; that when at such a moment you stand on the crest of a hill at the threshold of your cottage, you might believe yourself in heaven, the whole world open beneath your feet; and that the lights of cottages scattered across the hillside opposite wink at you, as do those of Hrozenkov from a hollow between hills, like a babe in its cradle. Everyone knows of everyone else, regardless of the distance between them. They are alone, yet together.

That would have been a proper beginning for her dissertation, showing how magical Kopanice in the White Carpathians was and that only in such a place could something as special as the goddesses originate and develop.

In an academic work bound by strict rules in which aesthetics counted for naught, there was no place for it, however. She didn't attempt it because she imagined the five pairs of eyes of the comrades of the examination committee, at least one of whom would be apprised of her cadre profile. "With all due respect to our working people, comrades, and please believe me that I am not acting out of a failure to assume the viewpoints of different classes, quite the opposite, in fact . . . But this is unacceptable; it falls entirely beyond our scale of evaluation, and it does not apply the criteria for the scientific process. I can't imagine anyone but a shop assistant writing such a thing. All due respect to her dutiful work in the service of our homeland, but let this be at the co-op store!"

So the start she made was a very different one.

Religion versus witchcraft

Religion and superstitious witchcraft have been treated many times in studies by leading theoreticians in ethnography and ethnology, who, on the basis of scientific materialism, have produced sufficient evidence to prove the falsity of belief in supernatural powers. Their argumentation shows clearly that the idea of higher beings and their supernatural abilities (e.g., God in the case of Christianity, forces of nature in the case of witchcraft) means the renunciation of reason and subsequently of justice, leading inevitably to the enslavement of humankind.

For a consideration of the question of the so-called goddesses of Žítková, however, it is necessary to address these categories and, to this end, to distinguish consistently between religion and witchcraft. Only then will we be able to understand the synthesis of the two in the magical activities of the goddesses, who have taken the Christian God into their rituals.[1]

Although this principle appears to be antagonistic, thanks to an extensive study by Dr. Čeněk Zíbrt,[2] it is today not unknown. Indeed, on the basis of his research, it is possible to prove various forms of interaction between the Christian faith and paganism that have occurred throughout the cultural life of Europe.

It can be stated that initially, this concerned the combining of the new faith with existing pagan religiosity (e.g., coincidence of church festivals such as Christmas with the winter solstice, Easter with the spring equinox). Only later did a church backed by the ruling class begin to distinguish between significantly different bodies of faith, make new, unusual demands, and dictate a strict network of ethical principles that included the rejection of ancient customs and rituals. Nevertheless, Zíbrt has proved that throughout

1   Hence the name "goddessing," the magical process of divination on the basis of which advice is given, diagnosis is determined, etc. "Goddessing" means the making of supplication to God for manifestation of what the subject seeks. The mediator of such manifestation is called a "goddess."

2   Zíbrt, Čeněk: *Seznam pověr a zvyklostí pohanských z VIII. věku*. Česká akademie císaře Františka Josefa, Praha, 1894.

Europe, there were families that long persisted in preserving the original teachings of their ancestors; they passed ancestral wisdom from generation to generation, notwithstanding the fact that this wisdom was termed pagan and thus heretical.

Representatives of the Church were aware of this. From the dramatic, often remarkable religious confessions contained in fragmentary records that survive from early medieval times, much is known about actions to unify the population within the system of a single faith. These actions were directed against those who maintained pagan traditions. The greatest threat posed to the Church by such traditions was represented by the fact that people who turned to them believed them to have a power that originated in knowledge of ancient secrets and an ability to draw into their activities the (newly) acknowledged power of the Christian God. Thus dual knowledge and dual abilities became far more important than priests and monks, the official representatives of the Church.[3]

For this very reason, treatises were written in which ritual and magical practices were misinterpreted so as to present them as a danger to Christian society. Most members of Christian society had a low level of education and took horrific images of advocates of paganism making pacts with the devil at face value.

One of the best-known treatises of this type is *Malleus Maleficarum*, otherwise known as *Hammer of the Witches*, by the Dominican friar Heinrich Kramer

---

3   *vide* Baroja, J. C.: *Die Hexen und Ihre Welt*. Ernst Klett Verlag, Stuttgart 1967.

(Henricus Institor).[4] Although the University of Cologne, under whose auspices the author attempted to have the work published, rejected it as the product of a mentally disturbed cleric, from its first edition in 1486, it was distributed widely; in the course of the next two centuries, it appeared in twenty-eight new editions throughout Europe. Before long, its content was being cited at times of natural disaster or epidemic so as to provoke hysteria, resulting in a search for culprits. It is no surprise that these were found among adherents of the pagan tradition, who, in the shape of devil's helpers, sorcerers, and witches, enforced their will on Earth with the intention of destabilizing their community or the whole of Christian society.

Let us assume that there was something in this. Dora could well imagine that were one to mix what she knew about the arts of the women of Žítková with well-directed rabble-rousing and dashes of hysteria, fear, and stupidity, the resulting blend would be explosive enough to hurl women like the goddesses—women like Kateřina Shánělka and Kateřina Divoká—into the flames or onto the block.

Their heads dropped into baskets made ready to receive them, and their blood spurted up to a yard away; their bodies transformed into ash, as did those of many other victims of witch trials. But there was a difference between them and the women of Žítková. These images stayed in Dora's mind as she went through the surviving "blood books"

---

4   Heinrich Kramer (Henricus Institor; 1430–1505), prior of the Dominican house in Schlettstadt and author of the three-volume treatise *Malleus Maleficarum*. It was once believed that *Malleus Maleficarum* was coauthored by Jakob Sprenger (1437–1495), prior of the Dominican house in Cologne and professor of theology at the local university, but this has been disproved.

of other Moravian towns, which recorded verdicts passed mostly on women who were sentenced not only for *crimen magiae* but for accompanying crimes that were capital offenses: infanticide, termination of pregnancy, poisoning, theft, adultery, bigamy, incest—committed for the most part by women on society's margins, beggars, and the mentally ill. There were exceptions, of course: the most famous trials were at Velké Losiny and Šumperk, which were unleashed by a Mr. Boblig of Edelstadt, whose sick carryings-on caused the border with Poland to be lined with the charred corpses of mostly honorable townspeople.

Other exceptions to this were women from Žítková, whose sentences comprised an enumeration of sins highly abstract in their substance, doubtless generated by the agitated imaginations of plaintiffs with awareness of their true arts. This Dora knew not only from her reading of individual records but also from her own experience. The women who came before the court in Bojkovice should not have had any charges to answer. Unless it is a crime to know things that others don't.

Dora pressed the button on her computer. While she was waiting for the display to resolve itself into a deep blue, she waved to the waiter and ordered another glass of wine. Window after window opened before her eyes until at last the cursor clicked on one titled "Healing." She took her time as she searched through the individual files. Then she opened the notes she had taken at her interviews with contemporary witnesses, on ancient recipes passed down through the generations. She read on until she came to what she was looking for. Surmena's advice to Baglárka.

> If you wish to inflame man's desire and so aid conception, strip bark from the trunk of a young oak, in spring when the leaves are not yet sprouting and the sap is rising. Grind to a powder, add pieces of Maral root, pulp of birch catkins, and two teaspoons

of caltrop leaves infused in ten drops of vinegar. Mix with lard, bring to a boil, and leave to congeal. Rub on your husband in the evening. Twice a day have him drink tea decocted from caltrop stems. If this is too hot, mix it with spirits.

It was the recipe that Kateřina Shánělka had given Fucimanka. But in Baglárka's case, it had worked: she had mothered three children. The "Healing" folder was full of such instructions and advice. Once these had been their only methods for making people better. Such a pity that in the hysteria of the witch hunt, people had come to see them as wicked practices to be eradicated as quickly as possible. Along with respect for those who knew them—the goddesses, who came to be seen by their neighbors as witches. No doubt other of the goddesses' reported abilities served to strengthen this belief.

Dora clicked on a file named "LOVE MAGIC."

The screen revealed a photocopy of the written verdict passed on Kateřina Divoká, Shánělka's great-niece, whose magic had carried a man called Talaš into her arms. Wax pouring and exorcism? Use of herbs to create illusion and mischief with love? Although Dora believed Kateřina Divoká to have done all this, it hardly justified her execution. In this regard she considered her as guilty as her granddaughter Zuzka Poláška, who, more than half a century later, was tried in Bojkovice for the bewitching of Jura Řehák, *"an honest blacksmith from Bystřice, whom she caused to become infatuated with her, enticed away from his wife Marina, whom she then tortured to death."* They failed to establish that Poláška was the murderer of Řehák's consumptive wife, but on suspicion of other magical practices, she was convicted and fined five guilders. That was in 1741, by which time ordeal, torture, and execution were no longer the order of the day for purported witches in the courts of Moravia. Poláška's life was spared, unlike those of her predecessors.

Dora believed in the guilt of both, as she did in that of many other goddesses. Indeed, she knew them to be guilty: even in her time, girls had come running to the Bedová in the hope of turning the heads of their chosen ones.

She remembered them coming to Surmena, mostly in the evening when the light was failing so that even if seen, they wouldn't be recognized. They came shyly but full of hope. Surmena would take them out into the dark, guided only by the flickering flame of an oil lamp, which Dora's gaze would follow from the window until it disappeared beyond the crest of the hill.

Surmena always locked Dora and Jakoubek in the cottage so that Dora wouldn't think of going after her; apparently, this was not something she should see. Her exclusion made Dora all the more curious, and she never fell asleep until after the return of Surmena and the girl. And she never learned what the two had been doing out there; all she heard was the rustle of dried herbs being tipped into a bag, then words of thanks from the girl before she hurried out into the night.

Then Surmena made the mistake of forgetting to lock the door. She was lying wrapped in a woolen shawl next to the hot stove when tapping on the cottage door roused her from her doze. She hastened to strain the herbal decoction that had been bubbling on the stove and to put her things into a cloth bag. Still in a state of mild confusion, she hurried into the night without having secured the door; Dora, wide awake as ever, went after her. Hidden by the darkness but guided by the flickering light, Dora followed in Surmena's footsteps to the edge of the woods, where the spring rose into a well.

Dora came close enough to see and hear what was going on. She saw a girl she recognized from Hrozenkov squatting naked in the well while Surmena poured the brew, now mixed with spring water, over her.

"I wash you with five fingers, with the palm as the sixth so that the chosen one will come to you . . . to make you most precious to him, the

dearest of all virgins, so that he cannot eat, cannot drink, cannot sleep, cannot smoke tobacco, cannot make merry, can come only toward this Hanička until he reaches her and enters into marriage with her . . ."

Surmena bent down to the well and then straightened up again, making sure that Hanička was thoroughly wet. She washed her hair and rubbed her arms and legs.

"So that for him an hour is not an hour, family is not family, a sister is not a sister, a brother is not a brother, a mother is not a mother, a father is not a father, so that nothing is dearer to him than his chosen one. With God's help let her be placed before his eyes."

Hanička began to pray.

"Thus I perform this enchantment," Surmena continued as she moved around the well and made the sign of a large cross over it. When she had finished, she wrapped the girl in a canvas grass-carrier that she had brought in her linen sack. When she had dried the girl and the girl was dressing, she asked, "When will you have your monthly bleeding?"

"In a week," said Hanička, her voice shy and faltering.

"I see. On the very first day, add to the yeast three drops of your blood collected from the cloth and one hair from your pubis and leave the dough to rise. After baking, take all the prettiest cakes and hold them for a short time in your armpit. A few minutes should be enough, while they're still warm, but not while they're hot so that you don't scald yourself. Put them on a plate. When young Lipták is passing, offer them to him, telling him to take a few if he likes the taste of them. Not so many, though, that he'll share them out—he must eat them himself, as you know."

As she put on her blouse and skirt, Hanička hung on Surmena's every word, nodding again and again; she didn't want to get this wrong.

"When we get home, I'll give you Saint John's wort and ground pine, and amaranth for you to wear so that you'll smell sweet. To him in particular."

Hanička laughed with delight, then sang a Kopanice song in a low voice. *"How you boys do not know / Why you run around me so / For I'm wearing ground pine / Attached to this fine pinny of mine . . ."*

"That's right," said Surmena, nodding.

The light of the paraffin lamp over the well illuminated only the stage on which this scene was played out, together with its two actors. Dora was rapt with wonder.

Some months later Dora again looked on, incredulous, as Hanička—in a wedding dress, with a great crown of flowers in her hair—was led to the altar at Hrozenkov by one of the Lipták boys. Was she imagining things, or were Surmena and Hana exchanging special smiles?

This memory first occurred to Dora as she was reading the judgments against Kateřina Divoká and Zuzka Poláška. It occurred again whenever she came across a case that demonstrated the special love charms practiced by the women of Žítková.

In the pages of a registry of births and deaths, for instance, she found an entry stating that Marie Juračka, granddaughter of Zuzka Poláška, made a good marriage with a rich farmer from the Hanakia region, who had picked her out at a fair. It came to her again when she happened upon a record of the exhumation of Marie's sister, known as Perchaňa, who, having died before her young lover, pestered him every night until they dug her out of her grave and drove a stake through her heart, believing her to be a vampire. At the time of her exhumation, she had lain in the ground for over three weeks, yet reportedly, she had rosy-red cheeks, and her hair and nails had grown. And again when she learned of what was said about the son of a Jihlava industrialist, to whom was summoned the healer and unmarried mother Dorka Gabrhelová, daughter of Marie and sister of Kateřina. So successful was the treatment that he rode out to see her every summer and continued to do so till the end of her life. There were still some people in Kopanice who remembered him following her around like a dog; he was so captivated by her that he saw and heard no other woman. When Dorka Gabrhelová died, so they said, her daughter and successor Anka was preparing the ground around the cottage for vegetable beds when she dug up a lock of hair that was turned toward Jihlava; it was an exact match for the hair of the industrialist's son. Only after she burned this hair did he desist in his visits to Kopanice.

Dora clicked on another folder. Moments later a family tree spread wide across the screen.

Slowly she moved the cursor from Kateřina Shánělka, to Kateřina Divoká, to Zuzka Poláška, and then to Marie Juračka, who, after the death of her husband, returned to Žítková (at the end of the eighteenth century) to entrust her trade to her daughter Kateřina; after that it passed down to Kateřina's two daughters, Marina Gočiková and Dorka Gabrhelová. The branches of the family tree spread into the nineteenth century, reaching Marina's daughter Anna Struhárka, who was known as Chupatá and became a midwife whose reputation stretched well beyond Kopanice. It was she who, early in the twentieth century, gave birth to a daughter, Irma. The goddesses of the Hodulík line never forgave Irma for enticing her husband Jan away from his family. To this day, Irma lived on the Černá hill, which Dora walked past every Friday on her way to the Bedová.

The second branch went by way of the unmarried Dorka Gabrhelová to Anka, who, it was claimed, never erred in her divination. It was said that she foresaw the Great War and listed almost all the Hrozenkov families who would lose sons in it. Baglárka had once told Dora that Anka's prophecy had been fulfilled to the letter. Although some of the Hrozenkov boys she named were then small children and others not even born, every one of them would fall. Today these names were carved on the memorial to the war dead in the square. The few names Anka did not see were those of her son-in-law and grandsons. It was said that Anka's daughters, Pagáčena and Justýna, inherited the healer's art from their mother, and that when they looked into someone's eyes, they were able to see everything in them: illness, misfortune, and wrongs, events past and present. Supposedly no one was able to hide their secrets from them. Dora could well believe this. She remembered how Surmena's eyes, which folk said were exact copies of her mother Justýna's, could get under the skin like two black leeches.

Dora's gaze returned to the family tree. The name of Justýna Ruchárka was connected by the two last threads to those of her daughters, Surmena and Irena Idesová.

And below these was Dora's own name. This made her feel uneasy. So how was it with her?

She couldn't have claimed to have always known her true place in this chain of names that had been formed over centuries. It was complicated, after all. Some might say that she was the last surviving goddess in a direct line of descent. But she wasn't. In Dora, there was nothing of what had made the women of her line famous, dormant or otherwise; she knew little about herbs, she was no healer, she could not see the future. Surmena had not chosen her as her successor, nor had she taught her anything of what she knew herself—because Dora had been different, suspicious, and full of doubter's questions picked up down at the school in Hrozenkov. Later, Dora had had to conduct her own laborious search. For many years she had fumbled in the dark. Then, as time passed, her dreams had begun to show her the way.

This came to her again early that morning, when she awoke with the screams of Kateřina Shánělka in her ears. She stared at the ceiling of the darkened room, troubled by the question of why her overworked imagination wouldn't allow her a good night's rest. It struck her that these dreams contained too many details, that her sense of the lives of people hundreds of years dead was too keen for it all to be the work of her imagination. Now, for the first time, she asked herself: What if these were no ordinary dreams? What if what was bothering her was not her lively imagination but tiny remnants of what her ancestors possessed?

Fragments of the goddess's art? What if what resonated within her was a common heritage, a shared consciousness reaching down the centuries from Kateřina Shánělka and passing to her, Dora, through Surmena and her mother? At that moment she sensed she had found the key to a door that had been locked for years. But no sooner had she opened it than she was confronted with her true role, and suddenly she guessed what it wanted of her and how she was to contribute, as the only one who stood where two worlds met—with one foot in the world of science, yet deeply rooted in the life of the goddesses. It was her task, she told herself, to dig out and tell the life stories of all the women of her line, no matter how long ago they had lived, and most importantly, to tell the world of the extraordinary art their enemies had tried to erase from the face of Kopanice all through the ages. It was up to her to ensure that their legacy was not lost.

That night she felt immense relief. From that moment on, she knew that it was not for nothing that her name was at the end of that family tree.

Again she studied the individual names and the threads that linked them.

This genealogical gem was Dora's secret. So far no one else had seen it.

She had started putting it together for her dissertation, but the sight of her own name on the last line, all alone, had discouraged her from appending it to the text. Reluctance to wash her family's dirty linen in public was only part of the reason why she had excluded it. The main reason for rejecting it was the fear that her work—her aim—would be threatened by allegations on the part of the board of examiners of personal involvement and perhaps even bias.

She was convinced that in keeping this secret for herself, she had done the right thing.

She was roused from her thoughts by the waiter, who was inquiring politely if she would like another drink. She nodded. Only then did she realize how much her eyes were stinging from staring into the computer all evening. She rubbed them wearily.

She looked up to see a man watching her from the other side of the room. At first she was startled by the firmness of his gaze; then the corners of her mouth twitched into a shy smile.

Nighttime Travails

*I*n truth, she would have been amazed if it had lived up to her expectations. Or at the very least, extremely surprised. How many mornings-after had there been in her life when she hadn't woken up disappointed? Two? Three at most.

It is as if they do it to her on purpose. Hardly has the bedroom door closed behind them than they are at it like soldiers or mechanics, rolling her and squeezing her as though she were a piece of dough, their hands clumsy, grubby, with no trace of imagination, desperate to get inside her as quickly as they can, like racing dogs. Any hope that she has had of arousal melts like a snowflake over a flame, to give way to embarrassment as a sweaty male body toils away wearily on top of her. This body knows no method and lacks all subtlety; it makes no attempt to get their hips to move to a shared rhythm, which might just bring her to the realization that this could work out after all. But the man never tries to bring her to this realization. It means nothing to him—all he wants is for her to be there, with her sex open to him. No more than that.

It is like this almost every time. Before she knows it, it is all over. He is rolling over and lighting a cigarette, or proudly slapping her thigh and reveling in the sense of a job well done, while she is staring at the ceiling as the fury wells up inside her. Why is she like this? Why doesn't she like it? Why is she not like other women? Why isn't she content with what men have to offer? She would like to get up and run out of the room, which now stinks of their secretions. She would like to run as far and fast as she can, making herself too tired to think about anything, especially herself and her degeneracy, the perversion it makes her sick to imagine, and the poor souls who prove to her again and again how little it is all worth.

Instead of running she lies and stares at the ceiling, trying to suppress her anger. Sometimes she succeeds; usually she doesn't, as the man next to her, the man who slid out of her a few moments earlier and is now lighting a cigarette, feels the need to say something because that's what people do; they don't like silence. And these words cause the simmering anger she is trying to suppress to crash out in a wave that breaks against the stinking mound at her side; it hits him so hard it is a wonder he doesn't choke on his cigarette. Most men are out of the door before they can pull on or button up their shirts, shouting, "You stupid bitch!" or something similar because they know now that she doesn't share their view of their sexual prowess, nor is there any chance that they will see her again.

She knows that this man in Pardubice won't be bothering her again because their paths will never cross. But her disgust with herself and the scorn she feels for her own body and its unsavory, monstrous desires will remain, even after she has washed it carefully with the fragrant hotel soap that foams everywhere, even between her toes. Everywhere but in her memory, which will remain stained and greasy with shame so that, for a time, Dora will try to shut her memory down so as not to think about it. A week or two or three will pass before the urge returns, and one evening, she will fall into the arms of someone she has just met, in the hope that this time it will be different, that the spark inside her will catch and burn, that she will yield to a man as a normal woman, as she should, as is right, at long last . . .

Archive: Day Three

On Friday morning her name was again the first entry in the visitors' book. The archivist had Surmena's file ready for her.

"Just for the morning today," Dora said.

The archivist shrugged his indifference.

Quickly she settled into her usual seat and began to read. She had to manage as much as possible before she left for the midday train and to pick up Jakoubek.

126
to the District Department of State Security in Uherské Hradiště, Third Division
FAO Officer Švanc
PROGRESS REPORT ON CASE: Surmenová, Terézie
Submitted by: s.c. "BOLETUS"

> On Sunday, November 14, 1976, duty nurse comrade Františka Kudlová reported that an attempt had been made to visit the patient Terézie Surmenová. The petitioner was a young woman of about twenty years, of medium to tall height, and with long, dark hair and brown eyes. This woman claimed to be a relation of Terézie Surmenová, although she produced

no documentary evidence of this. The duty nurse did not deny that Surmenová was staying on the ward, but she refused to admit the woman without the required documentation. Then the woman asked for information regarding the documents she would require, which the nurse gave. Then the woman went away.

I await further instruction at your earliest convenience so that I may apprise the duty nurses of how to proceed should the above-mentioned woman again attempt to visit.

142

to the District Department of State Security in Uherské Hradiště, Third Division
FAO Officer Švanc
Processed by: code name/file: INTERPRETER/15701
Type of cooperation: operative worker
Registered state security authority: Uherské Hradiště

Record of meeting with s.c. "BOLETUS"

On December 10, 1976, a meeting took place with the secret collaborator with the code name "BOLETUS," as always, at the "Peace" services on Highway 47 (in the direction of Křenovice). The above-named presented himself on time, as usual. During the interview he was friendly and accommodating.

The beginning of the meeting comprised a consultation on the Terézie Surmenová case. In answer to my inquiry about Surmenová's state of health, BOLETUS stated that since the fourth series of electric shocks, it has been stabilized, and there is no need for us to worry about her condition. He added that although the patient suffers typical post-therapy health problems, such as shaking and epileptic seizures, it is proving possible to keep these under control.

Further, BOLETUS wished to know how to proceed on the matter of visitors. He explained that Surmenová had been placed on an open ward and that her state of health permitted visitors; as a result, the consultant had several times considered this matter and several times spoken about it with BOLETUS, the attending physician. Now that a relation is demanding the right to visit and is likely to take her claim to the consultant, BOLETUS believes that such a visit can no longer be prevented. He challenges the argument that Surmenová should be moved to a closed ward for more serious cases, claiming that this would raise suspicions.

Further, he added that at the present time, there is no need to worry about visits, however: due to the patient's el. shock treatment, her condition renders her incapable of concentrated speech, and this incapacity can easily be intensified by more medication. BOLETUS is looking forward to hearing our opinion on this matter.

The meeting continued with a description of his personal relationships in the workplace, which he states have improved in view of the fact that he has recently been promoted to the position of deputy to the consultant. Asked whether anything unusual is occurring in the work collective, he replied in the negative, stating that everything is now as it should be and that everyone is working in accordance with regulations. He added only that his colleague comrade Dr.

Brousek does not demonstrate the kind of attitude to our Socialist order that one would expect from a doctor of his standing and that in some matters of ideology, his opinions are unprogressive. Asked to specify in which aspects the opinions of Comrade Brousek are unprogressive, he stated that Brousek expresses the view that the position of medical doctors in capitalist countries, specifically in Austria, is better, from which BOLETUS deduces that his attitude toward Socialist medicine is not good and that he favors the exploitative system of the imperialist West over the national health system as defined by the Ministry of Health of the CSSR. BOLETUS indicated that he would be interested in knowing how Comrade Brousek is able to make such a comparison. He received the assurance that we would look into this matter.

Conclusion: By his actions and behavior, BOLETUS continues to prove his suitability in the role of secret collaborator. He demonstrates high levels of motivation and interest in collaboration.

Operation ended on 12/10/76 at 6:45 p.m.

Total expenses: 162 Czechoslovak crowns

145
from the Local Council of the National Committee in Žítková to the District Department of State Security in Uherské Hradiště, Third Division
FAO Officer Švanc

At your request we are sending copies of registry documents that affirm the kinship of the respondent Dora Idesová and Terézie Surmenová, application for which was made at our LCNC on 11/26/76 by Dora Idesová, resident at house no. 28 in Žítková.

Further, we confirm that we will issue a statement of this kinship at your recommendation by 5/1/77.

In this regard it is pertinent to remark that the respondent Idesová has also applied for a certificate of kinship in relation to Jakub Ides, currently resident at the Social Care Institution for Mentally Handicapped Children at Brno-Chrlice, citing as her reason her intention to assume joint custody of him.

Responsible operative: Čermáčková

1/17/77

148
State Social Services Office in Brno
file no. 124 007/JMK Bo 02
to the District Department of State Security in Uherské Hradiště, Third Division
FAO Officer Švanc

At your request we are hereby submitting a report on our ward Jakub Ides, DOB 2/16/61.

The above-named is registered by us as a social welfare case who is a semi-orphan and suffers from mental and physical disabilities. Following the death of his mother in 1966, he and his sister, Dora, were entrusted to the care of his aunt, Terézie Surmenová, at her request. For the care of a disabled individual on the basis of ordinances of the Ministry for Work and Social Affairs of the CSSR (Act 182/1961 Coll.), Surmenová was granted a pension of 498 Czechoslovak crowns per month. At the same time, both minors were granted orphan pensions of 456 Czechoslovak crowns, which until 6/30/74 were remitted monthly by postal order to their guardian, Terézie Surmenová. Subsequent to her hospitalization in the State Psychiatric Hospital in Kroměříž, Jakub Ides was made our ward at the behest of the County Public Prosecutor's Office in Uherské Hradiště; on 6/18/74 he was given into the custody of the Social Care Institution for Mentally Handicapped Children in Brno-Černovice (Brno-Chrlice site), where he remains to this day.

On 5/4/77 the State Social Services Office in Brno (Central Office for the Region of South Moravia) received an application from Dora Idesová (DOB 10/30/58; resident at house no. 28 in Žítková) for **Joint Custody in the Guardianship of a Third Party** with regard to the case of Jakub Ides. Along with her application, Dora Idesová submitted her birth certificate as proof of her having attained the age of majority, a Certificate of Kinship in relation to the minor Jakub Ides, and an Employer's Statement as proof of her proper employment; further, Idesová stated that she is now the only relative in a position to provide such care.

At your request we have enclosed the psychiatrist's report from the Medical Assessments Department of the State Social Services Office in Brno.

Responsible operative: Magdaléna Kavková
5/7/77

Enclosure
PSYCHIATRIST'S REPORT
Jakub IDES, DOB 2/16/61

Family anamnesis: Psychosis identified in family (aunt currently confined at State Psychiatric Hospital in Kroměříž with diagnosis of acute psychotic disorder). Alcoholic father.

Personal anamnesis: Operations and serious illnesses—0. Diagnosis of insufficient personality development, intermediate oligophrenia, imbecility with IQ 46. Ineducable; incapable of concentrated manual work and orientation in complex world, which confuses him. This in combination with Apert syndrome, accompanied by typical phenomena of premature fusion of cranial seams and hypoplasia of middle part of face. Eyes at variance with facial axis; syndactyly in hands and feet, causing motor difficulties. Heightened suggestibility.

Patient's state is permanent; no expectation of conspicuous improvement.

Abuse of addictive substances: Not found. Does not drink alcohol. Nonsmoker.

Social anamnesis: Impoverished social background. Mother died 1966; father serving prison sentence. He and sister entrusted to care of aunt 1966–1974. Lives in limited world; contacts or bonds other than with caregivers not established. Brought up to believe in God.

Education and employment: Ineducable but has developed self-serving habits; legally incompetent. Most of his biological needs fully satisfied.

Attitude to the Socialist order: None.

State on admission to hospital: Patient delivered by staff of State Social Services Office on 6/18/74; minor hematomas, vomiting. Behavior suggestive of disorientation; anxious; incapable of communication with or concentrated perception of any attending authority. Uncooperative. Possibility of seizure with loss of consciousness and convulsions warned of by Social Services Office staff, who also stated that patient demonstrates occasional bursts of behavior when he falls into state of excitement and loses self-control (described as "frenzy").

Medication: So far unmedicated. Hormone therapy indicated—cyproterone (2 mg daily) to decrease libido, diazepam in event of seizure.

Dora already knew the documents that came after this report. She had copies of them at home, in the bottom of her documents drawer. Once they had been a cause for joy to her, and she had been loath to throw them away. She slowly leafed through them but lingered only over the last of them.

161
State Social Services Office in Brno
Dora IDESOVÁ, house no. 28, Žítková, Uherské Hradiště district

Ruling

Pursuant to Article 45b/1963 Coll. of the Family Law, reassignment of the care status of the minor Jakub Ides (DOB 2/16/61) from **Social Care Institution for Mentally Handicapped Children (year-round) to Social Care Institution for Mentally Handicapped Children (week-long) is permitted**. The following person becomes a designated caregiver by law:

IDESOVÁ, Dora, DOB 10/30/58, resident at house no. 28, Žítková, Uherské Hradiště district, sister of the minor Jakub Ides

Given that the above-named has completed a mandatory course in work with a mentally disabled person, including crisis management, has undertaken by her signature to abide by the Constitutional Regulations, and has been instructed on the diagnosis of the minor Jakub Ides, his medication, and daily regimen, the disabled person is entrusted to her joint custody from 6/1/77.

Ward of the Social Care Institution for Mentally Handicapped Children in Brno-Černovice (Brno-Chrlice site) Jakub Ides will be released from institutional care on Fridays from 1:00 p.m.; he will be readmitted to institutional care on Sundays by 5:00 p.m. at the latest.

Signed: Ing. Vlastimil Kovář
5/7/77

173
to the District Department of State Security in Uherské Hradiště, Third Division
FAO Officer Švanc
Processed by: code name/file: INTERPRETER/15701
Type of cooperation: operative worker
Registered state security authority: Uherské Hradiště

Report on investigation of Dora Idesová

In June 1977 the subject assumed the joint custody of her brother, the mentally disabled minor Jakub Ides, of whom she takes care from Friday to Sunday. She collects him regularly on Fridays at 1:00 p.m.; at 2:20 p.m. they depart by train to Uherské Hradiště, from where they depart on the 5:15 p.m. bus in the direction of Starý Hrozenkov, alighting at their destination stop, Žítková. On Sundays the subject delivers her brother to the institution at 5:00 p.m. sharp. During the working week, the subject lives in a rented apartment at 112 Francouzská Street in Brno; apart from her employment at the co-op store at 72 Cejl Street, she attends, in the evening hours of Tuesday, a class in German language at the State Language School at 1 Koliště Street. She has few other contacts, presumably owing to the fact that she moved to Brno only recently.

Conclusion: I verify the projection that logistics and the volume of work with her mentally disabled brother prevent all contact between the subject and Surmenová, as the subject is not able to reach the hospital in Kroměříž during visiting hours.

Surveillance ended on 9/30/77

Jakoubek

At the time, everybody said that God only knew why he had sent such misfortune down on Jakoubek. As everything he did had a reason, perhaps it would become apparent later. The expression on people's faces as they said this was among Dora's earliest memories.

He was delivered by Surmena, of course. Dora and her father waited for a long time on the other side of the door, wrapped up in bulky coats, stamping their feet to keep warm, until at last Dora's mother gave a long, drawn-out cry, followed by quiet, agitated weeping. There was no other sound. For a while Dora's father paced nervously about, until he could stand it no longer and burst into the cottage. He collided with Surmena in the doorway.

"Before you do anything else, fetch Irma Gabrhelová," she told him.

Dora's father wanted to see the newborn first, but Surmena wouldn't let him in. He was sober. Had he been drinking, she wouldn't have managed him. So he went away and wouldn't return for at least two hours; the Černá hill, where Irma lived, was almost an hour's walk away, and in the February snowdrifts, it would take longer still.

So apart from her mother and Surmena, Dora was the first person to set eyes on her brother.

Her mother was crying.

She was holding him in her arms, already washed and swaddled. He was lying exhausted at her breast, and the tears that were trickling down her cheeks were falling onto his head. Dora did not understand her mother's distress until she climbed onto the wooden bed. The face of the child in the swaddling clothes scared her half to death. This was the first newborn child she had seen, and she had never seen anything so strange.

"Why are his fingers like that?" she asked. Out of the hands that rested next to the baby's head, there grew three nail-less stumps. Dora's question made her mother sob all the harder. Surmena took Dora aside, over to the table.

"As God decides, so it shall be," Surmena said. "It is for us to bear the load he has given us. And we—you, I, your mother, and your father—will bear it bravely. Promise me that."

Dora nodded obediently, even though she was not sure what "to bear something bravely" meant.

What it meant *not* to bear something bravely she would soon learn from her father's reaction.

At first they both wept—he and her mother.

Meanwhile Irma and Surmena paced the room, not knowing what else to do. Dora sat on the bench by the range, upset, trying to make sense of this incomprehensible scene, until the heat of the oven became too much for her and she nodded off.

Perhaps there were moments when she came out of her doze, or perhaps it was all a dream. She didn't know.

She seemed to remember her father taking two bottles of brandy from the shelf and going off into the woods. Irma and Surmena sat down next to her sobbing mother and the silent baby; with their solemn, pensive expressions, they looked like the Fates of myth. Only the occasional word was spoken. Dora heard the word *waster*.

Never would she be able to rid herself of the belief that that evening, as the Fates sat on and she dozed by the oven, her mother, too, would have preferred not to have the child with the deformed head, the sunken face in which the nose was almost lost, and the eyes that rolled unhappily to the sides.

"Maybe he'll die all on his own. The roof of his mouth hasn't knitted," Dora heard.

Then Irma, or perhaps Surmena, said in an excited whisper in which the sibilants were emphasized, "Is it a sin?"

What did she mean by "a sin"?

She came out of her doze and walked quietly to the bed, where Irma and Surmena were leaning over the baby, who was lying in his mother's lap. She couldn't see what was going on because the women's sturdy backsides were blocking her view, so she squeezed between them in order to take a look.

"Is it a little sister or a little brother?" she asked, giving the three of them such a shock that they gasped. At that moment Jakoubek gave a cry, which sounded hollow because there was a cloth over his face. Then he started to wriggle and the cloth slipped off, and for the first time, she had the feeling that he blinked at her, ever so quickly, before the pale-blue eyes were again wet, narrow cracks.

"A brother," her mother said softly. Then she pulled the sobbing child toward her. Surmena and Irma stepped back from the bed.

Today Dora knows that tiny babies are unable to see. Even if they could, Jakoubek wouldn't have seen her with his right eye; he has never been able to see much with it. But his left sees so well that he notices details that escape Dora. And he is able to smile with his left eye, too, although it sits so deep in his skull that it tends to make strangers queasy to look at it. He always smiles like this on Friday afternoons, when she comes to the institution for him and he finds her waiting in the ice-cold reception room. He smiles with his left eye and twitches his stub of a nose, making his face still more twisted and sunken. Then he makes a braying sound and says something like "*A-ast*," or her name, "*Do-a.*" He articulates like this because the roof of his mouth never knitted together properly.

She knows today that these are all symptoms of Apert syndrome.

But no one in Žítková knew about Apert syndrome in those days. Nor did they know about it in the days when the social services took Jakoubek from her. In those days they had only one name for it: *monster*.

"Do-a! Do-a!" he shouted that Friday afternoon, too, when she appeared at the doorway of the institution's waiting room. Yet she was the more delighted of the two: she needed to be diverted from her thoughts, which revolved endlessly around Surmena's file and what she might yet find in it. A weekend with Jakoubek in the quiet and seclusion of Žítková was just what the doctor ordered.

Jakoubek was escorted by a smiling nurse and ready to go.

"So we'll see you on Sunday at five, OK?" the nurse confirmed as she transferred Jakoubek into Dora's care.

Dora and Jakoubek embraced. She kissed him on the forehead while he held her tight and shouted over and over, "Do-a! Do-a!"

That's something that has certainly changed for the best, she thought. In the past Jakoubek had been handed over by a stern nurse who was impervious to all complaints; Jakoubek had been agitated, then visibly relieved when he realized that Dora was taking him out of the awful environment of the Socialist institution. After the revolution, when job placement no longer applied, these harpies were gradually replaced by younger, more patient nurses who were at least kind, even if they were nothing else. Whether this was because they had chosen the job of their own free will in the knowledge of how difficult it would be or because capitalism forced people to earn a living by working rather than their mere presence, Dora didn't know. In any case, Dora could see that Jakoubek's mood was no longer dark when their weekends were over and she returned him to the institution; indeed, he sometimes expressed pleasure to be back there. This change brought Dora enormous relief.

Earlier she had feared that Jakoubek was the victim of injustices similar to those she had suffered at the hostel; now, several years after the revolution, she was quite relaxed about his care. Even happy with it. Her sense of guilt at being unable to provide Jakoubek with all-day care had been overtaken by the recognition that he was actually quite glad to be at the institution. Certainly he wasn't suffering. So she decided to stop torturing herself. Their lives developed a pattern, which was a cause of happiness for both of them.

Their bus left from the nearby Zvonařka station forty minutes after they left the institution. There was enough time to go there on foot. They would have a sweet snack on the way: ice cream from a nearby stand when it was warm, chocolate from Dora's weekend backpack in the winter. They would enjoy the first moments of reunion with all their senses.

It was autumn and already dark when they arrived in Hrozenkov. This time, too, they succeeded in getting to the only shop before it closed. As usual, Jakoubek grabbed the handle of the first cart in the line and yanked it to and fro until Dora came to his aid and pulled it free. Then they moved slowly along the wide shelves of groceries. Patiently she returned all the things they didn't need that Jakoubek was throwing into the cart with a regular rhythm. She only just managed to catch a jar of pickled vegetables that would not have survived a collision with other goods.

"He's a man-mountain now, isn't he?" Tichačka called from the other side of the meat counter.

"He is indeed," said Dora with a smile.

"How about some smoked ham? The very last bit. Look how lean it is!" Tichačka said, waving the meat above her head.

"Why not?"

"I'll pack it for you. And you ought to go to Mass, you know," Tichačka said, raising a warning finger as she packed the ham. "I haven't seen you in church for at least two months."

"You know how bored he gets there. He makes a nuisance of himself," Dora said apologetically as she gave Jakoubek a gentle nudge in the back to get him to turn the cart toward the meat counter.

"I know, but you can put up with it once in a while, can't you?"

"I suppose so," said Dora with a sheepish grin as she reached for the meat.

"See you on Sunday, then. And make sure you're there because I'll be bringing you some cakes for your walk back."

Dora wanted to refuse these politely, but instead she dropped the packed meat into the cart and nodded goodbye. Dora didn't need to turn to know who was the source of the mighty silhouette she saw from the corner of her eye and the strange, pungent odor. Immediately behind her, Janigena was waiting to be served.

"Hi," Dora whispered as she worked her way around this neighbor from the distant Pitín hill as quickly as she could.

Janigena uttered an awkward, mumbled greeting while Tichačka looked on with suspicion from behind the meat counter.

Dora turned away quickly and wheeled her cart to the checkout.

Jakoubek trotted behind her in alarm. He was even more confused by the time she had hurriedly paid and thrown the contents of the cart into her backpack.

Usually, she would buy a plastic bag, and this last chore would be his. He would then carry the bag carefully up to Žítková. It wasn't like that today. Dora threw the straps of the chock-full backpack over her shoulders, grabbed Jakoubek's hand, and pulled him out of the shop. They stopped only when they reached the cemetery, where the steep path to the Bedová began.

Jakoubek was scowling.

"OK, then," said Dora, wearily shaking off the backpack.

Jakoubek's face lit up. He grabbed the straps of the backpack and, with Dora's help, heaved it up onto his shoulders. He gave a delighted grunt at the weight. The bottles of milk, she remembered.

Now they went on their way happily. This was how the weekend was supposed to begin.

Archive: Day Four

*T*hree days later, on Monday morning, she again rang the doorbell for the reading room. It was answered by the familiar voice. As usual, she made her way up to the second floor.

"I hope this will be the last time," she said to the archivist as she received Surmena's file. Moments later she was leafing through it to the few pages she had yet to read.

192
to the District Department of State Security in Uherské Hradiště, Third Division
FAO Officer Švanc
PROGRESS REPORT ON CASE: Surmenová, Terézie
Submitted by: s.c. "BOLETUS"

On Sunday, October 9, 1977, the patient Terézie Surmenová received a visit from her previously mentioned niece Dora Idesová, who, having presented all the necessary documentation, was admitted by duty nurse comrade Eva Frolková. Surmenová was in a long-term stabilized state corresponding to the consequences of her electroconvulsive therapy.

The visit, which was of forty minutes' duration (Idesová arrived three-quarters of an hour before the end of visiting hours), proceeded without incident. Patient and visitor met in the common room and were under constant staff supervision. Although Idesová spoke to Surmenová, the latter was not able to reply owing to the influence of the sedative medication that is always applied on weekends; according to the witness of the duty nurse, however, the patient appeared to be unusually restless. When Idesová departed she was visibly disturbed by her aunt's condition; in answer to Idesová's questions, the nurse told her that Surmenová was suffering from severe psychosis and that no improvement was expected. As Idesová was not satisfied by this answer, the nurse advised her to telephone the attending physician for a consultation. This call took place the very next day (Monday); the questioner was apprised of the insidious nature of the mental illness from which Surmenová suffers, and her doubts were thus dispelled. At the end of visiting hours, the patient's restlessness came to a head; hence, she was given a sedative IM. In the days immediately subsequent to Idesová's visit, Surmenová was seen to be in a state of heightened restlessness. Her medication was adjusted accordingly.

Dora was again overwhelmed by the weight of a guilt she had succeeded in banishing during her weekend with Jakoubek. A single document was enough to bring it back.

She pictured Surmena as she was then, the first time in years she had seen her. She barely recognized her. A trembling old woman dressed not in the colorful folk dress of Kopanice but the blue uniform of the hospital. A shrunken old woman who would not have made it to the table in the middle of the visitors' room without Dora's help.

Dora was horrified. She had been expecting to see a sick woman, but the person sitting opposite her was a wreck whose face resembled Surmena's only remotely. As far as Dora could tell, Surmena did not even understand that this was Dora, here after all these years; Dora, who had made it here to her after a long struggle. By accident. Had Baglár not paid a call to the Bedová and announced that he was driving to Brno, she wouldn't have managed to drop off Jakub at the institution so early before dashing to the bus station and catching her connection to Kroměříž. After the very brief visit, on the way back to Brno, she did nothing but wonder about what could have happened in those not even four years in which they hadn't seen each other.

She calculated that Surmena was now sixty-seven. Not a great age, but an age at which some people quickly became a shadow of their former self.

One day later she had telephoned Kalousek, and now she remembered his gentle, kindly voice. He had spoken to her as if to a child.

"I'm afraid the science comes up short. Dozens of teams of doctors are working on it, in Czechoslovakia and in the Soviet Union. I'd be glad, too, for some conclusive results at last. You can't imagine how glad I'd be! It would be wonderful to be able to give relatives more concrete information. It's not easy, you know, day after day, with no proper explanation to give suffering families. With no comfort to offer stricken patients—except for the medication, of course. Regrettably, the brain is still a great mystery to us. All I can tell you is that cases like your aunt's—when a healthy person gradually becomes someone quite different—are actually pretty common. Sometimes the progression is quick, sometimes slow . . . and medication can address the process only partially. Much depends on the patient and how

he or she reacts to the medication. Sometimes—and your aunt is a case in point—the patient doesn't react well, and the illness develops quickly and soon reaches its terminal phase. Well, you've seen her for yourself. And you must have noticed other such cases on the ward. But I can assure you of one thing. Your aunt is not suffering. Truly. At this moment your aunt doesn't care about anything, not even you. She has lost the ability to think logically; she has no notion of time or the people around her, and she is indifferent to the world. I'm sorry, but it's not going to get any better. Try to look on the bright side: basically, she's quite happy. In that regard her illness is merciful. Believe me. It's just the way life is."

The bastard had convinced her. Still, she read all the literature she could get ahold of, but the facts of Surmena's diagnosis she found there didn't offer any encouragement.

So she came to terms with it.

Earlier, perhaps, than she should have. But in those days Surmena's illness was not the only thing on her mind: there was her new job, her new life in the city, adapting to the difficulties of traveling between homes with Jakoubek, the cottage in Žítková . . . it was a struggle to manage it all. Quite simply, she lacked the energy to doubt what Kalousek had told her.

Dora's first visit to Surmena was followed by several more.

She made the last of these on a sunny day in spring 1979. Patients in faded hospital gowns—alone or in the company of their visitors—were wandering about the park that surrounded the building. Dora couldn't resist asking the nurse to let Surmena out too. Her request was granted. In the state Surmena was in, the staff members were confident that there was nothing for them to worry about.

Slowly they shuffled their way to the lift. At ground level they followed the gravel path to a bench under a lime tree in blossom. The air was scented, and there was a buzz of insects from the treetops. Dora remembered the joy she felt at sitting there with Surmena, holding Surmena's restless hand in her own while taking in the fragrance of the lime and the warming rays of the sun.

She certainly wasn't ready for Surmena's outburst.

It began with the shakes. But this wasn't the kind of systematic shaking associated with Parkinson's, where the limbs vibrate to a regular rhythm, but a different, far more powerful phenomenon that traveled through her body in waves. Suddenly Dora's daydream was obliterated as her hand was caught in Surmena's frantic grip. She looked at her aunt in horror.

Surmena's face twitched as one small seizure followed another. The corners of her mouth formed themselves into a grin that flooded her face and then dissolved; this happened several times. Dora sank to her knees in order to see Surmena better. Over and over she asked what was the matter, although there was little hope that Surmena would break her silence now. But to her great surprise, Surmena answered.

"Don't go."

At least that was what Dora thought she heard, but perhaps she was dazed by the spring heat.

Don't go. It would never have crossed her mind to go, so paralyzed was she by the sudden change in Surmena's state. But was it really Surmena's state that had changed? Perhaps it was she, Dora, who had fallen into a sort of dream, a mystical hallucination, that had drawn them together for the communication recorded in scribbled, agitated, tension-racked script in Dora's diary. As the case may be, in those few minutes, it happened, and Dora grabbed at the words of a rasping voice, produced through a crack between lips that were usually clamped shut. The words came out in gasps, as though Surmena was preventing herself from gagging.

Surmena's wheezing delivery was halted by a nurse and an orderly, who had been looking for them. Obviously it was long after visiting hours. Not until it was all over did Dora realize that the park was empty and the other patients were back in the building. Before that the orderly had seized Surmena, even though Dora had yelled at him to leave her alone. Ignoring Dora completely, he had hoisted Surmena into his embrace as though she were a sack of potatoes and set off with her toward the building. The nurse stood in front of Dora and screeched at her in a high-pitched voice: by violating visiting regulations, she had disrupted the patient's routine and provoked an attack of nerves, which . . . Meanwhile Surmena was thrashing about, her eyes round, her toothless mouth open wide, reaching out a hand to Dora. Then she disappeared behind a bend in the path.

With some force the nurse shepherded Dora to the gate before shoving her off the premises. Behind her the click of the closing gate was like a threat.

Dora took two steps and then collapsed. She missed her bus to Brno.

It was a struggle for Dora to banish these painful memories. But as time was pressing, with a sigh, she reached for the next document.

207
to the District Department of State Security in Uherské Hradiště, Third Division
FAO Officer Švanc
PROGRESS REPORT ON CASE: Surmenová, Terézie
Submitted by: s.c. "BOLETUS"

A death at the State Psychiatric Hospital in Kroměříž

At 10:00 p.m. on May 12, 1979, the patient Terézie Surmenová, since 6/17/74 hospitalized in Department 5A of the State Psychiatric Hospital, died.
Cause of death: heart failure

The body of Terézie Surmenová was examined at 7:30 a.m. on 5/13/79 by Dr. Pavel Petera, a physician employed at Dept. 5A of the State Psychiatric Hospital, who issued a medical examiner's certificate and subsequently reported the death to doctors in Uherský Brod and the National Committee in Žítková, the place of residence of the deceased. The corpse is now in the morgue of the State Psychiatric Hospital; in the coming days, it will be given up for cremation or burial.

216

to the District Department of State Security in Uherské Hradiště, Third Division
FAO Officer Švanc
Processed by: code name/file: INTERPRETER/15701
Type of cooperation: operative worker
Registered state security authority: Uherské Hradiště

Record of the funeral of Terézie Surmenová

On 6/19/79 an urn containing the remains of Terézie Surmenová was collected from the National Committee in Žítková. At the initiative of Dora Idesová, niece of the deceased, at 11:00 a.m. on that day, the urn was interred at the cemetery in Starý Hrozenkov.

The funeral service was conducted by Antonín Šesták, priest at Starý Hrozenkov, in the presence of the church secretary of the National Committee in Žítková. The funeral was attended by twenty-one persons.

At the end of the funeral service, niece Dora Idesová thanked those present with the following words: "I thank all of you who accompanied our aunt on her last journey, even though it is many years since you saw her last. She would certainly be glad to know that you haven't forgotten her. I am sure that everyone here knows where she spent the years before her death. I wish to say just one thing about this: please do not remember her as a madwoman but as a person who put herself at the service of others throughout her life . . ." After this Idesová was no longer able to speak. She was embraced by two women attired in the local costume (Irma Gabrhelová and Alžběta Baglárová), who covered her mouth and face with a handkerchief, thus preventing her from making a further statement.

No complications arose at the funeral. At the end of the service, the citizens present went their separate ways, Idesová and her brother departing by bus for Brno, where the latter returned to the institution as usual.

Operation ended on 6/19/79 at 5:45 p.m.

Total expenses: 96 Czechoslovak crowns

Dora perused the copy of the death certificate and the bill for the cremation that was stapled to it. It was the first time she had seen these.

She had found out about Surmena's death two weeks after it had happened. No one had let her know. She had presented herself at the nurses' room only to have its door slammed in her face.

"You've got to be kidding!" she shouted, pounding on the door with her fists.

A scream came from one of the rooms off the long corridor.

"You've got to be kidding!" she shouted again. She renewed her pounding, and the door was flung open.

"What are you yelling for? Don't you know which ward this is? You've got to keep quiet here. Can't you read?" The nurse waved a hand in the direction of a noticeboard.

"What you just told me. You were kidding, weren't you?" said Dora.

"Of course I wasn't kidding! You saw her yourself when you came here. She was on her last legs. You have my condolences. If you want to know more, phone the doctor tomorrow."

The door was closing again when Dora shoved a foot into the gap. "Where is she?"

"What do you mean, where is she?"

"Where is she buried? Where are her remains?"

"She was cremated, of course. It's the law for people living alone without next of kin. Maybe if you go to the crematorium, they'll let you have the urn. Ask at your National Committee office; they should know. And please move your foot—I can't stand here talking to you all day!"

Dora did as she was told. She was overwhelmed by a feeling of helplessness. Surmena had meant so little to them that they hadn't made even one extra phone call on her behalf.

This had happened when Dora was in her twenty-first year. She hadn't had the faintest idea what to do next. She'd had no idea where to turn and whom to complain to. Surmena's death had been imminent; having seen her in such a dreadful state on her last visit, Dora was in no doubt about that. But they should never have cremated her. She should have had a memorial service attended by all the people of Kopanice. Her cortege would have gone through the whole village, and they would have seen her on her way with handshakes. Her last journey would have been in the company of all of them. The priest would have spoken, and little boys would have craned their necks in the expectation that this goddess would fly out of her coffin like all those before her. The last goddess to do this was Krahulka, and Dora had been a witness to it. The pallbearers had been so nervous and full of courage-inducing brandy that their legs had been all over the place; it would have been a wonder if they *had* held on to the coffin. One of those at the front—Uncle Ruchár or Burget—must have stumbled and tripped. The coffin had fallen next to the grave, the lid had popped off, and Krahulka's corpse had sprung out so that half of it was hanging over the pit. The angle of her stiffened arms in relation to her shoulders had been very unnatural. Everyone had screamed with horror, and the kids of Hrozenkov, including Dora, had had nightmares about it for the next month.

But Surmena would have no such burial. She would have no burial at all. In cremating her they had deprived her of her body, and she certainly wouldn't have wanted such a thing. Her belief in the resurrection had been strong, and besides, no one would ever be able to dissuade the people of Hrozenkov from the belief that someday they would return to their earthly bodies. The thought of this was as natural to them as the thought of taking one's coat from the wardrobe and slipping it on every autumn. All of them could do this, all of them except Surmena.

This thought tormented Dora to this day.

Compared to a burial, how sad was the interment of the urn, that small gray thing containing Surmena's dust! And they hadn't even allowed them to perform this ceremony in private, Dora realized.

Which of the people who had stood around Surmena's grave had been the interpreter? she wondered. The faces of the mourners had long ago merged into a single image. Besides, at that time, Dora had had no mind to ask those she didn't know to identify themselves. She had assumed they were either distant relatives or people Surmena had once helped.

With a sigh, she put the interpreter's account of the funeral on top of the stack of read documents.

On the right-hand pile, only a few pages remained. She flicked through the official records on the handling of Surmena's estate, which she knew already, and her own letters, in which she haggled with the authorities over the dilapidated cottage on the Bedová, skipping over their negative replies. All this she did at great speed; she didn't want to reengage with something that had caused her great distress. Even the little Surmena had left they had taken from them and rented out as though it had belonged to a stranger. In the end she lost patience with all this and jumped to the end of the file.

279

District Department of State Security in Uherské Hradiště, Third Division

Final report on the "TERÉZIE SURMENOVÁ" case
File no. PO—KT3 30 987 was opened on 9/10/53 on citizen of Czechoslovak nationality:

SURMENOVÁ, TERÉZIE, DOB 7/24/10, resident at house no. 28, Žítková, Uherské Hradiště district (orig. Uherský Brod district)

For reasons of her operation of an illegal medical practice threatening to the health of Czechoslovak citizens by which she made an undeclared financial gain and robbed the economy of Czechoslovakia and the Czechoslovak people under Article 221/1 of the Criminal Code:

After the investigation was taken over from Public Safety authorities in Uherský Brod, it was established that Surmenová was identical to a subject under surveillance from 1945 to 1953 as part of an action with the cover name "GODDESSES." This action investigated persons suspected of internal activities hostile to the state and attitudes opposed to the democratic republic of Czechoslovakia for reasons of contacts maintained during the occupation with hostile German authorities specially commissioned by the SS and who were not subjected to adequate investigation by the People's Court in 1945.

In the GODDESSES action, the authorities focused primarily on identification of certain visitors in former times and the present. There existed reasonable grounds for suspicion that through the network of clients created by Surmenová and other subjects of investigation in the GODDESSES group, the leaking of information to hostile powers was facilitated. It was supposed that this was performed by the conveying of information supplied by persons coming to Žítková from various parts of the republic to foreign persons presumed to be parts of a hostile agency network. It was later established that visitors included a member of the diplomatic corps of the Republic of Austria (who visited Žítková in 1948) and several citizens of the Hungarian People's Republic (1945–1949) and the Polish People's Republic (1946–1950). Unfortunately the action did not succeed in securing relevant reports on the contents of visits made to the subjects of investigation by persons suspected of subversive activities because any pertinent information was conveyed in private and orally and was thus unverifiable (it proved impossible to place covert listening devices in the homes of the subjects of investigation). A person with the cover name SOOTHSAYER was the only subject of investigation to be prosecuted, convicted of spreading scaremongering, mendacious reports on representatives of the USSR and the CSSR derived from the process of divination by wax casting (supposedly she prophesized the deaths of Comrade Stalin and Comrade Gottwald).

Due to a lack of evidence regarding the deeds of the subjects in the years of the Protectorate, to the moderation of the activities of the subjects of investigation after the prosecution of SOOTHSAYER, and to the termination of visits made by foreign visitors to Žítková, the investigation was halted in August 1953.

One month later a new investigation was launched, its subject Surmenová, who was continuing her reactionary activities through her illegal medical practice.

It did not prove possible to verify certain reports from the Department of Health of the District National Committee in Uherský Brod drawing attention to Surmenová's dishonest dealings until, in 1974, an informant with the cover name WITCH, who had been a significant collaborator of ours on the GODDESSES case, alerted us to an instance of unlawful performance of an abortion and resulting death, alleging that this crime was perpetrated by Surmenová in the course of her medical practice.

Having presented herself for questioning regarding this incident, Surmenová refused to cooperate and exhibited such a high level of aggression that the investigating authority concluded that she was not of sound mind; hence, she was taken for examination at the State Psychiatric Hospital in Kroměříž, where she was found to be suffering from a psychiatric illness that developed progressively until her death from heart failure in 1979.

Between 1974 and 1979, it proved possible to prevent Surmenová (as a special case) from receiving visitors, through whom she might have continued with her sabotage. For this reason we believe that all subversive activities of the subject of observation ended in 1974, before the definitive end of 1979.

Evaluation: Terézie Surmenová's attitude toward the social order was a hostile one. Her activities were difficult to expose because she acted on a strictly individualistic basis and took numerous security measures. For this reason it took several years for her activities to be proved. Subsequently she was successfully separated from the healthy collective and thus prevented from causing further damage to Czechoslovak society. Surmenová transferred neither her opinions and unprogressive worldview nor her attitude toward nonspecialist medical practice to the children to whom she was guardian from 1966 to 1974, as these children were then too young to learn or even understand her practices. Today Dora Idesová works as a sales assistant at the co-op store on Cejl Street, Brno, to which city she moved in order to be closer to her brother, Jakub Ides, who is an inmate of the Institution for Mentally Handicapped Children in Brno-Chrlice and lives a peaceful life. Concerning the matter for which Surmenová was placed under observation, Dora Idesová does not appear to represent a danger; hence, her observation is suspended.

It can here be stated that the case of the internal enemy SURMENA has been successfully concluded.

Thus I make this **APPLICATION** for the consigning of file no. PO—KT3 30 987 to the Ministry of the Interior Archives.

Officer: J. Švanc

7/15/79

The GODDESSES Case

*T*he last page of the file lay read and facedown, although the heavy type was visible through the paper. Dora was sad. It was as though Surmena's life had ended again, this time in a different way.

On the other hand, she was glad. She'd had as much as she could take of cooked-up reports and statements and new findings about Surmena's life, starting with her children and ending with the GODDESSES file.

As she ran her fingertips along the plastic back of the final page, she wondered who was SOOTHSAYER and who was WITCH.

Now all that remained for her to go through was a half-empty blue folder labeled "GODDESSES CASE (materials relevant to the SURMENOVÁ case)," which was secured to the back of the file with paper clips. Slowly and wearily, she pulled this toward her, opened it up, and tipped onto the desk a number of newspaper clippings and a few handwritten and typewritten pages.

She flicked through the papers until she stopped at the last of them. This was of interest to her.

So this was what Anna Struhárová—renowned goddess, midwife, and mother of Irma—looked like. The journalist had misspelled her name, but that hardly mattered now; besides, it was likely that Anna herself hadn't been sure of the correct spelling—indeed, she may not have been able to read and write at all. Dora looked closely at the furrowed face. In spite of Anna's obvious mistrust of the camera and its operator, Dora had the feeling that her face exuded goodness and knowledge. She would entrust herself to Anna Struhárová, as she entrusted herself to her daughter Irma.

She recognized the woman in the second photograph. As a child, Dora had sometimes seen Marie Mahdalová at church on Sundays. The church in Hrozenkov had been the closest for her even though she had lived in Potočná, on the Slovak side. Marie and her whole family used to sit right at the back. Dora remembered her slight figure and how her sons had often made a nuisance of themselves during Mass. And she remembered the dark, piercing eyes Marie had turned on them whenever their paths had crossed. As though she were ridiculing them, Dora used to think. But then she would tell herself that that was nonsense: this goddess was a stranger, and as such, she had no reason to laugh at them.

She turned her attention to the article next to the photos. At its mention of black magic, she wanted to laugh. She remembered a neighbor once telling a story of how, as a boy, he and some friends had been spying on a goddess; they had seen a client leave her house and, immediately afterward, an imp fly from the chimney. This had been accompanied by sparks and lightning, and it was a wonder that the boys hadn't broken their necks in the rush to get away. Black magic indeed!

Dora put the newspaper article aside and picked up a slip of paper with a note in an old-fashioned hand.

Check

re: Archive MM Brno: Gestapo, collection B-340 (Staatsgeheime Polizei Zlin)
re: Archive SNA Bratislava: Gestapo, collection NS-42 (Staatliche Sicherheitszentrale Preßburg)

1. Activities of goddesses (1939–1945)
2. Their postwar political orientation, esp. relation to fascism and bourgeois capitalism

Again the nonsensical association of the goddesses with the politics of the Protectorate and the occupiers. Had they meant it seriously, or had they just needed to find a reason to tread on the goddesses' toes?

Dora couldn't remember a visitor ever asking Surmena about her nationality or political convictions. Not only had she had no interest in such things, but she had struggled to remember who the president was or who was in the government at any given time; basically, she had known nothing about all that. And why would she? As a healer, such knowledge had been useless to her, and she had helped anyone in difficulty, regardless of whether they were Czech or German, Slovak or Hungarian. Dora could have sworn that nothing but healing had passed between Surmena and the people who visited her, during the war or after it. That Surmena had collaborated with an enemy agents' network—an accusation made in the concluding statement in her file—seemed to Dora far-fetched in the extreme. Had she not read this with her own eyes, she would never have believed that such a fiction could take root. Not only had it taken root, but under the supervision of an ideologically consistent officer, it had developed into the GODDESSES case and later borne fruit in the surveillance of Surmena.

The young archivist walked meaningfully through the reading room, bending to the computers in the corner and switching them off one by one. Opening hours were again coming to an end.

Dora placed the article, the slip of paper with the handwritten note, and several other pages—the notes of some journalists who had written about Surmena, an expert's assessment study several pages long—back in the folder. The last document she picked up was a strange one—a copy of an official letter written in German sent at the beginning of the war to the Protectorate border police. Its subject was another of the goddesses, Josefína Mahdalová, probably a relative of the Marie Mahdalová she'd just had cause to remember. But there was something else in the letter that caught Dora's attention—Josefína Mahdalová's maiden name: Surmenová. Dora's eyes swept across the lines.

From the State Security Police, Bratislava headquarters

re: Mahdalová, Josefína, née Surmenová; born Sept. 20, 1893, in Žítková, juridical district of Bojkovice; resident at house no. 269, Drietoma—Potočná; sorceress

We know from experience that the above-mentioned is known in the borderlands of Slovakia and the Protectorate as "the Goddess." The local people refer to her as "the soothsayer" or "the witch."

It is said that M. engages in "death sorcery." In one case she was sent an anonymous letter containing locks of a girl's hair in which the sender promised a reward for sorcery that would bring about the girl's death.

As the house of Mr. and Mrs. Mahdal is located in the hamlet of Potočná near the border with the Protectorate, there exists a danger that M. practices this occupation on the territory of the Protectorate.

I request the taking of appropriate action to ensure that the practicing of this occupation, should it encroach on the territory of the Protectorate, is prevented and political and police redress pursued.

As Dora turned the letter over to see what was on the back, the silence of the reading room was shattered by a resolute voice. "Closing in five minutes!"

Agitated, she looked up at the clock on the wall. It was true; she had only five minutes left. She turned to the few lines of text she hadn't yet read.

> Of the activities of the above-mentioned M. we have notified the SS-H-Sonderauftrag Department of the Ahnenerbe Institute, which has been conducting research on the matter in hand on the territory of the state of Slovakia and has requested information on such cases. Expect a visit from a special commando in the next few days.
> Ignaz Mielke, Hauptkommissar
> Staatliche Sicherheitszentrale Preßburg

Having completed her reading, Dora continued to look at the letter.

So this was how the goddesses had gotten close to the SS! And if the special commando really had paid that visit, then obviously the State Security Police's pursuit of the oracles of Žítková for fraternizing with the Germans and the whole GODDESSES case were not without foundation.

These thoughts were interrupted by the sound of throat-clearing from the impatient archivist. Reluctantly, Dora put the letter back in the folder. Her mind was racing. What did the letter prove? Nothing that pointed to Surmena as a collaborator, as its subject was a different goddess. So why was the letter in her file? Because of Mahdalová's maiden name, Surmenová?

For a moment Dora wondered what to do next. Then she made up her mind and got to her feet. With the blue folder in her hand, she hurried to the window behind which the archivist was sitting.

She placed the file on the returned loans shelf, then turned pleading eyes on the archivist as she handed the folder to him. "Would you mind copying this for me? It's only a few pages. I wouldn't want to come all the way from Brno just for this, you understand. It'd be ever so kind of you."

The archivist was caught off guard. It was against the rules to make copies of documents from personal files. But then he made a dismissive gesture and said, "Very well. Hopefully I won't get shot for the sake of a few sheets of paper."

From under the lid of the copying machine, a light flashed four times. When Dora ran down the spiral staircase, it was one minute past five. She skirted the park and caught her train back to Brno.

Part II

The Hostel

*I*t is impossible to imagine how helpless a person feels when she doesn't know what has happened to her loved ones. Surmena left on that June day in 1974, and she never came back. Then they took away Jakoubek, and no one would let her know the slightest thing about either one of them. The wardens maintained an impenetrable silence. Several times Dora phoned the National Committee office at Žítková, to no avail. She sent letters to Baglárka in which she begged for news of their whereabouts. She received no replies; she wouldn't have been surprised to learn that the letters were intercepted at the hostel office.

Right from the beginning, it was much worse than she possibly could have imagined.

They shut her up in an enormous room with bare walls coated with glossy pale-green paint. The room contained eight iron double bunks, whose rickety legs made marks on the stone floor, and a row of sixteen narrow metal lockers. The lockers—she was given the second one from the end—had four shelves, two at the top and two at the bottom, and a door peeling its paint; the door was fitted with a small padlock with a key. What remained of her life was supposed to fit inside this locker. She unpacked her only bag under the impatient gaze of a policeman and a social worker. As the door of the locker creaked shut on her meager possessions, fifteen pairs of cold eyes were fixed on her back.

After lights-out she sobbed into the rough material of the bedcovers, the edges of which bore the name of the hostel in blue. The other girls hissed at her and cursed her until they raised Hrtoňová, the night warden. Before long, this woman would rid Dora of her nighttime weeping. She pulled Dora into the glaring white light of the corridor and made her stand there—the first time for an hour, the second for two, the third until morning. Woe betide her if she leaned against the wall.

At first she had no inkling of what she had done to so antagonize Hrtoňová. But it was always Dora who attracted the warden's attention or ire. Dora's defense of her self-esteem in the face of slights and wrongs usually began first thing in the morning.

Hrtoňová was in the habit of rousing them just before the wake-up call, and Dora was her instrument. She would enter the dormitory quietly, tiptoe to the sleeping Dora's bed, then pull the quilt off her. And she always had plenty to say—about the stink that was coming from Dora, about the position she was lying in, most of all about what she had done with herself in the night. Before she was even properly awake, Dora was being screamed at and made to feel ashamed. She wanted to answer back, but in the beginning, she didn't even know what the woman was talking about. It was not until much later that she realized Hrtoňová was referring to the sighs and moans that occasionally came from the beds of the older girls; it was later still when she understood what caused these sounds.

Hrtoňová also went through Dora's locker, replacing her sanitary pads with cheap cotton wool so that she could punish her for soiling the bedsheet. At the time, Dora didn't understand her motivation in terrifying her by locking her in the showers and turning out the lights, or in pulling up Dora's nightdress in order to check that her privates were well washed before pushing her back into the showers and spraying her with icy water until she was blue with cold. Dora couldn't understand why, for years, Hrtoňová turned everything that went on at the hostel against her. Anna Stolařová received a package that went missing from her locker the next day; Dora was blamed for it. The new sneakers Lenka Rybářová's parents had sent from Canada disappeared, and Dora was blamed again. When Marie's money was stolen, Dora was the only possible culprit.

Back then, she thought it was because she had resisted the house rules from the start, that she refused to play the role of weakling in the face of the mighty. Or perhaps because she stayed on over the weekends when most of the girls went home.

Today she knew what was in Surmena's file, so she understood why those primitive women entrusted with bringing her to maturity had used her as a lightning rod for their own anger. She had read the note in file 82—it was etched in her memory so that she knew it verbatim. *"For her further education, proceed with special reference to the matter of her relation to our Socialist society and her ideological principles."* The women had followed Švanc's instruction.

During the course of those years, Dora learned to fight. In the evenings the other girls would return to the subject of her alleged crimes. Now she knew why none of the wardens ever came when the fights were at their fiercest. Now she knew why they would wake her with glee, saying, *"Did you get a good hiding, then?"*

Dora got a good hiding many times, which was why she ran home to Žítková. But running away was futile. For a few days, she holed up in their little house and roamed the neighborhood, but as time went on, she felt more and more lost. She had no one to turn to. Her solitude was amorphous and boundless, and she was ever more fearful of the future. And she was hungry, of course. In the end she was glad when the chairman of the National Committee office, whom she'd visited in the hope of learning something about Surmena and Jakoubek, refused to let her leave the room. For six whole months after that, she was denied every freedom: she was taken to and from school like a prisoner. She submitted to this like a lamb to the slaughter, seeing no reason to fight, or even to live.

It was around this time, when she could bear the emptiness and loneliness no longer, that she started to write a diary. With no one to turn to, paper was the next best thing. It absorbed all her pain and the constant repetition of her unchanging sorrows. The love she felt for her diary was almost physical. Which was why she was so devastated when they took it from her.

Had she left her locker unlocked, or had someone broken into it? Had the wardens dug out her diary when she was at school and left it lying in the dormitory? Or had some of the girls taken it? It didn't matter because one day, she had returned to the dormitory to find everyone poring over her notes. All that remained of the diary was an empty shell. It had been taken apart page by page, and these pages were doing the rounds. There were some terrible things in it. About her. And about them. About what she liked about which girl, about what she found attractive; all her hopes and fears set down on the page, including her speculations on whether she was normal.

She could put up with their rage and contempt. But their mockery was like salt in an open wound that stung more with each new name they thought up for her. Pervert. Bloke. Queer. Lesbian. The wardens would use these words, too, happily.

After that she kept no diary until she found a place to hide it beyond the hostel. All the things she needed to communicate, she buried deep inside—for months and years.

She found another outlet for her emotions. At first rarely and then with greater regularity, she would steal and destroy hostel property and the other girls' possessions, or—even better—things belonging to the wardens who called her names. Then she would look on with delight as these things burned in the wastebasket while everyone ran about screaming, as though what was on fire was not a bucket but the roof.

She burned a lot of stuff. And she cut it up, punctured it, slashed it. She knocked it over accidentally on purpose: a bust of Comenius shattered right next to Hrtoňová as she was leaving the building with her bike, whose inner tubes someone had punctured. She got away with that. It was the stupid light bulbs that they caught her for, and they also drew the (right) conclusion that she was responsible for plugging the washbasins with towels and flooding the washroom and dining room beneath it. For that she was almost sent to the youth detention center; she wasn't bothered one way or the other. All that did bother her was the fact of her failure, in getting caught.

For this she gave herself a punishment that far surpassed all her earlier ones. Not an elastic band wound so tight around her wrist that her hand went blue; not sleep or food deprivation or the swallowing of saliva; not fifteen minutes under an ice-cold shower. It was three cuts: vertical, horizontal, vertical. An *H*, because she was a halfwit for getting caught; an *H* for the hyenas who kept her there and had her over a barrel; *H* for Hrtoňová, who never let Dora out of her sight and wanted to crush her. It was enough to sit on the toilet, cross one leg over the other at the knee, dig the sharp manicure scissors into the soft flesh of her thigh, and tug. Vertical, horizontal, vertical. The blood that dripped down into the toilet bowl was washed away, along with the hatred she felt for herself and for all of them, including those who were not there, like her mother. At least for a while.

In those endless years at the hostel, when she hated the whole world, Dora thought of her mother much more often than before, when she was still with Surmena. Again and again she imagined what it must have been like when the sharp blade of the ax split open her skull—the skull of the woman she had loved with all that was in her, the woman she'd have done anything for. But her mother had done nothing for her, to protect her from what had happened. Dora thought then that if anyone was to blame for how things had ended up, it was Irena.

Irena Idesová

"It was never easy with Irena."

Their hill was bathed in the light of the midday sun, casting shadows under Dora's feet. The air was tense with heat. The silence of the glade was disturbed only by the tireless chirping of crickets and the call of the indomitable lark. It was the last school day of that dreadful June that reduced her family to a rump. Perhaps she'd forgotten to tell Surmena that her day would end early, with the handing out of end-of-year reports. No one had come down to collect her, so she'd gone up on her own. Through the window she saw shadows by the stove. She stood there and listened. There were two voices. Were they really speaking about her mother?

"She had no patience. She had no interest in learning either—it was as if she didn't need it. She was so full of herself that she never listened to a word Mother told her. 'Why should I?' she used to say. She had a will of her own and other guides, too, as you well know."

From deep in the kitchen area came the screech of a chair being pushed back from the table, followed by footsteps and the clink of a ladle on the aluminum pail that brought water from the well.

"Drink up; it's hot today."

"As a kid, I was scared of Irena," said a quiet female voice. "She was somehow wild, and that terrified me. You never knew what she was thinking and what she would do next. Sweet as pie one moment, nasty the next. And I still don't understand what those angels of hers were about."

"I know what you mean," said Surmena.

The chair screeched again, less urgently than before.

"She reckoned she was able to talk to them."

"Did you believe her?"

There was a short silence.

"There was something special in Irena, you know. The trouble was, there was too much of it. I don't think she understood herself. When the angels were with her, it was just about OK. When she was all on her own, it was worse."

"So you believed her, then?" The woman's voice was surprised.

Surmena cleared her throat. "I did. At least, I believed that she experienced something, but whether it was angels she talked to, I don't know."

The woman gave a shriek of surprise. Dora now recognized the voice as Baglárka's.

"Well, I think Irena was a bit crazy. Do you remember when the word got around? All the whispering that she'd got a screw loose. Speaking with angels, for heaven's sake! She was mad; something must have snapped. She'd flipped. The priest was beside himself. He'd never heard such blasphemy."

Dora imagined Baglárka crossing herself.

"For three Sundays his sermon was all about humility and the true faith. And he wouldn't leave Irena in peace. Many times I saw him having a word with her after Mass, and she would walk away in tears. She went to confession as if she was going to her execution."

"That was Father Hůrka, wasn't it? No, Irena didn't make things easy for him," muttered Surmena. "But he was wrong to behave like that. Whatever was the matter with Irena, he was never going to put it right by browbeating her. Nor was Father going to fix it by using the strap on her. It's hardly surprising that Irena went into herself."

Baglárka mumbled an expression of doubt, but Surmena went on. "I've never understood why there was always such a gulf between Mother and Irena. I'm not sure that it was there before Irena got her angels, but maybe it was. She never did as Mother told her. She was abstract and impatient. Gathering and sorting herbs was torture for her. She had no interests, and she didn't want to learn anything. She had her own little world. She didn't need anyone, except perhaps the dog we had at the time. She used to walk him on the slopes. She'd sit with him under the lime where the ways part or by the rocks on the hilltops, and she'd talk and talk. We used to think that she was talking to that dog. It was only later that we realized she was speaking with the angels. Maybe Mother thought that Father and the priest would tame her with their beatings and threats, and that after that, she would come to her, humbled. Perhaps that's why she didn't intervene. But things took a turn for the worse, not the better. Irena ran wild. She was calm only when she returned from her talks with the angels. Even I didn't understand her."

The bottoms of the empty cups clacked against the tabletop.

"Things didn't get any better. It was worse still once our parents were gone. She went from cottage to cottage after men. Sometimes she stayed out all night. She made an exhibition of herself at dances. In the end she found herself in the family way. I tried to keep her in hand, but she wouldn't listen to me. She was old enough to do what she wanted, she said. I came to terms with the prospect of a baby in the cottage, but otherwise, I expected everything to stay as it was. But come the next Sunday, the banns were out. I didn't learn who the groom was until the priest told me. Believe me, I'd far sooner have kept her at home with me than given her to Ides. But nobody asked me what I thought. At least I could keep an eye on them on the hill opposite as they fixed up the cottage our parents had left to her."

"I'd tear my daughters to shreds if they made a show of me like that, God knows I would," said Baglárka. "And with a man like Ides, for pity's sake!"

"That was Irena's biggest mistake. I tried to talk her out of it. We all did, but she never listened, even when folk spoke to her nicely. I wouldn't be surprised to learn that her angels, too, tried to talk her out of it, but even they couldn't move her. Maybe she refused to speak with them; maybe she finished with them then because after that, everything was different. Judging from our rare meetings, when Ides allowed her to come to me, her life was like one long fall into an abyss. Not even children could save her. She lost the first, she lost the second, and then came Dora. The day after the birth, I went to check on her. She had a split lip, and one side of her face was so swollen that you couldn't see the eye. He'd beaten her and then cleared off. He didn't come home for four days. Irena couldn't bear such a burden; that much was obvious. Who on earth could have managed to pick her way around the twisted rules of a drunkard? He kept her down for so long that he broke her will and robbed her of all common sense. He was free to beat her as and when he chose, to come home drunk, to gamble away their property. Whatever he did, she always blamed herself—for missing something, for failing to do something, for spoiling something, for the kids she'd had by him. A girl . . . and a *monster*. She bowed down before him, panicked, went into a frenzy. There was no way that things would end well."

Dora licked her cracked, dry lips. She was roasting in the midday heat.

"Poor Irena," Baglárka sighed.

Surmena made a clicking sound with her tongue. "Anyway . . . Mother should have paid more attention to her when she was little. While she was here, there, and everywhere attending to others, the rest of us left Irena to her own devices. As she was too young to be put to work, we sent her off to play on the hillside. Who could have guessed then that it would end so badly? We didn't see the problem until it was too late to do anything about it."

Could Dora hear Baglárka sniffling? Was she weeping? But maybe Dora was the one who was crying—for Irena, the mother who, it turned out, she had barely known. The woman she remembered was different—beautiful, very beautiful, with curly brown hair she released from her bonnet and embroidered headscarf only rarely. But she was unpredictable too. One moment tender with love and running about the room with them, out into the sunshine, back inside, all in a vortex of song; the next possessed by a sudden rage, pelting them with pots and pans, screaming things that Dora didn't understand.

"Tell me, Surmena, why didn't you warn her? If you'd poured the wax and read the future in it with her, Irena might still be alive! If she'd known what would happen, she'd certainly have had second thoughts about Ides. It's a great power that you have, but you use it too sparingly on your own family."

It was a long time before the kitchen gave up Surmena's answer.

"Because it's not possible. For any of us. You can't read your own future or that of your family. Irena wouldn't have let me pour wax for her anyway. She was a goddess herself, remember."

"What a pity."

"No, it isn't, not really. Fate is fate. I couldn't have helped Irena even if I'd known what was going to happen. She departed from the right path very early, and she scorned the gift that would later destroy her. She channeled her abilities inside, not away from herself, and that could never have ended well. Something had to happen. We couldn't prevent it. But with Dora, I can reverse it. Maybe the gift's in her, too, and if so, I'll take care to make sure that she knows how to handle it. Or I can convince her not to accept it. I haven't made my mind up yet."

There was another pause before Baglárka spoke again. "Do you ever . . . think about what they say? About Mahdalka in connection with Irena?"

Baglárka's words were drowned out by the sound of a falling chair. Something must have happened inside. The sound of footsteps was followed by an exclamation of alarm from Jakoubek and some muttering from Surmena. It was plain that the talk about her mother was over.

Dora couldn't be sure that what she remembered was what she had actually heard. It was quite possible that her memory presented something slightly different each time it replayed the scene, and that these shifted ideas then overlaid the true image of her mother that she held in her mind. What was for sure, as time went by, her recollection of her mother shrank until there was nothing left but a madwoman who had talked to herself from childhood and been lost in her own world. Had they not said that this was a hereditary condition that had afflicted her family for centuries, surfacing every now and then in the form of a complete lunatic? What else was Jakoubek, after all? How many of them had there been? They must have mentioned others because they had said that for every exceptional woman in the family, there had been a doomed man preyed on by sisters and mothers, who transformed the power they took from him for the goddess's arts. It seemed that in her own mother, it had all come together—although she was exceptional, she had been consumed by madness.

That day Dora had been found under the kitchen window in a state of delirium. Burning, gasping for water, in a semiconscious swoon. It had taken her three days to get over the sunstroke. A little longer, Surmena had said, and there would have been nothing left of her but dust.

Mr. Oštěpka, Antiquarian Bookseller

*H*ad it not been for Mr. Oštěpka and his quiet, dusty antiquarian bookshop crouched in a narrow street leading to a disused synagogue, she wondered how she would have survived her years at the hostel. From the day she first entered the shop, it offered her a hiding place away from the prying eyes of the wardens. Every day after school, she would hole up there for hours at a time until she had to report back at the hostel.

There was never anyone in the shop, apart from Mr. Oštěpka. He sat behind his high counter, with its stacks of dusty old books and a greasy, tattered napkin containing a bread roll and the crumbs it left behind. The scent of the books was overlaid with the crude, sharp smell of salami.

At first she tried to slip into the shop without being noticed, taking care that the door didn't creak as she entered. She would conceal herself among the shelves so that Mr. Oštěpka had no idea she was there. She was afraid that he would tell her to leave: sitting and leafing through books you had no intention of buying was something you did in libraries, not antiquarian bookshops. But she was mistaken about this shop owner—his interest in selling books was no greater than his interest in whether his salami was in a roll or between two slices of bread. He was interested in additions, and if his favorite books stayed right where they were, all the better. His wages were paid come what may, out of the generosity of the Socialist state, and anything beyond that was not his concern.

He explained all this to her later, the day of their first conversation. Then he invited her to the back of the shop and showed her its whole dusty wealth from the seller's perspective. Before long the territory beyond the counter was her preserve too. Sometimes she would sit at Mr. Oštěpka's back, on the top of the low wooden steps, reading a book and listening to his quiet, slow chewing.

Mr. Oštěpka's domain was aviation, and he protected it anxiously. Under the counter he stored an abundance of books and ragged magazines on the subject, their pages teeming with drawings of hot-air balloons and a wide range of hovercraft and aircraft. Dora was most attracted by the ethnography shelf. She found folk art and folk customs a fascinating topic, although so much of it was new to her. She admired the photographs of folk costumes from villages all over Moravia, and she wondered at the variation in customs, which differed from one place to the next. Her pile of books included works by Zíbrt, Niederle, and Václavík, and they brought back memories of Žítková.

From time to time, Mr. Oštěpka would dig something out on Dora's home region, and she would always receive this with delight. Once he placed before her a package wrapped in newspaper. It was a set of loose pages in a front and back cover that were missing their spine.

"Look at this. The Goddesses of Žítková, " he said, as if passing a casual remark. He laughed at Dora as she grabbed the book from him.

A slim volume with faded pages. The author was Josef Hofer. Dora made a start on it straightaway. Although she was enraged by Hofer's nonsensical maligning of the goddesses, here and there she smiled at a portrait of the peculiar people of Moravské Kopanice. It was as though she knew every character, every man and woman, intimately. They behaved in a way that was familiar to her; they were dressed as a few aunties in the village still dressed; they spoke a dialect that was still current in Žítková. When she left the shop that day, she was already halfway through the book. For the first time, she opened the zipper on her small purse and placed a few coins on the counter. Mr. Oštěpka waved them away. This was the kindest thing anyone had ever done for her in all her time at the hostel in Hradiště.

She was forced to stay there for three years.

At first she didn't believe that she would be institutionalized for longer than a few days. A few weeks at the most. It didn't cross her mind that she would reach the age of majority as a detainee of the hostel.

That moment was etched in her memory. She officially became an adult on October 30. The morning was dreary, as though she had a whole century of rough life behind her. Although her childhood had ended the day before, it seemed so far away it was as though it had never been.

Many things changed that day. Among the best was the fact that the strict rules of the institution no longer applied to her. Suddenly she became a person with full rights, for whom the institution should serve as a base only until she finished school. After that she would at last be allowed to live her own life. From one day to the next, no one cared by how many minutes she was late for dinner; indeed, no one checked whether she turned up for dinner at all. The old prohibitions were no longer in effect, and no one thought up any new ones. Now, from her birthday on, no one could do anything to her. She prepared impatiently for the coming Friday.

She took the first bus of the afternoon to Žítková.

As she approached the National Committee office, her heart was pounding. She looked down the broad hillside of dried, wind-whipped grass, at the dense woods of the hills opposite, at the cottages scattered about the slopes. One cottage she couldn't see, as it was beyond the ridge, was Surmena's—theirs.

She was nervous because in a few moments, she would find out everything. They couldn't put her off any longer; they couldn't, as so many times before, refer her to someone else or transfer her to another line, at the end of which no one would know anything. They couldn't brush her off with the kind of embarrassed shrug she could sense even over the phone in the post office booth, the phone that for so many years she had used to so little effect.

Twice Mrs. Gorčíková, who worked at the National Committee office, had ended a call with the words: *"Perhaps when you're an adult, Dora."*

That Friday her time had come: she was an adult. And she was more determined than ever. Not even wild horses would have driven her out of the place before she found out the whereabouts of Surmena and Jakoubek. Not even wild horses, she told herself as she knocked on the door of Mrs. Gorčíková's office and stepped inside. Mrs. Gorčíková sent her straight to the chairman, whose office she left almost half an hour later.

"So now you know, I suppose," said Mrs. Gorčíková.

Dora nodded before settling in the chair Mrs. Gorčíková offered her and accepting a glass of elderberry cordial.

She could never have imagined that after so many hopeless, failed attempts, she would find out everything all at once, without the need to demonstrate the anger that had built up inside her or to use the dozens of arguments she had practiced in her head. There was no need for her to do anything but sit and listen to the chairman, who was obviously well prepared for her arrival.

"I won't drag it out, Dora; neither of us deserves that. You'd find out from the district office, in any case, or even down at the shop. So here it is: they put Jakoubek in an institution in Brno and Surmena in a hospital in Kroměříž. Both of your houses are empty. The municipality didn't want

them. What would it do with such ruins in the hills? You can visit them whenever you like. We've kept the keys here. Here you are, take them."

There was no need for Dora to say a word. Then she came out and slid into the chair opposite Mrs. Gorčíková, helpless, still clutching the two bunches of keys.

"Keep your chin up, girl. You're going to need to be strong," said Mrs. Gorčíková as she patted Dora's knee and pressed the glass of cordial on her.

And so she would. Because the suffering connected with her discovery of Surmena's and Jakoubek's whereabouts was far from over. It was a fair while before she was able to visit her loved ones on Sundays. After that the few Sunday afternoon hours in which she was permitted to see them became the center of her universe, giving her remaining months at the hostel their only moments of meaning. This flash of light in an otherwise dark week gave her strength and the hope that finding them was a step toward their life of before. She was determined to bring them back together.

But she needed to work out how to do it.

In dozens of nights spent tossing and turning as the other girls slept, dozens of lessons in which she failed to concentrate on the matter at hand, a great many afternoons spent wandering about the town, this was all she thought about.

Then came the end of the school year. She departed the hostel with her school-leaving examination diploma and her certificate of apprenticeship in a bag the same size as the one with which she had arrived. And she knew what to do. It was the most important decision she would ever make. She did not move to Kroměříž to be closer to Surmena, but to Brno, where she would pull out all the stops to have Jakoubek delivered into her care. Then they would return to Žítková, and one day Surmena would come back to them, as soon as she was well again.

When she closed her eyes, she saw their cottage clearly. Jakoubek was sitting on the doorstep, and Surmena was standing behind him. They were giving her a cheery wave as she approached. At that time she didn't yet know that the only images she could summon were firmly anchored in a long-closed past.

Josef Hofer

The thin, newspaper-covered volume from Mr. Oštěpka was to play a big role in Dora's later life. She took it with her to Brno and stored it on a shelf in the small, cold room that would be her home for the next few years. She could have recited the stories it contained backward. At that time they were as close as she could get to the days of Surmena's childhood. They presented a mosaic not only of Surmena's life but also that of her grandmother Justýna Ruchárka, Justýna's sisters, and other goddesses that Josef Hofer had made the antiheroines of his stories.

This book was Dora's first study material. Others soon came along, and within a few years, she was quite knowledgeable on the subject. More important than this, she had formulated the desire to turn her private passion into her profession. She applied to a Brno university for admission to an evening course that aimed to bring the intelligentsia and the working class closer together.

One of her first essays addressed the relation between parish priests in Starý Hrozenkov, Josef Hofer, and the goddesses. It was clear from the beginning that this would form the basis of her dissertation.

She sought the advice of the current parish priest, who in the distant past had served Hofer as an altar boy. He suggested she take a trip to Luhačovice, the home of Hofer's sons, or to Brno, where, he had heard, Hofer's papers were kept.

She made energetic inquiries until she discovered that these papers were in the archive of the Institute of Ethnography, on the very floor where later she would have an office of her own.

Over several long afternoons, she worked her way through boxes labeled "JOSEF HOFER (1871–1947)." They contained official documents, sermons, and articles in draft form, along with Hofer's private correspondence and diaries. With all this material in hand, Dora found it easy to reconstruct his life.

Josef Hofer, the second of seven children, was the son of a farmer from Snovídky in southern Moravia. In his writings he claimed that his stubborn and stormy nature was inherited from his father. Judging from family photographs, Hofer's ugly aquiline nose was also a legacy from his father. His sense of smell was apparently poor, as it led him from the path of righteousness on more than one occasion. He strayed first in his student years, when he ran away from the theological seminary. People probably explained this act with words to the effect that "everyone can have doubts." His parents were relieved when he resumed his studies. But what else could he have done? His elder brother had come into the farm, and the remaining siblings would have to provide for themselves. Because his studies were his lifeline, he completed them and accepted with gratitude the post of parish priest in Polanka; a few years later, he became a curate in Zábřeh nad Odrou. While he was in Zábřeh, Stázka, the eldest of his younger sisters, ran away to join him; she was soon followed by the others. Judging from the correspondence, the sisters quarreled with their brother and even more so with his avaricious wife.

Had they joined him earlier, he may not have achieved all that he did; he may not have dared to rise up as his stormy nature commanded. But by the time Stázka knocked on his door, the wheels were already in motion, and he couldn't reverse them. Not that he would have wanted to. It was clear to Dora that he was consumed by his success, that he was drunk on it, that his hand itched to take up his pen in the evenings and write more scathing criticism. He was Josef Hofer alias Josef Hříva, Jakub Posolda, or Rectus (the "Righteous One"), assuming multiple identities to achieve, by the stinging application of his pen to the pages of magazines, including the Olomouc organ *Pozor*, the removal of the Jewish dog who had bribed and politicked his way to the archbishop's seat.

"This Kohn," Dora read in Hofer's diaries, *"occupies a post that should be granted only to the best of us, and certainly not to an immigrant fop whose grandfather was circumcised."* Hofer was not alone in the trembling indignation of his diaries and magazine criticism. And his robust diction probably gained encouragement from an ironic utterance made by Austrian minister-president Viscount Taaffe when he received news of the choice of the archdiocese of Olomouc. *"Und hat er sich schon taufen lassen?"* (And has he been baptized yet?)

In a letter Hofer received from his Viennese friend Manlich, these words were underlined in red ink and reinforced by several exclamation points in the margin. Dora was quite sure that all this had been added by Hofer.

Hofer had tracked the career of Archbishop Kohn in the form of newsprint clippings. On reading these, Dora understood that the dissertation in which Hofer proved his devotion to the church community had also worked against a more merciful acceptance of Kohn. He had called it *De infallibilitate Romani Pontificis* (On the infallibility of the bishop of Rome). Hofer and others of like mind were scornful of this infallibility, claiming that to accept it was tantamount to sycophancy. Apparently, Kohn had wriggled out of this debate, which had been making waves in church circles since the end of the previous century; instead, Hofer wrote, he had made a glittering impression by his servile work, thus establishing a position for himself with the highest authority.

"The man knows no shame!" an angry Hofer wrote one summer. He berated Kohn for going from parish to parish and censuring those whose support gave his office its power, for approving dozens of suspensions, for invoking protocol for the interrogation of priests before imposing uncommonly heavy penalties, for impeding the creation of catechists— in fact, for making himself a nuisance to the servants of the Church all around him. According to Hofer, Kohn was a nuisance to ordinary people, too, in that he refused to consent to their shortening their way to Mass by crossing fields that belonged to the archbishop's palace. Woe betide the man who took so much as a twig from his woods! *The Jew in him is there for all to see,* thought Hofer as his alter ego Rectus spewed out article after scathing article.

Perhaps he would have gone on spewing to no great effect had Kohn himself not drawn greater attention to him by ordering an investigation to uncover the writer of the philippics. On the basis of a graphologist's recommendation, an arrest was made not of Hofer but of the innocent František Ocásek, priest at Velké Kunčice, who was thrown into a priests' prison. When the voice of Rectus sounded again—with a condemnation of the archbishop's ruthlessness in punishing an innocent man—it was heard as far away as Rome. The apostolic nunciature in Vienna informed the Holy See, and in December 1903, Kohn was summoned to an audience with the pope. At this time Hofer wrote that he had heard whispers that if Kohn would not abdicate of his own volition as soon as he returned, his office would be taken from him.

Rectus celebrated victory. *"Rectus the Righteous! Rectus the Incorruptible! Rectus the Almighty!"* wrote Hofer in his diaries. Dora was disgusted.

This was the end of the battle but not of the war. No sooner had Hofer rid himself of Kohn than he looked around for his next opponent—and this time he set his sights on Rome. *"Can man live a moral life without God and his Commandments? The Church of Rome in disarray. Rome, the Czech enemy."* As these and other articles appeared in *Pozor*, it was obvious that Hofer was ceasing to be a useful fellow warrior and becoming an inconvenient faultfinder. Dora understood the simplicity of the solution. The people of the White Carpathians were strange and inflexible. In Bojkovice they heard nothing but complaints about them. Let them teach him a thing or two!

He arrived in winter 1910, just as the January frosts hit with full force. Three horse-drawn coaches pulled up in front of the presbytery at Starý Hrozenkov. From these vehicles jumped five young girls wrapped so thoroughly in scarves that only their eyes were visible, and a man dressed in a large, shapeless fur coat. Chance passersby stopped and formed themselves into clusters; the steam from their whispering mouths hovered over their heads. Six feather quilts, a cupboard, two wooden beds, and a number of unwieldy chests of various shapes and sizes were unloaded from the coaches and carried into the house. The door to the house closed behind Hrozenkov's newest residents. The conveyances set off immediately on their return journey. The gathering reached the realization that the new priest had arrived and that he was no lesser a personage than he who had achieved the deposition of the archbishop of Olomouc.

As he stood behind the altar on the first Sunday in February, dozens, perhaps hundreds, of eyes were on him. So this was the rebellious priest who had been ordered to come here because no one would come by his own choice. The church was bursting at the seams. But could this dry beanpole of a man with a receding hairline, a pince-nez, and an enormous nose really be the hothead who had unseated the archbishop?

Hofer's mind was racing. His diaries make it plain that he was horrified. From the pulpit he looked into the faces of women in beautifully embroidered but cheap local dress; some of the children had holes in their clothes, and some wore rags instead of shoes. As for the men, they had turned up drunk for a church mass.

As Hofer examined the faces of his new parishioners, his mood became ever gloomier. Not infrequently his gaze snagged on an expression of unusual dim-wittedness.

This was perhaps the moment that his contempt for the people of Moravské Kopanice was born. How was he to learn to live with their broken morals, alcoholism, and ineducable children? He felt contempt for the whole godforsaken region. And this contempt would cause many wrongs.

"The goddesses are a result of your stupidity! This stupidity works in their favor: they make better livings off it than many of you who do an honest day's toil!" Hofer thundered from the pulpit.

He wrote the following in the local gazette and also in his book on the goddesses:

> Every day the goddesses are visited by up to fifty people asking for their help on a wide range of matters. I repeat, fifty people. The destitute in their smocks, respectable women in gold chains, ladies with silken veils over their faces. Our "sensitive" goddesses have a friendly word, "good" advice, and a "wholesome" cure for all of them. The goddesses open a door to the past, draw aside the dark veil of the future, summon the dead from their dark graves as witnesses. In short, for money they know and understand "everything." These artless founts of wisdom earn by their "goddess" activities as much as a Rank Eight civil servant, and they live their lives accordingly.

In this way he sowed a seed of envy among his parishioners. Every Sunday he worked the soil in which the seed lay, until it sprouted in unprecedented proportions. The people of Hrozenkov began to treat the goddesses with reserve. Word got around that they took advantage of the unhappiness of others. But not a single family failed to send for them when the need was great.

The goddesses received as many visitors as before; the falloff in neighbors' visits created greater capacity for nonlocals. But their lives took a turn for the worse. Suddenly their neighbors treated them with resentment and envy rather than respect and gratitude. Their homes closed more tightly around them, and before a goddess admitted a stranger, she considered the matter long and hard. The knock at the door might be dealt by a constable tipped off by Hofer in the confessional, investigating whether a certain parishioner had discussed an offense against the law with a goddess rather than at the station. *The goddess said, the goddess thinks, the goddess advised* . . . The priest was always galled to hear words such as these through the wooden grille. That the mutterings of women with minimal education should count for more than the word of God! Or even the word of Josef Hofer. It was unacceptable.

He denounced them and maligned them; he refused to baptize their children, introduce them to the faith, or otherwise provide for them. For the deeply religious goddesses, this was a calamity. They found themselves at a parting of the ways: Hofer's will or their own demise.

At the thought of the escalation in the conflict, Dora's heart ached for the goddesses. She read draft sermons filled with scorn and wounding denunciation, directed, too, at those who continued to visit them. She read Hofer's *Stories from Kopanice* and *Kopanice Stories*, works he had composed thanks in large measure to the goddesses and their deeds but that cast them in a light of his own making. These books, published in quick succession, reported to a wide readership on the injustices practiced without a shred of conscience for the simple wretches of Moravské Kopanice by the wily, insidious female charlatans. Indignant readers sided with the shrewd, inventive narrator, who at the end of each chapter taught one of the goddesses a lesson. This just narrator was the books' hero, and he was none other than Josef Hofer, parish priest at Starý Hrozenkov.

Dora wanted to know the source of Hofer's vanity, animosity, and imperiousness. In a man who had promised himself to God, surely they could not have developed without encouragement.

As her search progressed, she went through the archived magazines Hofer had worked with and the literary remains of his writer friends, reading all the letters he had addressed to them. Before long she came across the collection of František Sokol-Tůma and his forgotten novel *Celibacy*. Now she was shown a chapter of Hofer's life that was new to her.

The man who stood before her now was not the one who had taken spiteful advantage of his position in a community of uneducated mountain dwellers; it was a lonely, unfulfilled man who had lacked the courage to mold his own fate and so live in accordance with his convictions. In this regard his story was unexceptional; in fact, it was exemplary, shared with many other talented men with no property whose lives would have developed along dissimilar lines if their circumstances had been different. Hofer's lack of means had left but one course open to him. A teacher in Snovídky had suggested that bright, gifted Josef be sent to a Jesuit seminary, thus relieving his parents of the burden of paying for his education.

Irrespective of whether young Hofer was sympathetic to faith and its obligations, he was required to come to terms with them quickly. That he was unsuccessful in this was as clear from his letters, in which he claimed that celibacy was the worst cruelty a man who aspired to be a good servant of God could endure, as it was from his behavior. His first attempt to cast off the yoke of his obligations was his flight from the seminary. Having realized that he could not make his way in life alone and without resources, he surrendered and reconciled himself to a future in the service of others, the Church's flock. But the powers that held him in check would have a fight on their hands. His first challenge centered on the figure of the archbishop of Olomouc, after which he would take on the whole of the Catholic Church. By now Dora knew how all this had ended up. Relegated to the hills of the White Carpathians and sentenced to oblivion, he poured out all his anger on those who defied him. The goddesses. He staked out a new battlefield. Although he could never have defeated the shackles of the Catholic Church, in this private battle, his victory was assured.

But the word *never* continued to trouble him. The closer he got to fifty, the more it troubled him. Had fate not offered Hofer this chance, his burden would have been too much for him, Dora thought. He may even have been at the point of doing something foolish when he was saved by the breakup of the monarchy and the formation of Czechoslovakia. At the first opportunity, he left the Catholic Church and became a member of the Czechoslovak Hussite Church; furthermore, he became one of the new church's loudest promoters.

In Hrozenkov, hardly had the word of Hofer's defection got out than the whole place was buzzing. Women stopped each other in the street and sent their children out to the fields for their husbands. Slowly the pub filled up. Everyone saw it as a betrayal. They didn't call him a hothead; they called him a Judas.

For ten years he had kept his parishioners on a tight rein so as to make good Catholics of them. They had turned a blind eye to the fact that he had given Anežka a child; after all, he wasn't the first priest to behave in this way, and nor would he be the last. But to betray his faith? And then to marry another, who was already expecting, right under their noses, in Uherský Brod?

Early that evening the curate called on Hofer with a warning. He had overheard talk in the pub to the effect that someone would get his throat slit. The newly converted priest thought it best to circumvent the indignation of his flock. In secret he packed up and quit his parish. And he never returned—at least not while he was alive. For many years he moved from one South Moravian village to the next, scraping together a living as a teacher. After a long illness and a protracted retirement, he was brought back to Starý Hrozenkov in a coffin. In his last will and testament, he had made it clear that he wished to be buried there and nowhere else, amid his former parishioners and the goddesses.

Hofer's friends and family were astonished by this directive. Everyone was astonished but the locals.

In Moravské Kopanice, Hofer's legacy was a living presence. No one there was surprised by his final act. They had been expecting it, in fact.

As soon as word got around that Hofer's body was on its way to Starý Hrozenkov for interment in the churchyard the next day, everyone knew who had sent for him. Pagáčena, Justýna, and Chupatá—the goddesses he had tormented most, by now rotting in their graves for many years—had unfinished business with him. This was confirmed by local men shortly after Hofer's body was washed and dressed. Apparently, it had turned slowly black, from the feet up to the waist. This phenomenon was the talk of the village. Perish the thought of what would come to pass when the whole body was black! Would the goddesses rise from their graves to meet him? Was the devil on his way?

Perhaps none of the villagers knew the cause of death, as entered on Hofer's death certificate: gangrene. But even if they did know, Dora was quite sure that they shrugged it off and continued to believe that their tormentor was punished thus by the will of the goddesses. For the sin of conversion, the people of Moravské Kopanice approved of such retaliation. Dora was in favor of it, too, although not for the same reason. She approved because of what Josef Hofer had perpetrated on the region's greatest wealth—the goddesses.

In the days after Dora read Surmena's file and the blue folder containing extracts from the GODDESSES dossier, she thought a lot about Hofer. Because of his damaging interference in the lives of the goddesses but also because of a name that kept cropping up in the files. Josefína Mahdalová, née Surmenová.

She had seen this name before. At the university, when she was collecting materials for her work on Josef Hofer. At that time she had not seen anything suspicious in it. Surmena/Surmenová was quite a common name in Moravské Kopanice, and there were many people with this name whom Dora didn't know. Only after reading the pages in the blue folder did it dawn on her that the name may have some deeper connection with her Surmena.

Josef Hofer kept a diary from his adolescence on. Although most of his notes related to his passionate pursuit of his career, he devoted quite a lot of space to his dreams, which he recorded with unfailing regularity, practically every second day. Descriptions of his dreams included details of surroundings, colors, even smells. Dora had read these descriptions carefully. One particular dream, which Hofer had recorded in his last year at the Hrozenkov presbytery, came back to her as she was studying Surmena's file:

> It was late afternoon and darkness was descending on the mountain slopes into the valley at Hrozenkov. I was walking along the main road from Bojkovice. On rounding a bend, I saw the church bell tower. I noticed a huddled figure at the main door. I narrowed my eyes so as to see more clearly in the gloom, and I quickened my pace. Could it be that a traveler was lying injured in front of the church? As I hastened along, I heard the rustle of my cassock and the howling of dogs. In the cottages of the village, almost everyone had a dog to watch over their dwelling when they were not at home, but could there have been so many of them as to make such a commotion? In any case, where were their masters? The streets were deserted.

When I was a hundred yards or so from the church, I looked again at its door. I was alarmed to discover that no traveler was lying there. Where was he? I looked about but saw no sign of him. Then above the rustle of the cloth about my legs and the barks of the wild dogs, I heard a feeble call. *"Re-ta!"* This was the word by which the people of Kopanice called for help. From its sound there was no doubt that the voice was a woman's. Frantic, I looked about for the source of the call, and at last I saw her, a good way off, beyond a bend in the road, where it branches off in a path that leads to the churchyard. Swiftly I ran to her, fully convinced that she was injured.

I had almost reached the woman when she began to slither along the ground and then to move about on all fours. It was as if she was afraid that I had followed her with the intention of doing her harm. Her dread at my approach was palpable, and so I called to her: *"I've come to help you!"* The eyes that this very young woman turned on me were terrified. With still greater desperation, she clawed her way along the clay path, up to the churchyard. Perhaps she was seeking refuge among the trees, where her suffering would not be seen. By now I had reached the path and was following her along it. I was curious about and also moved by the girl's plight. What could have happened to make her so fearful of people? Who had done her harm? I was afraid that by the state she was in, she would do more harm to herself. She reached the top of the path and crawled beyond the churchyard gates, seeking a refuge that was hidden from my gaze. I hurried after her and found her on the ground, wretched and pathetic, weeping copiously but silently. Still she pulled away from me, frightened half to death. I sank down next to her and took her in my arms. *"What has happened to you, my child?"* Her answer was to cling to me and let out a heartrending sob. Perhaps now she knew that I would not hurt her. She released her despair and wept into my chest. I stroked her hair and soothed her, prepared to wait until she was calm and could tell me what was troubling her. I do not know how it happened that I was overcome with desire at a moment such as this. Avid, fierce, uncontrollable desire. Perhaps it was because of the girl's thigh, which glowed white amid her rags; perhaps as I held her tight, I caught the scent of her sex; perhaps it was her warm, submissive body with the enticing curves of which I could not fail to be aware. To my surprise, she did not resist. Suddenly she was compliant in my arms. I felt passion in my stroking hands. Her weeping subsided to be replaced at last by sighs of longing to which I could not fail to respond. There was a fierce pressure in my loins, and she knew it. She touched me there and a contented sigh escaped her throat. Then she opened her thighs and invited me in with such sincerity that I was powerless to resist. And so we lay together, wild and passionate, concealed by the brick pillars of the churchyard gates. I held her by shoulders that had slipped free of the dark fabric of her torn dress; she revealed to me her small, full breasts, and I kissed them.

I do not know how it happened that we found ourselves in a clearing lit by a clear full moon. In dreams places are transformed and time does not matter. I realized that we were at this special place just before her womb received my manhood's mighty explosion, which was almost painful for the groin and abdomen but also gave infinite relief. At that moment she was towering over me, her whole body tense, her head thrown back, moaning with pleasure, until the final surge. Then she collapsed onto my chest, and her face came close to mine. My God, it was Josifčena! Josifčena Surmenová, the girl who fixed me with suspicious eyes from the pews beneath my pulpit. Her laughter was so wild that I took fright. I was induced to look about, and now I realized that we were on top of Sacrifice Hill, where the pagans once made their blood sacrifices; and we were at the center of a ring of fire, beyond which figures stood hand in hand. Josifčena Surmenová was still sitting on me and fervently rubbing against me, and still she was laughing. The people beyond the ring of fire were yelling and dancing. And then I awoke, covered in sweat.

Taming the Storm

Bundles of herbs gathered for Saint John's Eve were hanging from a spar under the roof and swinging from side to side. The wind was playing with them; several times a fierce gust drove the dry tips of the faded blooms against the wall of the cottage. Jakoubek was sitting below the bundles and following their movements. Every day, weather permitting, he sat in the same spot, waiting for Dora to come back from school. He never left the Bedová on his own. He spent day after day there with Surmena, whose trips down to Hrozenkov were rare. Why should she go there, except to church and to the shop? Everyone came to her. And what she needed, they brought to her.

As Dora advanced slowly up the hill, she saw Jakoubek waving wildly at her. His knees were pulled up to his chin and held there by the embrace of the arm that wasn't waving. Dora waved back and quickened her pace, powered by the wind at her back.

A storm was brewing. Although it was still afternoon, Žítková was cloaked in gloom. The first drops of rain were due any time now.

"Hey," he said to her by way of greeting, when at last she was standing in the little garden in front of the house. Jakoubek motioned with his chin toward Hrozenkov. Dora turned and saw that what he had been watching so intently was not her approach but the endless jumble of storm clouds rolling slowly toward them. Like a living mass, like an uncontrollable beast capable of destroying everything in its way in a moment, the heavy clouds twisted and poured into one another. And the beast's way was all the fields on their side of the hills of Žítková: the Bedová, the Koprvazy, the Hudáky, the Rovná, the Černá.

"Hoo-oo," said Jakoubek as he buried his chin between his knees.

From a distance, the ringing of the smaller of the church's bells carried to their ears. If its rich tone was intended to disperse the clouds, it would surely fail, Dora thought. The first cold raindrops kissed her bare arms.

"We should go inside," she said, urging Jakoubek to stand up.

He looked at her in surprise before shaking his head and pointing with the middle of his three fingers at the path she had walked up. Again she looked back and down. Amid the vortices rolling across the meadows and the swallows trying frantically to fly away, she spotted a woman in glowing white clothing, the traditional dress of their home. The scarf she was holding above her head was pulled hither and thither by the wind, giving little protection from the rain.

Most likely it was one of their neighbors, on her way to Surmena. Dora went indoors to look for Surmena, but she found the cottage empty. She slipped off her school bag and returned to Jakoubek. "Where's Auntie?" she asked.

Jakoubek shook his head awkwardly. The wind had risen to such a degree that his hair was a Medusa-like shock.

A woman's call reached their ears. "Surmena!"

A few moments later, a breathless Baglárka sank onto the doorstep. "Where's Surmena?"

"We don't know." Dora shrugged, and Jakoubek imitated this gesture.

"It's terrible, this is," said Baglárka, gesturing toward the storm and then shaking her head sadly. "Everywhere, all of a sudden. Next thing we know, we'll be pelted with hailstones. How are we supposed to go back into the fields after a hard day's graft? God forgive me, but what's he bringing down on us now? Next year it won't even be fit for sowing. Where can Surmena have got to, kids? Could she be with the animals?"

Dora doubted this because if she had been, she would have answered her call, but she stood up anyway and walked around the cottage to look. There was no one there. In the shed the cow was shuffling her feet, her calf rubbing its body against the rough plaster of the inside wall. She stroked both heads, then closed the little door carefully behind her, fearful that the animals would be frightened by the storm and try to run out.

Dora gazed at the hillside that rose above the cottage. Right in the middle of the steep slope stood a small woman, bolt upright, looking as though she would be pitched over and sent tumbling down at any moment. To get a better view, Dora walked over from the shed and screwed up her eyes. To her astonishment, she saw with certainty that the woman was Surmena.

It was obvious to Dora that Surmena was struggling to keep her balance as she braced herself against the wind.

Without a second thought, Dora set off toward her. What was Surmena doing, standing with her arms raised to the coming storm, waiting to be whipped by the first torrents of rain? Had she gone mad?

Dora clambered up the steep hillside, tearing at the grass to quicken her progress.

"Auntie!" she yelled.

But from her position on high, Surmena did not see her. All her attention was directed at Hrozenkov and the eye of the dark element.

Impelled onward by the gusts at her back, Dora accelerated, concentrating all her energies on the task at hand. There was no doubt that a storm was on its way. When Dora was close enough to read Surmena's expression, she was shocked by the ferocity she read in it; this was new to her.

"Auntie!" she called again. No reaction. Instead of looking in Dora's direction, Surmena raised her arms slowly, as though wishing to embrace the devastating power that would soon be upon them. At the same moment, she started to mutter, but the wind took the words from her mouth so that Dora heard nothing of what was said.

Dora moved closer before the wind took hold of her, turned her around, then caught her by surprise by rushing at her from the front. Startled, she landed on the ground, suddenly aware of how powerless she was to prevent her body from scraping against rocks and thorns or being thrown against the trunk of one of their limes or the door of the cowshed. Again she fixed her gaze on Surmena as her hands clawed at the grass.

Surmena looked like she was dancing. As her arms embraced the wind, her hips swayed in wide circular motions. At the beginning of each motion, she clenched her fists as though trapping a gust; then she made a sweeping movement to send it back the way it had come. The grass around Surmena began to undulate in the semicircle her gesture was describing. Evidently the wind was turning around her.

Suddenly Dora heard snippets of words, carried by the reverse current. But she did not understand these words. Encrypted in a song she was hearing for the first time, they were worshipping someone she did not know.

"Oppose the storm, heavenly Father, Almighty God! Oppose the storm, his beloved Son! Oppose the storm, Holy Ghost! Hagios O Theos, Hagios Ischyros . . . Holy, holy, holy Lord God of heavenly hosts . . . Heaven and Earth are filled with thy majesty and thy glory!"

Now with a sweeping, top-to-bottom, left-to-right gesture, Surmena was making the sign of the cross.

"Banish these turbid clouds and this violent air, with all their harmful vices, their hail, their thunder, and their lightning . . . We beseech you, God Almighty, to dispel and despoil them!"

The wind tumbled across the hillside, carrying away clumps of soil and dry grass and tearing the heads from meadow flowers. Dora's eyes and mouth were full of dust.

"I enchant ye in the name of the Day of Judgment, in the name of God Almighty, Conqueror of all evil, that ye turn your hail from these crops and gardens to the hills, the rocks and the water, where no one sows, plants, or grafts."

At this point Dora was struck by a gust so strong that the tufts of grass came away in her hands and she was propelled twenty feet down the slope. Her vision dimmed as the wind tossed her about like a sheaf of hay. She was quite helpless; this was surely her end . . .

But her slide was halted by a rock. Pain brought tears to her eyes.

"Help!" she yelled into the wind. "Help!"

Surmena did not move, and far and wide there was no one else who could help her. Dora clung desperately to the rock, her shoulders around her ears as she attempted to hide from the gale, from the flying grass and twigs that whipped her face, from her fear. In her helplessness, she started to pray.

"Our Father, who art in heaven, hallowed be thy name . . . ," she gasped, on the verge of tears. She went on with her prayer even as her mouth filled with dust, even through the coughing this brought on. *"On Earth as it is in heaven . . ."*

A dusty vortex passed over her head. And still the words flowed from her mouth, at first quietly, then louder, until she was shouting for all she was worth and quite beside herself. *"Forgive us our trespasses, as we forgive those who trespass against us . . ."*

Then the wind swirled up one more time, lost and then gained strength, turned swiftly against itself, gave one final blast, quietened, then fell silent.

In the new calm, Dora's and Surmena's voices merged as one. *"Deliver us from evil. For thine is the kingdom, the power, and the glory, forever and ever. Amen."*

It was over. As if by magic, the gale had vanished. Dora sat up and looked about in confusion. She saw that the clouds were in retreat, that their heaving, menacing blackness was rolling toward the uninhabited woods of the Kykula hill, beyond Hrozenkov and away from Žítková.

She was at a loss about what to make of all this.

"Come on, get up." Surmena was bending over her and sighing. She took Dora by the arm and helped her to her feet. Surmena's hand was shaking, and when Dora turned to look into her face, she saw that it was drawn with fatigue.

Each leaning on the other, they slowly made their way down the hill. Baglárka was standing by the cowshed, waving with delight, and Jakoubek was racing about and yelling.

Baglárka's words came out to meet them. "You did it, Surmena! You did it! You drove the storm away!"

"This time I got some help," Surmena wheezed, glancing at Dora as Baglárka put an arm around her.

That evening Surmena drank a little more than was her habit.

Alžběta Baglárová

Thirty years had passed since the warding off of that storm. After that it happened several more times, and Dora became used to people from Žítková believing that her aunt was able to control the weather and drive away wind and rain.

Today she had another vivid recollection of it. As on every Friday, the bus was taking her up into Moravské Kopanice, but this time the autumn rain was teeming down, and the sky was dark, menacing, and ever lower.

The bus windows were streaked with thin, meandering columns of water. Jakoubek was tracing these with the tip of an index finger, beginning again whenever the individual paths merged into one. Dora was looking past his head at a landscape bending low in the teeth of a wind that the passengers could feel.

She wondered if Surmena would have been able to deal with such rain. Since the time Surmena had warded off that first storm, Dora compared it with every storm she experienced.

The bus climbed up to and beyond Bánov before passing Bystřice pod Lopeníkem and proceeding to Hrozenkov, where they usually got off. But because of the downpour, they would stay on until Žítková.

She signaled for the driver to stop only once they were right at the top, but even so, they had a long way to walk along the ridge to the Bedová, which they would reach by way of the Rokytová and the

Hudáky. Dora helped Jakoubek get his rucksack on before slinging the bag containing her laptop over her shoulder and opening her umbrella against the onslaught of the wind.

The gravel path had long ago disappeared into the mud. Hunched under the umbrella, they did what they could to avoid the puddles. From time to time, they looked down at the slopes of the Slovak side, which rose again a little farther on, becoming a great hill. From the woods, steam was forming into a cloud that was slowly making its way up the narrow valley; soon it would be under their feet. Although the rain was now easing off, still it was whipping against their trousered legs. They were captivated by the view and paused awhile to take it in, the discomfort notwithstanding.

They were surprised by a voice.

"Dora! Jakoubek! It's been a long time since I last saw you two."

It was Baglárka. The umbrella had concealed her approach from their view.

"We've come from Brno, Auntie," Dora said.

She was pleased to see Baglárka. And there was something she wanted to talk to her about.

Baglárka pulled her yellow raincoat tighter around her body, although its hood remained high above her forehead. "How about coming to my house for lunch tomorrow?" she said. It was as if she had read Dora's mind.

Dora turned to Jakoubek and smiled in encouragement. "We'd love to, wouldn't we?"

Jakoubek nodded enthusiastically.

"See you tomorrow, then. With any luck this awful weather will have passed by then and you won't have to slide about in the mud. Shall we say twelve o'clock?"

With that, Baglárka moved quickly away. She was already on the path down to the Rokytová hill, where she lived, when she called back to them: "I bet you've been wondering, too, if your aunt would have let this happen."

Dora didn't hear what she said next as her words were carried away on the wind.

That evening, when the calm breathing of the sleeping Jakoubek came from his place on top of the stove, Dora opened the clothes chest and from its false bottom fished out her old diaries. These were the ones she had found the courage to write after leaving the hostel. The entry she was looking for was from the day following her last visit to Surmena.

Slowly she flipped through the pages. *How different everything was then,* she thought with relief. Today things were as she had dreamed they would be in the days when her adulthood had begun so abruptly. She read several entries with concentration before flipping in haste to the one she was looking for. It was dated early May 1979:

> It was awful. Awful! When I led her out of the building, she was beside herself, just like the last time. It was like I was guiding a puppet. This was just a ghost, not Surmena. Some person with a vague similarity to my aunt. We sat next to each other in silence practically the whole time. Again I wondered if there was any point in saying anything at all . . .
>
> But then something changed. It was as though something came apart inside her. She was trembling, twitching, her breath was rattling, and the look she gave me almost scared the life out of me. And what was she saying? I held my ear right up to her lips, and still I couldn't make it all out. What was it she was trying to tell me?
>
> Who was I supposed to avoid? Who was I supposed not to trust? The people here or the people at home?

And what did she mean by black magic? Not goddessing, surely? That would be crazy—not even a priest would sermonize on that, so why would she say such a thing? And those goddesses whose names she rasped, Mahdalka and Fuksena. Why them? I don't even know them. I've never seen them in all my life. And the child. Which child did she mean? I couldn't understand who was supposed to have hidden it and where. If the worst came to the worst, it could be made use of, she said. But it was all so confusing, that might not be what she said at all. It was impossible to make head or tail of it. In her muddled mind the scraps of ancient memories just didn't fit together. It was only when she mentioned Germans that I knew the time she was speaking of, but she didn't listen to me when I told her she was mistaken, that there were none of them about now, that all that was over and done with and that she had nothing to fear from it today. The terror of it gushed out of her still. I have to write all this down even though it's so terrible, even though I don't want to believe it. Has our Surmena, *my* Surmena, gone mad? Because there's no other explanation for what I witnessed yesterday.

It gives me the creeps. Nothing is as it used to be, because she isn't as she used to be. What I wanted so much—to go back to living as we used to, the three of us on the Bedová together—is out of the question now. Because Surmena lives in her own little world, pursued by terrifying thoughts that I don't understand, that I'm too weak to deal with. It's unthinkable that I should take her into my care and look after the two of them. I wouldn't manage . . .

Dora pressed her palms to her cheeks for some time before bringing them together to form a shell that covered her nose and mouth. For several minutes she sat without moving, overwhelmed by self-reproach. She, too, had thought that Surmena was consumed by her illness; she, too, had taken Surmena for a madwoman.

Now Dora herself was at risk of going mad. In being so easily fooled and believing the lies, she had left Surmena in it on her own. Surmena, who had done so much for them!

She blinked away her tears and again concentrated on her diary. Now she was looking for the entry that reported Surmena's incomprehensible message. Although now she knew so much more about the background to the case, still she did not understand what Surmena had been trying to say.

Whom should she avoid and not trust? And the mention of Mahdalka. Dora was now almost sure that they and Mahdalka had had something in common. Which child had Surmena spoken of, and how could it be made use of?

More and more questions were racing around in her head. She didn't have an answer for any of them, and they were making her cranky and weary. At that moment all her hopes were pinned on Baglárka, whose misty memories, Dora believed, might hold the key to the truth behind Surmena's words.

For lunch Baglárka had prepared her famous cabbage soup. After the meal Dora sat on the bench in front of the cottage, watching Jakoubek run about by the path beyond the field as she clutched a large mug from which she was slowly sipping piping-hot chicory coffee. The door creaked open, and Baglárka appeared with a plate of cakes. Having sat down, she draped a wide knitted shawl over her shoulders; she was sensitive to the cold. As Baglárka stretched out her legs in their thick stockings, Dora heard the gentle cracking of her bones. *She's getting old,* she thought.

"So you say that the secret police kept an eye on Surmena? That they were the ones who had her locked up in the madhouse? That's just terrible." Baglárka sighed. "In all those years, I never noticed a thing."

As Baglárka meditated on this, Dora sipped her drink in silence.

"But you know yourself how many strangers came this way. Not only to see Surmena but to see Irma Gabrhelová, too—and Kateřina Hodulíková, Krasňačka, and all the rest of them, when they were alive. Who would have noticed if someone was watching her? I didn't use to ask people who came to see the goddesses who they were and what they were up to. So how could I know if they were going to Surmena for something other than advice or help? I minded my own business. But for your peace of mind, I can tell you that I never heard any talk of the police taking a special interest in Surmena."

Baglárka paused before adding in haste, "Well, they called on her occasionally, of course. Just as they called on all the goddesses. Not everyone was satisfied with the services they offered, you know. Especially folk whom the goddesses found out—thieves and swindlers, that kind. The philanderers they uncovered weren't too keen on them either. So from time to time, that sort would put the authorities onto them. But it was never anything serious, squabbling, really—there was never any threat. Fortunately, things were never as bad again as they had been in Hofer's day and after the first war. In those days goddessing was a much more dangerous occupation, and every goddess spent a few weeks of each year in prison. Apparently, Dorka Gabrhelová had the constables and the doctors to thank for the fact that she died so young. But later, in Surmena's day? Well, I thought that things like that didn't happen anymore."

Dora rearranged the wool-covered cushion under her bottom. The miserable weather of yesterday had given way to a warm autumn day, although by now the sun had lost all its strength.

"As I know now, they did use to happen," Baglárka went on. "They watched her, and in the end, they got her. And me and you, too, by convincing us that she was sick."

Baglárka gave a wry little smile and shook her head, as though wishing to soothe a fractious child.

Dora was surprised and hurt by this gesture. "So you think my aunt really was ill? That they had good reason to keep her in that place, I mean?"

"Hmmm. I . . . I'm not so sure about that," Baglárka said. "But there's one thing I do know: the goddesses had terrible luck. As far back as I can remember, none of them ended well. You know what happened to your mother, and she hardly did any goddessing at all. Kateřina and Irma had daughters who abandoned them because they were ashamed of their magic-making. And Irma lost two sons as well—through her own fault, they say. It would have been enough for her to pour the wax and she would have seen the future and told them not to take the car that day. Both boys died, along with their wives, leaving four little orphans. Such a tragedy. And from the stories my mother and grandmother used to tell, the older goddesses suffered misfortunes too. So it's somehow fitting that Surmena ended up in a mental hospital. It's not so important whether it was because she was sick or that someone was keeping her there. There was never any chance of her ending well."

Dora shuddered at these last words. Baglárka had to be kidding! She was about to object when Baglárka went on.

"Knowledge comes at a cost. I suppose you've heard of Fuksena?"

Dora was taken aback. "Fuksena? Well, yes . . . a bit . . . Surmena mentioned her once when I went to see her in Kroměříž, but by then she wasn't making any sense. It sounded like she was trying to warn me . . . But she was so full of pills, you know, that she probably didn't realize that Fuksena was long dead."

Baglárka nodded.

"She never mentioned her any other time," Dora added.

"That doesn't surprise me," said Baglárka carefully. Then she went on as if against her better judgment. "Talking about the bad luck of the goddesses, her fate is a case in point. The greater the gift, the more bitter the life and the grimmer the death. Fuksena died right at the end of the war. Her end was terrible. She was beaten like a dog."

Baglárka screwed up her face at the outrage of it so that her top lip was almost touching her nose.

Dora was astonished. Fuksena had died during the war? Like a dog? She had never heard anything about this.

"Beaten to death? Who did it?"

Baglárka was obviously uneasy.

"No one knows, my girl. The front was moving this way. The woods were full of strange types. The locals were solving their disputes without bothering the courts—you must have heard about that. How Trmelák burned his neighbor in his bed—that was in the newspaper not even a month ago. That sort of thing can only happen in Moravské Kopanice. Probably Fuksena died at the hands of someone who was getting their own back. She lived with the Mahdalkas, you know, and they were an evil lot . . ."

The Mahdalkas? Wasn't Mahdalová the married name of Josifčena Surmenová?

"Fuksena lived with the Mahdals, you say? And who were these Mahdals?"

Baglárka was plainly taken aback by the curiosity in Dora's question. "The Mahdals?" she said as if hearing the name for the first time. "A strange family from Potočná, that's all."

Dora waited in case she was about to continue. When she didn't, Dora asked, "Were the Mahdals related to the Surmenas, by any chance?"

Baglárka flinched, and Dora heard irritation in her reply. "Related? I don't know about that . . . All I know is that there was no love lost between Surmena and the Mahdalkas. There was nothing strange in that; quite a few goddesses weren't on good terms, and anyway, no one liked the Mahdalkas. They were the craftiest kind of riffraff you can imagine. That's all I know."

With this, Baglárka rose heavily, straightened her skirt, and went back into the cottage.

Dora had the feeling that Baglárka was keeping something from her. It was as though there was some secret around the Mahdal family, and Dora was pretty sure Baglárka, in spite of her denials, knew what it was. She was ready to ask again, but as soon as she came back out, Baglárka spoke up.

"The goddesses were always quarreling among themselves. They envied and bad-mouthed one another because that's what competitors do. They fought each other for clients, and to prove that they were the best, they did whatever they had to do. Take Irma and Kateřina. Sisters-in-law, and neither would so much as utter the other's name. That only came to an end with Kateřina's death."

Dora knew that Irma and Kateřina, the last of the goddesses, who were active until only a few years ago, had not even greeted each other. She had known them both as women stooped with age, always friendly and helpful, until someone happened to mention the other, at which point the hatred burst forth and they appeared capable of spitting venom.

"The bad blood between them shook their family, and their occupation drove their own children from them. Which does not excuse the children, of course. No one should condemn their own mother to keep in with their cadre. As I said, goddesses don't have life easy."

Baglárka fell into a solemn silence, which she broke unexpectedly. "But don't worry, my girl, it won't affect you. Besides, you don't know how to goddess, do you?"

Dora shook her head. Why on earth had Baglárka said that?

"It's good that you never learned it," Baglárka said, palpably relieved as she put her arms around Dora's shoulders. "You don't goddess, so there's no bad end ahead for you. It's best to let the gift sleep, you know. You're better off without it."

Dora shrugged. She'd had no choice. Surmena had never started on her, and after that it was too late.

Jakoubek made his way up to them. He was frustrated, slashing about with a switch he'd found somewhere in the woods; Dora shouted at him several times to stop, but he wouldn't. It was time to go home.

"I haven't helped you much, have I?" said Baglárka as they were preparing to leave and she was pressing a plate of cakes into Dora's hands. "But do you know what you should do if you want to know more about Surmena or what life here used to be like? Go to Irma. She's still doing well, even though she's almost ninety-five. Take her some bread and salami from the village and ask away. She won't refuse you. From what I can remember, she and Surmena were good friends."

Irma Gabrhelová

*I*rma sat at the table, her head set at an angle by the ailment that afflicted her back. She was wearing the local working garb with an apron over it. Her sparse hair was covered by a bright-red scarf, in which her small, grayish face was lost but for the deep black eyes, which darted about and drew one's gaze as though they were two magnets. The ends of her trembling fingers toyed with the hem of a sleeve whose embroidery was faded but still beautiful, whose tiny stitches Dora found delightful. Dora listened to Irma's deep, rough voice, the kind of voice no one would expect from a little old woman.

"The war was something terrible. Particularly toward the end. The uncertainty. And the worry—you could almost feel it, you know. People were afraid to go to sleep at night. All kinds of people knocking at your door—partisans, smugglers, Financial Guard—we saw a lot of them, I can tell you! My old man did a bit of business. Well, times were hard, you know; he had to provide for us somehow. We had the first five kids by then, and his bedridden father was still with us in the cottage. But then he brought that horse back with him, and I was scared. It was complete madness to parade about the mountains with a stolen horse, what with the Financial Guard right under your nose! At the time I almost threw him out of the cottage, but he listened to me, and after that it was just the distilling of spirits and a few trifles I never asked about—food and smokes, I suppose; what else could it have been? Everyone wanted smokes then. He'd leave them in the fruit-drying shed, by the woods over there. His smuggler pals would come for them after dark, and sometimes they'd bring along someone for me. A chap with a leg sprain, say, or someone who'd been shot. A goddess can perform miracles, they thought. And that would provoke the Financial Guard, who would search the whole cottage. Then on top of all this, in forty-four there were the flyovers. What a racket they made day and night. A bad time, it was."

Irma sighed sadly.

"The flyovers started in the summer, and toward the end, in August, there was a disaster. I can remember all the details like it was yesterday. It was the twenty-ninth, and summer's end was in sight. It was particularly cold in the mornings that year, as if autumn had come early. We'd got used to the flyovers by that time—sometimes they flew for the sake of it; sometimes they'd drop leaflets. Nobody'd been expecting a massacre like the one that happened that afternoon. There was a deep rumble in the sky before you saw the few dots approaching through it. Those dots were American bombers. It was all over in a second. The Germans rushed out from Trenčín in those fighters that looked like hawks and shot the large, heavy American planes to pieces. They got them all. They were gathering up the poor men all the next week, from Bošáčky to Slavičín. Apparently, there were more than forty of them, and more than half of them didn't survive. Some of them were burned and swung from the treetops in their parachutes for two days. Everyone searched the woods for them. The German police came out from Zlín, as did the Czech police; the partisans searched for them, and our people did, too—that is, those who didn't have other things to worry about. That morning brought a great wave of sadness to Hrozenkov.

"Andulka Zindulová from Vyškovec, for instance—she caught it. She was working in the field with her kids, just as they always did, and it was all swept away. They didn't pull her out of the wreckage until evening. By the time they'd run for water to put out the fire and cleared things out of the way, all that was left of her was charred bits of flesh. When they were plowing that field two years later, they found a hand. Bones. They didn't know if it was Andulka's or someone else's, from one of the planes that had burned with her. So they buried it under the American memorial at the cemetery in Slavičín. By this time—it was forty-six—all the servicemen's bones had been sent to America. But at least there's that hand there, under the monument.

"It was dreadful, too, at the Šopíks', who live toward Bošáčky. There are more memorials to the Americans there than anywhere—three of them. Where the planes fell, at the very places they plowed into the earth. The roof of the Šopíks' cottage was smashed to pieces, and two of them were buried under it. I can't remember now which two, but one of them must have been very young because his coffin was carried to the churchyard by brides in black. I remember that they called for my mother. In those days folk called for her more than they did for me. While she was alive, there was no better goddess. But even she was helpless. When they'd put out the fire at the cottage, they found nothing but charred remains. Of two of the Šopíks and one airman.

"You should know that one fell near us too. Harry, his name was. That was the only thing we knew about him for sure. Apart from the name, we didn't understand a word he said. But to grasp what was the matter with him we didn't need to understand him. His face was covered with burns, all his hair was gone, and he had grazes all over his body. He had a deep wound on his back, and there was something wrong with his leg; obviously he couldn't walk. He was lucky to fall so close to my mother's cottage. At night he dragged himself there, and she took him in—by then she was on her own; my father had died, and all of us had our own places. As there was no one about who might report her, she told herself she would help him. You were taking a great risk, you know, if you harbored an American soldier, and not many folk had the guts. My mother did. She was courageous, and she felt sorry for him. He was in such a sad state that he didn't properly understand where he was. When I got there, he was delirious. That was on the morning of the second day. I stopped at Mother's on my way back from Hrozenkov—she'd sent word to me through the neighbors. As soon as I got there, I knew there was something the matter. The door was bolted shut; that never happened. And Mother didn't come even when I banged on it. I was beginning to get frightened when she opened up, darted a look outside, and pulled me in. And there he was. Naked, lying in the corner on a pile of straw because my parents never had a bed; we always slept on the kitchen range or in the attic. He lay there groaning. It was enough to make your heart stop to see him like that, all suffering and disfigured. And for us, for Czechoslovakia, Mother said to me. She sent me for Surmena, who would fix his bones. I ran straight out and fetched her.

"Surmena took one look at the American before she knelt down, put her hands on him, and told us to get some brandy. We thought she wanted this for herself, but she lifted his head and poured half the bottle down his throat. Then she left him alone for a while. As he quieted down, she took hold of his leg, rested it on Mother's shoulder so that she could move it freely, sat on her haunches, and wrapped her hands around his knee. Then she tugged at it and turned it, and the joint slotted into place. The American was so startled that he didn't even have time to yell; he just made a gurgling sound and then fell silent. This gave him a bit of relief at least. We finished the rest of the brandy there and then. It was no joy for us either, you know. Mother and Surmena were all sweaty with the exertion and I with the fear that someone might pass by and hear something. We waited a while before we went on with the job. The night before, Mother had washed him and put crushed herbs on his burns, but he had a fever and his skin was blistering, and he needed tending. I supported him while Surmena lifted his limbs and Mother washed and peeled the scaly skin from his burns. He whimpered like a puppy. I feel pain even now when I remember it. We bandaged him up and laid him down to sleep. By now it was clear to us that such a patient was unlikely to make a quick recovery. It would take weeks, Mother said. And she was worried. It was one thing to heal a patient like this but another to keep him a secret. She and Surmena conferred on what they were going to do with him, having sent me for more herbs and a hen for the soup. It was getting dark when I got back. It had taken me a while because I'd had to get the kids organized, and besides, from the Pitín side of the Černá, the walk takes over an hour. I rushed into the cottage, the slaughtered hen dangling at my waist and pouches of herbs and a bottle of brandy in my basket. To nothing. Where the American had lain, there was a pool of blood. The man was gone. Mother and Surmena were sitting by the range. In silence, holding hands. 'Where is he?' I asked, surprised. They didn't say anything. I had to shake them to get them to wake up. They didn't speak until they'd each downed a couple of shots. When I heard it, I almost collapsed; in those days I was still sensitive and hadn't been through much. That evening we drank all the brandy we had. I'd never felt as bad as I did the next day.

"They'd come round about an hour after I left. The American had at last fallen asleep, no doubt thanks to the brandy and the fact that the pain had gone from his leg. Mother and Surmena were discussing how to get him up into the attic and out of sight in case anyone came when they heard a car. There was nothing they could do but snatch a large cover off the range and throw it over the American. Then they were inside. An inspection. They—the German Criminal Police Department in Zlín—were driving around the woods, pastures, and cottages, searching for airmen. Mother was petrified. Suddenly she was confronted by a man in plainclothes and three men in uniforms— there wasn't room for any more of them in the cottage—and they were staring at her. There was a dreadful commotion. The men inside changed places with those outside, and the new ones yelled at Mother and Surmena. They could have done this till kingdom come without either of them understanding a word that was said. So they pushed the plainclothes man back in, having called for him by the name Schwannze, Mother said. She remembered this because it sounded a little like the German word for *pig*. Schwannze spoke Czech, so he went through it with them. When had they found him? What was the matter with him? What had he told them? Mother and Surmena told him everything. Why would they deny it? It was obvious at first sight. Except they didn't mention me. They said he hadn't told them anything because he had a fever, and even if he had said anything, they wouldn't have understood because he was an American. Hardly had they blurted this out when something worse happened. One of the uniforms pulled the cover off the American and looked at him lying there naked. Then he shouted, *'Jude! Der ist Jude!'*

"Mother told me later that at that moment, she thought they were finished. That they would be dead by evening. She said she and Surmena threw their arms around each other and started to pray while someone barked an order, and the bandaged American, by now awake and terrified, caught the discharge of the gun barrels that were pointing at him. There had been no time for goodbyes. Then the guns were pointed at Mother and Surmena. The barrels drove them out in front of the cottage, into the clutch of furious Germans. A whirlwind of questioning descended on them, but they understood only the bits barked at them by Schwannze, who had probably been given the order to interpret. He was redder in the face than the officer who jumped out of the car. Did they know that they were aiding enemy forces? Did they know that they were aiding a degenerate race? Did they know what they could expect for this? Mother and Surmena said nothing. Only when Schwannze began to beat them, because an officer's questions cannot remain unanswered, did they force out some utterance. Mother couldn't remember what it was till the day she died. Surmena said something that caused the barrage of slaps, kicks, and shouts to stop. It seems that Schwannze translated it in passing to the officer, and the officer immediately barked, 'Halt!' and everyone froze. Into the silence that followed, he asked Schwannze, and Schwannze translated, 'Are you goddesses?' Mother got up from the ground, but because she was old, she fell down again; still, she managed to gasp yes. She was a goddess, and so was Surmena. The officer just nodded, and two uniforms bent down and picked her up. Then Schwannze asked a question in a strange, serious, quiet voice. The answer the officer gave made him shake his head in disbelief, protest, and wave his arms about. He was so furious that at that moment, they feared him more than they did the German.

"What the two of them said to each other, we'll never know, but we know for sure that Schwannze then shouted at Mother and Surmena that they shouldn't go far from their cottages, that the matter was not dealt with. And that was all. Mother and Surmena couldn't believe their eyes. They were shoved against the wall, beaten but alive. The dead American was carried out of the cottage by two soldiers, who dropped him on the platform of the open car, where another crumpled body lay twisted up in the cables of its parachute. Then they jumped into the car, started the engine, and drove away. Only the officer looked back, and he appeared thoughtful. Understanding nothing, they went into the cottage and sat down, and this is how I found them. Then they waited. They waited, but nothing happened. No one came to them all winter; perhaps the Germans had bigger things to worry about than two mad old women. At that time they were in hot pursuit of partisans in the Carpathians and the Beskids; then the news got around about Ploština and Prlov, which are right next to Kopanice, and then suddenly the Russians rolled in, and it was all over. Mother lived for another year. By the next winter, she was in her grave."

Irma's voice trembled with emotion. It became more and more hushed until it wasn't heard at all. Dora, who had been listening to the old woman with bated breath, dared not say a word. She waited, huddled, until Irma chose to continue.

"I always wondered what was going on in that officer's head that he let those two women live. I can't help but think that Ferdinand and

Rudolf had a hand in it. Those two good-lookers who hung about Kopanice earlier. They were here for a long time, and then they went back. They were the biggest military brass who ever showed up here. But I don't know much about it. Just that the Financial Guard would bow down before them, and even the Gestapo in Zlín. And that they bowed down to the goddesses, especially Mahdalka and Fuksena. That's right—the Mahdal family!"

Having suddenly recalled what Dora had asked, Irma shooed away the memory of Chupatá, her mother, with a wave of her hand.

"It was because of them that you came, wasn't it? That's why I keep going on about the war . . . Well, you see that I know. I know all sorts of things about them. But the story's a bad one, really bad. Do you truly want to hear it?"

Although Irma's question was almost sullen, Dora nodded excitedly.

Irma sighed. "Before I go on, take some tea and pour me some too. It's made from nine flowers." Suddenly she perked up. "But I should be giving you tea from Saint John's wort, shouldn't I? Lovers' weed, we call it. So that you get yourself a handsome chap. How about we pour out the wax? Now there's no one left but me to pour it for you. No one else can do it, so you might as well take advantage while you can. Don't try to wriggle out of it; you should be long married. Let's take a look at him, the chosen one who's out there waiting for you."

Traces of mischief had appeared in Irma's eyes.

The sweet tea in Dora's mouth was suddenly bitter. "First tell me about the Mahdalkas and Fuksena, Auntie!"

"The most interesting thing about that family is what happened to Fuksena," said Irma once their mugs were full. "Surely you know who Fuksena was? And that Pagáčena was her mother? That's right, the famous goddess who kept giving birth to sons and almost didn't have a successor. She was so well known that before the first war, they came from Vienna, Budapest, and Kraków to see her. She'd spent months on the Hungarian side doing seasonal work, and she'd made a name for herself there; only after that did she come back home and get married. That's what they used to say, anyway. My own mother used to say it, too, but who knows how it really was? Perhaps she said it out of jealousy because they didn't travel such distances to see her. But I took it as a fact.

"I remember, for instance, a factory owner coming from Vienna in a coach to see her. She treated him by getting him to fast for a month, and because of that, they put her in prison for three weeks, even though the factory owner pleaded for her. She'd helped him, he said. I can actually remember all this. You've read Hofer—may that scoundrel rest in peace!—so you know that he writes about it. Oh, how he chased us and tormented us! Most of all my mother and Surmena's, and Pagáčena—the three who were heard about most and who did the most, which probably bothered him more than what he was preaching against. His sermons were all about obscurantism, superstition, and the fictions we drew from the wax just so that we could hoodwink honest, trusting people. What bothered him most was that the goddesses were paid. Of course they were paid! Think about how many souls they saved! It goes without saying that they should be paid. That apostate who left four mouths to feed just couldn't forgive them for being better off than he was."

Irma was shaking her head in anger.

"Not everything he said was wrong, of course. Not all the goddesses used their craft for the benefit of others. I lost count of the times I was called out to a poor little thing who'd asked for help with an unwanted pregnancy, and sometimes it was too late. Or the times I heard that a neighbors' dispute had gone to court because some goddess or other had seen that neighbor A had bewitched neighbor B's cow or stolen something from him. Yes, there were bad goddesses too. Ruprechtka, for instance. She had a goddess in her service, so she was aware of how many people visited that woman and what she got out of it. Even though there were no goddesses in her own family, Ruprechtka turned the woman out and started goddessing herself. Her cottage was in the right spot for it—she could intercept folk as they were heading up to Žítková. It goes without saying that she caused lots of damage. But Hofer saw no differences among us; he thought all of us frauds, and he treated us accordingly. You've read his books, haven't you? So you've read what he had to say about Pagáčena. He tormented her, poor thing, and it's not as if she had it easy in the first place. Her father was a drinker, and she had to leave home when she was practically a child. Not that there's anything unusual in that—no one in these parts will turn down a drink. You can tell that by looking at the kids. I used to tell them all, men and women: 'Don't drink so much brandy, especially when you're expecting.' But they drank no more and no less than would make the child stronger, they said. It would be a strong sleeper, that was for sure, and you can see for yourself how it grew up. It breaks my heart to look at some of them, they're so stupid. Anyway, folk wouldn't listen to me any more than they would listen to my mother and her mother before her. As far back as anyone can remember, no one in our family has ever been able to do anything about it. Not that we didn't enjoy the odd swig ourselves—good brandy is life itself, as you know. But the pregnant women, the expectant fathers . . . Anyway, about Pagáčena's father. It wasn't just that he was a drinker, but that when he was around her, he was up to no good, they used to say. My mum told me once that old Anka Gabrhelová, who became Anka Ruchárová, herself a goddess, bore one child after another until she'd had as much as she could take of old Ruchár, so there were certain things she'd turn a blind eye to. Who knows what truly went on? But it was nothing good, that's for sure. So as soon as she could, Pagáčena ran away, to the Hungarian side. As a servant girl. She didn't come home until Jura brought her back. She'd come across him in Pest, when he was on his way home from the army, and they made an agreement. As soon as he had his own cottage in Kopanice, he wrote to her, and she came happily. Apparently, their marriage was a fiery one, as both of them liked their own way. But they were happy together, and they produced their kids out of true love. Pagáčena gave birth to one boy after another, making Jura very proud. He used to boast that he'd make an infantry unit out of them. Had the poor man known the future, he'd never have let those words out of his mouth. Every last one of them was called up. Jura died right at the beginning of the first war. Pagáčena's sons were sent to the Italian front. None of them came back. But she never knew that—she died in the last year of the war, of grief, they said. I was still a child at the time, but I remember her funeral. Hofer did so much to spoil it that they held it against him for years afterward. It was blowing a gale, although it was summer, and there were claps of thunder. Folk were huddled together, afraid of being blown from the churchyard and down the hill. The pallbearers had a terrible job. Those at the front were going too fast for those at the back. The hat of one of those at the back was blown off. Then the coffin went down, and its lid came off. And there she was: Pagáčena. Every great goddess jumps out of her coffin—that's the way it is. But instead of bidding everyone a dignified farewell, Hofer sermonized over the open grave about superstition and trickery, ridiculing folk who believed that the forces of nature were taking leave of a goddess. He was laughing at folk who, moments earlier, had screamed with horror and now had tears in their eyes for their good neighbor Pagáčena, who had helped all of them many times—to give birth, to get well, to make difficult decisions. Fuksena was there too. She was about five at the time. Just imagine that poor little orphan looking up at the priest as he railed against her mother over her grave! It breaks my heart even now, just to think of it . . . They used to say she'd be the most powerful goddess in Žítková because she was born on Christmas Eve, all wrapped up in the fetal membranes. Pagáčena almost died giving birth to her. Such a shame that she had only five years more to live! But although her mother wasn't given the time to teach her, Fuksena didn't escape her fate. Mahdalka took her in, and they moved out to Potočná. That was bad, very bad. What a terrible pity that Mahdalka got to her before your grandma Justýna Ruchárka did! She was Fuksena's aunt, you know."

Irma sipped some of her tea.

Dora thought this strange, so she asked, "Why was it a pity, Auntie?"

Irma thought for a moment before she answered. "They used to say that the Mahdalkas were witches. People were afraid of old Mahdalka, Josifčena, her name was. Her enchantments always had an effect. Cows would lose their milk or suddenly make enough for two; boils grew or healed themselves under her hands; she could make women into heifers, and she could also help those who were barren. She could do anything. Woe betide anyone who cheated her, who tried to outsmart her, or who did anything against her family. If anyone knew dark magic, then she was the one. They used to say she made a widower of the man who would become her husband; that she would do her dark witchcraft for whoever was willing to pay for it; that her power was as black as night. Perhaps you remember her daughter-in-law, Marie Mahdalová, who died not long ago. She used to call herself a goddess, too, claiming that she learned under her mother-in-law. It wasn't true. Maybe the old woman helped her along a bit, but Marie had no powers of her own, that's for sure, because she wasn't born to be a goddess. That's why Mahdalka took Fuksena in—she wanted her successor to be of her own bloodline. She'd had only one son, when she was very young, maybe by a man other than her husband, they used to say. Anyway, after that she couldn't have any more kids. So she grabbed Fuksena. Took her there and then at the funeral, from under Justýna Ruchárka's nose. Then she wouldn't let Ruchárka into her house. They'd quarreled, you see, and now they couldn't stand the sight of each other . . ."

Irma stopped short before adding quickly, "But that's all a long, long time ago, and there's no need to poke about in it anymore. Besides, I think Fuksena lived well enough with Mahdalka. She treated her kindly. You can't replace a mother, of course, but Mahdalka formed a mother's attachment to her. She taught her right from the beginning. And she didn't spare the rod to spoil the child. They must have gone for their herbs on the other side, the Hungarian side, along the Drietomica, toward Trenčín, because we never saw each other. Except at church and then later at dances, but even that not very often.

"Fuksena was beautiful. Tall, well built, with abundant hair the color of the dark sun. You don't often see hair like that here. Folk used to say she was the most beautiful girl in Kopanice. All the young men had thoughts of her, and quite a few went after her. But she wouldn't give any of them the time of day. She stuck to Mahdalka and wouldn't hear of marriage. Folk used to say that it would serve them right if someone set fire to their cottage. You know what people around here are like— hotheads, the lot of them. It's not so long ago that they burned the roof from over the head of the widow Pavlicová because she'd take neither the young one nor the widower, remember? We'll never know which of them did it. It might even have been both of them; folk had heard them talking in the pub about how conceited she was. As there's nothing so unusual about things like that here, folk got to wondering about when Fuksena would get her comeuppance. And get her comeuppance she did. But in a way different from what anyone was expecting.

"When they turned up that day, everyone thought they were from the tax office. They were wearing dark uniforms, so obviously they weren't the lot we were used to, but they put them up in a new building belonging to the tax office, which they'd built right by the border, at the end of Hrozenkov, where the brook flows next to the road. So we assumed they were tax officials. And in the first few days, they always had a tax official with them. But we found out later that he was only showing them around. They bustled about the place for a while, measuring things and walking about the hills. Then they drove away, only to come back a month or so later. That time they knew what they were here for. They went straight to Mahdalka's. Folk said that they had their fortune told, paying more for it than anyone here in Kopanice had ever seen.

"It was also said that the Mahdalkas once received a very important visitor. From the Reich. One night a commando stopped in front of their cottage, and two men went in with someone wearing a mask. The Hošťálek boys blurted all this out in the pub the next day, not bothering to hide the fact that they snooped about Fuksena's place at night. Then on the way out of Mass, young Mahdalka let something slip about the visit, to the women. Why shouldn't she brag about it? At that moment she couldn't care less that folk here hated the Germans. So she bragged about the strange visitor. Apparently, he asked them very politely to tell his fortune, even though he was someone important. He wanted old Mahdalka to tell him everything about his past, and he wanted to know about the future. The graying hair old Mahdalka had not had time to brush hung about her face as she melted wax over the fire. At the table, Fuksena prepared the water, into which the old woman then cast the wax. As the cast took shape in the bowl, Mahdalka froze. Young Mahdalka said that she herself was scared because she'd never seen the old woman look so grim. So her expression must have been really something! Then she began to tell the excited guest's past. She saw his birth in a prosperous region, bright sunlight after a storm with one hundred and sixty-eight lightning strikes that bore away a long friendship severed by betrayal; she saw the birth of innocence, of a child, and surely many other things besides. As she told him all this, the visitor did not say a word. Then she told him things that sound strange, but you know yourself that tellings cannot be commanded; all you can do is hear them out. The sense of them opens up slowly, gradually, like the opening of a flower, and even then, how much of it comes out depends on how receptive the person is and how keen he is to reach his goal. So Mahdalka felt along the edges of the set wax, trembling from the cold that followed the man's path, which led only upward and never dipped, to the very top, where she saw the silhouette of a large, crumbling castle filled with mysterious halls and great men. She also said that on that path, she saw a second betrayal just as great as the first, thanks to which his life had taken a great leap forward. But this was a betrayal that he and other men of influence, one of whom was the traitor, would live to regret. Marie Mahdalka said that for the first time in her life, she heard her mother-in-law break her rules: she told the visitor that she could tell him more if he wished, but beyond this point, she could see his end. Well, you know that no goddess should speak of death, even if the person asks her to. The path seen by the goddess is not a closed one. The wheel of fortune can turn in another direction at any moment. As this is a rule a goddess will never break, young Mahdalka was amazed to hear the old woman speak of the visitor's end. Either she bore him ill will or she wanted to warn him, young Mahdalka said. We'll never know. Old Mahdalka told him that if he looked long to the east, he would find his death there. And that if his death should come from there, in future generations his own blood would run together with the blood of those he now held in chains. The visitor was so startled by this that he jumped up from the table. It took Marie and Fuksena a long time to calm him. They poured brandy down him to quiet his nerves. Apparently, Fuksena went over Mahdalka's telling time after time, with explanations and corrections, until it was blurred by a flow of words that it is pointless to consider. They succeeded in calming him to such a degree that his defenses came down and he complained of how tired he felt. They gave him a blend of ground rosehip, stems of knotweed and mint for his strength, and a special pouch with oregano, angelica, and Saint John's wort to free his thoughts. When at last he went away, he was apparently thoughtful but at peace. He threatened no punishments or reprisals—quite the contrary, in fact. As he parted from them, he asked what he could give them for their services. Before young Mahdalka could refuse this offer—she was too afraid to name a price—Josifčena shouted from the room that she wanted the return of her son, who had been put to work somewhere in the Reich. The visitor said nothing to this, just clicked his heels and touched the peak of his cap with his fingertips. Then he got into his car, followed by the two men, and they drove away. No one here ever found out who the visitor was. But the other two showed up again. The rumor was that one of them no longer slept at the tax office, but with Fuksena. He had a posh name, Friedrich Ferdinand. He was the older of the two but the junior in rank: he called the other not *'Herr Doktor'* but *'Herr Obersturmbannführer.'* I think his name was Levin, but it's so long ago I'm not sure I remember well.

"I think it was because of those two hanging around Fuksena and the Mahdalkas that my mother and Surmena got off so lightly. Those two weren't ordinary SS, even though they wore the uniforms. They were well educated. Fuksena once said that they were conducting research. Research into what? Well, the goddesses. Don't ask me what kind of research—I've no way of knowing. But what I do know is that this research seemed to have some kind of divine protection; God forgive me for saying so. It was known about as far away as Zlín. That's why that officer left my mother and Surmena alone, regardless of what Schwannze, that swine—no one knew whether he was Czech or German—said about them. He left them alone because different rules applied to the goddesses. At least, that's what I think. Today no one can tell us for sure.

"Do you know what happened to Fuksena? Better not to know; it's an ugly story. Everyone here tried their best to forget about it. Do you know how the woman who many thought the most powerful goddess in Kopanice ended up? She was beaten to death.

"The two SS men went away before the end of the war. A few months later, a baby was born at the Mahdalkas. It was the time when partisans were roaming the hills, and the first Russians were appearing among them, taking on new recruits, fanning flames of hope, so everyone was caught up in it, and it wouldn't leave the men in peace. In the midst of all this, a girl who had spurned the locals and consorted with the Germans gave birth. You should have seen how furious this made some folk! When the front came this way and the whole village fled to the Kykula hill or the woods around Pitín, fearful that the brutes who flooded the place in the first wave would kill them, Fuksena simply disappeared. Only some days later, once folk had made their way home, did they find her, mutilated and broken. Apparently, they buried her straightaway, without a funeral. After the liberation there was a call for her to be placed in a grave like a good Christian, but no one even knew who had found her and where. The child—a girl—disappeared as well. They said that Mahdalka was so beside herself that she was practically apoplectic. Now she'd lost the successor she'd been nurturing for years as well as that successor's daughter, the last goddess of her bloodline. It must have been dreadful for her: all she had left was a daughter whose blood was not hers and a son in the army somewhere in the Reich. She didn't even have grandkids."

Irma shook her head before turning abruptly to look at Dora. "Now you know everything about Mahdalka and Fuksena. So shush and I'll cast the wax for you. Don't say a word. A year from now I might not be here anymore, and you won't know what's ahead of you."

These words brought Irma's narrative to an emphatic close. She stood up from the table. But immediately she checked herself as her eyes clouded with suspicion. "Or do you know it already?"

Dora was startled. "Know what?"

"Maybe you, too, can see! You *are* Surmena's niece and Justýna Ruchárka's granddaughter, after all. It's in *your* family as well. Do you feel it?"

"Feel what, Auntie?"

"That special power. To see past and present, and other things besides."

Dora shook her head. "I don't."

Irma nodded, seemingly satisfied. "That's good. Although it's also a shame. Because it really does mean that I'm the last of the goddesses."

Dora started to smile, only to turn serious again when Irma went on in a tone of bitterness. "My daughters were supposed to carry on the knowledge, at least for some time. But life here wasn't sweet enough for them, and they left to live in town. So they know none of it. Their choice. But don't you get to thinking that she who sees the future can escape what fate has in store for her!"

Irma gave Dora another searching look. Again Dora shook her head.

"Be that as it may. I'll cast the wax for you anyway."

A little while later, an intoxicating steam of tree bark and herbs was rising to the ceiling from a painted bowl on the table. The strange and spicy scent, the silence, and the hot tea with which Dora had filled her stomach were making her drowsy, as were the slow gestures with which Irma was preparing the utensils she needed for her divination.

"Soon you'll know it all, my girl," Irma mumbled.

When everything was ready, Irma stood solemnly over the table and blessed the things on it. Then she fetched the heated wax from the stove and poured it slowly into a pot of "happy water" from the well above the cottage. While she was doing this, she chanted: *I do this not by the power of evil but by the power of God, in the name of Our Lord Jesus Christ . . . Tell me, wax of knowledge, with God's blessing, of dear Dora, this lovely girl. What has been, what will be. Of her health and happiness. I invoke God on her behalf for the first time.*

Then Irma leaned over the ceramic bowl. In the cold water, the wax was solidifying. A moment later she fished about in the bowl and brought out a flat wax cast containing many twists and turns. Briefly, she weighed the cast in her hand; then she slowly began to run the fingers of both hands over its intricate shapes.

The silence in the room was broken by Irma's sigh, which lingered in the air, almost tangible.

217

Then Irma spoke. "You're bewitched good and proper, my girl."

Dora looked up at her. She was uneasy.

Irma was chanting again. *"In the name of the Father, the Son, and the Holy Ghost, let the Blessed Virgin come and bring health, happiness, and God's blessing to Dora . . ."*

Irma's monotonous voice was so lulling that Dora became drowsier still.

She was roused by words spoken straight at her: "I know how hard it's been for you. Everyone here knows it. And it's all here. Death in the family, being left alone, always alone. As I say, it's all here. Jakoubek too. He relies on you, and he walks the long path with you. It's all here like an open book. Look."

Irma thrust a piece of the honey-colored wax in front of Dora's eyes. Dora barely had time to focus on it before Irma's attention turned to other shapes in the wax.

"Oh, my girl, my girl," Irma said again as Dora tried to shake off her drowsiness and concentrate on what was being said. "You've done some bewitching, too, haven't you?"

Now Irma was looking at Dora with concern. The drowsiness was gone. Bewitching? She had bewitched herself?

"There's great evil in this," said Irma as she studied one of the points in the cast. "And all pain for no gain. There was nothing to be done but to live through it. You could have spared yourself the bad blood. That's what has given you the weak stomach. It bothers you, doesn't it? Well, I'll give you herbs for it."

Dora nodded, although she disagreed with what Irma was saying. Bad blood to no avail? If Irma meant the hostel, nothing of what she'd done there had been to no avail. It had been impossible simply to live through it. Dora had acted to defend herself, and she would do the same again. Hadn't their ridicule almost destroyed her?

"It's better now, isn't it?" Irma went on. "Life is calmer now. Everything is going as you wish. There's a sense of order . . . But don't forget that life can't be managed in tidy portions, day after day, week after week, never changing. You're living as though you were already dead. That's wrong; it really is. Especially at your age. You're flesh and bone. There's blood coursing in your veins. You're a woman full of a strength that must well up somewhere. Don't set yourself against it."

Irma fell silent and looked at her hands. Then she cried out in surprise, "Now I see it! It's not like that at all!"

Her fingertips brushed frantically against the points of the wax cast. They kept returning to one place, as though she couldn't believe that it was really there.

"Well, I never . . . What I see here . . . it's terrible."

With a shocked look on her face, Irma struggled for words, shaking her head. "Though she looks like she can barely count to five, she's a real handful. Do there have to be so many of them? Couldn't you choose just one and at least remember his name?"

This question contained an accusation, which she must have regretted immediately, as she went on sadly, "It's the fear that does it, isn't it? You think they're all the same, don't you? You think they're all like your father. I'm right, aren't I? But you're on the wrong track, believe me. You can't run from them because you think they're all like he was. They're not."

She spoke these last words with urgency, shaking her head as she saw Dora mustering the courage to protest. Dora's benumbed mind gathered thought after thought, but she had no idea where to begin. She was about to open her mouth when she became aware of Irma's puzzled expression. All will to speak left her. Instead, she closed her eyes and kept them closed, tight. It was clear that someone was pounding on the door of the thirteenth chamber of her life story.

"That . . . that woman here . . . I don't . . ." Irma's voice was quiet; she was incredulous. Carefully she studied the wax cast, examining each of its ridges, one after another, taking in every crack, bulge, and twist of it, searching for an explanation. Perhaps at last she found one because she said in an astonished, perhaps terrified voice, "So that's how it is!"

Yanked from her blissful torpor, Dora sat there with eyes clenched shut, trying to concentrate on breathing. In, out. In, out. Her lungs were filled with the bitter scent of burned bark and herbs, her heart was pounding, shame was racing through her veins. She felt hot blood in the tips of her thumbs and the blush of her cheeks. How could Irma have seen?

She swallowed hard before daring to look at Irma with all the self-denial she could muster. But Irma was too busy studying the wax cast. Traces of agitation gradually faded from her expression. Obviously, her thoughts had moved on, into another chamber of Dora's being. She was looking through the window of her open palms, and it was as though she was speaking with someone through that window; through her mouth there issued a stream of what sounded like gibberish. Only after some time did it give way to phrases that made some kind of sense.

Now Irma's whisper was compassionate as she muttered, "It's not going to be easy for you, I know. But don't be downcast. Not all of us can be a mother. It's not an obligation. There's nothing to blame yourself for . . . You have something here, but it's not that."

Irma was swaying from side to side, as though drunk and struggling to keep her balance. But apparently, she was convinced by what she was saying. "Something big, which draws you in . . . You should go after it; it is the right way. It'll give you what you need—you'll see."

Now Irma was nodding; she was almost happy. It was as though she had found absolution at the very center of the cast. Perhaps understanding that it had nothing more to tell her, she waved a dismissive hand before embarking on a last invocation. *"I call an invocation on this girl, Dora, baptized and blessed by the Holy Trinity . . . On the bleak Černá hill, I call on you troubles and worries to move away, to retreat, to get out of Dora. You have no power within her, day or night. I do this not by my own power but by the power of God and Our Lord Jesus Christ . . . In the name of the Father, the Son, and the Holy Ghost. Amen."*

Then Irma and the room were silent again. This silence was broken by the creaking of the wooden bench as the old woman sat down on it, then by the hiss of the bark and herbs as she poured cold water from the bowl over them.

Dora was about to explode. She was ready to give the old woman her opinion straight out, to tell her how wrong she was. She was ready to shower Irma with explanations and excuses before the old woman could grab and reveal her private thoughts.

But Irma was ahead of her.

Without warning she reached across the table and stroked the back of Dora's hand. This tender, maternal gesture was something that Dora had not experienced for many years. She was confused by the forgotten feeling it aroused; a wave of gratitude washed over her.

She raised her eyes to Irma's. Irma's gaze was warm and somehow full of understanding.

"I know how to help you, my girl. I know where you need to start. And I'll advise you. If you do as I tell you, you'll feel much better, trust me. It doesn't have to be the way it is now."

"What is it?" said Dora, bewildered.

"You know what it is, Dora. Don't worry; I'll help you find the right way. I think you have an idea about it already, don't you? It'll all sort itself out, so don't you worry. Soon you'll be entirely sure of it. So don't worry; we just have to start unraveling it from the right end. But before I tell you about it, you must promise me that you'll do as I say. Promise me, Dora."

"All right," Dora said cautiously. "I promise."

"You're doing the right thing," said Irma, nodding. "Believe me, everything will be different. You'll feel much better and find your peace. But there's something you have to do first. Go there and speak with him."

"With who?" said Dora uncertainly.

"With your father, of course."

Father

She'd assumed that after what happened, she would never see him again. Following his arrest, she tried so hard not to think of him, and he dropped out of her memory completely. It was as though he had literally ceased to exist. It never crossed her mind that it might be otherwise. But a few months before her graduation, he came back.

That afternoon when she and Jakoubek got off the bus, the square in Hrozenkov looked just as it did every other Friday. Standing around the stop were a few neighbors waiting for the bus to Bojkovice. On the bench near the co-op store sat a few old men smoking pipes and basking in the afternoon sun; on the nearby playground, boys were playing football.

Dora entered the co-op with her pack on her back and Jakoubek in tow. They needed supplies to take up the hill. As always, she picked up a basket in the corner of the store. Dora greeted loudly and received the usual greetings in return. But something wasn't quite right. She couldn't have said what this thing was, but she sensed it. It was hanging in the air and revealed itself when everyone in the store looked at her at once.

She took pasta and two tins of vegetables from the shelves and a loaf of bread from a plastic bin. She leaned over the cooler for milk in a bag printed in blue. She went to the meat counter and asked for an offcut from a roll of salami.

"Could you wrap it, please?" Her voice echoed through the quiet store. Embarrassed, she turned to leave. "Good afternoon, Mrs. Janková."

The greeting was part of her attempt to get past her stooped neighbor, whose long, bony flank was thrust into the narrow aisle as she looked significantly at the half-empty row of fruit syrups.

"Hello, Dora. Heading home?"

"That's right."

"Take care, my girl. And make haste. It'll be dark soon."

Dora smiled. It wasn't as if she was going up to Žítková from Hrozenkov for the first time.

"Just so you know," said Tichačka, as she reached from the till for the contents of Dora's basket, "your father's back."

The bag of milk slipped from Dora's fingers and landed with a plop on the striped linoleum. Tichačka looked up at her, and Dora saw her mouth tighten with embarrassment.

"My father?"

Tichačka nodded.

At the end of this day, when dusk fell on the Koprvazy pasture opposite, a light really did go on in their old house. In the darkness interwoven with thick threads of rain, a shy, barely perceptible little light emerged and shimmered; it was a signal for her, telling her he was there, that he really had come back.

She sat in the middle of the dim room, in which the only sounds were Jakoubek's regular breathing and the tap-tap-tap of rain on the roof, and watched that faint light through a narrow slit of window. She sat there until she realized she was surrounded by darkness, by which time nothing would have made her get up and switch on the light, thus reciprocating his signal to her: I'm here.

Meanwhile, her confusion kept producing the same thought: What now? So thoroughly had she forced out the fact of her father's existence that she had forgotten to prepare herself for a situation such as this. She was caught out. Gooseflesh crawled up her arm as she imagined how close he was. It would be enough to go down the Bedová to where the paths joined, then up and along the smooth trench that marked the municipal field toward the wild orchard but missing it to the left, and she'd be standing in front of the cottage that contained him. Or it might be the other way round. If he went out now, he'd be at their door in less than a quarter of an hour.

This knowledge filled her with dread.

What if he tried it?

As if summoned by her thought, the outside gate creaked softly. Dora's heart lurched. She dared not so much as breathe so as not to miss the next sound. A moment later she registered the approach of a few muffled steps. Then someone knocked on the door. Dora froze. The staccato rap came again, followed by a muffled "Dora?"

Before she could answer, the door handle turned to point at the floor, and Janigena crossed the threshold tentatively. She was soaked to the skin. No sooner had she entered than a golden arrow of lightning hit the ground with a deafening crack.

That year they spent most of their weekends in Brno. Her fear and reluctance to encounter her father did not permit her to go to Žítková more than twice before winter arrived and temporarily cut off the house on the Bedová from civilization. They returned in March. But even then Dora could find no peace there: the house had become a cage.

Every day she asked herself if it wouldn't be better to withdraw from Žítková altogether while he remained there, simply not go there at all. This thought made her sad, not least for Jakoubek's sake, but slowly she began to embrace it. Then something unexpected happened.

She wouldn't have gone there if God himself had asked her, she told herself. Until Baglár turned up that morning and said, "If you don't go, I'll bring him here. It's no one's responsibility but yours."

So she went.

She and Jakoubek came down from Surmena's cottage and then up to the Koprvazy, dragging their feet in Baglár's wake.

He turned back to them. "Don't much want to, do you?"

She shook her head.

The gate that gave onto the small yard was open. Weeds and tall grass grew through the paving; the service tree next to the house was bothering the thatched roof, seemingly wishing to lean against it. The house was a hive of activity.

When she went in, everyone turned to look at her. Baglárka, Janigena, the coroner. She didn't see her father's body. Only his boots under the bench by the stove. Boots like the time before.

Then they made way, created an aisle, a triumphal arch to take them straight to their father. Dora walked this alone; Jakoubek stayed by the door.

He was lying on the kitchen table. His arms were folded across his chest, and an elder-wood cross had been placed under them. There were lacerations on his neck and stiffening traces of pain on his face.

"It was over quickly," said the coroner. "He was drunk as a skunk again. He's better off now."

"We shouldn't speak ill of the dead," muttered Baglárka.

Baglár chuckled.

Dora stepped up to the table. After so many years, it was strange to look into his face. She looked at him without blinking; she felt that there was nothing behind his features she wanted to think about, nothing she wanted to remember. No memories except for one. And this came to her when she was least expecting it—now, for instance. The chopped-off heads of kittens, each wearing a ghastly grin, the necks oozing blood and sprouting shreds of flesh and skin covered in fuzz. The heads rolled across the canvas of her blurry gaze, one after another.

Scared, she blinked and stepped back from the table.

"You should sit down," said the coroner. "Here."

A chair was pushed toward her, and she sank into it. Her father was inches away from her; had she reached out, she could have touched the tips of his toes in their thick knitted socks. He'd had nothing, so where had he gotten such good socks from? she wondered.

"When did it happen?" she asked.

"It must have been during the night," said Baglár. "After midnight, I should think. He spent the evening in the pub. I was there too. It was plain that something was eating at him. He sat there still as a statue and spoke to no one."

Dora nodded. "Who found him?"

Janigena cleared her throat and said in a deep voice that suggested annoyance, "I did."

For a moment it looked as though she would say no more. But when she saw that everyone was waiting for her to describe her discovery in detail, she went on. "Early this morning I was walking along the lower path. The way your service tree stood out against the sky was different. It was sort of bent to the ground, as if carrying a weight. It looked like a sack. It was him hanging there. I hurried up to him, but there was no helping him anymore. He must have been hanging there half the night."

Janigena kicked the tip of a muddy boot against a raised floorboard. Some cow muck came off the sole; she'd just finished the early shift at the farmers' cooperative, and the smell of it was on her.

The room remained quiet. All they heard was a peeling sound as Jakoubek tore splinters from the doorframe.

"I'll help you get him ready," said Baglárka at last. "There has to be a leave-taking; there's nothing else for it."

Seeing that Dora was not about to object, she began to assign tasks. "Baglár, you measure him up and go with the coroner to the presbytery and the carpenter in Hrozenkov. Janigena can go around the neighbors and bring the singer. In the meantime, we'll wash him. Our Lidka can make some yeast cakes. We'll tell all the neighbors we meet to bring brandy."

That afternoon Dora paced the room restlessly while Baglárka heated water, prepared a salt solution, and undressed the corpse. Before Dora could stop her, she snipped at his underpants with scissors, pulled them away, and threw them into the open oven.

"They would have stunk the place out," she said. "He shat himself."

The body of Dora's father lay before her as God had made it—with a tiny scrotum between its legs that in turn had made her. A naked, hairless, gray body. The body of her father.

Dora's stomach was tight.

Baglárka went on with her work relentlessly. She tossed a rag to Dora, then took hold of the pot of hot water and set it down on a chair next to the table.

They washed each of his limbs. One held, the other wiped. Everywhere. As Dora worked at his body with the rag, a part of her wanted to dig her fingers deep into the flesh. To tear into him so that the blood poured out of him. Like her mother's blood. But she did nothing of the kind. They washed him and laid him out as he was, until his laundered clothes on the range were dry.

By the time the darkness came, he was ready. Washed, shaved, dressed, his hair combed. They laid him on a white quilt in the knocked-together coffin that Baglár had brought on his cart at midday, together with chairs that he had arranged around the room.

They were putting plates of yeast cakes on the surface of the cooled-down range when they heard the first snatches of song.

Baglárka lit a candle and placed it next to the corpse's head. "Time to get started."

Dora was suddenly nervous. Up to that point, she'd been able to focus on her work. Baglárka had dictated her regime and never stopped talking. About everything: the harvest, the weather, the livestock, the new parish priest. The steady stream of words she produced freed Dora from the need to think about what she was doing. She was about to slip out of the rhythm created by mindless work. It was expected that she would begin to behave as a daughter—a person she hadn't felt herself be for a long time.

She turned to Jakoubek. "Are you hungry?"

All day he'd been watching her from above the range, his favorite place at their home on the Bedová too. He nodded and scrambled down slowly. Baglárka pushed a plate of yeast cakes toward him.

"My goodness, we almost forgot. Take two. You'll get more later when they bring some."

> *The day's work is done,*
> *Rest, brother*
> *Await the glorious Resurrection*
> *Thou hast died in Jesus*
> *Who is life itself . . .*

From outside the cottage came long, drawn-out notes of song, followed by the entry of Janigena in the company of the singer, with some neighbors behind.

Dora stood up. Jakoubek grabbed her hand and held it tight.

Baglárka bade the mourners welcome and handed around the plate of yeast cakes. Everyone took a cake, stroked Dora's and Jakoubek's hair, and put a gift down on the range, whose surface was soon crowded with bottles of spirits, a variety of vegetables, milk, even brawn. Many men from the neighborhood dropped by for the leave-taking, and soon there was nowhere to stand. The top of the range was occupied by kids. Later arrivals had to stand beyond the threshold by the open door.

Dora and Jakoubek were seated right next to the table. The singer positioned himself beyond the corpse's head and faced his audience.

"I welcome you all here," he began, speaking to the room at large, which went quiet immediately, "who have come to take their leave of the unfortunate Matyáš Ides. I welcome relatives and neighbors, and I welcome his unfortunate orphans."

Heads turned to him and them; Dora felt from the back and sides that all eyes were on them. They wanted to see how they would behave. Whether they would cry. Weeping and wailing were a duty. The old-woman weepers were there to make a noise that would complement the tirade of her wails. But she didn't wail; she didn't so much as sob.

"Let us say the first prayer."

The people in the room began to pray.

Dora, too, folded her hands and moved her lips silently. She wondered what had inspired Uncle Machala to become a singer for the dead. And when he had become one. She could remember no other singer in their hills but him. Had he inherited the role from his father? Or his grandfather? Did he assume of his own free will the burden of conducting leave-takings with the bereaved? He brought awful trouble on himself. He climbed to the most remote hills in summer and winter, when the paths were choked with drifted snow, and it was his job to manage the last things of the deceased. How had he learned to identify with the deceased that he could interpret their last thoughts to their relatives? Dora doubted he knew the last intentions of her father.

The common prayer ended. A bottle of spirits that was moving about the room reached her from the left. She was about to refuse, then thought better of it and took a few sips. The strong liquor burned her throat, and she was grateful not to choke on it.

Now the singer's plaintive tones were filling the room, having sliced into the silence with a song about the travails of Jesus Christ and torments that await unrepentant sinners in hell. During this song the wailing was supposed to start. But the room remained eerily quiet.

Light my candle boldly
My dearest friends
I part from you in sadness
I leave you now in God.

At the end of the last verse, Machala fell silent. He gave Dora a searching look. As she looked back at him coolly, he realized that she was not about to wail. He closed his eyes and took a deep breath. When he reopened his eyes, it was clear to everyone in the room that the dead man was about to speak.

"I, the unfortunate Matyáš Ides, offer you, my dear family and friends, a warm welcome to my home. I am glad to see you together like this. I am glad indeed that you have not forgotten me and have come to say goodbye to me and to start me on my way. I do not know what is before me, and I am a little afraid of what will be when I leave this place, whether it will be a long journey, or forgiveness, or torment. The Lord God knows how many times I have erred. I have sinned against his Commandments. But I trust in sweet Jesus for my forgiveness. Was not Peter a saint, and did he not err, and was he not forgiven? As Lord God forgives sinners, may you sinners forgive me. As I have erred, you, too, have erred. Are we not the same?"

From behind Dora there came a gentle sob. Followed by others. The old-woman weepers, fortified by the spirits being passed around, were getting to work without regard for Dora.

"So before anything else I ask—for the sake of God the Father, God the Son, God the Holy Ghost, and for the Five Wounds of Christ—that out of love, you forgive me all that has made you angry with me.

"First I turn to the other side and ask for the forgiveness of my poor wedded wife, Irena. I ask forgiveness for the sin with which I shortened your life. I ask your forgiveness one thousand times, my dear. Believe me, what I did to you, I did also to myself. I never ceased to regret what I did, and that self-reproach was with me to my last breath. Please forgive me, and believe that I often prayed that you would find peace in the Lord and a more contented existence than I provided for you here.

"In the second place, I turn to you, my beloved firstborn daughter. I loved you as my own soul, yet by taking your mother from you, I did you great harm. Believe me when I say that I mourned this till the end of my days. If you can, forgive my crime. I was a man with many faults, dear

Dora, but a lack of love for you was not among them. Forgive me for marring your childhood and leaving you to grow up among strangers with the burden of your brother's care. Forgive me, although I know that you accepted your lot with courage. Forgive me if you can, and learn from my mistakes.

"And I ask the same of you, Jakub, my son. I turn to you, too, with a plea for forgiveness for the taking of your mother and my never having made things good between us, for my having been a bad father. Believe me when I say that I, too, suffered by this, especially in later years, when not a minute passed without my reproaching myself for everything I brought on you and Dora. These reproaches and the loss of your love drove me to this act unworthy of a Christian, the taking of my own life. It is better for me to burn in the fires of hell than to witness your silent reproaches. So I ask you once again to forgive me."

Someone behind Dora tapped her on the shoulder with the bottom of a bottle. She took another sip. The spirits no longer burned in her mouth, and a pleasant glowing sensation spread down her throat.

The singer's moans didn't move her in the slightest; plus, she doubted that these could have been her father's last thoughts. So there was no question of forgiveness. She longed to have the whole charade over and done with. She wished she'd insisted on a normal funeral, with no leave-taking, no singer, no weepers. It would have been her right, after all.

"So I ask you all a second time—for the sake of God the Father, God the Son, and God the Holy Ghost, and for the Five Wounds of Christ—that you forgive me all that has made you angry with me.

"I ask for the forgiveness of all of you whom I ever wronged. As I take my leave of you, I wish you all the best and ask that you say the Lord's Prayer for me three times."

The gently sobbing weepers suddenly fell silent. Then the room resounded to the chanting of the Lord's Prayer.

Furtively, Dora studied the intent faces of her neighbors at prayer. Her gaze slid from bowed heads to clasped hands and finally came to rest on Janigena in the corner of the room. Janigena was staring at her. Dora was startled by her grim expression. It flashed through her mind that there was something odd going on, but then Janigena nodded in the direction of Jakoubek, and she understood. His hands were folded in his lap, and in them was a bottle of brandy that was now only two-thirds full. Probably one of his jolly uncles had slipped it to him; let the poor kid have some too. So he did, and now he was swinging about on his chair, bumping against the backrest, lurching backward and forward. Dora just managed to catch him before he slid to the floor. She snatched the bottle from his hand; a few drops sprang from its narrow neck. He smiled at her, in a daze.

The third chanting of the Lord's Prayer came to an end.

"Stay as long as you wish, good neighbors. Eat, drink, and think kindly of poor Matyáš Ides. The priest expects us at ten tomorrow morning."

The singer's role was over. Exhausted, he dropped onto the bench at the table, across from Dora, and smiled at her ruefully over the top of the coffin. A hum filled the room as people moved about. Plates filled with refreshments and more bottles of spirits circulated through the crowd. The weepers sat at the corpse's head and sang drawn-out laments. Mothers chivvied their children down from the top of the range and said their goodbyes to their neighbors.

"Tomorrow at the churchyard, then."

"God be with you, Dora. And you, Jakoubek."

"Have a good cry. You know it's the right thing to do."

This made Dora shudder. Had they still not got it? She would be crying for no one. Tomorrow all the old dears would be muttering about how she hadn't shed a single tear. Let them.

Concerned, she scanned the room in search of Jakoubek. He'd rolled away from the table with the coffin to the corner, where he hiccuped and spluttered every time someone said goodbye to him. People stroked his fair hair and he snatched at their hands, blissfully unaware of the reason why neighbors who mostly avoided him were treating him like this.

Janigena pushed her way through the crowd with a bottle of spirits. Dora took it from her and drank.

The room was filled with the conversation of neighbors intending to stay the night and the song of the weepers, which was becoming more rhythmical. There was a seemingly endless supply of spirits. The plates were emptied of yeast cakes, and there was an occasional trill of laughter. Now no one was paying attention to the coffin and the lately deceased; it was as though he had fallen asleep and the others had decided not to wake him.

The last things she remembered seeing before Janigena led her out were the drunken weepers singing a Csárdás and Baglár whirling about in the middle of the room with Tichačka, stepping on those who, like Jakoubek, had curled up on the floor and fallen asleep among the empty bottles and the broken plates.

The next day was much better. From early morning Dora performed one task after another under Baglárka's supervision. She was up at the Koprvazy at five to wake all those who were still in the cottage; she flooded the stale-smelling room with her élan.

Having done no more than wash her face in cold water, she set about her work. Attending strictly to detail, she made all necessary preparations for the bearing away of the deceased. To the weary song of the weepers, she tidied the kitchen and threw all leftovers and rubbish into a fire in the oven, ensuring the dead man would have nothing to return for now that the leave-taking was over. Before they closed the lid on him, she put two small coins on his eyelids to pay the ferryman. She stood attentive guard over the hammering of the nails into the coffin:

she didn't want him forcing his way out because of bad workmanship. She made sure that the deceased left the house feet-first and the bearers knocked the coffin against the threshold exactly three times, ensuring that the dead man took proper leave of the house. She turned her apron inside out to show the deceased that she was letting him go. Then she joined the coffin-bearing procession down to Hrozenkov.

She would never have imagined herself adhering so scrupulously to all the traditions and carrying them out so convincingly. But concerning her father's eternal sleep, she did everything to the letter; she needed to feel that his return was truly impossible.

The church service was a short one. There were not many kind words that could be said about the deceased, nor was there any reason to comfort the bereaved. Dora was fidgety. Several times she looked over at Janigena; several times she glanced at her watch. In the end Baglárka gave her a nudge and told her in a whisper that she was behaving inappropriately. *Be that as it may,* thought Dora, *I just want to get out of here.*

She made her way to the churchyard in the same absentminded state.

The coffin slid quietly into the grave. Dora had ordered no music, and after their exertions the day before, the weepers had no more tears. Her gaze turned more to the branches of the trees around the graveyard than the few black-clad neighbors who, one after another, threw clods of earth into the pit beneath her family's headstone. She hoped that someone in Hrozenkov would die soon and relieve her father's soul of its patrol among the rustling leaves, allowing it to pass into hell.

Dora did not calm down until later, in the pub. She ordered two bottles so that she, Baglárka, Tichačka, Janigena, and the priest could flood the dead man's eyes. And a beer for each of them. This included her father, for whom a chair was reserved at the head of the table. She kept an eye on this throughout, unable to shake off a feeling that he was somewhere watching her, a feeling much more insistent than the one she'd had when his body had been lying in front of her. But what of it? The beer in front of the empty chair went flat as the shot glasses continued to be refilled.

Had he truly disappeared from their lives? Was she really free of the fear that she might meet him, simply run across him? As indeed had once happened.

It was the second month following his release from prison. She and Jakoubek were on their way up to Žítková, weary from the journey from Brno. They spotted him as he was coming down the path from their house on the Koprvazy, stooped, older, gray, but otherwise the same as she remembered him from her childhood. Still a good-looking man. She grabbed Jakoubek and quickened her pace to such a degree that she was practically dragging him along. They passed their father when he was but a few yards from them. He stood at the fork in the path, looking like he'd seen a ghost. Dora and Jakoubek went on without greeting him and didn't look back, even once. In the months that remained until his death, he made no attempt to see them.

On the way back to Brno, she wondered why not. He might at least have written them a letter. But he never did. Not from prison, nor after he came back. She put all this on his account, but in the end, she got angry with herself. How come she still thought of him at all? He'd disappeared into the ground, and that was the end of it, she told herself. What was done was done.

After that she thought of him only once. The Saturday after, when Baglárka told her that the rope he'd hanged himself with had disappeared. The one who stole it must have been due in court. He who has a hanged man's rope never gets found out. He wins every judgment.

The Letter

After Dora's father had been lying peacefully in his grave for several years, Irma now wanted Dora to speak with him. Had she gone mad? Speak with her father? Total nonsense.

She fled from Irma as fast as her legs would carry her.

She called at Baglárka's to collect Jakoubek and didn't finish the cup of chicory coffee she was given. She hurried on and up, urging herself home. But her bitterness did not subside. As she was slicing bread for supper, she cut her finger. She wasn't able to concentrate. She ran about the room with her bleeding finger in her mouth, trying to find a bandage.

Jakoubek was bewildered. All he did was sit in the corner and watch her.

That night she struggled to get to sleep.

As she tossed and turned, the squeaking of the bed's oak boards disturbed the otherwise silent night. All those who had come to take their leave of her father paraded before her. She saw all the faces, Janigena's last of all. She was the only one who didn't care. Dora longed for Janigena to appear and take her out of her gloom, as she had first done then.

Come to me, come . . . She wished hard.

But the minutes passed and nothing happened. She was wasting her time. If she went out for a while and breathed fresh air, she might find it easier to fall asleep. She got up, slipped on her coat, and stood out in front of the house.

Her exhalations were vaporous; in this cold autumn night, she felt winter. She fixed her gaze on the clear crescent of moon that hung high in the star-studded sky. All kinds of thoughts whirled about in her mind. Try as she might to shoo them away, always they came back to what Irma had said. Only now did it dawn on her that she had run from Irma without having asked about the most important thing, the thing she had come about, so much had Irma's last words upset her. She'd wanted to know about Surmena and what she and Mahdalka had shared.

She continued her morose watch on the doorstep a little while longer, until she was truly cold, then prepared to go back inside. Her hand was on the door handle when she heard a muffled sound from the path below. It was Janigena, whose tall, broad-shouldered, loose-jointed frame was moving across the moonlit meadow. Her fiercely brushed long hair was contained in a fleecy cap. She was waving an arm above her head and whistling weakly to herself. She pointed toward the Koprvazy. Dora didn't hesitate. Pulling her coat tighter around her, she went to meet Janigena.

Dora's bad mood persisted into the next day. She and Jakoubek went for a walk in the hills, and it was with her the whole time. It was not dispelled by the sight of Jakoubek merrily tearing off dry grass, collecting leaves of different colors that had blown to the meadows from the woods and studying their veins in amazement.

"Next week we'll go to the woods," she promised when the time came to stop the fun before they caught the bus to Brno.

Later that afternoon, with Jakoubek back at the institution, Dora headed home. At the entrance to her building, she opened her mailbox out of habit. She was hardly expecting to find anything in it on a Sunday evening, but find something she did. It must have arrived on Friday. It was from the Ministry of the Interior. Hurriedly, she tore open the envelope and pulled out a sheet with three folds in it.

Dear Ms. Idesová,

On October 18, 1998, you requested permission to view the personnel file of an agent of the State Security Police (StB). At the present time we cannot allow you to view the personnel file of Agent JINDŘICH ŠVANC: pursuant to Act 140/1996 Coll. files kept on secret operatives of the StB may be shown only to authorized applicants, i.e., persons subject to observation. In the case of the file with the code name "SURMENA," the person subject to observation is Terézie Surmenová. Pursuant to Art. 4, Para. 1 of Act 140/1996 Coll., subsequent to the death of a person subject to observation, the right to view a personnel file of an StB agent passes only to persons authorized to claim protection for the deceased. Unfortunately, you do not fulfill this condition of the law.

The same conditions apply to permission to view the file on the "GODDESSES" case, although we hereby inform you that this file was destroyed by shredding in 1974.

Yours sincerely,

Mgr. Karel Dolejší

Head of the Department for Archive

Administration and Records Services

Ministry of the Interior of the Czech Republic

A perfect disappointment and a fitting end to a thoroughly unpleasant weekend.

Dora read the letter again before putting it back in its envelope and slowly climbing the stairs to her apartment.

If she was not authorized to protect Surmena, then no one was.

She was filled with a sense of bitterness and desperation. By the time she was beyond her front door, she was in the grip of an oppressive sadness.

A while later, drops of hot water were jumping onto her body from the powerful stream gushing from the tap. As the water level rose, the gooseflesh that had been coaxed out by her cold bath was slowly washed away.

She was thinking hard.

The letter made it clear that she had nothing more to expect from this course of action. The very people whose jobs were meant to shed light on past crimes were invoking officialdom in order to put obstacles in her way.

By now the hot water lay heavy on the curve of her belly and had made a shallow lake of her navel. Abstractedly, she watched her hands clumsily clear a path through the column of water. One of her wrists had a faded red bangle around it, a gift from Surmena. Her aunt. Could there be any other reason for why they were making it impossible for her, a blood relative, to pursue a direct course in her investigation of what happened to Surmena? She was assailed by fragments of what she'd heard of the hidden identities of former StB agents who were active in today's "apparatus." But surely a senior government official couldn't be a former StB agent, she assured herself. Wasn't she just being paranoid?

In an effort to drive away such thoughts, on a sudden, surprising impulse, she set about making a whirlpool of the bathwater, gradually creating a mountain of foam and bringing out the scent of lavender. She didn't desist until a snowy cloak covered her whole body. Now she was still but for her weary gaze flitting from place to place. "Calming emulsion," it said on the label of a plastic bottle next to the bath. She'd just washed out all that was left in the bottle, but it hadn't made her any calmer.

She closed her eyes and lay there quietly for a while longer. All that was audible in the bathroom was her breathing.

Then she took a deep breath and ducked her face and hair into the foamy water while her knees rose in the opposite direction. If it wasn't going to work out through the help of those who were there to help her, it would work out some other way, she decided. With a loud swish, her head came back up. She would track down the person responsible for what had happened to Surmena on her own.

Josefína Mahdalová

When at last she succeeded in catching Baglárka at home, spring had long since given way to the heat of summer.

They sat down in the pleasant, cool shade of the limes behind the house.

"Where have you been, Auntie? I've been here looking for you a few times."

"It's those doctors. They'd like to cut everything out of me. They kept me in the hospital for nearly a month. At least here they leave me in peace. Irma gives me some herbs for it, and it's healing well."

She reached under her washed-out summer apron and tapped her left side.

On her autumn visits to Baglárka's and Irma's, Dora noticed how neither of them wanted to continue with the story of Fuksena's instructress. She knew full well that they were prevaricating as they spouted story after story; whatever she asked them, she got no answer. What was this secret involving Mahdalka that no one wanted to touch? Dora gave it a little more thought but then could contain herself no longer. She turned to Baglárka with a direct question.

Baglárka was unsure in her reply. "Mahdalka? Irma hinted that Fuksena was a relative of hers and Justýna's, did she?"

Dora nodded with conviction.

"Well, perhaps she was . . . But to tell you the truth, girl, I'm not sure I can remember."

Dora was annoyed by this. "Auntie! I'm Justýna's granddaughter; I've a right to know who my relatives are! And who but you—my godmother—can tell me about them?"

Baglárka gave an embarrassed shrug, then said, "Well, what of it? The fact of the matter is . . . I think Mahdalka was your aunt."

Dora's eyes opened wide. This was unexpected, and she was taken aback. Baglárka was alarmed and silent.

"My aunt?"

Baglárka went on nervously. "Um, yes. Surmena's elder sister. But you couldn't have known her. She was only young when she went down to the Hungarian side, even before your mother, the youngest, was born. They said that the Mahdal she married in Potočná was a widower because of her, but who knows the truth of that? So she became known as Mahdalka . . . Anyway, she started to goddess there."

Dora was astonished. "Can you remember her, Auntie?"

Baglárka waited a moment before she spoke. "Yes, I can."

"What was she like?"

The old woman turned her face away. "Never speak ill of the dead."

Dora cleared her throat and said, "Irma said she was a witch. Is it true?"

"Irma said that? Really?" Baglárka shook her head in wonder. When she went on, there was irritation in her voice. "The truth is, they said some pretty bad things about Josefína. It's a pity that Surmena never told you. Maybe she should have."

Now that the subject had been broached, Baglárka realized that Dora wasn't about to let her off the hook. She went on calmly: "They said there was an evil force in Josefína. They called her a witch, not a goddess. They used the same insult for others whose goddessing they didn't like. But with old Mahdalka, it was different. They said that she could invoke possession by evil spirits, that she could bewitch people, that if someone displeased her, she could bring sickness on him. I don't know how much truth there is in this. I remember only what we went through with Surmena. It was sometime after the war, in the early fifties, I think, when I took a woman to her. A stranger. I'd met her down by the churchyard. She was wandering along the road, lost, walking straight ahead and then back again. I was pretty sure she was seeking a path to one of the goddesses. I decided to take her to Irma, Kateřina Hodulíková, or Surmena, depending on what she let on. Do you know what it was about? She was from Zemianske Podhradie, and Mahdalka had bewitched her—that's all she told me. That was all. She looked peculiar: untidy, white as a sheet, worried sick. Without a second thought, I took her by the arm and led her up to the Bedová. It dawned on me straightaway that if she really had been put under a spell from Mahdalka, then Surmena was the only one who could help her. Surmena and Mahdalka had been taught by the same mother, Justýna Ruchárka. And I was right. The woman explained that she and Mahdalka had disagreed over the price of some sorcery, and right away, Surmena knew what was what. At breakneck speed Surmena set the water to boil for the potion, got the woman to lie on the bed, put the eiderdown under her legs to support them, and ordered me to get all clothing off her that could get caught around her body. I untied her headscarf, pulled off her skirt, unlaced her shoes, made sure that she was comfortable. Then Surmena gave me a cloth, which I was to drape over her face. Although the woman was as weak as a kitten, she started to wriggle. The cloth on her face was burning, and she wouldn't be held down. For a few moments, I struggled with her. I was terrified and needed Surmena. But Surmena was still standing by the red-hot oven over an earthenware pot. Into this she was tossing maybe a dozen different herbs. She was muttering. Although I couldn't understand what she was saying, I knew it was something coarse, something dark, and it gave me the shivers. How was I to know that the worst was still to come? You should have seen what happened when Surmena made the woman drink the potion, when she put her hands in it and splashed it all over her body. To begin with, I thought the woman was screaming because it was too hot, but then I realized that Surmena had her hands in the pot and was not making a sound. The woman was roaring as though she were being pounded with hot coals. She roared and roared and thrashed about like a wild horse, but she never left the straw-filled mattress. You'd have expected her to get up and run away, but she didn't. What it looked like was the kind of exorcism priests used to perform on witches in the old times, to drive out the devil. And here was Surmena doing it in a cottage on the Bedová. After she finished, the woman lay still. She was covered in sweat, and Surmena opened all the windows and the door. I told her this was foolish; the woman would catch cold. She said that didn't matter—the main thing was that it should leave her. I preferred not to ask what she meant by 'it.' The woman stayed there overnight. I went back to my own folk. When I called on Surmena the next day, I found her alone and unusually morose. I asked, 'What's up? Didn't she give you enough?' She waved my questions away, saying that didn't matter, that she hadn't wanted to wait. 'Wait for what?' I asked. She replied that the woman had said she didn't want to wait until the evil spirit tried to get back inside her. 'Evil spirit?' I said, surprised. She was possessed, Surmena told me then. She was possessed by an evil spirit that was fighting for her body and kept trying to return to it. 'That crazy woman felt wonderful,' said Surmena. 'Told me she was quite well now. Thanked me and then marched across the field and down the hill. She wouldn't listen to a word I said. Within the week she'll be back; you can bet your life on it.' But she didn't come back. I left Surmena's and went down into Hrozenkov, where I stopped off at the pub. Some men from Trenčín had just come in. Down by the path, they said, in the Drietomica brook, they'd found a woman, although you wouldn't have been able to tell that it was a woman if it hadn't been for the headscarf under what was left of the head and if the body hadn't been wrapped in a skirt. It looked like she'd been caught up in some kind of vortex in the river and tossed against the rocks. She was tattered and torn. It was that woman, of course. I hurried up to the Bedová to tell Surmena. All she had to say was that Josifčena had always been stronger than her and that it was not advisable to take chances with her demons. I didn't understand this much, but it sort of made sense in the light of what others said about Mahdalka: that you should keep your distance from her. Whatever else she might have been and done, that bitch had consorted with the Germans. But what do I know about it?"

Dora left Baglárka's in a state of confusion. She was surprised that Kopanice—where she knew every rock, every tree, every hillside path— still had something to hide from her. And that this thing should be so close to her. Her own aunt.

On that balmy summer evening, she and Jakoubek trudged slowly up to the Bedová. Dora couldn't shake the sense that she had been betrayed. Why had they never told her about Mahdalka? Why had all those who could remember her kept quiet about her? Why had she found nothing about her in the great variety of documents that had passed through her hands in the archives? It struck her as extremely suspicious that in all her years of research, she had turned up nothing about Mahdalka. Even though her study focused primarily on earlier centuries, in all her various sources, she had come across mentions of every goddess who had ever lived in Kopanice, from the earliest to their very last successors, from the most important to the least powerful. All were mentioned but Mahdalka, her daughter-in-law, and Fuksena. That strange little family was cloaked in silence.

Then it dawned on her. They had lived in Hrozenkov, but on the other side of the brook. In a place called Potočná. And Potočná came under the jurisdiction of Drietoma. Now it was clear to her why she had found nothing in Czech archives and registries. Any records on them would, of course, be kept by authorities of Slovakia.

Magdaléna Mĺkva

*D*ora's approach to the preparation of materials for her dissertation had been painstaking. She had traveled the republic and scoured every Czech archive for sources related to magic and witchcraft. She had even handled the book of case files for the district of Bojkovice, in which were recorded details of crimes committed in the municipality of Žítková, and she had been astonished by how many statements denouncing the goddesses she found among them: for failed treatment, for deception in readings of the future, for inspiring a belief in the inevitability of victory in a plaintiff who had gambled away his cottage and livestock, for intentional misrepresentation by an unfulfilled prophecy that a girl would win the heart of the man she loved. Dora had also found a record of an investigation of a brawl between clients at the home of a goddess; there were records, too, of brawls between goddesses.

Dora smiled: human folly and thwarted schemes. But why had it not dawned on her that in Slovakia, too, there would be books full of cases such as these? Clients had flocked to the goddesses on the Slovak side just as they had flocked to those on the Czech side.

She spent the next few days in her office, searching for sources, the droning fan on her desk chopping the still, stifling air. By the end of the week, she had answers from the archives in Trenčín and Bratislava. She was expecting something, but not much.

A few days later, she was sitting in an air-conditioned reading room in Trenčín with a pile of books on the desk in front of her. These were the chronicles of the municipality of Drietoma, the department casebooks and the casebooks of the District Police Station in Trenčín—a stack of records of cases that played out in the municipality that neighbored Hrozenkov, albeit over a border. She spent the whole day leafing through these. And her leafing was not in vain. Some Slovak citizens, too, had believed that the activities of the goddesses had worked to their detriment. The many cases included accusations of unsuccessful treatment, an official complaint citing defamation of character made by a man who had been declared a thief, and a petition for the sale of herbs that had proved ineffective as a bringer of beauty. Then at last, as she was going through records of criminal acts from the late 1920s, she tracked down Mahdalka.

The "Crime" column stated: *"Josefína Mahdalová: 1927/234-SkS/ Aug. 26—attempted murder."* With a trembling hand, she filled in a requisition form.

Although it took several weeks, the archive of Trenčín District Police Station did indeed come up with a folder containing records of unresolved cases from the year 1927.

Skalica Police Station
no. 234-SkS/26.8.1927

Statement by Magdaléna Mĺkva claiming that her husband Izidor Mĺkvy (dec. Aug. 7, 1927) was killed by Josefína Mahdalová and Alžbeta Baleková
Record of interview with witness

> I, Magdaléna Mĺkva, born Magdaléna Kavková on July 3, 1905, resident in Skalica, declare that five years ago, when I was as yet unmarried, my relationship with my future husband Izidor Mĺkvy was already of an

advanced nature. The relationship was not without consequence. Since I was still young, my pregnancy caused me to feel great shame, and I mentioned it to nobody. On the advice of my godmother Alžbeta Baleková, I sought out the witch Mahdalová, who lives in Kopanice, as Baleková told me that only Mahdalová could help me with the unwanted child. I went to Mahdalová in early April, in the fourth month of my pregnancy. I told my parents that my godmother and I would be paying a visit to friends of hers, to which they had no objection. That Friday Baleková and I went to see Mahdalová. As Baleková had told Mahdalová to expect us and what we were coming about, she began with her witchcraft straightaway. She made her husband leave the cottage, and then we poured hot water into a tub she had ready. They immersed me in this up to my neck. They had me drink something that tasted of tobacco and nutmeg. There were other herbs in it, too—I saw Mahdalová boiling them all up—but I can't remember what they were. After an hour or two when I kept drinking the liquid and they kept pouring hot water into the tub I was in, the fetus left me. After that I was allowed to stand and dry myself. For safety's sake we stayed with Mahdalová on Saturday, as I was feeling weak. We left early on Sunday morning, by which time I was well. For this service I paid 110 crowns and promised to send five cubits of white cloth, which I did as soon as I got home. This took place in 1922, the year before I married the above-mentioned Izidor Mlkvy. A year after the wedding, our son Justín was born; he was perfectly healthy and of normal development. I began to work hard again almost immediately after the birth. As a consequence of this, my uterus dropped, whereupon I began to suffer severe pain during marital intercourse, which I then tried to avoid, making my husband resentful. We began to quarrel, and soon he started to drink and then to beat me. Eventually he found another woman.

I took this problem to my godmother Baleková, who suggested that we pay another visit to the witch Mahdalová, which we did, although I told my husband that we were visiting relatives in Brno. Mahdalová assured me that I had nothing more to fear from my husband and that she would help me to be rid of him. At first I was afraid, but both Baleková and Mahdalová assured me that no one would see through it; it would appear that my husband had died of natural causes. Baleková then reminded me that it had been two years since her husband had died of a stroke and that no one had suggested that his death had come any earlier than God had wished it, whereupon Baleková and Mahdalová laughed and I realized that they had experience with this kind of thing.

Mahdalová's sorcery proceeded as follows: into a blend of earth, wax, and other things she had ready on the range, she dropped hair and nail clippings from my husband, which Baleková had told me to bring with me. She added something to the mix and said some words over it that Baleková and I did not hear because we were sitting in a corner of the cottage at the table, where I was sewing, making an undergarment of my husband's into a shirt. Then I had to make the mix Mahdalová had prepared into a doll with the shape of a man and dress it in the shirt I had sewn with my own hands. After that we waited for midnight. The whole evening Mahdalová had some special smoke running through the cottage, and we were all drinking brandy, so as midnight approached, we were feeling tired and sluggish. I couldn't say what was caused by the brandy and what by the herbal fumes. At midnight Mahdalová pushed the doll toward me and ordered me to stick pins and needles into it, and to stab and claw at it in the place where the heart would be. When I hesitated because I was afraid, Mahdalová took the doll and did this instead of me, all the time chanting words I do not remember; all I know is that there was something in them about releasing the soul. Then, using a candle, we set fire to all four of the doll's limbs, soaked it in water, and set fire to it again. Then we went out into the woods and dropped the doll on an anthill. Then we went to bed.

In the morning, Mahdalová poured out the water that remained in the pot after the boiling of the doll and gave it to me with the instruction that I should put drops of it into my husband's food on nine consecutive days. She also instructed me to give her 180 crowns for nine masses, to be served on the days when I put the drops into my husband's food. I gave this money to Mahdalová, as well as five cubits of cloth, which she demanded on top. Then we went back home, where, over nine days, I did as Mahdalová had instructed. A month later my husband died of a heart attack, although he was only thirty-four years old. This scared me so much that every day I went to the home of Baleková, where I wept and said that we could not leave it like this, we had to report it, I had to turn myself in, if God would not stop Mahdalová, then the police should, as her sorcery was very dangerous. Baleková implored me not to go anywhere, even to confession, and to tell no one, as by so doing I would do harm to her, myself, and Justín, and in any case, I could not make it right. I could not bear it, however, and still wanted to go to the police. When I told Baleková this, she said that if I did that, she would go to Mahdalová and that the next person to suffer a stroke would be me. This scared me out of my wits, and I hardly knew what to do. When I found out that Baleková was again visiting relatives in Brno, although I knew no such relatives existed, I thought she must have gone to the witch in Kopanice. So on August 26, I have come here to the station, where I am reporting what happened. I am confessing my guilt in the murder of my husband and sincerely wish to atone for my deed. All I ask is that my son, Justín, be entrusted to the care of my parents, Jozef Kavka and Anna Kavková, in Skalica.

Signed by Magdaléna Mĺkva

Notice from Skalica Police Station
no. 234-Sks/29.8.1927
For Drietoma Police Station

Please find in the enclosure a transcript of a statement about the activities of Jozefína Mahdalová, resident of Drietoma-Potočná. Please verify its contents and inform us of the results of the verification at your very earliest convenience.

Signed: Sgt. Krejza, head of station

Notice from Drietoma Police Station
no. 234-Sks/12.9.1927
For Skalica Police Station

On September 10, 1927, an interview was conducted with Jozefína Mahdalová, née Surmenová, pertaining to case no. 234-SkS/29.8.1927.

Mahdalová denied that she knew Magdaléna Mĺkva, and she denied that she had ever received a visit from the above-named. On the day given by Mĺkva in her statement, Mahdalová claimed to have been in the field, where she was working with her family. This claim was corroborated by her husband, Ján Mahdal, and her mother-in-law, who lives in the same household. We confirm that the Mahdals cultivate a field of approx. 1.5 ha by the labor of the three adult persons named above.

Further, we report that Jozefína Mahdalová is known in the town of her residence as a practitioner of some sort of magic and that she is feared and referred to as a "witch." For this reason, it is known that she often receives visits from people from the locality and elsewhere; she claims that she helps these people.

Mahdalová has been questioned several times previously in connection with criminal acts pertaining to her activities, specifically in 1919 concerning the suicide of a woman possessed by an evil spirit; in 1922 in the case of bodily injury (broken neck) sustained by and the subsequent death of a man from Horná Súča, whose horse she allegedly bewitched and frightened; in 1925 concerning the spread of an infectious disease; and in 1926 concerning an act of arson. Mahdalová's involvement in any of the above-mentioned crimes has not been proved.

Signed: Sgt. Lukšo, head of station

**Skalica Police Station
no. 234-Sks/23.9.1927**

Application for deferral of a case

On August 26, 1927, Magdaléna Mĺkva, née Kavková, visited the Skalica Police Station to report a criminal act of murder whose victim was her husband, Izidor Mĺkvy, who died of heart failure on August 7, 1927. Mĺkva stated that she was a co-perpetrator of this crime and that her fellow perpetrators were Alžbeta Baleková of Skalica and Jozefína Mahdalová of Drietoma-Potočná. She alleged that the act had been planned by Mahdalová, who had prepared a potion that Mĺkva then put in the food of the deceased.

The investigation conducted by Sgt. Lukšo of the Drietoma Police Station has not proved that Mahdalová knows or has even met Mĺkva or Baleková.

The investigation conducted by Sgt. Krejza of the Skalica Police Station has not proved that Baleková knows or has ever visited Mahdalová.

Baleková confirmed that Mĺkva had often come to her to complain about her life with her husband, Izidor Mĺkvy, which had brought her great suffering; according to Baleková, Mĺkva had often said that it would drive her mad. Baleková stated that Mĺkva had seemed to her to bě mentally unstable and that her state had worsened after her husband, Izidor Mĺkvy, had allegedly taken a mistress. Baleková did not know who this mistress was. Further, Baleková stated that in recent years, she had several times been to Brno to visit a relative, namely, Rozálie Píšová, resident on Koliště Street, at whose home she had once spent the night with Mlkva.

An investigation conducted by Sgt. Benda of the Police Station for the Province of Moravia in Brno has proved that the above-mentioned Píšová is Baleková's cousin and that Baleková indeed visited her and stayed at her home overnight on the date given by Mlkva.

A medical report written by Dr. Stejnohom of the town health center in Skalica confirmed that Izidor Mlkvy's cause of death was heart failure. An additional postmortem examination showed that Mlkvy had had a defective heart valve and that death by heart failure was inevitable.

Thus the claims made by Magdaléna Mlkva in her statement were not proved. Owing to the fact that Mlkva died while the investigation was in progress—on September 21, 1927, due to a traffic accident—it was not possible to present her with the results of the investigation.

We recommend that case no. 234-SkS/29.8.1927 be deferred.

Signed: Sgt. Krejza, head of station

Dora snapped shut the folder and then sat still, just looking at it. An accident?

Did the deaths of Izidor and Magdaléna represent a coincidence? Would they have happened like this if Mlkva had not been to see Mahdalka? Sergeant Krejza had obviously thought so. His world was built on rational foundations and governed by indisputable physical laws. There was no place in it for witchcraft. Dora, too, lived in such a world. Indeed, the world of Dora the academic had the same firm lines as the world of Sergeant Krejza. But Dora's Kopanice world was different; behind the walls of strict order and distinct, tangible things, there was something else, something beyond the world of clear dimensions. Something that led her to believe that the concurrence of so many remarkable events could not be coincidental. The little white snake was gnawing at her.

When she left the archive, she was convinced that there really was something behind the talk of evil that had slumbered in Mahdalka. And she couldn't shake the feeling that that evil also applied to her.

Part III

The Blue Folder

Almost a year had passed since the Pardubice archive had made copies of the contents of the blue folder for Dora, a slim document enclosed right at the back of Surmena's file. For almost a year, she had known that what she had believed for over twenty years was not true.

In the course of that year, she had returned several times to the blue folder. She had read its contents carefully and searched for literature available in the Czech Republic that might shed some light on their context. Surprisingly, there was very little of it—just sketchy reports, fragments, nothing that comprised complete information.

On the internet she found rather more: records of studies in the German professional press, such as *Historische Zeitschrift* and *Zeitschrift für Historische Forschung*, copies of which she could read at the Deutsche Nationalbibliothek in Leipzig; several tabloid articles that mentioned the archive of the witch trials in Poznań; brief information on the archive's website written in Polish. Poznań's Archiwum Państwowego had gathered quite a lot of material. She spent several days plowing through the catalogues before realizing that she wasn't going to find an answer to the question she was asking. She abandoned her vain quest and submitted a general query email through the site. Then she waited.

Now, after a sparse exchange of letters lasting several months, she could truly appreciate the flexibility of Czech archive institutions and the staff's willingness to help. Indicative of these high Czech standards were Mr. Bergmann at the archive in Uherské Hradiště, who worked into the night, helping her go through stacks of written records he had brought to her on eight overloaded carts, and Mrs. Borová of the Wallachian Museum, who stayed on beyond her working hours in order to send Dora photographs of documents from the late eighteenth century concerning the locally held trial of a goddess who had been moved there from Žítková. Or was it that a mention of the goddesses of Žítková worked some kind of humanizing effect? This seemed to be the case when she made a call to a certain regional museum and had the feeling her words worked like a magic spell.

"We don't usually do this, but as you say, you're doing research, so let me take a look for you," said the archivist on the other end of the line. "My grandmother told me about them, you know, when I was a child. I was fascinated by what they could do. Will you let us know when you finish your work?"

For her answer from the archive in Poznań, however, Dora had to wait a month. But after those four weeks of uncertainty, during which she began to wonder if she had written to an address that was no longer current, she got her first message, and the correspondence was up and running. Printouts of those letters were now piled in her lap, as were the copied contents of the blue folder from Surmena's file in their entirety, which she was giving a cursory reading. She was sitting on a bus, the nighttime service from Brno to Poznań, which would bump its way north for the next nine hours.

The aged Czech-made Karosa, which differed from those used on domestic lines only insofar as it had reclining seats, crawled along the narrow county roads, through the towns of Svitavy and Litomyšl, before entering the mountains, where it bounced along a badly maintained road and occasionally tossed back Dora's head and caused her eyes to slip from the undulating lines of print.

STRICTLY CONFIDENTIAL
Certified translation of an accompanying letter found at the site of the Zlín headquarters of the Gestapo; card index file D
For original, *vide* GODDESSES file

Mein Reichsführer,

I am sending present results of field research in the borderlands of Moravia and Slovakia, which verify fully the premise of the existence of an autochthonous German population and of the mystical practices of local women who apparently are personified relics of Old Germanic natural gnosis. The rituals the women engage in and the knowledge at their disposal seem to be—although the women do not realize this to be so—modified and modernized versions of Aryo-Germanic customs and magical rites as we have succeeded in reconstructing them from the Edda Teutonic sagas and as described by Guido von List in his studies on the Wotan priesthood. Many of the rituals practiced by the so-called "goddesses" in their magical ceremonies are consistent with descriptions of rites defined by von List in his groundbreaking *Die Rita der Ario-Germanen* and developed by Lanz von Liebenfels and other Aryosophists.

Mein Reichsführer, we have before us unique and wholly viable evidence stemming from prehistoric times, which, owing to adverse natural and social circumstances, is in a state of perfect preservation. It is possible that these women represent a devalued remnant of the Armanenschaft, while the place in which they live shows all signs of the exalted Halgadom, and the composition of the local language contains whole elements of German. If our hypothesis is confirmed, we have achieved a staggering and groundbreaking discovery that will underscore the direction in which we are heading, demonstrate the power of a Teutonic element that held firm over centuries of subversive Judeo-Christian imports, and above all demonstrate the authenticity of this race the length and breadth of Europe; it will also enlighten us on many hitherto unknown points concerning the original Aryo-Germanic people.

Please receive in the documentation compiled by SS-Sturmbannführer F. F. Norfolk all records on the anatomical sufficiency of persons living here, including data from craniological research. Sturmbannführer F. F. Norfolk remains in the field in order to conduct more detailed research on the Hexenwesen under observation. Thanks to his study in progress, you will in the near future be able to acquaint yourself with the definitions and organization of practices that these beings apply in their visionary and healing activities. My study, which is also a work in progress, will contain documentation (including statistics) compiled on the basis of research found in the archives of the Protectorate on the subject of the witch trials held on the territory of the Protectorate of Bohemia and Moravia. In other countries of the Reich, the rest of the Hexen-Sonderauftrag task force continues to conduct its research; I shall acquaint you with its conclusions in the interim report that we are preparing for issue at the end of this year.

In respect to the momentousness of the discovery of Hexenwesen in Starý Hrozenkov and the importance of this discovery for the Reich, I recommend the retention at the Starý Hrozenkov site of a research company of at least two members so that it may perform the monitoring of the subjects under observation (the Hexenwesen Fuksena and women of the Mahdal line, Surmena, Krasňačka a.k.a. Polka, and Struhárka a.k.a. Chupatá). I will be in a position to submit a personal report with interim results of the work of this team in the course of the coming month, which I will spend at Ahnenerbe headquarters in Berlin.

Eternal glory to the Reich! Heil!

SS-Obersturmbannführer Dr. Rudolf Levin

SD-Außendienstelle Zlin, Protektorat Böhmen und Mähren

Aus Alt Hrosenkau, den Juli 11, 1942

STRICTLY CONFIDENTIAL
For original, *vide* GODDESSES file
Authors: Assoc. Prof. Věnceslav Rozmazal, CSc, Prof. Rudolf Vejrosta, CSc
Department of Ethnography and Department of History, Moravian Museum, Brno
November 12, 1949

Statement

On the basis of a letter by Dr. Rudolf Levin of the SS, which was entrusted to me for appraisal by Comrade XXXXXXXXX on June 17, 1948, inclusive of a translation into Czech, I have, in cooperation with Professor Rudolf Vejrosta of the Department of History of the Moravian Museum, produced the following statement on the research intentions of the aforementioned National Socialist researcher.

References in the letter make it clear that the research project conducted by Dr. Levin's team was concentrated on selected women from the Moravské Kopanice area. These women are known as "goddesses."

From the point of view of research workers today, these intentions are very surprising, not least for the emphasis Levin and his superiors placed on issues that our ethnology considers to be marginal to such a degree that no academic has ever paid close attention to them.

There are but two possible explanations for this: (1) that the true nature of their research remains hidden from us and that during the war, these enemies of world peace found themselves in a position of such desperation that they had no hesitation in engaging a team composed of several pseudoscientists whose research on superstitious charlatans in the White Carpathians should support the claims of the Third Reich to the European space, as we infer from several references to theories of autochthony; (2) a surmise based on interpretation of the contours of Dr. Levin's research that draws on the contents of his letter, as outlined in the paragraphs below.

Area of research interest: MORAVSKÉ KOPANICE
Historical and anthropological excursion

Moravské Kopanice is located on the border of Moravia and Slovakia and comprises a small number of villages that are scattered about the slopes of the White Carpathians. This is an area in which traditions of folklore are vigorously upheld and where such traditions remain in fully archaic form, mainly owing to the fact it is largely isolated from the outside world. The standard of living of the people there today borders on poverty, as this is an area of no natural or economic potential; a lack of education prevails (according to the last prewar statistics, while the rate of illiteracy in 1930 in the First Czechoslovak Republic as a whole was 13.2 percent, in Kopanice it stood at 52 percent); and the rhythm of the life of the local population is determined by the Catholic Church, which has strong roots there, and folk customs that follow the course of the year. As to these customs, the "goddesses" under investigation, bearers of specific rituals that are practiced on specific occasions, play an indispensable role.

Subject of research: GODDESSES

In the region in question, the subjects of the investigation are widely believed to have uncommon abilities that allow them to heal illnesses in humans and animals, see into the past and the future, and reveal information hidden to ordinary people. They are known to our ethnology through ethnographical publications that include works by Václavík, Bartoš, Dúbravský, and Niederle. On a nonacademic level, this group is complemented by a collection of short stories set in the Kopanice area by Josef Hofer, who was a priest in Starý Hrozenkov; a reference in a novel by Alois Jirásek, and the popular book *Gabra and Málinka* by well-known author Amálie Kutinová.

It is owing to their purported abilities (which, from the viewpoint of scientific materialism, are a simple

fraud that has endured only thanks to the obscurantism of the local population) that these women came
to and held the attention of the researchers Levin and
Norfolk.

As can be inferred from Levin's letter, he believes
the subjects of the investigation to be representatives of an indigenous, autochthonous population
assumed by National Socialist historiography to survive in small enclaves in largely mountainous regions
with low accessibility. These enclaves survived even
after the region was settled by the Slavs in the fifth
and sixth centuries and the Germanic population then
displaced. Autochthonous theory tells us that these
Moravian mountain dwellers may be descendants of
the Germanic Markoman tribe, whose presence in the
region is documented to the first century AD. Due to
the Germans' well-known inclination to build a heroic
mythology for themselves and an adoration of its oc-
cult and esoteric aspects that verges on the perverse, I
believe that the research team may have constructed a
far more extensive premise for the significance of these
goddesses than mere confirmation of autochthonous
theory. Judging by Levin's enthusiasm and emphasis
on the significance of the discovery and what his team
established about the lives of these women, it is as
though he were writing of Norns rather than simple
citizens in a rural community, their special abilities and
Germanic origin notwithstanding.

It should at this point be noted that on the basis
of our scholarly inquiry, we, the assessors, have established the existence of a conflict in the intentions (as

we assume these to be, as they are not expressed in the letter) and the findings.

It is generally known that the social organization of German aggression has always, even in Old Germanic mythology, been founded on strongly patriarchal patterns. Although Germanic mythology (much emphasized by Levin in his references to Aryosophism) shows us many goddesses who played an important part in the system of religion, and European anthropology presents instances of priestesses who were indispensable to Germanic tribal organization, we are puzzled by the fact that the National Socialist leadership was welcoming of research that would corroborate a position for German women as known from the context of Moravské Kopanice. Conditions there are founded on a deep respect for motherhood and the feminine principle per se, as proved by the respect in which the subjects of the investigation and women in general are held. It is not uncommon for a man there to move his place of residence to the cottage home of a woman, and the contempt for women who give birth out of wedlock that is typical elsewhere is altogether absent there. The community's female principals occupy positions at the tip of the social pyramid as they provide essential functions in many of life's more difficult situations: of midwife, of healer familiar with the effects of a great variety of herbs, as advisors and decision-making authorities in the resolution of disputes between local residents, in which they apply some kind of divination.

Had the research team of Dr. Levin published these research findings highlighting the feminine principle, such an act might have been interpreted as the conservation of the status of a hierarchy typical of an Old Germanic community; from our point of view, this would necessarily result in the destabilization of the functioning patriarchal principle that existed in the Third Reich. Owing to a dearth of information in the material supplied, we are not able to provide a satisfactory explanation for this apparent conflict of interests. Hence the true breadth of the research intention remains unknown.

Evidence of the Germanic origin of the subjects of investigation

In several places in the letter, there is mention of autochthonous theory and how study of the goddesses of Kopanice could serve to support this. The most important basis of this theory should be proof of the Aryan origin of the goddesses, to be demonstrated by results of craniological measurement.

It needs to be stated here that there is no question that uniformed members of the SS could not have performed extensive craniological measurement without the knowledge of the subjects of the measurement. It follows from this that if the subjects of investigation indeed underwent this measurement—as the letter testifies—at least to some extent, they must have been apprised of the research intentions of National Socialist scientists, and there must have been direct personal contact, and thus cooperation, between them.

It can be concluded from this that those of the goddesses who were measured were declared sufficiently long-headed (of the dolichocephalic skull type, which is elongated and narrower at the back, thus in concurrence with typical German anthropometry) and that they had blonde hair and fair skin, blue or light-brown eyes, and a tall, slender figure. In order to be declared sufficient, these women must have become volunteer or paid collaborators of this hostile team of researchers.

Dr. Levin also refers to the linguistic specificities of the region. This question could be addressed adequately only in an independent study by a specialist in comparative linguistics. On the basis of my own experience of the Moravské Kopanice region, I can state that the local language, known as "Kopanice speech," in some instances stands beyond other so-called Slavonic dialects to which the group of dialects of southern Moravia belongs. Exceptions occur, for instance, in word formation, which draws on many expressions from German, and in syntax, which contains interrogative sentences that are formed in accordance with German-language sentence formation.

Conclusion: An outline of research intent and its practical application

We consider the original research intention to be verification of the autochthonous theory of the preservation of a Germanic population in Moravia, which was one of the main and most well-known motivations of research supported directly from Amt VII—Weltanschauliche Forschung und Auswertung, the office by which, we believe, the activities of the Ahnenerbe (an organization with which we were hitherto unfamiliar, whose representative was Dr. Levin) were covered. This research was particularly important for reasons of propaganda; ultimately, it could serve for defense of the claims of the Third Reich to the Central European space.

In the White Carpathians, Dr. Levin's research team found territorial conditions in which selected members of the population possessed physiognomies that verified their theory; in addition, the subjects were adjudged to possess abilities that came to form the basis of a theory on the survival of Old Germanic priestesses. Their further research should, in the words of Dr. Levin, "enlighten us on many hitherto unknown points concerning the original Aryo-Germanic people." Subsequent research by this National Socialist research team was performed in the context of mythology, history, and Aryosophist philosophy, entailing archive study on the subject of the hunting of witches, as these women were often termed in the past.

As to the exact characteristics and direction of this research, on the basis of the short text available to us, which is no more than an interim report on the research performed on selected women, we are not in a position to offer a conclusion. For us to reach such a conclusion, it would be necessary for us to acquaint ourselves with the two studies contained in the dispatches to which Dr. Levin refers.

In conclusion, it remains to be stated that in the context of recent wartime events, we can imagine vividly the deep significance that National Socialism and its main representatives (to whom the letter is evidently addressed) would attach to such an all-encompassing idea and factual evidence in support of it. It would certainly be possible to use this for purposes of mass propaganda in justification of aggressive National

Socialist policy, on both a historically horizontal level (liberation of the Volksdeutsche of the day and their return to the homeland) and a vertical level (the region's age-old affiliation to the Third Reich). Thus we consider the use of autochthonous theory for propaganda purposes and the seeking out of individuals to corroborate this theory to be the main reason for the support given by leading representatives of the Third Reich to Dr. Levin's research team.

Uherské Hradiště District Department of State Security, Third Division

On the basis of the above statement by Assoc. Prof. Věnceslav Rozmazal, CSc, I deem it necessary that a survey be conducted on the activities of the subjects of interest of the hostile research team of Dr. Rudolf Levin, namely:

KRASŇÁKOVÁ, Žofie, a.k.a. Krasňačka or Polka
MAHDALOVÁ, Josefína, a.k.a. Mahdalka the Elder
MAHDALOVÁ, Marie, a.k.a. young Mahdalka
SURMENOVÁ, Terézie, a.k.a. Surmena

Due to the above-mentioned voluntary cooperation with an SS research team, we assume that these persons had a positive attitude to National Socialist ideology that was not revealed in the immediate aftermath of the war. The above-mentioned persons thus represent a serious threat to our people's democratic republic because they may still be points of contact for foreign intelligence agencies that could make use of their wide network of clients.

The examination of the above-named citizens shall be concentrated on their activities and connections in the period of the National Socialist occupation and also on their activities since 1945. This inquiry shall be carried out by local organs of security (in this district, the Department of State Security in Uherský Brod) in such a manner that the subjects do not realize that they are being investigated. The local National Committee office shall prepare a report on the reputations of these persons—ref. "Anti-state activities of the GODDESSES group"—to be delivered to the officer of the Third Division responsible within one month of the opening of the inquiry.

Officer responsible: Švanc

September 17, 1950

Hexenarchiv

Dora had thought that the interior of the building in which Poznań's archive was housed would be caught in the vise-like grip of the Middle Ages. She had imagined walls decorated with images from the torture chamber and sketches from the hangman's manual, perhaps even an exhibition of instruments of torture. She entered the building with anxiety that would be tantamount to that of a victim of the rack.

She was rung in at the automatic door to find herself in the bright hallway of a slightly shabby building with a patina of the 1980s, when the archive was founded. There was no sign or evidence of dramatic events connected with witch hunts. She took the elevator up to the reading room, which was in no way different from its Czech counterparts. The man behind the glass of the issue counter corresponded exactly with her idea of what archive staff should look like. He beckoned to her—she was alone in the reading room at that time—and pushed the visitors' book under the glass toward her. She filled in all the columns he indicated with his finger.

Her Polish–Czech dictionary in hand, she asked slowly and clearly for the card index for witch trials that concerned Moravia. The man nodded. A short while later, he set down before her the complete inventory of the collection and other subinventories divided by dates of trials and limited geographically to the territory of the Czech lands, including Silesia. Uncertainly, she reached for the first few pages. The introductory text to the collection was in Polish, but a little further on, she found a German translation of it. This was a great relief to her; although Polish has a lot in common with Czech, she found German much easier to understand. Her eyes started to move across the lines.

Hexen-Sonderauftrag

The Hexen-Sonderauftrag (Hex-SAT) collection, which contains files with specific information on individual witch trials dating from the ninth to the eighteenth centuries, is the result of nine years of work by the SS-Hexen-Sonderkommando unit. This special unit was part of the Seventh Division (Weltanschauliche Forschung und Auswertung) of Himmler's Reich Security Main Office (Reichssicherheitshauptamt), which concentrated on historical research. The work of the Seventh Division was pursued further by other divisions, whose task it was to put its theoretical conclusions into practice. The main issue was the taking of steps toward a historical justification of the superiority of the Germanic race, whose leading representatives should be confirmed by intensive genealogical research as descendants of Old Germanic rulers with roots reaching back into Germanic mythology. The eugenic singularity of the Germanic race should then be reinforced by the ensuring of its purity (so-called "racial hygiene") and freeing from the influence of entities hostile to the Übermensch. The entities were divided into three categories (from genetic to ideological) whose ordering respected the ordering of materials of the Hex-SAT collection.

I. Hostile races

II. Enemies of the nation

III. Politico-ideological enemies

   a. Church

   b. Freemasons

   c. Communists

Dora went straight to Part III(a).

Activities of SS-Hexen-Sonderkommando related to the theory of attempts by the Church to annihilate the Nordic race are archived in the Hex-SAT collection under inventory no. III(a), comprising 4,017 boxes with registration numbers Hex-12-c/1.1935—Hex-12-c/312.1944. The boxes are sorted into thematic groups that coincide with the thematic areas of activity of SS-Hexen-Sonderkommando.

Sorting of inventory III(a):

1. Materials on particular witch trials

Heinrich Himmler intended to make use of these materials as an instrument of anti-Church propaganda. In a planned trial, the Church was to be demonstratively found guilty of conspiracy against Germanic women, millions of whom it was alleged to have murdered in witch trials over several centuries, and also against the Germanic race, whose dissemination it sought to hinder. It contains cards on particular trials with detailed information on the murder victims, including descriptions of trials obtained from the black books of particular towns. This provides evidence that in these trials, the Church prosecuted mainly women who deliberately cultivated Old Germanic gnosis. Dates: 850–1785 AD.

2. Materials on research of Old Germanic rituals whose practices were generated by studies of the witch trials collected in III(a)(1)

Essays, studies, notes by members of the research team, photographic material.

3. Materials on practices of torture used during witch trials; studies on instruments and methods of torture

Descriptions, studies, notes for Heinrich Himmler recommending the use of certain procedures within SS activities.

4. Character of Old Germanic gnosis today

Materials on research concentrated on the seeking out of surviving relics of Old Germanic religious practice. White Carpathians region, Protektorat Böhmen und Mähren; dates: 1940–1944 AD.

Dora skimmed a few more pages about what the collection contained. The movement of her eyes across the lines slowed at a detailed description of the history and activities of the Sonderkommando.

SS-Hexen-Sonderkommando (also known as Hexenkommando only) was founded officially in 1935, becoming a part of the Reichssicherheitshauptamt (RSHA) and, as such, falling under the direct command of Heinrich Himmler. It was housed at Wilhelmstraße 102, where the first card index was created.

The Kommando was commissioned to perform research on witch trials conducted in the Middle Ages and early modern times under the leadership of Dr. Rudolf Levin, who had at his disposal a team of eighteen experts, most of whom had university degrees in history. Each of these researchers was responsible for one of the regions of Germany (and later also the occupied territories), in which they were required to conduct research. Research should produce exact statistics on executions performed as part of the witch hunts, including descriptions of circumstances in which trials were held.

For purposes of research, Dr. Levin produced a manual with precise details of procedure that included several different comprehensive form-type cards into which details of trials should be entered.

Each card (Hexen-Blätter, A4 format) contains fifty-seven questions that determine the name, surname, age, confession, and family and social circumstances of the victim, plus questions concerning the process of the trial, the name of the main prosecutor (inquisitor), the estate of the victim as forfeited to the court, etc. Not all cards could be completed to the full extent; in many instances it proved impossible to gather relevant information on a trial held several centuries previously. Other cards, however, are supplemented with several pages of precise descriptions of a trial, including witness statements and/or writings of a local clerk who was reflecting on the trial after the event.

The material discovered by members of the Kommando in the course of their research in the archives of particular towns in the Reich and the Protectorate (especially in black books, blood books, court records, etc.), and which today is comprised in III(a)(1), grew over the years to a total of 33,846 cards.

In the course of the nine-year existence of the Kommando, these 33,846 cards were allocated to

3,670 folders, of which 3,622 have been preserved to this day. They contain information on trials conducted between the ninth century and 1944, mainly in German lands but also in Belgium, Czechoslovakia, Denmark, England, Estonia, France, Greece, Hungary, Iceland, Ireland, Lithuania, the Netherlands, Norway, Poland, Portugal, Romania, Russia, Scotland, Spain, Sweden, Switzerland, Yugoslavia, and even India, Mexico, Transylvania, Turkey, and the USA.

In its later years, the Kommando concerned itself primarily with issues collected in III(a)(2)–(4), with the greater number of its activities generated by Dr. Rudolf Levin, whose intention it was to sit for a higher doctor's degree at the Faculty of Arts of the Ludwig Maximilian University of Munich, and Dr. F. F. Norfolk, at that time a successful writer from the Sudetenland of Moravia, who actively published professional literature and fiction, much of which addressed the survival of an archaic cult surrounding witchlike beings (Hexenwesen).

Nevertheless, the activities of the Hexenkommando lagged behind its stated objectives. One cause of this was a lack of professional ability on the part of researchers, although the main failing was the setting of aims that were too high and thus unattainable. There was an absurdly exaggerated estimate that 9,500,000 German women had been executed at the initiation of the Church in the course of a witch hunt lasting several centuries, as stated by Alfred Rosenberg (and before him Mathilde Ludendorff, albeit without recourse to figures) but unsupported by argument. The Hexenkommando never succeeded in substantiating the estimate. Its research was able to establish only tens of thousands of executions, which RSHA leaders considered a professional failure. For this reason the activities of the SS-Hexen-Sonderkommando research team were officially wound up on Himmler's orders in early 1944.

In defense of the research team, we should add that it was very difficult to find material in a Europe afflicted by war, while correspondence shows that individual researchers came up against slow and reluctant cooperation on the part of the archives they addressed. The material that Dr. Levin's team succeeded in securing was acquired on the basis of protracted negotiations with archives, antique dealers, traders in archivalia and old prints, etc. Of interest in this connection is the matter of a black market for archivalia, for which Levin solicited funds from the RSHA. For the forging of archivalia borrowed from state archives, see records on proceedings at the Nuremberg trials, re testimony of inmate of Sachsenhausen concentration camp Herbert Blank; further, see ledgers of SS-Hexen-Sonderkommando, inv. no. V(a)–V(b).

The last records of the activities of the research team are from January/February 1944, although some researchers continued to correspond after this; such correspondence is contained in card index no. VII, sorted in alphabetical order by researcher's surname (VII[a]–VII[m]).

It is probable that the extensive archive of the SS-Hexen-Sonderkommando was evacuated and hidden by one of its members in the final year of the war. In 1946 it was discovered in Sława Śląska on the territory of today's Polish Republic and filed in Archiwum Państwowego in Poznań. A copy of the archive can be found in the state archive in Frankfurt am Main.

Until 1985, documents of the collection were professionally processed and folioed; in 1987 a collection entitled "Kartoteka procesów o czary" (Card index for witch trials) was made available to the public.

Dora returned to the counter and asked the polite archivist, a small man with round glasses, to produce the whole of section III(a)(4) as well as personnel files VII(a) to VII(m).

"Everything?"

"Everything," Dora replied.

"I can get ahold of section III soon enough, but the personnel files will take a little longer to prepare. Until about three o'clock. Are you able to wait?"

"I'll wait."

The File of Hexenwesen Surmenová

*D*ora took a short break over a cup of vending-machine coffee before the archivist handed her several squat paper boxes. Some contained just a few scraps of paper, whereas others were much heavier. She was tense; in the next few moments, she might uncover the secrets of women she knew or had known in Kopanice. And maybe the secrets would be Surmena's.

She placed the boxes carefully on the desk and studied their labels. Hexenwesen Gabrhelová, Krasňáková, Mahdalová, Struhárová. At last she lifted the lid of the box labeled "Hexenwesen Surmenová."

It contained a slim dossier; its pages were bound together at the sides with decomposing string. Eagerly, she fished it out, untied the ribbon, and opened the cardboard cover. The title page stated:

III(a)(4) Character of Old Germanic gnosis today
Materials on research concentrated on the seeking out of surviving relics of Old Germanic religious practice.
White Carpathians region, Protektorat Böhmen und Mähren; dates: 1940–1944.
TEREZIE SURMENOVA

The next page was a lengthy form sparsely filled out in an uneven hand. As she scanned its lines, Dora smiled bitterly at the German thoroughness that ensured no detail of the life of the person under observation remained a secret. There was no comparison between this and Surmena's Czechoslovak State Security Police file; where the official in charge of the Czechoslovak police file corresponded with multiple sources in effortful pursuit of information on his subject, German investigators got by with preprinted columns that were eerily similar to the Hexen-Blätter used for the confessions of witches four centuries earlier, illustrations of which she had just seen, although somewhere along the line, their theme had been transformed.

She flicked through the form concerning Surmena's case, checking data that, according to the entry in the box for the name of the investigating research worker, had been compiled by F. F. Norfolk.

Surname: SURMENOVA
Christian name: TEREZIE
Born: July 24, 1910
Status: single, runs a household
Place of residence: Schitkowa 28 (Alt Hrosenkau, Kopanice), Bedowa hill
Specializations: healing, remedying fractures, herbalism, divination, repelling storms
Category: A

There followed a description of the subject inclusive of previously determined information, all of which was known to Dora: about Surmena's family background, her siblings, her lack of basic education, the strength of her faith in God and her regular church attendance, her relationship with Ruchár (who at that time was a regular visitor to the Bedová), her living in the cottage only with her sister Irena since the deaths of their parents. Irena, Dora's mother. Excitedly, Dora ran her fingertip along the lines, searching for further mention of Irena Surmenová, who at that time would have been about seventeen. She found nothing. It appeared that the younger sister of Hexenwesen Surmena had not been placed in Category A. Disappointed, she gave up on the form.

Beneath this was another sheet with an Ahnenerbe letterhead, this one for craniological data. It was blank. Dora was surprised that the sight of an uncompleted form could affect her like this; then she sighed with relief. So Surmena had not collaborated with them. Surmena was clean, she told herself several times.

With a feeling of triumph, she proceeded through the dossier until she came to some photographs glued to an A4 sheet of card. They showed their cottage on the Bedová—she recognized it immediately; it looked exactly the same today—photographed from all sides. Then a number of photographs of Surmena in various situations: in the throng at the front of the church, in the churchyard by the family grave, in front of the cottage hanging out the washing. *How pretty she was when she was young,* thought Dora; the Surmena she had known was nothing like this. Raising the photo closer to her eyes, she realized with amazement that the thickness of Surmena's shape was caused not by poor-quality photography but pregnancy. Dora knew from Surmena's file that the photo must have been taken in 1942.

Immediately beneath the photographs was a *Beobachtungsprotokoll* with a Reich eagle letterhead; this statement must have originated just a little later than the picture of the pregnant Surmena.

Beobachtungsprotokoll vom 27. Juni 1942
<u>New findings on activities</u>

On the night of June 23–24, 1942, Surmenova organized a meeting for the purpose of gathering herbs, in spite of the fact that a nighttime curfew and martial law were in force. At about 11:30 p.m., seven women residents at different smallholdings in the village of Schitkowa presented themselves at Surmenová's house, equipped with baskets and sacks. At around ten minutes after midnight, these women set out in the company of Terézie and Irena Surmenová toward the Bedová hill. Zubringer AH-12 states that on reaching the hillside, the women undressed; in their naked state, they gathered herbs until about four o'clock in the morning, at which time they dressed and walked down to Surmenová's cottage, where they left the contents of their baskets and sacks. Before daybreak, they parted and returned to their homes.

Based on further field research, it can be stated that such an action is in accordance with Saint John's Eve custom in this region, where it is believed that herbs are at their most potent between midnight and daybreak on the Feast of Saint John. The effects of the herbs are said to be stronger if they are gathered by nine, preferably naked, young virgins.

The participants in this night's activity were Irma Gabrhelová and her mother, Anna Struhárová; Kateřina Hodulíková; Žofie Krasňáková; Josefína Mahdalová, Marie Mahdalová, and their ward, Marie Pagáčová a.k.a. Fuksena (see personal files on the above-named).

The women centered around Terézie Surmenová were not apprehended during the curfew by the security authorities. We will not be reporting this breach of curfew determined in the course of our research; clearly this nighttime outing was for the pursuit of practices under our investigation, not subversive activity.

Signature: F. F. Norfolk

Dora chuckled. Then she closed her eyes and imagined Surmena and a group of naked women darting about the moonlit hillside, just as she herself had done some years later. She imagined the reporter of the Sicherheitsdienst on duty that night hiding somewhere nearby; if he was not a local person, he must have been taken aback. She imagined him pursuing the women under cover of bushes, then across open land, extolling the virtues of a dark night that allowed him to sneak up close, but also the brightness of the moon, which shone on the exposed female curves like theater lights. She saw him grabbing his fly, and she heard his hot, muffled sighs as he took in a scene at once pure and profligate. That night he would not have been complaining about the informer's cruel lot.

An elderly man entered the reading room and uttered a quiet greeting, tearing Dora from her thoughts. She glanced at her watch. If she wanted to catch the night bus to Brno—and judging by how Surmena's file was thinning out, she thought she might manage it—she would have to quicken her pace a little.

She flicked through several more Beobachtungsprotokoll statements that contained brief and uninteresting notes on observations. Surmena's baby was stillborn and buried unchristened in the family grave. Ruchár ceased to visit her home following a disagreement of some kind. And so on. Nothing truly excited Norfolk's interest, and thus all was captured in a few terse sentences.

Only much later did he give more attention to Surmena, when his term in Žítková was past the halfway point. Dora came to a more extensive Beobachtungsprotokoll, which bore a pencil inscription in its top right-hand corner: "AMULET!!"

Beobachtungsprotokoll vom 14. Oktober 1943
New findings on activities

On September 29, 1943, M. Lechová of the village of Bojkowitz was taken into custody in connection with the black market for food coupons. In the course of questioning at the station of the Zlín Gestapo, the investigating officer discovered around Lechová's neck some kind of amulet, the origin of which he attributed to one of the goddesses of Žítková. It was then established that this was a protective amulet made by Surmenová. The amulet was delivered to the H-Sonderauftrag station with the following statement for the record:

"I went to see her to relieve myself of fear. I'd been having evil thoughts. For some time I'd been having nightmares in which my husband—who died under a fall of rock at the Hrozenkov quarry over three months ago—returned to me. I couldn't sleep at night even though I was dead tired by day. Every time I closed my eyes, he made a grab for me. So I went to the goddess Surmena and asked her for help, and she gave me a mixture of herbs and told me to take it. She also gave me a pouch in which she mixed some herbs; a drop of my blood, which she took from a cut to my middle finger; and a piece of paper with something scribbled on it. All this she mixed with her finger on a piece of linen before tying it all together. She instructed me to take the herbs and wear the pouch around my neck for nine days and nine nights. Since that time I've had no more nightmares. To be on the safe side, I never take off the pouch."

The pouch in question is indeed a kind of amulet reminiscent of a phylactery, which was banned by the Church as a relic of pagan practices incompatible with a Christian conception of the true faith. The aforementioned piece of paper bears a drawing that I believe to

be derived from a rune of the Elder Futhark alphabet
that can be interpreted as "day." Included for analysis.

Signature: F. F. Norfolk

After that Norfolk paid much more careful attention to Surmena.
And he was not the only one.

The Beobachtungsprotokoll forms continued to record new, minor
findings on the customs Surmena respected. But now they were teeming
with something else: statements of denunciation that were arriving at
SD headquarters in Zlín.

*"I declare that Terézie Surmenová, who lives on the Bedowa hill in
the village of Schitkowa, receives a high untaxed income from spiritual
activities and illicit divination, a trade she has operated since her youth
and continues in today irrespective of the fact that in the Reich and the
Protectorate it represents a crime,"* stated one of the claims.

*"I declare that Terézie Surmenová, who lives on the Bedowa hill in
the village of Schitkowa, performed the illegal slaughter of a heifer in May
1942,"* stated a second.

A third claim was more serious still: *"Surmenová of the Bedowa hill
should be investigated—she is claiming that Germany will never win the
war: there will be no Endsieg. In so doing she is undermining the morale of
the people who listen to her."*

Beobachtungsprotokoll vom 6. Dezember 1943
New findings on activities

Between March 1942 and November 1943,
Surmenová's activities were denounced in a number of
statements (see enclosure). These denunciations arrive
at intervals of several months at the address of the
Zlín SD-Außendienstelle, which always and without
delay sends us a copy of the denunciation statement
to the H-Sonderkommando center at the customs

office of the finance patrol at Hrozenkov. This office has accepted our stipulation that it should not subject the person under observation to investigation that is not part of H-Sonderkommando research while said research is in progress, unless she should commit an extraordinary and unacceptable offense against the laws of the Protectorate.

We see no conflict between our approach to this case and cases of other goddesses, although in the case of Surmenová, an official procedure may be unavoidable in the future.

Investigating authorities under the leadership of SS-Sturmbannführer Reinhardt Glütschke have not yet succeeded in determining the identity of the informer. It may be that he/she is a dissatisfied client. We have been able to eliminate Jan Ruchár from our considerations: he is illiterate and thus incapable of writing letters.

Signed: F. F. Norfolk

Dora studied the rest of the denunciations carefully. The offenses they mentioned were of greater and lesser import; had it not been for protection from above, some of them would surely not have escaped the Gestapo's attention. Irma was right, and Dora had the evidence to prove it. Norfolk had taken the goddesses under his wing, and he must have been granted the authority to do so by the general staff. Thanks to him, the goddesses were untouchable.

Dora leafed through a few more Beobachtungsprotokoll statements and so came to the end of the records of Surmena's case. The last items were letters partly tucked into a too-small envelope. Judging by their stamps, these were from a time after the operations of the Kommando had been officially terminated, which explained why they were sent to Norfolk's private address, a villa on the outskirts of Leipzig.

There was no Beobachtungsprotokoll to go with these letters. In its place was a short description written on the back of the envelope:

10/9/1944: Received two documents on the case of Hexenwesen Surmenová—see Enclosures 1 and 2. Graphoanalysis performed—see Enclosure 3.

Dora pulled the enclosures out of the envelope and began to read the first of them.

ENCLOSURE 1
Letter
Addressee: F. F. Norfolk, VILA EVELYNE, Am Strand 12, Leipzig 2, Deutsches Reich
Sender: Reinhardt Glütschke, SD-Außendienstelle Zlin, Protektorat Böhmen und Mähren

> Ferdinand,
>
> I greet you warmly and look back with pleasure on your last visit. So far not a single week has gone by when I haven't dug into the recordings you brought me—especially the chants, which I've played ten times at least. Divine!
>
> Just a few days ago I received a package from Vienna with the Bach and the Haydn I was telling you about. You must come soon because I want to play them to you. When are you coming back, by the way? I was expecting you before this.
>
> Still, I can't really blame you for not turning up in the last few days. As you probably know, things have been rather unsettled here. We managed to shoot

down some American bombers above Kopanice, but the whole thing caused chaos, mainly with the mood among the population. Which is really why I'm writing.

It's about your research—specifically, two of the women you mentioned to me. I'm sorry to say that in connection with the downing of the aircraft, they became involved in a situation you would not wish to see them in. I had no choice but to put them under observation; to be frank with you, if they make one more mistake, I won't be able to get around it, as I did in the previous instances.

This time they went beyond the pale: they hid and treated an American airman—and what's more, he was a Jew. It was only because of your research that I didn't have them executed on the spot. I hardly need to describe to you the unpleasant nature of the situation I found myself in—in front of my own men, too—especially as here at the commissariat, we now have those new criminal police assistants from Charlottenburg to keep an eye on criminal activity. It was a struggle for me to defend my position, I can tell you. Thank goodness I had your Geheime Reichssache authorization, with its communiqué from the Reichsführer!

What I can't guarantee, however, is the level of personal safety of your Hexenwesen. I have reason to believe that they have something to fear—not only from us but also from the local people. I repeat: this is a fraught time here. There are partisans in the Carpathians; two weeks ago, Bandenbekämpfungsstab der ZbV-Kommandos 1, 9, and 24 began operations here; meanwhile, a variety of unidentified types keep coming over from the nearby Beskids, where the situation is worst of all. In conditions such as these, the disappearance of a woman, or more than one woman, will not be viewed as important. The main thing is, I won't find out about it in time.

The behavior of one of my Vertrauensmänner showed me just how much danger they are in. When we found the American Jew in the care of the two Hexenwesen, it was a battle for me to hold him back; the punishment of the Hexenwesen was apparently of extraordinary interest to V-Mann B-7. As I said, had I not been in command, they would have been executed summarily.

V-Mann B-7 Schwannze comes from this region. He puts a convincing case that the activities of the goddesses have been to the detriment of many people here. I would not be surprised if someone were to take advantage of the wildness of the times to settle scores with them, and I suspect that Schwannze is just such a person. The keenness of his involvement in the action against the goddesses, and the information with which he later provided me in a private interview, seem to me somewhat exaggerated. I have nevertheless assigned him the task of writing a report on the anti-state and antisocial activities of the goddesses and indicated to him that should we acknowledge the risks of these activities, he will be appointed head of a Hexen-Jagdkommando unit. You should have seen his reaction—he was bursting with pride.

I must emphasize that although the prime motivation for these Vertrauensleute from the local trash is the monthly allowance, if you give them the smallest function in the apparatus, you gain their undying and absolute loyalty. Schwannze is now the most servile officer the Zlín SD has. If our people in the Protectorate were all like him, we'd have a much calmer time of things.

I am sending you his report, which comprises five pages and attends to the smallest detail. His network of Zubringer and Gewährsmänner is broad, and he himself is extremely active, so they have dug up many things about the goddesses. I believe he gives an excellent treatment of what you have been working on in secret these last two years. And something more, as you'll see in the part where he writes about the harboring of partisans.

In this context you must hope that Schwannze is mistaken—that could not be tolerated, as I'm sure you can imagine. Furthermore, it would go way beyond my authority; partisans are now the responsibility of ZbV-K.

Quite simply, Ferdinand, I advise you to keep an eye on those women of yours. It could be that there are difficult times ahead for them. You need to ensure that there is still something for you to study the next time you turn up here. Send me a telegram before you do. I hope that it will be soon.

Best wishes, Heil,

Reinhardt

Dora put the letter down and eagerly pulled out the five-page enclosure—Schwannze's analysis of the situation and proposals for how to proceed.

His irregular, ugly script had little respect for ruled lines. The report seemed to her an unstructured, hastily written jumble. Without salutation, it went straight into a stream of denunciation, accusation, rumor, and half-truths concerning the past and present of the goddesses of Žítková.

I, Heinrich Schwannze, a German national and faithful associate of the Third Reich, since 1936 a member of the SdP, since 1938 a member of the NSDAP, since 1940 engaged by the Zlín SD-Außendienstelle, present for your attention information acquired by long-term field observation in the region around Alt Hrosenkau. Here in the hills live women who call themselves goddesses and who engage in alleged healing activities. These activities, however, are nothing better than charlatanism, and they harm decent people—they will always find superstitious and gullible folk to deceive with their divination, and they have no shame in taking fat fees for their lies. It is said that one of them demanded a cow to restore by magic the health of a Jewish girl with a tumor that made her head twice the normal size. Of course the filthy Jewish vermin gave it to her. It happened in the 1930s, meaning that these treacherous elements were able to continue to sponge off us.

In this regard the worst of them was always Surmenová of the Bedowa hill, who demanded the highest prices for her services and had no aversion to taking the shirt off the back of a mother of sick children, as happened with a certain Mrs. Kamenická from Pitín. A Mr. Sopouch from Krhov was robbed of his last crown after she claimed that he had cancer;

he went to Surmenová for years for exorcism, even though he was as fit as a flea . . .

Dora's gaze jumped over the lines and sometimes skipped a whole paragraph; this slanderous nonsense disgusted her. She flipped to the last page:

. . . irrespective of the fact that in 1941 such practices were prohibited in the Reich and the Protectorate. They have been illegal ever since. Although these women have claimed over and over that they engage in herbalism, not divination, we know what we know—using blobs of melted wax, they tell the fortunes of idiots who are willing to pay. This is a punishable offense! These women are no better than vagabond gypsies. I propose a thoroughgoing course of action that would see this dirty scum tolerated no longer and dealt with . . .

Finally, I should add that a young man was seen to spend two nights at the goddess Surmenová's cottage. In all likelihood this was a partisan whom Surmenová was providing with shelter and her so-called healing services.

In my opinion we should understand the deceptions by which she draws financial benefit and ruins the lives of gullible locals and the help she has given to the dirty Jewish race and now partisans as behavior inimical to the Reich. This should not remain unpunished!

To ensure further familiarity with their practices and the local environment, I venture to suggest the formation of a squad of several men that would

examine the criminal activities of these women and
bring them to justice.

Eternal glory to the Reich, Heil!

H. Schwannze

Attached to the report was a sheet that listed the addresses of all
active goddesses at the end of 1944.

Laying aside Schwannze's pamphlet in disgust, Dora turned her
attention to the clean white page of the final enclosure, a brief statement
in a careless hand.

Beobachtungsprotokoll vom 29. Oktober 1944
New findings on activities

> Assessment by a handwriting expert has confirmed
> a match between the handwriting of the report by
> H. Schwannze and the letters of denunciation sent
> from the SD-Außendienstelle in Zlín to the SS-Hexen-
> Sonderauftrag center in Starý Hrozenkov. Assessment
> enclosed.
>
> Signature: F. F. Norfolk

Not only did the informer Schwannze try to steal a position for
himself as head of a Hexen-Jagdkommando by the official route, but
he supported his efforts by sending in anonymous statements. Dora
looked at the short paragraph with still greater distaste than that she
had bestowed on Schwannze's report a few moments earlier. Why did
he do it? There were other routes by which he could have made himself
a career, so why through the goddesses? And why through Surmena in
particular?

She went through the dossier in search of the statement by the
handwriting expert, but it wasn't there. She went through the whole
file again, and she still didn't find it. She was sorry for this, but she

was hardly surprised by it; by the time it was made, everything had changed. Norfolk would have had bigger things on his mind than his filing system.

Dora got up to ask the archivist if she could photograph the documents she had just been looking at. He nodded without hesitation. She took her camera out of her bag and photographed all the correspondence from the too-small envelope.

I hope this went on your account at the end of the war, she whispered grimly as she put the informer's letters back into the dossier. At the same time, she felt relief wash over her: in terms of her Protectorate past, Surmena was clean. In that slim folder, Dora had found nothing that could discredit her; there were no unexpected secrets. Absolutely nothing, she said to herself. She handed the cardboard box to the archivist with a feeling of elation. She'd found nothing on Surmena at the Poznań archive, thank God.

The File of Hexenwesenfamilie Mahdal

*D*ora had again shed a little more light on Surmena's past. On the desk before her now was a row of cardboard boxes that stored the fates of other goddesses. Dora passed over Krasňačka, Struhárka, and the others and reached for the box labeled "Hexenfamilie Mahdal." Maybe at last she would succeed in finding out what linked that family to hers.

This box was much heavier than all the others. After removing the lid, Dora found a file several times thicker than the one kept on Surmena. Plainly, the two German researchers had taken a far greater interest in the Mahdalovás.

At the front of the file was a page Dora knew already from Surmena's file—a letter from the *Sicherheitszentrale* in Bratislava to the closest SDs in the Protectorate, demanding an investigation into the activities of Josefína Mahdalová. She skipped this, as she did the detailed questionnaires on all three members of the family. But she saw at a glance that their way of life was no different from that of the other goddesses. What was different was their specialization (also Category A), which included the note: *"black magic, ability to harm, seiðr (?)."* She came to documentation on the establishment of cooperation with members of Levin's team of researchers.

Beobachtungsprotokoll vom 19. November 1941
New findings on activities

Cooperation established with the family.

Collection of craniological data has confirmed the original observation that especially Mahdalka the Elder and Fuksena show Aryan features.

Signature: F. F. Norfolk

Beobachtungsprotokoll vom 20. Februar 1942
New findings on activities

Concentrated research includes the making of an offer to rent one room in the house of the Hexenwesen Mahdal family, under the pretext of the impossibility of finding accommodation in Alt Hrosenkau. Offer accepted. Cost: 100 Protectorate crowns per month.

Signature: F. F. Norfolk

Beobachtungsprotokoll vom 9. Mai 1942
New findings on activities

Subjects of observation have agreed to closer cooperation and authorized hidden involvement in the process of their magical activities. Observation conducted from entrance hall.

On May 9, two visits recorded: clients coming for advice. For a detailed description of these meetings, incl. ritual, see special study.

Invocation accompanying ritual not yet deciphered: spoken in local dialect, quickly and quietly, hence impossible to perform transcription. This will be a subject of further research.

Signature: F. F. Norfolk

Beobachtungsprotokoll vom 12. Oktober 1942
<u>New findings on activities</u>

Observation of the everyday life of the subjects has established the following: the subjects' actions submit to the Roman Catholic faith—prayers are conducted morning and evening, God is praised before the taking of food, the subjects attend Mass on Sundays in the church at Alt Hrosenkau, etc.

Alongside conventional religious practices, their behavior includes practices that are incompatible with the traditions of the Catholic faith. We chose two of the deviations we observed and succeeded in deciphering them. On the basis of detailed analysis, we consider these relics of paganism.

<u>Incident I:</u> We consider the most distinctive feature that differentiates the typical weekly life of the subjects of observation from the regimens of ordinary Catholics to be their veneration of Thursday as the day on which most important activities are performed. On this day the subjects do not receive visitors, nor do they devote themselves to strenuous work in the fields, as on other days apart from Sunday. In common with Sunday, for the subjects, Thursday is a sanctified day, although when questioned about this, they do not appear to know exactly why.

The latest knowledge on Old Germanic society and its spiritual culture tells us that our ancestors venerated Thursday as a day sanctified by Donar, the god of thunder and lightning—hence "Donnerstag." Guido von List claims that on Thursdays, our ancestors devoted themselves to their personal faith, not their worldly concerns. We believe that this tradition has been passed down to the subjects of observation from pre-Christian times and that their honoring of the day is intuitive, even if they do not understand the original significance of this veneration.

Incident II: The drawing of strength from surrounding natural phenomena represents another connection between the faith of the subjects of observation and that of the ancient Teutons. Our subjects recognize a certain tree—an ordinary local lime—as a sacred symbol of the strength of their line; this tree stands close to their house. The subjects explain their reverence for this tree in purely practical terms: it provides them with healing properties they need for the preparation of their herbal potions. Yet this extreme reverence for the family tree demonstrates an awareness of the respect in which Teuton priestesses held trees consecrated to tribal societies.

Another case in point concerns the spring that rises in the woods near the dwelling of the subjects of observation, in the direction of Wischkowetz. It is said that the Mahdal family has cared for this since time immemorial because of its "happy water," which in combination with certain herbs is said to have therapeutic properties. As we know, springs and watercourses played an indispensable role in the rituals of the Old Germanic peoples, as was demonstrated in many various magical ceremonies, including some for purposes of healing.

In answer to my question as to why on the night of the spring equinox, the subjects went off into the woods in the direction of the spring, Hexenwesen Fuksena explained that this was for purposes of magic and healing. She described a purification ritual that honored the water source and how their nighttime bath in it washed away the ills of winter.

We believe that the closeness of the subjects of observation to nature is a remnant of Old Germanic gnosis, which placed primary emphasis on initiation into the mysteries of nature, for which the necessary rituals were preserved and performed by dedicated priestesses.

Signed: F. F. Norfolk

Beobachtungsprotokoll vom 14. März 1943
New findings on activities

An interesting finding regarding portents of tragic misfortune and/or death. As in the cases of the stelae found in Niederdollendorf in the Rhineland and the Tuchola heath in northern Prussia, here, too, the snake is considered a symbol of death or disaster. In this locality it takes the form of a "white snake" that is said to live in the walls of every home.

Its appearance is a harbinger of disaster or the death of a family member, whose demise prefigures the downfall of the family line.

The subjects of observation do not know the origin of this awareness of the white snake; they claim that it has always been so.

Signed: F. F. Norfolk

Dora's throat was tight. She had seen the crushed body of the snake and the expression of horror on Surmena's face. She thought it best to turn a few pages of the file, to the next report of greater length.

Beobachtungsprotokoll vom 15. August 1943
New findings on activities

Notes on clients' visits.

Incident I: A woman (about forty years old) comes with a request for help. She believes herself to be in danger from a neighbor, who she claims has placed her under a spell.

The magical ceremony starts as usual with the preparation of water from the spring, into which melted wax is poured. Fragrant herbs are burned, and an incantation is spoken whose extent and content are similar to that of the incantation as conveyed by the informer (see enclosure from 9/11/42). The visitor's assumption is confirmed by the reading of a wax casting, followed by the taking of further steps for the removal of the evil spell and other protection. A smashed porcelain cup, shards placed in an ordinary preserve jar along with nails, a needle, and a broken razor blade. The visitor is bidden to urinate into the jar; she goes out into the yard to perform this. On her return the jar is sealed, and all the women go toward the forest in order to bury it. On their return the visitor is given selected herbs that she should take for a period of nine days. Hexenwesen Mahdalová the Elder accepts a payment of 10 Protectorate crowns.

Incident II: A male visitor (about forty-five years old) is convinced that he has been cheated in probate proceedings. He wishes his unmarried brother to die so that the remainder of the inheritance will fall to him. He offers the high sum of 200 Protectorate crowns to ensure that he is kept out of his brother's death.

As in previous cases, a ceremony is performed in which wax is poured and used for purposes of divination. The visitor is told that the act can be carried out only by the administration of a certain herbal potion, which the subjects of observation are able to prepare; it must be administered, however, by the visitor himself, on two consecutive Sundays. The visitor is reluctant to do this, saying again that he wants no involvement in the process. The ceremony, led to this point by Hexenwesen Fuksena, is joined by Mahdalová the Elder, who bids the visitor to abide by what is given or to leave immediately. After this intervention, the visitor is agreeable. He receives a promise that the mix of herbs will be prepared; he should collect it on Friday and administer it to his brother on the following Sunday. Mahdalová proposes he invite the brother to consecutive Sunday lunches on the pretext of reconciliation and to mix the herbs into his food. The visitor agrees with reluctance; he makes a payment of 100 Protectorate crowns and undertakes to deliver the remainder on receipt of the mix of herbs.

When I ask what this mix will contain, I am told that this is irrelevant because the man will not return. To the day of this record, he has not returned.

Signed: F. F. Norfolk

Greedily, Dora took in word after word, until her dry, tired eyes stung. The next incident files detailed very similar cases. In most instances people came to the Mahdalovás with something that was in conflict with the law; very few visitors sought them out for reasons of illness or the simple desire to have their fortune told. Norfolk's case studies teemed with the requirement to harm relatives, neighbors, and rivals in love; applications for acquisition of the property of others; and so on.

Dora was particularly engaged by one of the more innocent cases, not least as the visitor was someone she had once known in Hrozenkov. It concerned family property buried somewhere in the woods by an owner who feared for it because of the wildness of the times. Not expecting to die anytime soon, the poor man got entangled with a horse, took a hoof to the skull, and died before the priest could be called. He had no time to say where the family fortune was buried.

The Mahdalovás' visitor wanted help in determining where the property was buried. What then took place could only be described as the summoning of the dead man's ghost. According to the record, this took place not in Potočná but in the cemetery at Hrozenkov, at which the claimant undertook to appear before midnight with items that had belonged to the dead man. Apparently, he was able to muster the courage to do so, as Norfolk's report testified to a meeting of four individuals over the grave of the relative; in a magic circle made by the joining of hands, they underwent something the writer designated a "necromantic séance."

He described its beginning as a long process of preparation whose success was revealed by the sudden appearance of swarms of fireflies over the grave. Then the claimant was called upon to make sense of a stream of barely intelligible words spoken in a sort of trance by Mahdalová the Elder, who had become the medium through whom the world beyond the grave would be reached. The dead man named a place at the foot of the Kykula hill; here the claimant should conduct his search. With this the séance ended, and the terrified man promised a reward amounting to one-third of the recovered property.

The record did not state whether the place specified was the right one or if the visitor returned with the fee. It noted the need for a broader study, but Dora did not find this in the rest of the file, which comprised only one incident file after another.

Dora was taken aback. Apart from the claims of Baglárka and Irma, which were little more than exaggerated rumors, she had first come across evidence of rituals that did harm in the case of Magdaléna Mĺkva. This was the first tangible proof that the Mahdalovás engaged in black magic. But still, it might have been an isolated case. Now she was confronted with a dossier filled with similar instances, some of which were evaluated as successes.

Dora took a deep breath.

Not for the first time in the past year, she saw the goddesses and their small Kopanice world in a different light. By now they were not at all the obliging women she remembered from her childhood, women who gave to anyone who knocked on the doors of their cottages. These widely different individuals included dangerous characters who did not hesitate to bring harm on total strangers if the price was right. Were their actions an empty witches' comedy that did not trouble their consciences, as they knew them to have no consequences? Or did they willfully employ their abilities that they knew to be extraordinary? Whether one thing or the other, their determination to do harm was terrifying.

Deep in thought, Dora leafed through the remaining papers in the Mahdalová file. As with Surmena's dossier, the last record was from the end of February 1944, when the Kommando was taken out of commission. With the closure of the story of the Mahdalovás, Dora felt disquiet and also a trace of disappointment. The enlightenment she'd been hoping for had not been delivered; she was still no wiser as to why and how the fates of Surmena and Mahdalová the Elder had become entwined.

It was now just after half past two; the materials on the German scholars would not be delivered from the storeroom until three. She waved to the archivist to let him know that he could return the boxes on her desk to their shelves. Then she walked down the narrow aisle and out of the reading room.

Researchers with a Special Commission

*B*ack at her desk, Dora found a box containing files on each member of the Hexen-Sonderkommando. Digging into it eagerly, she pulled out the file labelled "VII.g: Forscher der Hexen-Sonderauftrag F. F. NORFOLK." It was filled with Norfolk's correspondence.

Ferdinand,

How are you? How is your research going? Any new findings? To be frank, new findings are the very thing we need at the moment; the atmosphere here leaves a lot to be desired. I have the feeling that the Reichsführer is coming under pressure to make cuts to the Ahnenerbe, and I hardly need to tell you that we are the first in line. From seven years of research, no relevant outcomes, no studies, no witches' trilogy— you should have heard the icy tone of his voice; the receiver practically froze in my hand. Thank goodness we still have his cousin between us! If it wasn't for him, I fear we'd have been shut down long ago.

Every day I think about my dissertation. If they accepted it, I could get it published and put this whole Auftrag behind me. But those haughty old men, those academic asses . . . Oh well, as long as they stay out of politics.

In any case, we can't get away from the trilogy. I'm waiting for news from the others on how their papers are coming along. From what I can tell, only Merkel's is ready. Yours too? I hope that you're not putting your new novel before your paper—that would be the last thing we need! As for me, I've finished the first part on the Church's conspiracy against Germanic women. But to my surprise, the numbers are giving me all kinds of trouble. So far I've got statistics from 1200 to 1790 from Bavaria, the Saarland, and Brandenburg, and I can't account for any more than two thousand executed. If I can't push that figure up, I'll go crazy, as will the Reichsführer—you know how much he's expecting of this; it's as though his ancestress at the stake is keeping him awake at night.

On top of all this, I now have to prepare some materials for the Minister of Propaganda, to support his campaign for National Socialist women. There is some connection with Lebensborn; the need for more fighters means that it is in the interests of German women to mobilize mothers, mothers-to-be, and female workers. What drives the Ahnenerbe at the moment is the emancipation of German women and their greater involvement in the war effort. You would have to be here, my friend, to see how they are starting to fish in all waters imaginable, even the very shallowest. For us this means the delivery of our study—needless to say, the sooner, the better.

So please try to send me your data on the position of women within the structure of the Old Germanic tribe and to add to it the paper on the model structure of Kopanice society. And don't forget the drawings and photographs—you know how everyone here loves that kind of thing. (Try to photograph Fuksena in the act of divination; I think that that would make an impression.)

Please work as quickly as you can and send these things soon.

Best wishes,
Rudolf
Berlin, June 15, 1942

Ferdinand,

Thanks for sending the paper, but to tell you the truth, I was expecting something more. You must surely admit yourself that such a brief survey of data is hardly representative of seven years of work. I submitted it to the Reichsführer as a "draft" of a more exhaustive study to be submitted very soon. I hope this is how you see things too.

Otherwise, I agree, of course, with your conclusions regarding the trilogy. I like your chosen examples of the oppression of women by the Church on the territories of the Protectorate; the precise tabulation of data in a century-by-century overview is particularly impressive, and it illustrates beautifully how the Church escalated its aggression and how sneakily it did so. I feel immense pride in the knowledge that without our research, this conspiracy would have remained hidden behind more attractive historical events.

The response of the Reichsführer was a declaration to the effect that your draft is of benefit to Goebbels. I enclosed for his perusal the first results regarding totals of women executed in certain lands of the Reich; I have to say that this caused me some anxiety, as they do not amount even to one-tenth of the figure the Reichsführer presumed. It is becoming clear that we have no chance of counting up nine million victims. Six, Merkel, Biermann, Eckstein—all have come up with immoderately, *monstrously* low figures. As many different archives are not cooperating—they have nothing to cooperate *with*—we can delay matters a little . . . But even so, we should meet at headquarters—and soon—to decide what to do in the case that we fail to reach a total that will satisfy the Reichsführer.

Heil!

Rudolf

P.S. I have yet to receive your paper on the structure of the Old Germanic tribe.

Berlin, November 24, 1942

Ferdinand,

Perhaps our time has come! This is an opportunity too good to miss. Is there any way of getting Fuksena to Berlin? It is crucial that I introduce her to Reichsheini. Have you heard about the Wannsee Five? I can't imagine that you have—only a few top RSHA leaders have access to the experiment. In brief, this is what it is. The Reichsführer has had two clairvoyants, a diviner, an astrologist, and a graphologist brought to the villa at Wannsee. After the flight of Hess in '41, all of them ended up in labor camps for failing to give warning of it. I was told this yesterday by Haselhuhn—in confidence, of course. Haselhuhn himself selected the five, and now they are his responsibility. Although I have not seen them, from what he tells me, most of them are not capable of half of what our goddesses do. A circus clown, a comedian with a crystal ball, a woman who purports to soothsay from coffee grounds, and two pseudoscientists. Distinctly third-class when compared to what we have.

Now what do you say to this? It is their task to soothsay and submit a report before every action that is not to the liking of Reichsheini or the Führer. Apparently, the first falls in and out of a trance, the second gazes into his ball, the woman babbles on about the visions she reads in the grounds, the astrologist makes a horoscope . . . and every day all this rubbish is delivered to headquarters and has a bearing on staff decisions! When I think about the possible consequences, it chills me to the bone . . . Now just imagine what would happen if we introduced Fuksena to the machine, with how she looks and all that she knows! The practices of the Mahdalovás are something like seiðr, am I right? Can you imagine what that would mean to the Reichsführer? Do you get my point?

Prepare her—this is our big chance.

In the meantime, I'll work on Haselhuhn to get her into the Wannsee group.

We simply must not miss this opportunity, Ferdinand.

Heil!

Rudolf

Berlin, July 8, 1943

Rudolf,

I'm sorry to say that none of them will consider it. They are enormously afraid of leaving Potočná, comparing it to the exodus of the Jews from Hrozenkov. Besides, they still have not heard from Mahdalová's son, who has been conscripted. Try as I might, they will not be moved. What's more, they argue that they can draw on their greatest powers only here in the hills of the White Carpathians; something to do with magnetic waves. Just imagine three women, two of them illiterate, making such a claim! Try to get me someone with a knowledge of geology and physics who is able to study the locality; I'd be very interested in what he might discover.

What do you suggest?

As you will understand, I am wary of resorting to violence.

Ferdinand

Starý Hrozenkov, August 19, 1943

Ferdinand,

Your letter made me truly angry. You lack neither funds nor time and should be coming up with far better results, especially as your involvement in your fieldwork and the enjoyment you take from it goes far beyond the call of duty! I fail to understand your answer to my last letter. By this time you should have every member of the Mahdal family wrapped around your little finger. It is we who set the conditions, not they!

At first I thought that I'd pay no heed to what they do and don't want and let you sort it out yourself; your concern. But the situation has changed.

I was at headquarters, where I had a private audience with the Reichsführer. This went as usual. He is not at all satisfied with our work. Not at all! And he hinted that if we do not submit the trilogy immediately, the Hexen-Sonderauftrag project will be terminated by the end of the year.

All I could give the Reichsführer to improve his mood was the comprehensive report on some of the research at Starý Hrozenkov. His reaction to this changed my intention to bring them here at all costs. For the time being, we have another way of playing it. He wants to meet them—straightaway. I told him how you feared what would happen if the women were torn from their proper place. Surprisingly, he took this as a fact, even adding something about recurrent paranormal phenomena happening only in certain places, where special energy is cumulated. And he sees no problem in his breaking his planned journey to Preßburg (to take place a few weeks from now, on October 9 at the earliest) by stopping off at Starý Hrozenkov. I shall come with him, so you and I will see each other. I'll ask for funding if we need it.

I'm sending this express in the hope that you will receive it in time to make the necessary arrangements. If I were you, I'd be careful not to tell the women more than you need to. I want them to behave and act as they always do. I don't want silly geese who are too afraid to open their beaks, all right? Do what you can. Now everything is riding on how much our goddesses can impress Reichsheini.

Heil!

Rudolf

Berlin, September 12, 1943

Ferdinand,

Great news! It worked! The Reichsführer said nothing at all on the way to Preßburg, but in the evening of the next day, he summoned me. He told me how impressed he was and that he would certainly be calling for the inclusion of the family in a more detailed program of research. He indicated that while we should deliver an evaluation of research objective A as soon as possible, he would recommend an objective B to come into immediate effect: the conducting of research on Old Germanic rites and the Hexenwesen.

As I was leaving, he again stressed the importance of our discovery, saying he would continue to take a great interest in the women. We really did it! For the time being at least, the risk of cancellation of the Hexen-Sonderauftrag has been averted. Deadlines for the submission of studies for the trilogy still apply, however.

Heil!

Rudolf
Berlin, October 15, 1943

The correspondence part of Norfolk's file ended as suddenly as it had begun. In common with all the research, it was discontinued when the commission came to an end. The final item in the folder was a yellowing scrap of paper—a telegram form, to which was glued the following message, written in block letters.

TELEGRAMM

1 Für: F. F. Norfolk, Ahnenerbe, Wilhelmstraße 102, Berlin, Deutsches Reich

2 Von: Marie Pagacova, Alt Hrosenkau, Protektorat Böhmen und Mähren

TEXT: Our beautiful daughter has same birthmark on forehead as you. Christening 9/24/44. Come. Fuksena.

Friedrich Ferdinand Norfolk

*H*e did not reply to Fuksena's telegram, nor did he go to the christening. He would not have gone even if he had been able. His notes to self, his marginal notes on official documents, the wording of his interim reports and studies—all made clear that it would not have been his wish to go. The end of the research meant the end of his relationship with Fuksena. Apparently, she was nothing more to him than a subject for research; that this study should have produced a child was in the nature of a small accident. Besides, according to his personnel records, Norfolk was married.

Norfolk was not his real name. He was Ferdinand Soukup from Frývaldov—a Czechoslovak German and winner of the 1924 Mährischer Literaturpreis. His adoption of the name Friedrich Ferdinand Norfolk was brought about by his phenomenal success and subsequent determination to conquer Europe with his stories of the bloody trials of the witches of Frývaldov and Velké Losiny. It seems he was helped along the way by fair-haired Evelyne and most of all contacts made by her father. Professor Hübsch was a teacher of literature in Leipzig, where Norfolk went on a short-term stay before relocating there permanently. His personnel records also reveal that he met Dr. Levin at the University of Leipzig in 1935. Levin invited Norfolk to join his new research project, which he had been commissioned to conduct by special order of the Reichsführer-SS himself.

Dora could almost sense Norfolk's joy at having his dreams come true.

From the small mountain town of Frývaldov—or Freiwaldau, as it was again called—he had worked his way up to a position at the center of an important Leipzig family and gained a toehold at that city's university; magazines were publishing his horror stories, and he had just become a member of SS-Hexen-Sonderkommando and was thus engaged in special research and was being paid for it. All for spending much of his time reading historical novels on the topic of witch trials and writing about them, which he would have done even if he hadn't been paid for it.

In the beginning the pay was nothing special. His work for Hexen-Sonderauftrag brought in only a few dozen Reichsmarks a month, once his expenses for travel and subsistence had been deducted. But after he and Levin happened upon Blank, this changed.

Correspondence shows this to have been Levin's idea. He had a relative who had access to extraordinary prisoners—*Sonderhäftlinge*—at Sachsenhausen. These particular prisoners were extraordinary in that they were "restorers"—falsifiers and forgers of all types. Due to special conditions and workshops with top-quality equipment, they could turn out anything from Gothic panel painting to nineteenth-century realism, from medieval illuminated manuscripts to government bonds from the 1920s, and graphics from Dürer to Daumier. It was quite within their capabilities to make a few duplicates of black books and blood books, items of archivalia borrowed from the Reich archives thanks to connections with its director, ordinances from city and ecclesiastical courts, Inquisition verdicts. And Rudolf Levin, his relative Karl, Norfolk, and Murowski (another member of the Kommando) divided between them the huge profits they collected from the RSHA–Amt VII library fund and on several occasions from the Reichsführer himself, who wanted valuable archivalia in his own collection. Unanswered reminders from archives that were victims of the robbery gave eloquent expression to their further trade with archivalia; these reminders were gathered in a box together with the Kommando's ledgers. This was a time of opportunity. Not least for Norfolk.

As a speaker of Czech, he was given a special order to visit the archives of the friendly Slovak Republic, from where he proceeded to archives in the Protectorate—in Cheb, Liberec, Opava, and eventually Frývaldov, which he knew so well. As the Czech lands had always been considered part of a Greater Germany, it was important to establish how many women—Germans and others—had lost their lives through the trials of alleged witches, alias pagan cult priestesses. It was Norfolk who was alerted by the Slovak authorities to the existence of the strange women known as goddesses. He knew immediately that he had discovered an academic V3 weapon.

> Rudolf,
>
> You're not going to believe this! Forget the moldy papers of the archives and the dusty, unread periodicals. I've discovered something quite incredible. They're alive! Do you get it? They're alive! The priestesses—goddesses, if you will—are alive, in the hills of the White Carpathians, and they still practice their Old Germanic rites! Tell the Reichsführer that I've found living proof of creatures we thought to be long extinct. And hurry: I am about to leave for Bojkovice, whose archive has a blood book, and from there I go to Starý Hrozenkov. I'll expect to see you there by the end of the month.
>
> Ferdinand

When he sent this letter, he was already on his way to Kopanice.

And so it began. After their first meeting in Hrozenkov, they stayed there together several times. The reports, sketches, and photographs that Dora found among the outcomes of their work—which were sent to the Ahnenerbe in the early 1940s—were ample evidence of their huge appetite for investigation of this unexpected source, and it showed that they were motivated by more than keeping the Reichsführer happy. Levin wanted to publish his research, whereas for Norfolk, the goddesses became a crucial source of inspiration. That the investigations began to pay dividends is evidenced by the awards Norfolk was soon collecting. In late 1942 he received the Kantate-Dichterpreis der Reichsmessestadt Leipzig for his epic about Germanic priestesses over whose heads an icy mountain sun sets. The nation was moved; Norfolk was its literary hero. While Evelyne swelled with pride at the official honors and her third pregnancy, Fuksena waited. Norfolk did not see the swell of Fuksena's pregnancy: in February '44, he—along with the other members of the research Kommando—was withdrawn from the field; not only had the Reichsführer run out of patience, but he had run out of time for the implementation of propaganda focused on the Germanic woman, having more important things on his plate than the rehabilitation of his immolated ancestress Margareth Himbler and the mobilization of German women, not least the ever-greater proximity of an Eastern Front that would soon overwhelm the building that housed the witch files, which fortunately had been borne away in time.

The Hexenarchiv and all library materials acquired by the SS-Hexen-Sonderkommando were hidden, and members of the Kommando scattered across the remnants of the Reich. They did not go into hiding—far from it, they conducted private correspondence using the addresses of their permanent residences.

"Did you hide the files? If so, where?" wrote an anxious Murowski, whom Levin and Norfolk had evidently removed from their team of black marketeers in archivalia. In all likelihood he received no answer.

"Are the files in place? Confirm," wrote Norfolk to Levin.

Later, Levin wrote: *"They're taking me to Nuremberg. I'm informed that we'll see each other there."*

And so they did. To their surprise, they were tried, along with Alfred Rosenberg, NSDAP ideologue and originator of National Socialist theories that included one about a conspiracy against Germanic women. Tried as members of the SS for crimes against peace and the dissemination of Fascist ideas and as scientists for the misuse of science in the interests of war.

Evidence was presented by Herbert Blank, member of the *Sonderhäftlinge* group in the Sachsenhausen concentration camp. The sentences handed down to these misguided researchers were not particularly heavy: a few years, in which they would reappraise the purpose of their scientific work. Prison, however, is not something for academics. Levin died in an accident at the end of 1945, Norfolk of exhaustion three years later.

Dora studied the photograph of Norfolk that was attached to his documents of authorization. A handsome, fair-haired man with a gentle smile, wearing a peaked cap. He looked somehow familiar. Where had she seen that strange birthmark on the forehead before?

Before the bus took her back to the Czech Republic, Dora wandered aimlessly about the city. There were things about Poznań that reminded her of Brno: its size, the way the river had been pushed out of the city center, the baroque and classicist buildings punctuated with modern glass structures as in the South Moravian metropolis; the people, whose features were similar, as were their frowns of indifference; and finally, the bus station and its spit-infested waiting room where she spent the last hours before departure, tired after an exacting day.

She wondered if the Mahdalovás had been aware of what they were colluding with by their involvement in Norfolk's research, of the danger they had exposed themselves to by letting him into their home and deciding to trust him. Had the monthly retainer of one hundred Protectorate crowns been worth the risk of putting themselves under the Nazi microscope? She wondered, too, how great a role had been played by Fuksena, who had fallen in love with the handsome man in uniform. How had they reacted to Norfolk's request that Fuksena go with him to Berlin? Had they been aware that he did not even have to ask, that he could have arrested them and taken them to Berlin at any time he chose? To be under the nose of the Reichsführer, who may have chosen not to visit them in their home environment after all but instead to have them brought to Wannsee, where they would soothsay at his command? And what if their predictions had failed to come true, once, twice, or three times? Dora was wondering this as her travel information came up in lights on the departures board.

Soon she was aboard a bus plotting a slow course through the night to Hradec Králové. The lights of Poznań were almost behind her, and the vehicle would sit more calmly once it came to the wide road south, to Bohemia.

Part IV

The Koprvazy

The relationship preyed on her for years. It robbed her of her appetite for life and her self-respect. She wished a thousand times that it did not exist, and a thousand times she had the feeling that she had snuffed it out, had trampled its presence inside her to death. But then it would come back with still greater intensity, searing her body and soul.

It began on the night she parted from her father on the Koprvazy, out in the open on the hillside—and it was a disaster for them both. What if one of the homeward-bound mourners had seen them? What then? Even today the mere thought of it tied Dora's stomach in knots.

At the time she regarded it as a coincidence—an unhappy coincidence brought on by slivovitz and the horror of what had just happened. It would not happen again, she told herself; she would suppress it, as she had suppressed it since her years at boarding school. She would handle it by willpower. Besides, she had Jakoubek and her research, which gave her a sense of fulfillment akin to happiness. She had all she needed.

Yet it lay inside her still, deep down, and sometimes, to Dora's horror, it bubbled up to the surface. So it was more than just the once. A few years later they found themselves in a similar situation, and it happened again. And again. After that they stopped relying on chance and the attendant risk that someone would see them. The cottage on the Koprvazy was still empty; they started to meet there.

She would never have thought she could do such a thing—not least as she did it in the room where her mother had bled to death. Yet she lay there naked as she would have lain naked anywhere, fully focused on Janigena and what they did in the two or three hours for which they had the courage to be together. They returned to their respective homes filled with dismay and remorse, all the time looking about to make sure that no one was following them. In the next days and weeks, they would try to wipe their memories clear of what had happened—to force it out so that it had never been.

"It would be better if you didn't exist," Janigena said to her once, before walking off into the dark night toward Pitín.

After that it was several weeks before Dora met her again, but this was nothing unusual. All she saw of her in the meantime was at Mass, kneeling at the front pew and mumbling prayers long after the last parishioner had left the church.

It was several months before the dark waves of revolt and disgust subsided and they could meet again on the Koprvazy, an hour after midnight on Saturday, as was their arrangement. Then again and again, week in, week out, the shock of coming together in passion—followed by another long fast and remorse as heavy as death.

In those weeks it was different, however. The honeymoon returned in a rush, driving them up to the Koprvazy Saturday after Saturday. On that quiet summer night, Dora climbed the moonlight-flooded path quickly and cautiously, driven by the desire to be with Janigena as soon as possible.

But Janigena wasn't there; the cottage was empty.

Dora, out of breath, dropped onto the bench next to the small house. To her right the hillside fell away into the hollow that contained the path that led to Surmena's cottage; to her left was the descent toward Pitín. The landscape opened up in front of her like a dark flower. The pleasure Dora felt in looking at it was all the greater for her knowledge that it would soon produce Janigena.

The night was calm and quiet, the only sounds the occasional whistle of an awakened bird in the nearby woods and the chirping of crickets in the grass. Above Dora's head the branches of the old service tree swayed in the gentle breeze.

Dora didn't know how long she had been waiting like that. All she remembered was Janigena suddenly standing there, her broad back blocking the crescent moon, her elbows sticking out because her hands were on her hips. Then Dora was closed up in a tight cage from which there was no escape. And how she wanted to escape! What she read in Janigena's face she had never seen there before; there was no shadow of guilt etching sideways grooves into her brow, there were no misgivings that narrowed the eyes, as though she was afraid to look at Dora properly. There was a rage in Janigena that tugged at her features and frightened Dora. Before she could catch her breath and ask what was going on, Janigena had her by the wrist, was dragging her toward the tree, was tying her to the trunk. Before Dora could fully grasp what was happening, she had loops of rope around her wrists and waist and was hugging the service tree.

Her protests were loud.

"Quiet, quiet," hissed Janigena.

Then, as suddenly as she had appeared, Janigena was gone.

Confused, Dora turned to the cottage. Janigena was in there. Dora waited. Several times she called out. Nothing. Janigena neither came out nor switched on a light. All was dark. But Dora felt sure that she was watching her.

Was this some kind of game? A kink? Dora didn't know, and her ignorance horrified her all the more. To say she had known Janigena for so many years, she knew practically nothing about her. She had never penetrated her hard shell, never broken the barrier of her silence.

Dora stood there twitching helplessly. Although it was not cold, she had goose bumps. As her anxiety grew, a great sense of injustice came over her. Her throat was tight, and her eyes filled with tears. She could do nothing but hug the tree her father had hanged himself in and listen to the rustling of its leaves.

Eventually the leaves attracted her gaze too. It was a while before she realized that her eyes were dry and that she was no longer thinking about Janigena. She stared up into the tree, unable to tear her gaze away from the branches in which her father had hung. It was as though something of him was still there. The thought flashed through her mind that perhaps there was. After all, before his departure from the world and the people in it, there had been no reconciliation.

She began to panic. The anxiety she was suffering from her inability to move was intensified by thoughts of her dead father. She tugged the rope this way and that, grazing her hands on the trunk as she tried to work them free. She called, yelled, pleaded for Janigena. Nothing. There was no movement from the house, although Janigena could surely see Dora's desperate thrashing. Then Dora began to weep.

Only then did Janigena emerge. But instead of untying Dora, she covered Dora's mouth with the back of her hand so that Dora's voice ceased to carry across the silent nighttime landscape. Against her back Dora felt the full weight of a mighty female body; against her belly she felt Janigena's right hand, which then slipped beneath the waistband of her skirt, hoisted her pelvis, and slid deep between her legs.

Everything ran together—panic, terror, a profound aversion for the tree into whose branches she was staring (her head tilted back by Janigena's grip), but also an unbearable desire that spilled to her loins and received with hunger the regular shocks dealt by Janigena's hand. When it came, she was beginning to wonder if she had lost consciousness.

She woke up on the ground, under the service tree. The exposed parts of her body were numb with cold: the ground temperature had fallen with the night. She sat up, pulled her skirt back over her knees, looked around. The moon was concealed behind storm clouds; only their rounded edges shone in the dark night. No sign of Janigena. No sign of anyone, anywhere. Silence but for the branches of the service tree above her head, which were swaying more vigorously than before; the murmur of their leaves was like the sound of voices. It was dark and menacing.

Standing up too quickly, Dora tripped on the hem of her skirt and went crashing into the trunk, uttering a scream as she grazed her face. Squeamishly, she pushed herself clear, as though from a person who wished to grab her, hold her, and never let her go. Then she fled down the hill, as though her life depended on it, without looking back. She heard the first rumble of thunder at her back.

After this incident Dora did not appear in Žítková for many weeks, until the scabs on her face had healed. She and Jakoubek even spent the last weekend of August in Brno. Dora kept wondering if her experiences on the Koprvazy were real. Could she have dreamed them? She didn't know; she was in the dark.

They first returned to Kopanice in September. But instead of leaving the bus on the Bedová as usual, Dora led them straight to the cemetery.

Having left Jakoubek at the entrance, she made her way on the sloping terrain among the dense jumble of headstones. At last she reached the stone with the inscription "IDES FAMILY." The first red-tinged leaves of autumn lay across the marble—and underneath it her mother and her father. As there had been no money for a new headstone, they'd had to reconcile, albeit in the earth.

As she stood there, she felt ill at ease. The will that had driven them there had not been hers, but her father's—together with the branches of the service tree she had looked up into, during an incident she could not banish from her memory. And the will of Irma, who had urged her to talk to him, which she now found difficult to believe.

Then it happened—naturally. Her first babbled utterance, before she knew it was coming. Followed by several more that flew into her head and came together in a stream. Others hurried to join them, and the stream became too strong to hold. It came in a rush along with her tears, like a waterfall, out and down and onto the ash-gray headstone. Hate, pain, remorse, and at the very end, sorrow.

Justýna Ruchárka

*I*n the early evening of the next day, Dora knocked on the door of Irma's cottage. For a few moments there was no sound, not even the distant but audible shuffle of Irma's steps. Could she have gone out? Dora knocked again, and seconds later, a weak voice bade her enter.

Dora did so. From the threshold she saw bare legs move from the bed. Irma was getting up to welcome her.

"I'm pleased to see you, my girl," she said.

"No need to get up, Auntie. I won't stay long."

"Why come at all if you won't stay long? Come on in and sit down."

Dora stepped into the room. It was scented with the resin of burning wood and warm and cozy, but it was untidy. On the table there were cups and plates and half-empty bottles of spirits. Dora picked up a broom from the floor and stood it against the wall in the corner.

"You won't mind attending to yourself. There's water in the pail, and you can help yourself to tea from one of those sacks."

Dora did as Irma told her. From a pail beside the range, she ladled water into a cooking pot, which she placed on the stove to heat. While she was tidying the cups and plates from the table, she asked, "What's the matter, Auntie? You're in bed so early."

Irma waved a dismissive hand. "It's been going on for a few days. Weakness, Dora. Not much longer now."

Dora looked at her closely. It seemed that Irma had shrunk some more, if that were still possible. Her cheeks had sunk, and her parchment skin had deep grooves in it. The hands that rested on her quilt were just bones covered with skin.

"Don't look like that. I am ninety-five, after all."

Dora blinked in surprise. Was Irma speaking of death?

"You'll get over it, Auntie. You'll be fine in a few days; I'm sure you will."

Irma made a face. "Why have you come to see me, then?"

Dora shifted her weight from one foot to the other.

"Something bothering you, isn't there?"

Dora walked back to the table, which was covered with a cloth of bright-colored Kopanice embroidery, and sat down on the end of the bench. But then the water in the cooking pot came to a boil, and the impatient hiss of drops hitting hot metal brought her to her feet again. Carefully, she poured the boiling water into her mug, over herbs she had taken in handfuls from the small canvas sacks that hung from a wooden pole above the range. She set the mug of fragrant tea and the ladle down in the middle of the table.

"Last time I was here, I asked you something."

"Hmm," Irma muttered.

"Why didn't you tell me that Mahdalová the Elder was our aunt? That she was Surmena's sister?"

Irma sat up straighter and propped herself against the pillow. Bony shoulders with a white nightgown hanging from them appeared from beneath the quilt.

"Why, you say? What business is it of mine? It's nothing to do with me, and I won't talk about it."

"Not even if I ask you to?"

Irma gave a snort of annoyance. "Why should I? Don't you know enough about your family as it is? If you were meant to know more, Surmena would have told you."

Dora shrugged. "Maybe she intended to and ran out of time. She went away so suddenly, didn't she?"

"Ran out of time? Is that what you believe?" Irma gave a sidelong glance. "Did she find the time to tell you about other relatives? Do you know who *they* are?"

Was Dora imagining the mild ridicule she read in Irma's eyes?

"Yes."

"There you are, then. You know all your relatives. You know who's whose relative from Žítková to Lopeník, and also everybody's godparents in the past forty years. You know everything that's important, and there's no point in trying to figure out what isn't . . ."

Irma wheezed as she cleared her throat. Dora wanted to get up and help her, but Irma gestured emphatically for her to remain seated. She took a few shallow breaths to calm herself. "It's nothing," she said. "Dog fat will put it right. Pour me some tea; I need to wash it down."

Dora stood up obligingly, picked up the ladle, poured the tea into a mug, and handed it to Irma. While the old woman sipped the hot drink, Dora wrapped her hands around her own mug, deep in thought as she formulated her question.

"Do you think Surmena didn't tell me about Mahdalka because she didn't have a good reputation?"

Irma's laughter carried through the room like the caw of a crow. An old, rough chuckle.

"She didn't have a good reputation, you say? That's funny, that is, girl." Then Irma fell silent as if something had cut her off. "I was afraid of her, and relieved when at last she passed."

These last words she hissed, and Dora was frightened by them.

"Who told you that Mahdalka was your aunt?" Irma asked angrily.

"Baglárka." There was a silence while Dora raised the courage to continue. "I found some documents in the archives that gave her maiden name, Josifčena Surmenová. And somewhere else I found records of a case from before the war, claiming that Mahdalka tortured to death a man called Mĺkvy, whose wife then died as well. Do you know anything about it?"

Irma lowered her head and said, "I don't think I ever heard of it, no. But that's not important—there were so many of them that it's difficult to remember them all. I told you she was an evil spirit, didn't I? So it's hardly surprising that she tortured someone."

Irma was silent then. She stared down at her hands as if looking for something in them. Then she went on. "I never understood it. Nor did my mother. Nor did Surmena. We had no idea where it came from— that evil power that flowed into her and she learned to subdue. None of the rest of us had such a power. Perhaps only Ruchárka knew what it was and how to treat it. It's a pity she never confided in anyone. After she died, there was nothing to stand in Mahdalka's way."

Dora was listening intently.

"But that wasn't what you forgot to ask me about, was it?" said Irma.

"No," said Dora. "The last time I was here, I asked about something, and you quickly changed the subject."

"Changed the subject?" Irma was visibly taken aback.

"You said that they had a quarrel. Mahdalka and Granny Ruchárka. What kind of quarrel?"

Irma dipped her small face into the mug and took a long drink. Dora began to fear she would say nothing more. When her hands returned to the quilt, her mug was empty. She dried her wet lips on the end of her nightgown sleeve.

"That was none of my business either. Nor is it now," she answered at last. "A quarrel is a quarrel, and they didn't like each other afterward, which is understandable."

Dora was silent for a moment. Then she said, "You think that it would be better for me not to know. But can you imagine what it is to live in the wreckage of a family you know nothing about? It's driving me mad. It's like someone is reading you only every fifth sentence of a story and refusing to disclose the ending. Surmena didn't tell me because she didn't want me to know about it. Maybe she thought it would be better for me not to know. But what she was trying to hide was perhaps not as well hidden as she thought and as it seems to you. I keep finding scraps, but they don't make any sense. But I can't go on like this—I've had enough. I don't want to come across it by accident. I want to put it together now, once and for all. I want to paste the scraps together, take a good look at them, and see for myself. So help me. Tell me!"

Irma turned her face toward the pillow and closed her eyes.

When she opened them again, she said, "Perhaps God will forgive me. Mahdalka is dead, after all . . ."

"Life in these parts was never good. Even today there's poverty everywhere you look. Folk on the Bedová had it particularly hard. Life was always wretched there, on the wrong side in the shade of the woods. The rocky earth couldn't keep a large family, but even so, Anka Gabrhelová—mother of Anna Pagáčena and Justýna Ruchárka—had about thirteen children. Some of them died, and those who were left preferred to run away to escape the poverty. Anna Pagáčena, too, had to leave, but for a different reason—perhaps you've heard that her own father wouldn't leave her alone. Apart from Anna, Anka still had Justýna, who came along after a long line of boys. Justýna was almost ten years younger than Anna.

"Anka taught them what she could. Later, both would be goddesses known far and wide. But before that something else happened. Pagáčena had gotten away from her father in time, but apparently, Justýna didn't manage to. Who knows what the truth of it is, but one day the news got around that Justýna was in the family way. This was odd—no one hereabouts knew of any man who was after her. More to the point, she wasn't even fifteen. In normal circumstances the police would get involved straightaway, but they were in no hurry to come up here, to the back of beyond. The whole business was hushed up. Justýna disappeared from view. They were like caged animals in that cottage, so she was given two choices: either she and the child would go to the one who did it to her, or if she wanted to stay, she would give the child away. That lovely young thing gave birth to a plump, strong girl who—so they said—already had teeth. You know what that means, don't you? An evil spirit, the birth of a witch. No doubt that was another reason why everyone pressed Justýna to get rid of it. She gave in. They devoted the child to the mother of Jesus by christening her Josefína Marie, and then they sent her away. I don't know where to, but it wasn't in Kopanice, where people would have known about it.

"Justýna was very unhappy, and she struggled to get over it. It must have preyed on her mind for all those years before she married Surmena, your grandfather. I remember that they always called her by her maiden name—she was always known as Ruchárka. Your grandfather was a young widower who'd been left with two small sons, which was why they allowed Justýna to take Josefína back. She fetched her straight after the wedding. By now she was getting on for six, and she was still a well-built girl. And she was—how should I put it? She was strange. She avoided other people, and she was stubborn, impossible to talk to. Not even Justýna could get through to her. Not even Justýna. Her own mother, least of all: Justýna was her archenemy.

"Who knows where Josefína—soon they were calling her Josifčena—spent her first six years? But it wasn't a good place, that's for sure. The child took it into her head that she'd been put there by a mother who didn't love her, and who could blame her for that? No one ever convinced her otherwise. It was probably wrong of Justýna to take her back. There were problems right from the start. And within a year, there was another child, another boy. Justýna had a troubled pregnancy, and the birth was somehow complicated, and after that—as is nature's way—she formed a strong attachment to the baby. Things had been tough before then, but now she didn't have even a second to spare for little Josifčena. Justýna lay there in the corner, and Josifčena, as the only daughter, had to manage the household. This didn't change when Justýna was up and about and ministering to all comers. As Josifčena watched her mother's delight in the baby she had struggled to bring into the world, she felt herself ignored. She had never seen anything like this before, and she didn't wish to see it again. But within the year, Justýna was pregnant again, and the whole thing repeated itself. How that child must have yearned for affection! After six years among strangers spent who knows where, her lot was hard work for no reward. It's no wonder she hardened—it's no wonder she turned out evil. Maybe even then she was getting ideas from her mother's ministrations and turning them to the bad.

"In the end, when she was about seventeen, she ran away. Justýna had just given birth to a daughter, the first after all the boys. In her delight Justýna let it slip that she was looking forward to having a little goddess in the cottage. I think the disappointment was too much for Josifčena to bear.

"Justýna had never thought of her firstborn daughter as her successor—perhaps because there were problems with her from the very beginning, perhaps because she felt threatened by her. Either way, Josifčena knew her position. Shortly after Justýna gave birth to your aunt Surmena, Josifčena packed up her things and left, turning up in Potočná at the home of a man recently widowed. Very recently, the whisper went around. His young wife had been strong and healthy, but something happened to her, and she was in her grave within the week. It was then that folk began to talk about the dark power within Josifčena, to refer to her as a goddess with nothing good to give. They began to fear her. I suppose you realize that apart from her mother, no one was in any doubt that she was a goddess. The powers of a goddess are inherited. Justýna realized too late that it was not for her to choose a successor from among her daughters; it was quite possible that she had two heirs. But by now Josifčena was in Potočná and had slipped out of her mother's control.

"Before long, Josifčena's reputation was such that folk were going to her with matters they wouldn't have taken to a good goddess. Folk who wished harm on others. The killing of livestock, revenge, hidden thievery, the quashing of rivals in love, to say nothing of the inflicting of personal injury. The mere mention of Josifčena's name was a cause of horror, and things only got worse after she stopped going to church. There were rumors that Josifčena had turned her back on God. That she had made a pact with the devil. I, too, believe them now. Perhaps *devil* is too strong a word, but it was certainly evil, the dark side of what we try to do as goddesses, that's for sure. And Josifčena was able to use it to her own advantage.

"There was one thing she failed in: she had no successor. A son was born to her, but after that, try as she might, she couldn't conceive. As the years passed, Josifčena began to fear that she was barren. That's how things stayed: she never had another child. That's why she was so attached to Fuksena, her only possible heir by blood. Right from when Fuksena was small, Josifčena did all she could to pass on to her everything she knew. Too bad she didn't warn her against making a pact with that German—things might not have ended so badly. But goddesses don't look into their own cards. Josifčena didn't consider what it meant that Fuksena's man was a German. It was enough that he had power and that the Germans were on top. It never crossed her mind that it wouldn't always be so. As you know, it came back to haunt them at the war's end, when Fuksena was beaten to death in the woods and her child disappeared. That's how things ended with Josifčena's line and her teachings. Then Josifčena died, when you were at boarding school or in Brno; I can't remember exactly when it was . . . And that's the whole story."

By now it was dark in the room. The silence was disturbed only by the crackle of fire in the stove and the beating of bare lime branches against the cottage roof. Irma was exhausted.

"That can't be all there is," said Dora suddenly.

"What?"

"That can't be all there is," Dora repeated. She looked with suspicion at the old woman wrapped up in her eiderdown.

"Why not?"

"Surmena didn't have the slightest reason to keep any of that secret from me."

Irma looked dubious, but Dora wouldn't be put off.

"There's nothing unusual in a sad family story. There are dozens worse in these parts. So why wasn't I supposed to know what you've just told me?"

Irma muttered a few angry words and ran a hand through her sparse hair. Irritated, she sat up straighter. Her resentment was growing.

"That's not the whole story," Dora insisted. "I asked you about a quarrel. What was it about? You didn't say."

Irma turned irritably in the bed. Then she looked hard at Dora and said, "Don't you try telling me that it's not in you! Maybe you don't know herbs, but there's a power inside you. You know there is. Listen to me, and now tell me truthfully: From time to time, strange things happen to you, don't they? Things don't turn out as you want them to . . . you have visions of what has gone before . . . there are strange coincidences and the like. Maybe there's still time for me to teach you a thing or two . . ."

"No." Dora pulled in her chin and shook her head. "Nothing like that. It's just that I still can't explain it. There's something missing. There's a reason why I've never been told the whole story. What went on between them?"

Irma sighed and asked for another cup of tea. "This is making my throat dry," she said, waiting to say anything else until she'd had more tea.

"The worst thing was what Josifčena said when she ran away from Justýna. All the brothers and her stepfather heard it, and one of them didn't mind his mouth—it soon got around. Maybe at first, folk didn't really believe it. But a few years later, Josifčena's reputation was stronger. There were reports here and there that someone had died or fallen ill as a result of her sorcery. Suddenly people saw what she said in a different light. You've probably guessed what it was by now. Josifčena left in such a rage that she did something to the newborn baby. Surmena. Not Justýna. She wished a life in everlasting fear on that little scrap and all others born as girls who came after it. She cursed them and passed sentence on them: they would grow to adulthood, but they would never bring anyone joy, and their lives would be filled with sorrow and ill fortune. Nothing substantial would be generated of and around them; their lives would remain barren, and their deaths would be so grim and filled with suffering that for years to come, the people of these parts would speak of the awful ends of those who angered Josifčena. Don't look at me so surprised! You're acting as if you aren't from this place. You know very well that it's possible here. I remember how folk would stand in front of the church after Sunday Mass and nod in the direction of Justýna and the children. The cursed ones, they'd say. Meaning Surmena and Irena. It's fortunate that Justýna didn't have any more girls. They carried that curse around with them like a pig's intestine, from birth till death; neither of them had things easy. When I imagine dying in pain and suffering, I think of Justýna's two daughters. One by the ax, the other in the madhouse. But I'm getting ahead of myself."

Irma swallowed with difficulty. "From the very beginning, all kinds of bad things went on around those two girls. Everyone knew they were cursed. Other children feared them, recoiled from them. That's why neither Surmena nor Irena went to school: they were shunned by other children. Justýna never forced them to go. Their family wasn't keen on schooling in any case, and besides, she was afraid for them and preferred to keep them close to the cottage. She tied them to her by worry and fear, and she cut them off from normal life. But this isolation did no one any favors.

"I hardly remember Surmena as a child and when she was growing up. I can't even remember what she looked like. She never left the Bedová. She never left the family, and she spoke to nobody else, even after Mass. Folk used to say that she was strange. And that the younger one—Irena, your mum—was even stranger. She shunned the family and lived in her own world. They said that she could speak with angels. I think they appeared to her because she knew that they were all she had.

"Justýna was an anxious type. She infected Surmena and Irena with her horror of the curse, which I'm sure they hated. Each of them dealt with it in her own way. Irena defied it. She pretended that the curse didn't exist, and she hated the fearful mother who reminded her otherwise every day. She had no interest in learning; she believed only in those angels of hers, and she thought they were all she needed. But she was wrong—it was because of her angels that the goddess in her perished. And that wasn't the only well that ran dry in the family, just as Mahdalka had foretold. Yes, Irena had children, but what children they were! Jakoubek's a poor thing. And you? Don't you wince, my girl—you're over forty, and what have you got? A head full of fragments, just like you said, but none of them fit together. You'll never have any children, and you didn't want to be a goddess. Irena's barrenness has stayed in her line. And her death? She carried it with her from childhood. She had nothing to do with anyone, so it's no wonder no one wanted her. It made her desperate; she was like a bitch in heat—I've never seen such a needy woman before or since. In the end she had no choice but to accept the only one who asked her. Everyone knew that all Matyáš Ides had was his debts and his drinking. He was the only one prepared to overlook the fact that his bride was mad and cursed. All he was interested in was her property. He thought that as the daughter of a goddess, she surely made good money, and that once they were married, she would pay off his debts. There was no talk of love, but even so he knocked her up practically the first time he touched her. After that it was headlong toward disaster. Ides had made a big mistake: yes, Irena got the cottage on the Koprvazy that old man Surmena had come into just before he died, but that was all. An old cottage that was falling down around their ears. It's still waiting for someone to fix it up properly. In those days everyone in these hills knew of his disappointment and the grudge he bore because of it. And they knew about the brutality of his beatings, which she was powerless to do anything against. She'd come to him entirely defenseless, lacking any experience of self-protection against movements of the human mind, and anyway, she loved him and looked up to him to the point of reverence. Before he closed her eyes with that ax."

Dora was looking at Irma wide-eyed, and she was having trouble breathing. This was not what she had expected.

"And Surmena? She defied the curse, too, in her own way. But unlike Irena she didn't deny its existence. She opted for caution and built a wall around her that kept strangers out. That's why she spent her whole life on her own. She became a devoted goddess because she was determined to defeat the curse by her own arts. She wanted to prove to people that there was no need to recoil from her and avoid her as if she were a mangy dog. She wanted to prove that she could be of use to people in spite of her ill fortune. She succeeded in this: people came to like her, even though the talk about her never stopped. But Mahdalka's words came true anyway. Surmena ended up barren, just as Mahdalka had said she would: her children died, and she was left with no successor to pass on her knowledge to. And her death? In a madhouse somewhere, who knows how? But no one would doubt that she died in suffering.

"Folk still whisper about how Mahdalka brought down her own family. If you ask me, you should take a good hard look at what's happening with you. How you're living an unfulfilled life that even the biggest gossips don't comment on. There's nothing to say: it's as if you weren't living at all . . . You weren't supposed to hear any of what I've just told you. Surmena let you live in ignorance to spare you the fear that wrecked her own life, and she minded others to make sure they let nothing slip. I think that was the right thing to do. Now you've lost your peace of mind."

Irma's small bony chest bounced to her irregular breathing, and she was having trouble swallowing. Dora worried that she had been overinsistent. Had she failed to realize how fragile Irma was and how much this effort might cost her? Herself upset, she remained seated at the table, waiting in silence for the old woman to recover her composure. She toyed with the plaited band at her wrist, which had lost its deep-red color years before. *"Never take it off,"* Surmena had told her when she gave it to her.

That had been at the time when they came for them, the time they had taken Jakoubek away. Many people in these parts believed that the red bracelet protected them from evil spells. Dora had almost forgotten its original significance; for years she had cherished it as a memento of Surmena. Now the sense of it came back to her with full force.

She raised her eyes to look at Irma. Once she was sure that the old woman's breathing was more regular, she dared to say, "It's nonsense, Auntie."

Irma's expression was one of surprise as she said, "What do you mean?"

"All that curse business. It's nonsense. Superstition. What you told me about Mahdalka is scary, I agree. But this? In this day and age? Auntie, I'm from this place, and I know what the goddesses can do, but I refuse to believe that I'm cursed."

A silence fell. An awkward, suffocating silence.

"I think that Surmena was wasting her time trying to protect me. It's crazy to believe in curses and live your life in fear as a result. Gossip never killed anyone!"

Dora sensed the anger that was building inside Irma. Her eyes narrowed to thin lines, and her face swelled with rage. Her voice, quiet but ice cold, cut into the tension. "It's up to you whether or not you believe it. But I won't tolerate ingratitude to a woman like Surmena."

"I'm not ungrateful. It's just that I . . ."

"Believe what you want," Irma hissed, interrupting roughly. "Doubt all you like the causes of subjugation. You'll know them well enough when you put your own fingers on the wounds, just as Thomas did. But as long as I live and breathe, I'll never hear another word spoken against Surmena. Do you understand? It's only thanks to her that you live your good-for-nothing life as you do. She forbade the folk of these hills from talking in front of you about what hangs over your family. Without her painstaking efforts to protect you from all the talk, you'd have been in pieces long before now, and no one would have been able to put you together again. Can you imagine growing up knowing that people were avoiding you because they believed without question that you were branded, peculiar, and dangerous?"

"But, Auntie! A few words can't bring about a person's death. Words can't have killed my mother or Surmena."

"Hold your tongue! People have died for far less than belief in words. If you believe in something and the folk around you believe in it, too, you're heading that way whether or not you want to go there. Mahdalka wouldn't have needed any special powers to manage her curse. Understand this: human faith in whatever, provided it is strong and unshakable faith, is tremendously powerful."

Dora was at a loss. So this was the essence of the secret that had been weighing her down over the past few months? Mean-spirited women's gossip first uttered around 1910, when Surmena was born? Still, she couldn't believe that a trifle motivated by human hate could resonate in her own life today. What had Irma said? That everyone believed it? That everyone was following her unfulfilled, barren life to see if the curse was taking effect?

Dora got up, ready to leave. In silence she cleared the table and headed for the door.

But before she left, Irma drew her back with a question. "How did things end up with your father?"

Dora smiled. "No one has ever given me more important advice."

Irma nodded and at once looked far happier than she had a moment earlier.

"I knew that it would make you feel better," she said before closing her eyes and turning her face to the wall.

The Red Bracelet

*W*hat Dora told Irma as she was leaving was true: no one had given her such relief as Irma had, by encouraging her to speak with her father. To think that at first, she hadn't believed her, had even been angry with her, and that in her mind, she had called her a cynical old biddy.

Now, as she walked slowly back up to the Bedová, she realized she felt similarly. Again it seemed to her that Irma was giving utterance to crazy ideas with their origins in superstitions. Didn't Dora know goddesses? Hadn't she seen for years what goddesses did? But a knowledge of herbs and advice to give relief to the human soul were one thing, a curse that was supposed to have brought about the deaths of her mother and Surmena quite another. That was complete nonsense. All the more so as Irma was convinced that it affected her, too, almost a century later, in a world run by computers where humankind knocked about on the moon because all the secrets of Earth had been revealed.

Foolishness, she told herself. There was nothing to be afraid of.

But hardly had she finished reassuring herself than she pulled up short. Had she really just told herself that? Did she really have the need to assuage her fear of something she didn't even believe in? If she did, she was separated by very little from the locals, who froze with fear at every mention of black magic. And she, an academic!

She was disgusted by these intrusive thoughts and shook her head in an attempt to expel them. She remembered an assertion she had come across several times during her studies: where science ends, the self begins. Only now did she grasp its meaning.

Let's get back to science, she told herself firmly as she continued on her way. Briskly, she skirted the fields and slopes of Žítková, which by now were cloaked in gloom. The faster she walked, the more forcefully she suppressed her doubts. Silly old wives' tales. What a fool she was to have been taken in by them even for a moment!

Emerging from the woods and seeing on the dark-blue horizon the ridge with their cottage, she was surprised by her feelings of relief. She was close to home, where she felt safe; close to Jakoubek, who was waiting for her there (probably still sleeping just as she had left him); close to her everyday life, where curses had no place.

At once, she was sure that her life rested firmly in her own hands—hands whose work had brought her where she was now, got Jakoubek back, fixed up the cottage, fixed her life and Jakoubek's. She looked at them. By the work of these hands, she had recovered their security; she totally rejected any reminder of earlier dangers. The red bracelet symbolized the absurdity of the story that Irma had told. This bracelet was suddenly odious to her, its presence around her wrist unwelcome, as it tied her to something she rejected. All the warm memories associated with it fell away, leaving only a distaste for the ridiculous superstition that had caused Surmena to make her wear it as protection against Mahdalka's curse. She could no longer bear it on her: she tugged at the small knot until the bracelet snapped.

So light as to be practically weightless, it traveled briefly through the air before landing next to the path, where it remained suspended on a tall blade of grass.

"I don't believe it." Dora spoke these words with resolve. Then she hastened up to the cottage. Before she reached it, their field, too, had been swallowed by the dark autumn night.

She opened the door quietly, so as not to wake him.

She heard nothing and groped for the switch, flooding the room with light. Immediately, she saw him. He was standing by the window, pants around his ankles, a hand at his erect member. Caught in the cold light of the bulb, he froze and stared at her, motionless apart from the penis in his hand, which was smaller with every passing second. Suddenly, he was cowering and bewildered.

This was nothing new to her. On each of several earlier occasions, they had managed it in an orderly fashion; it was natural, after all.

But this time it was different.

Jakoubek stood as if frozen to the spot. By the movements of his eyes and the tic at the corners of his mouth, she knew that he was unable to shake off his confusion. Had he been startled by the sudden noise and the glare? Had he been frightened? Or had he felt shame for the first time?

In those few seconds when he stood in front of her with his pants around his ankles, Dora tried to read his expression. But before she could assess the situation and offer him her usual words of comfort, something changed. Before, he had always stood up straight and smiled at her sheepishly, but now he started shaking and yelling. Then he jumped at the window and smashed it. A moment later, he was beating his head with his fists as well as lashing out at the jagged shards of the broken window, over and over, like a madman.

"Enough!" Dora screamed.

Then she ran to him. As though her scream had also been an instruction, he ran at her in the same instant. She could never have imagined that such an impact would be so overwhelming. It knocked the breath out of her and caused her knees to buckle. After she hit the floor, Jakoubek's full weight came down on top of her.

Both were overcome by panic. Deprived of the ability to stand by Jakoubek's spread-eagled body, Dora lost all self-control and began to scream and writhe. Her screams were joined by a roar of desperation from Jakoubek, whose arms were flailing and beating against her. Several times he caught her with an elbow; several times more, his weight fell against her chest or shoulder, bringing tears of pain to her eyes. Eventually, she succeeded in yanking her arms free and leaning her own weight against his shoulders. She caught her breath and forced out a few words.

"Be calm. We can do this! Calm down!"

Jakoubek did not respond. His eyes clamped shut, and he continued to twitch. Meanwhile, the deep-throated animal roar became a howl. As he bellowed and howled, the spittle from his mouth splashed against Dora's face; hampered by the pants around his ankles, he used his knees to deal Dora's thighs and lower abdomen blow after blow. In this confusion of writhing bodies, she at last managed to free herself by rolling him onto his side. She was gasping, and her nose was filled with a stink of spittle and sweat.

After that it was as though something came over him. First his whole body went tense; then he was thrashing about in a convulsive seizure, the wild movements of his body beating against the wooden floor. He looked like an absurdly animated rag doll, and there was no way of getting him under control.

Dora was overwhelmed by another surge of anxiety. Jakoubek was in danger of cracking his head open. In a desperate attempt to prevent him from injuring himself, she placed her feeble frame across his back and took his head in her hands.

They remained like this until the jerking became trembling. She got up quickly and went to the cabinet above the bed for the medicine box, which was secured with a strap to keep Jakoubek out of it, just in case he discovered it by chance. Her hands were shaking so much that she struggled to free it. She unzipped the box and emptied the contents onto the bed. She rummaged frantically, found the packet she was looking for, and dashed back to Jakoubek with a strip of pills.

His jaws were shut tight, his lips swollen and an unnatural, shiny purple. His battered forehead bore a trickle of blood from temple to chin. In a determined attempt to get Jakoubek's mouth open, Dora pressed down on his face, but try as she might, his teeth remained clenched. So she leaned over his exposed backside, pushed a pill from the strip, and used her finger to force it deep into his rectum.

Later that night she sat in a corridor at the hospital in Uherské Hradiště, rubbing nervously at the strip of lighter skin on the wrist where the red bracelet had been. Now that she had spoken to the doctor and telephoned Jakoubek's institution, there was nothing left for her to do. Although she felt empty, there was one terrible thought that she couldn't banish: this was her fault. Because of her skepticism, her doubting, her ridiculing of superstition and belief in curses. For having thrown away the red bracelet.

She rested her head against the tiled wall and closed her eyes. Only now was it dawning on her how wise Surmena had been to shield her from Mahdalka's curse, regardless of whether its threat was substantial or only in people's heads. Her family had borne so much ill fortune that the question had to be entertained: What if it was no coincidence that these things had happened to them? What if they really were the results of a decades-old curse, and this curse had now reached her and Jakoubek? How could she have reached adulthood in the knowledge of its existence? How could she have lived a normal life?

Every day of her life, she would have waited for the curse to be made real. Would some driver fail to brake as she was crossing the road in Hrozenkov? Caught up in a storm on the slopes, would she be struck by lightning? Would she have an epileptic fit and be left in a coma, as Jakoubek was now?

Věnceslav Rozmazal

$\mathcal{S}$he remembered him from her time at the university, and his class Changes in the Social Life of the Village Cooperative, which was obviously a cause of suffering to him. When she looked at his profile in the faculty book, she knew why: his dissertation had been titled "Defunct Instruments of Practitioners of Folk Music in South Moravia." His lectures on the Socialist village must have caused him as much anguish as they had caused his students. In those days he was renowned for taking practically no interest in his students. As he talked, his eyes would be fixed on a point beyond the window, somewhere out in the courtyard. It seemed unlikely that he'd even notice if all the seats in the classroom were empty. When he did turn to his students, he always faltered, gave a sad smile, then continued with his lecture to the window.

She came across him again in the early days of her employment at the Institute of Ethnography and Folklore, when, as a novice, she was given various small tasks to perform. One such task took her to the Moravian Museum, where he worked.

This was immediately before his retirement, and he was known for his bad temper and unwillingness to cooperate. His colleagues tended to give him a wide berth; he was passing his last weeks of employment in solitude, in an office cluttered with old musical instruments from the repository that he had held on to for years, for research purposes.

Nobody minded this. Lack of interest was widespread among staff, managers, and repository administrators; if some of the instruments had disappeared, no one would have noticed. She had heard that at that time—the end of the 1980s—there was a decent trade in such things. Outside of Czechoslovakia, of course.

Rozmazal was no trader, that was for sure. He was so crazy about his instruments that he wouldn't have let them out of his sight, or at least not out of the museum's.

At that time, he refused to see her; he needed all his remaining time for his instruments. He had some work to finish, she was told by the museum librarian.

Dora forgot about Rozmazal until she read his name under a report in Surmena's file.

For weeks she tried to contact him, determined not to be put off. But if he was not merely ill, he was in the hospital; his son, with whom Rozmazal lived, refused all her requests until after her return from Poznań, when at last he gave in. Early one evening she presented herself at a well-maintained two-story house in Brno's Židenice quarter, rang the doorbell, and was invited upstairs.

He was lying on a sofa by the window, half-covered by a blanket. He struggled to lift himself by his elbows to greet her. His every movement was cumbersome and accompanied by a tremor.

"Take a seat," he muttered between lips that then remained slackly open so that Dora found herself looking straight into his toothless mouth.

She sat down in a chair opposite the sofa. Between her and him was a small table with light refreshments prepared by Rozmazal's daughter-in-law.

"You say that we're colleagues? From the museum?"

"No, from the academy," Dora replied.

"So what brings you here? Are you a musician?"

"No, I'm from the Department of Ethnology. I specialize in the spiritual culture of the Moravské Kopanice region."

"I see," said Rozmazal, obviously confused. "So what is it that you need?"

"Your expert advice, Dr. Rozmazal," said Dora politely.

Rozmazal smiled weakly and then spoke slowly. "Oh yes . . . I used to be an advisor. I supervised quite a few dissertations and theses. I taught at the university, you know."

"Yes. I was one of your students, in 1985. You lectured on the Socialist village."

Rozmazal made a scoffing sound. "Dreadful subject." He paused to swallow hard before continuing. "We had no choice, you know, those of us who wanted to stay where we were. I wanted to stay at the museum. My work was with historical musical instruments; it was my passion, that and folk music. I couldn't have done without them. So you see, I had to teach about the Socialist village."

"I do see," said Dora.

"Do you really? Then you're one of few. These days people think of you as a coward if you kept your mouth shut, did your work, and didn't protest in the streets. At least that's how my son sees it. But I loved my instruments, you see, and nothing so terrible happened to me. Apart from the Socialist village, but that was only once a week for a few years. I could put up with that."

Rozmazal's voice was hoarse, and he was struggling to get the words out.

"Do you need a drink?" Dora asked.

"Y-Yes . . . But you'll have to hold it up to my mouth. That one there, with the straw. I can't manage on my own."

Dora stepped around the table, poured some water into the glass, and held the straw up to Rozmazal's mouth. He sipped through clenched lips, making an unpleasant sucking noise.

"Enough. Thank you. So why are you here?"

Dora sat back down in her chair.

"Because of what I'm working on."

He nodded.

"While I was collecting materials, I found a report you'd written. On the goddesses of Žítková."

"Žítková?" said Rozmazal uncertainly.

"That's right. Žítková, near Starý Hrozenkov, in the Moravské Kopanice region."

His eyebrows went up, and deep grooves plowed through the liver spots on his forehead.

"I'd almost forgotten about them. I never paid much attention to them, you know. The folk musicians of Kopanice, yes, but not the women."

"But you wrote an expert's appraisal."

"Appraisal? Perhaps I did. We had to write those reports. I applied to join the party, you know. That's right. But I didn't want to join the party; I wanted to be at the museum."

Dora nodded. She was afraid that Rozmazal's thoughts were drifting away from the topic.

"I understand that," she assured him.

"Yes, I suppose you are young enough to understand. To understand sincerely, as it were."

"It was a report on the goddesses of Žítková. You wrote it in 1949. It was about their activities during the war."

"Above all, I wanted to be at the museum. I'd just been awarded my higher doctorate. Can you imagine the use I'd have put it to if they hadn't let me stay on? Then there was my bourgeois origin. My mother's family had owned a tenement on Veselá Street, you know. But it was flattened in the bombings during the war, so when the Communists came to power, we had nothing to worry about: there was nothing left for them to confiscate. Anyway, above all, I wanted to be at the museum."

Dora kept an awkward silence.

"So the odd report I had to write seemed to me a lesser evil than the compromises my colleagues were making. Yes, it's quite possible that they gave me something to review and I wrote something about it."

Dora was relieved to learn that he was not entirely lost in his past.

"What was it about in particular? I can't remember a thing about it."

"The goddesses . . ." Dora faltered as she always did when she had to speak about them. "Remarkable women who used herbs to heal. Today we'd call what they did 'alternative medicine.' They lived in the White Carpathians and passed on what they learned from generation to generation. So far, I've researched the earliest documented members of a family, victims of the Bojkovice witch trials. Which is how the Germans came to know about them. They were studied by the SS-Hexen-Sonderkommando. Do you remember now?"

"*Those* women! Of course." But then he shook his head. "To tell the truth, it's going on fifty years . . . and as I said, my main interest has always been instruments. I remember very few details about the topic or my report on it."

Dora had a copy of the report with her. She pulled it from her bag and held it up. "Would you like me to read it to you?"

Rozmazal shrugged. "Very well, why not?"

After she finished, a silence settled on the room. Rozmazal's eyes were closed.

"I can't really blame my son, I suppose," he said quietly.

Dora was aware of beads of sweat along her spine. In a mood of reproach, her mind raked over Rozmazal's formulations. "*. . . on the basis of scientific materialism, have produced sufficient evidence to prove the falsity of belief in supernatural powers*" and "*The surrendering of practical reason leads necessarily to the enslavement of humanity.*"

But that would change because everything would change, and very soon, she reminded herself. She would not desist in her unraveling of the life stories of the goddesses until she had written her study—and this study would know no compromise. She cleared her throat loudly.

Rozmazal gave a start, opened his eyes, and said, "I wrote it for them, you understand. The tone and the diction are theirs. It's awful. I had to keep them sweet . . . When all's said and done, it was for them."

Weary eyes looked into hers.

"As you read, they were simple village comrades. Do you think I would have written those things if circumstances were different? I, a graduate in ethnology, a scholar of music who specialized in folklore? Would I have described those women at the heart of village society as comrades? Would I have written that whoever believed in them was an obscurantist? Of course not. I did it because I knew it was exactly what they wanted. It was perfectly clear. It had to be written from the right ideological perspective on progressive and nonprogressive tradition, and it had to be infused with a bit of their jargon. We referred to it as 'palm greasing' and 'using the right vocabulary.' If I did that, I could be sure that they'd leave me in peace. In peace and at the museum. That's why Professor Vejrosta and I wrote it as we did, even though we knew next to nothing about the subject. The letter by the German didn't give us much to go on. And in '49, even if materials from abroad hadn't been practically unobtainable, probably there wouldn't have been any on the subject anyway . . . So that's how the report got written." Rozmazal sighed heavily.

"I'm interested in something else," said Dora.

Rozmazal looked at her in surprise. "What?"

"I'd like to know who asked you to write the report."

He was taken aback. "Isn't the name given?"

"No. It's blacked out. Perhaps it was censored later. All I know is the name of an officer who was responsible for it at a later date: Švanc."

The old man shook his head. "Could you read me the first sentence again, please?"

" 'On the basis of a letter written by Dr. Rudolf Levin of the SS, which was entrusted to me for appraisal by Comrade'—this is where it is blacked out—'on June 17, 1948, inclusive of a translation into Czech, I have, in cooperation with Professor Rudolf Vejrosta of the Department of History of the Moravian Museum . . .' "

"It has to be the same man, doesn't it?"

"The same man?"

"Švanc. That's right . . . I remember that name. It was shortly after the war, and you were never sure whether to give a name a German or a Czech spelling. Perhaps I gave the wrong one. All this was nothing unusual, as you know: many a Czech Germanized his name during the war and then turned it back again afterward. I knew lots of people who adopted a Czech version of their name. So I probably spelled it wrong, and then they blacked it out."

Dora blinked to indicate surprise.

"No, really. I remember now. I met this Švanc and no one else. He gave me the letter—officially, through the museum—and asked for an expert's appraisal. Probably I wrote down his name in its German form, as 'Schwanz' or some such, and he then crossed it out because it wasn't the done thing. Because he was the one I submitted the report to. I remember how pleased he was with it. It was particularly important to him, or so it seemed."

Rozmazal started coughing.

The old man's daughter-in-law looked into the room. "Everything all right, Dad?"

Rozmazal gave a few last, smothered coughs and nodded. Dora got up to give him another drink. The woman closed the door quietly.

"My son would never have done it like that, you know. That's why he doesn't understand. All I cared about was my music. That's why I did things a person would normally refuse to do. Or do in a different way. That report, for instance. I knew he was a state security agent, so I wrote it in the way I assumed he wanted it. Yet I knew nothing about the women. It didn't matter to me . . . Did anything happen to them as a result?"

Dora shook her head. "Not as a result of that."

He was visibly relieved. "That's something, at least."

The next day, Dora arrived at her office an hour earlier than usual. The echo of her footsteps was muffled by the worn linoleum of the dimly lit corridors. Hardly had she taken off her coat—which was covered with constellations of ice flakes—than she stepped up to the shelves of books, files, and folders. The writings of the first folklorists; xerox copies of ethnographers' reports arranged by topic—A (Kopanice), B (Goddesses), C (Other); several issues of *The Czech People* and the *Foundation for Moravia Magazine*. Dora looked lower, for a file marked "SS-Hexen-Sonderkommando." She pulled it out and began to leaf through it frantically.

She found a transparent sleeve that bore a sticker with the words "HEINRICH SCHWANNZE." It contained several pages of handwritten notes, which she had taken in Poznań. Brief notes, because of all the names she had discovered there, she hadn't expected Schwannze's to be significant. During the occupation there had been dozens of informers like him. All that singled out Schwannze was his special interest in the goddesses.

"Schwannze, Schwannze," Dora said under her breath as she ran her finger along the words. This was what she was looking for: her notes on entries made on official *Sicherheitsdienst* forms.

He had signed these in early 1940. Starting salary 1,400 Protectorate crowns, which, by the end of the war, had risen to a respectable 2,000. Evidently, Schwannze was a procurer. Date of birth: July 20, 1913.

She put the open folder down on her desk and returned to the shelf. At waist height was a far more voluminous file containing notes on State Security surveillance of Surmena. She pulled this out and flicked through the pages in their transparent sleeves until she came to one with the highlighted designation "JINDŘICH ŠVANC." She took this out.

She'd had these photocopied pages in her hands perhaps a hundred times. They were supplemented with many notes on small slips of paper, several of which now fell out of the sleeve and floated under the desk. Dora turned to an article she had obtained from the clippings service of South Moravia's daily newspaper, whose publicly accessible archive went back to the mid-1980s.

> *Jarošov Herald*, February 21, 1986
> We'll Never Forget You, Jindřich
> This article appears exactly two weeks after our dear comrade and friend Jindřich Švanc departed this world. I could not allow his passing to be remarked upon only by those closest to him, of whom, regrettably, there were few. I feel impelled to give an account of his life—a life devoted to the fight against enemies of our Socialist homeland—to you, too, dear reader of the *Jarošov Herald*. I wish us all to be aware of this exceptional man who lived among us.
>
> Jindřich Švanc was born on July 20, 1913 near Horní Němčí. An avid sportsman from a young age, he was particularly keen on football and cycling. This came to an end, however, when he suffered an unfortunate injury at work: a painter and decorator, he was painting a room for a Horní Němčí bourgeois family that wished to save money by engaging too few workers, when he fell from a ladder.
>
> After a long period of recuperation, he found himself no longer able to practice his original profession; he was required to find another purpose in life. He found this in Marxism-Leninism, and he determined

to devote all his strength and efforts to converting its ideas into reality.

He was counted among those of us who endeavor to make real the profound thoughts of those philosophers who show us how to live in a healthy, friendly, honest society of workers and their children. He, Jindřich Švanc, did this not only in words but also in deeds, by which he fought for our collective happiness. Even during the occupation, he was already known far and wide for his daring: he was a smuggler of Communist leaflets, and as a result, he was persecuted by the Gestapo.

His brave deeds were not forgotten. Soon after the war, I met Jindřich among the Communists of South Moravia and made his acquaintance. After 1948 I got to know him better, as a fellow law enforcer with the National Security Corps. More than once I witnessed the good use to which Jindřich put the sense of fair play he had developed in his days as a sportsman. We became friends for life. In the 1950s we served in the same department and saw each other practically every day. We often discussed the difficult journey ahead for the young Socialist republic and asked ourselves what the future held. Jindřich was convinced that the future would be as we built it. For this reason he devoted himself to his work, allowing it to absorb all his free time; for the sake of the well-being of the citizens of Czechoslovakia, he never started a family. Work was everything to him. At the department, he was the first to arrive and the last to leave, and as far as he was concerned, there was no such thing as a weekend or a holiday. He worked tirelessly with 200 percent commitment. Thanks to his interventions, many hostile elements were foiled in their attempts to disrupt the peaceful life of the Czechoslovak Republic.

I am proud to have been Jindřich's friend, and I regret that I was unable to help him in his final struggle. But this struggle was personal, not public—with an insidious disease that devoured him from the inside. The struggle lasted several weeks, which he spent at home in the midst of the community he loved. Though he was a great fighter, Jindřich never made it to the hospital. He died in the early hours of February 7, 1986.

Jindřich, my comrade in the struggle, it was an honor for me to work alongside you. I promise on behalf of our colleagues and friends that you will never be forgotten.

Antonín Líček

So there it was: the two men were born on the same day. Dora sank back into her chair.

The last few months had passed at such a furious pace that she had been unable fully to process the flood of new findings. At the time she was deluged by Baglárka's and then Irma's memories, she was still digesting what she had learned from the file kept on Surmena. And on top of all this, there was Jakoubek.

Since receiving her letter from the Ministry and stepping up her investigation, she had made a number of small discoveries—of which Líček's article was the most significant—but nothing more. Her several telephone calls to police headquarters in Uherské Hradiště and the Jarošov district council drew a blank. She didn't know where to turn next.

But now one figure had popped up again—this time in far more textured form: Schwannze/Švanc. A man who had succeeded in bluffing his way from one regime to the next with such deftness that he had saved his own skin. The man who had trampled on the goddesses, on Surmena, for so long that he had crushed them.

She devoted the next few days to him. She made calls, asked questions, searched online, and read practically every finding of the Office for the Documentation and Investigation of the Crimes of Communism. Nothing. All anyone knew was the fact of his existence. All roads led nowhere.

But then, she got lucky.

Ingeborg Pitínová

At half past seven, Dora was standing in the square in Prakšice, which comprised a circle of withered, frost-coated grass with a spreading, bare lime at its center bordered by a few squat houses, all approached by a single road. The little village was hidden in the valley between vast fields. To all appearances, it was still sleeping.

She walked slowly so as to read the numbers on the houses. The house number in her notebook was 27, which she could not find. The end of the village was marked by dilapidated barbed-wire fences. A dog was running along one of these, barking in desperation, but although the fence was full of holes, it did not cross the boundary. Somewhere at Dora's back, a gate creaked and someone yelled, "Shut your mouth, you idiot!"

Dora was about to turn and cross the road when the man's voice asked, "What are you hanging about that fence for?"

"I'm looking for number twenty-seven," she said. "Mrs. Pitínová lives there."

"You're in the wrong place, then. It's on the other side. Back through the square, right at the church, and down toward the pond."

"Thank you," Dora called back before following the man's directions.

It was one of the last houses at the opposite end of the village. For a while Dora stood in front of it and looked at the open, undulating landscape that stretched out beyond it as far as the eye could see. While some fields were dark brown, those closest to the woods had retained a dusting of snow. In the hollow, the pond reflected the scudding clouds.

To get herself warm, she decided to walk to the pond and back. She had time to kill: it was far too early to call on a stranger.

Shortly before nine she rang the doorbell of number 27. Her finger was still on the button when she heard shuffling footsteps beyond the door, which was then opened by an old woman.

"Good morning. I'm Dora Idesová. I called you on Thursday."

"Yes, of course." The old woman dried her wet hands on a dishcloth. Dora noticed the varicose veins and the skin scarred with the dark spots of age. "But not here," the woman whispered quickly before looking about. "Go back to the square and I'll come for you there. Then we'll go to the cemetery. My son's not happy about it . . ."

Dora nodded, whereupon the woman closed the door.

A good twenty minutes passed before she came shuffling in Dora's direction.

"I didn't mention it to my son. He wouldn't want me talking about Jindřich to anyone. It's not right, he says, because of his reputation. I'm sure you know what I mean. I'm not especially proud of him, you know, but the whole thing doesn't seem to me to be as terrible as all that. It was a bad time; everyone did what they had to do to survive. Jindřich was always a good sort; it was just that his luck was bad. Yes, he was one of them—but that was just a way out for him."

Dora didn't know whether she was speaking of the Gestapo or the State Security Police, but she didn't think it right to ask, having only just met this woman.

"What brought you to me?"

Dora cleared her throat. "I read somewhere that your brother came from Horní Němčí. I called the registry office there because I wanted to find out his new address. They told me they'd had no address for him since the war. He must have been expelled, they said, because your family was German. But they told me about you. That you married in 1945 and stayed here. And that you live in Prakšice. They gave me your address. Please forgive me for contacting you out of the blue like this."

"There's nothing to forgive. I'm curious about why you've come. You must tell me everything. So the people at the registry office can tell you what they like? Like where I live now and that I was a German?"

"I don't know. They told me."

The woman started walking as she began to speak. "With a name like Ingeborg Schwannze, everyone knows straight off that you're a German anyway. Even now it's difficult to pass it off as a Czech name. Of course, today my name is Pitínová. Here they call me Ina. But you should have seen how they used to scowl at me in the old days when I showed my identity card. I got married straight after the liberation. It was obvious that the Germans weren't going to have it easy here after the war. And truly they didn't: most of them were expelled. But I'd had a boyfriend the whole war long. We'd been keen on each other since school. Ludvík, his name was. I lost him to cancer ten years ago. He married me in May, when we knew that something was about to happen. What with the wedding and the fact that it was spring, and with everyone being so happy that the war had ended, I fell pregnant straightaway. For me, the months after the liberation were a beautiful time. But for most Germans here, they were anything but. They must have hit Jindřich hard, too, because he didn't show himself here for four years, and we had no news of him. We tried different ways of looking for him, including writing to the Red Cross, but for nothing. Then in the early 1950s, the doorbell rang and he invited himself in for coffee as if nothing had happened. My husband wasn't too happy about it, I can tell you. The word had got around that Jindřich had been in prison before the war and that he may have had something to do with the Nazis during it. You know how it is; such talk doesn't do a man much good. But I knew how things were. Times were pretty hard for us, you know. People used to think the Schwannzes were well off—they owned a house in Horní Němčí and a piece of land, but that wasn't much, you know. The field's yield was poor, and during the crisis, we were glad that it even kept us fed. I don't remember much about it, you know—a little girl doesn't worry about money—but my parents told me later that we could be happy that we'd survived it. No savings and fear of the future—these were things we talked about a lot. And then there was one more mouth to feed—Jindřich got married. To a right trollop—goodness knows where he found her. She was pretty, but she was a slut. She must have reeled him in at some dance, when he was the worse for drink. Then she got herself pregnant, so what could Jindřich do but marry her? But he married her for love too. He'd fallen for her head over heels, like young men do. But they had to live with us, and another mouth to feed was a big deal. Lena—that's what she was called—was always arguing with Mother. And as Mother was every inch a woman, she wasn't prepared to put up with it. The year we all spent together, the year before they locked up Jindřich, was a terrible one. Poor man. He did it because of her, you know. Sick and tired of the constant arguing with Mother, Lena went on and on about how he should find them somewhere else to live. But for that he needed more money. I don't blame him for snapping. I'm convinced that all he intended to do was steal a few trinkets. I'm sure he had no thoughts of murder. It was an unfortunate coincidence that the old man showed up. Jindřich was a good man. He was incapable of doing anyone an injury, and that's why he didn't kill our neighbor. Anyway, he got caught, and they locked him up for five years. The floozy fled right after the trial, and she took the kid with her. I don't know where she went. It knocked the wind out of Jindřich. He had a breakdown in prison. I know that because Mother and I went to see him there several times. He was as miserable as a man can be.

"After they released him, just before the war, he gave himself up to his work. He was looking for a purpose, and he no longer trusted women. He was swallowed up by the new age and the good work it could give him, even though it was for the wrong side. To begin with, he traveled a lot as an interpreter—in those days interpreters between Czech and German were much in demand—and then he must have moved up in the world, been given more important jobs to do, because he visited us less and less. And then, like I said before, he stopped showing up altogether, until the early 1950s. Could you give me a hand with these, please? These days I find it difficult to walk with them."

They had reached the cemetery. She had been pushing a small handcart filled with a bag, some tools, and a large Advent wreath. Only now, as she was parking the handcart at the gates to the cemetery, was she prepared to accept Dora's help. Dora bent down, picked the things out of the cart, and slung the bag over her shoulder. Her arms filled with fragrant pine needles, she followed Mrs. Pitínová across the cemetery.

"Here's my Ludvík," the old woman said when Dora caught up with her. "I wanted him to have a light grave. He was a light person altogether. Hair, eyes, and most of all, his soul. Such a kind man! Such a shame he passed so early! But he was ill for a long time, so somehow you come to terms with it. Before long there'll be a photo of me here. Look, I had my name and the frame put on right away. When I die, they'll slip in my photo, and the stonecutter will add the date of death, and that's all. I'd prefer to go at the beginning of the year so that there's a single-digit number and it doesn't go over the bracket. I could have chosen a wider stone, but my son would have grumbled about that. He's a terrible penny-pincher."

Dora stared at the headstone. It bore the following legend in gold letters: "Ina Pitínová (6/17/1925—)." There was indeed little space left inside the brackets.

"I hope it works out for you," said Dora, embarrassed.

"So why have you come to see me? I've been doing so much talking, I still don't really know what you want to ask me about."

Dora had been waiting for this question. Since the moment she had learned of the existence of Ingeborg Pitínová née Schwannze, she had been considering what she would say to her.

"I want to find out about your brother's life after the war. I think he and my aunt used to know each other."

"Are you saying he had an affair with her? Jindřich? Well, I never! And he told us he was finished with women! Although I know for a fact that he went looking for Lena after the war. Not because he wanted her back, but to find out what had happened to the child. But I don't think he found her. After that, he never mentioned any other woman. So he might have had a relationship, you say? That would make us almost relatives, eh?"

"I'm not so sure that they . . ."

"Who was this woman? An aunt, you say? Was she pretty?"

"Well . . . my aunt was rather a loner. She never married. She brought me up, in fact. She died in '79, but I've only just found out that she knew your brother. Also, I wanted to ask you if he ever mentioned her."

"A loner? Then they would have got on. A woman like that would have understood him. But he never spoke of her to me. That's not saying much, though. We hardly ever saw each other. As I said, my husband didn't have much time for him, and for several years, we didn't even see each other at Christmas. Perhaps he was with her. I always thought of him at Christmas and wondered where he was."

"I doubt he was with her."

"What was her name? Where was she from? Maybe something about her will ring a bell with me."

Dora hesitated before taking the plunge.

"Her name was Terézie Surmenová. She was from Žítková."

Mrs. Pitínová had been raking the small, frozen stones within the rectangle that formed the grave's border. Now she straightened up.

"Žítková, you say? If she's the woman from Žítková I know about, he certainly wouldn't have spent Christmas with her. There was nothing between those two, that's for sure. She'd be the one he said he was going to kill when we went to see him in prison. But don't worry—Jindřich would never have done that; it was the anger talking. But your aunt must have been a right bitch. It must have been before you were born, and I doubt that woman would have bragged about it. But d'you know what? They probably wouldn't have come for Jindřich if it hadn't been for your aunt. He robbed that house and ran away. The old man survived, and a few months later, he went to see some madwoman in Žítková. Ugh! And that woman was your aunt! At one of their séances, she saw that the old man had been attacked and robbed by a neighbor. The one who was apparently the kindest to him. Jindřich was a nice chap who behaved warmly toward everyone, so they took him in for questioning. Then they found the stolen things in his room. He blamed it all on the madwoman, who called herself a goddess. If it hadn't been for her, that Jew would never have pointed the finger at Jindřich, and everything would have been all right again. He'd survived, after all, and he was still rich enough. He could have managed without the few things he'd lost. And Jindřich might have made a better life with his wife, and perhaps she wouldn't have left him. You can bet that's how he saw it. Hand me the wreath, please."

She waved her hand, and Dora leaned in toward her with the Advent wreath. Mrs. Pitínová placed it carefully before the headstone, in the center of the gravel area. Then she said, "I'm pretty sure that goddess stuck in his gizzard his whole life long. So you're her daughter? You look quite normal, you know. Do you call yourself a goddess too?"

"I'm her niece. And she was an herbalist, really. She used herbs to treat people."

"And that's why she called herself a goddess? Isn't that a little odd?"

"That's what the people from the village called her. There were quite a few of them around Hrozenkov. They practiced as healers and foretold the future."

"Hrozenkov? Žítková is near Hrozenkov?"

"Yes, in the hills above Hrozenkov. A few isolated cottages."

"He used to go there. I remember him mentioning it now. That was the one time I had hopes that he had a woman because he kept mentioning someone called Josefínka. I remember thinking how nice the name sounded, like a pet name. And if he was using a pet name, then it must be something really serious. But he just laughed at the thought and said she was a colleague or a contact or something. Older than him, apparently, so I wasn't to get any ideas. I thought, *So what if she's older?* What would that matter? He wouldn't be the first or the last. But he said she was an old woman, and in any case, he would never have had anything to do with a witch like her. She was probably strange. Or dangerous—the name might have been a code name. Who would have called an old woman by a pet name like that? I don't suppose you knew any Josefínka there?"

"Josefínka?" asked Dora doubtfully.

"That's right, Josefínka."

"Might it have been Josifčena?"

"Yes—Josifčena! I knew it sounded really affectionate. You're right; they called her Josifčena, not Josefínka. How nice it sounds! That's how I got the idea that there was something more in it than he was letting on."

"Maybe there was something more in it," said Dora.

Mrs. Pitínová struck a match to light the first of the four candles on the wreath. The weak flame flickered between her palms and then increased slowly in size.

"That's that, then," the old woman said with satisfaction before straightening up carefully. "I would have wanted it for him, you know. He was so lonely. He would have benefited enormously from the attention of a good woman, especially a calm, older one. Men can't be on their own. Loneliness drives them crazy. Jindřich died a bitter, unhappy man, and I'm truly sorry for him. Do you know where his grave is? In Hradiště. He wanted us to cremate him. He wanted a little plaque on a wall so that no one would have to tend his grave, as he didn't have family of his own. There's a photo of him there. He's about forty-five in it. Some time or other, our whole family had its photo taken, so I had him taken out and enlarged. Go and have a look at it. At least you'll see what a good-looking chap he was."

Late that very afternoon, there stood Dora, wrapped in a coat and a scarf that covered her hair. She had marched off to the cemetery in Uherské Hradiště like a machine, having taken it into her mind to go as soon as Mrs. Pitínová told her the location of the grave. Only now was it dawning on her that she had made a mistake.

Had she given it any thought at all? She had come straight from the hospital, where she had spent several silent hours at Jakoubek's bedside, hoping that somewhere in his deep sleep, he at least sensed her presence, but he gave no indication that he knew she was there. When she left, she was on the verge of tears. Now that she was battling the present, she was totally unprepared to delve into the past.

At the cemetery she was greeted by the soft, flickering flames of Advent candles.

Slowly and reluctantly, she walked along the perimeter walls, with their marble slabs the size of open books, until she came to Švanc's. It was mounted at eye level. Next to the small round frame with its photograph, in which a middle-aged man was looking over her shoulder and into the distance, was a name set in gold. In the December gloom, she had to stand very close in order to get a proper look at the image.

She stared at the round but regular face of a man whose bulging cheeks gave him a look of mild arrogance. She imagined that with the passing years, the cheeks had succumbed to gravity and blended in with the chin, which itself had merged with the neck. The eyes below the receding hairline were close-set; the lips were thin and, at the moment the photo was taken, standoffishly tight. It did not appear that he was enjoying the family get-together. He looked troubled and stubborn.

And he certainly wasn't good-looking. Nor, however, did he look like a murderer.

At the sight of him, something in Dora shifted, vibrated—she was afraid that this something would transform into weeping or yelling. She closed her eyes and took several deep breaths and so succeeded in quelling the pressure in her chest.

She looked at the face again. So this was him, she said to herself: the man who drove Surmena to the madhouse, which turned her into a wreck, a crazy old woman muttering last words that resonated in Dora's memory. *"Don't trust them!"* Words that to her ears were indistinguishable from hissing. Now, as if by the crack of a whip, she remembered other fragments of sentences that had issued from the toothless mouth. And suddenly, albeit slowly and in pieces, their content emerged from the fog and began to make sense.

"The Germans!" She must have meant Švanc. In the mid-1970s, she had looked him in the eye again, thirty years since the last time, when Harry was executed; they had put her in a cell and then in an institution in Kroměříž. She had remembered, which was why she had expressed such fear of the Germans during Dora's last visit.

"Mahdalka!" So she *had* wanted to tell her and warn her. She had spewed out the whole Mahdalka story, had even mentioned Fuksena and uttered the word *"child."* But Dora couldn't have known that the child Surmena meant was Fuksena's daughter, whose fate was known by no one, who apparently had never been found. *"Use it, if worse comes to worst!"* Surmena knew about this child, and she knew where it was. It was Surmena who had hidden the girl, as a move against Mahdalka, depriving her of all that remained of Fuksena—her daughter, her successor, the only one Mahdalka had managed to raise in the knowledge, her own blood, her last chance. And Surmena and Dora's ace in the hole.

Dora felt dizzy. By looking into Švanc's eyes, she was returned to those years when, by the force of his will, her and Surmena's lives had been torn apart. Suddenly she understood the events of that time; pieces of the mosaic came together in a clear picture. It was obvious that Surmena had believed in the curse and lived in fear of it, that she had been terrified of what Mahdalka had sent down on her, that she had dreaded her own end and had dreaded more than anything what would become of Dora—because she believed that Dora's fate, too, was a tragic one. At the last moment, Surmena had wanted to tell Dora about the curse and how to defend herself against it with the help of the hidden child. Surmena had tried her very hardest to tell Dora everything she knew—but it had been too late. Mahdalka's curse had caught up with her, in the form of Jindřich Švanc, whose expression in the photo had changed under Dora's gaze. His tight lips had widened into a malicious grin in which Dora glimpsed something that certainly hadn't been there a few moments earlier: a victor's smile.

Potočná

Two weeks later Dora made a trip to Potočná. The customs office took up the entire floor of a narrow valley that sat between the wooded hillside and the Drietomica brook. In front of and beyond the office building was a parking lot comprising wide strips of concrete, which in this place of meadows where dianthuses and protected varieties of orchids flowered in summer, with the White Carpathians rising all around, stuck out like a sore thumb.

Her documents at the ready, she made the crossing from the Czech Republic to Slovakia on foot. The customs official, an acquaintance from Žítková, did not emerge from the heat of the building; with a movement of the head, he indicated that she could proceed. She headed off to her right, toward Potočná. The asphalt road soon became an ordinary dirt track. The woodland around her became denser and the way quieter. She went deeper and deeper into the forest.

It was the first house she would see, she had been told.

A tumbledown cottage with a caved-in roof and boarded-up windows. She stopped in front of it. On the wooden gate that opened into the yard, she looked for a plate with the name of the people who lived there but couldn't find one. But this—the first house in Potočná—must once have belonged to Mahdalka. She turned the iron handle of the gate, which creaked open, and peered into the yard.

It was very untidy. In a corner lay bricks from a broken-down barn, and thatch and gutters from the roof reached almost to where she was standing. The debris included cracked mugs and scattered pieces of wood and stones; rags and the remains of plastic bags fluttered in the cold wind. A place of destruction, she thought.

She entered the yard and stepped across stones that had once made a path until she reached the cottage's front door. It was locked. She bent down to the doorstep and picked up a rag that was lying there, using it to wipe the small window in the upper part of the door. She wanted to see where Mahdalka had practiced as a goddess, but all she saw was a bare wall. Disappointed, she turned back to the small yard and examined what was left of Mahdalka's property. Then she left.

A child of about eight was standing at the gate. Dora was startled.

"What are you doing here?" asked the girl, who was wearing an ill-fitting, threadbare coat and a scarf tied under the chin.

Dora was caught off guard. "I . . . I was looking for the Mahdal family."

"The Mahdals haven't lived here for years. My gran says they moved away before I was born."

"Is that right?" said Dora with interest. "Does your gran live nearby?"

The girl nodded. "At the top. We all live there."

"Would you take me there, please? I'd like to ask her something."

The girl turned and led the way up into the woods, nimbly picking her way among patches of ice on the path. Perhaps water flowed this way, although Dora, who was walking behind, couldn't figure out where it came from. They walked for a good twenty minutes. The path narrowed, and the woodland around them became denser. Then, in the clearing ahead, Dora saw a cottage enclosed by a fence. The girl wriggled through the gate and disappeared. Dora remained at the gate, embarrassed. She heard sounds from inside the house and a commotion from the garden at the back. She waited awhile, but no one emerged from the house, so she pressed the bell at the gate several times.

The ringing hadn't died away when a man of around forty appeared in the doorway. He was wearing only a light T-shirt, and Dora shivered at the sight of him. Having opened the gate, he placed both hands on its frame and leaned against it in a brazen display of his physical superiority and self-assurance. Dora could smell the sweat and alcohol on him, and she felt very uncomfortable.

She asked him politely about the Mahdals.

"Get Mother!" he bawled into the house.

The noise inside increased, and a second man appeared in the doorway. He was a carbon copy of the man standing in front of her, though a little younger. Immediately behind this man was a third, his true reflection.

The man at the gate nodded in their direction. "My brothers," he said with a smile.

A number of children of various ages emerged from between the legs of the men at the door, including the girl Dora had already met.

"Our kids," said the man with another smirk.

Then an old woman appeared in the doorway. The hair under her headscarf was white, and she was wearing only a long, loose-fitting button-up apron. "Who is it?" she asked rudely.

"She's come to ask about the Mahdals," explained the man at the gate.

He still just stood there, as if he hadn't noticed the December cold. In the meantime, the children and one of the men had disappeared.

"So ask her into the warm. We don't want to be nattering out here on the doorstep," shouted the old woman into the house. "Miloš! Look after her while I get dressed!"

The man at the gate put a hand on Dora's shoulder and applied a gentle pressure that impelled her toward the house.

"I'm Peter, and this is Miloš," he said, nodding at the youngest brother, who was still in the doorway, now with a hand outstretched in greeting. As soon as she was in reach, he grabbed her hand and shook it.

"Are you single?" he asked, blushing. Then, without waiting for an answer, he said, "I am."

"Me too," Dora said, embarrassed.

By now the man from the gate had nudged her inside. She passed slowly through the hallway and into the living area, where children were shouting and two plump young women sat at a table. Someone at her back removed her coat and pushed her into a chair; at the same time, a shot glass of brandy appeared in front of her. The women stared at her without speaking.

Dora looked about the bleak-looking room, which gave no indication that Christmas was on the horizon. The bare plaster of the walls was smudged and in need of another coat; the mismatched furniture was on the industrial side. The upholstery of the chair she was sitting in was worn through to reveal the slats in its back, and it dipped along with her when she bent to the table. Everyone had an untouched shot glass in front of them.

Someone proposed a toast. "So, young lady—to Christmas and first meetings!"

"Dora. Dora Idesová from Žítková," she replied hastily.

The man who had introduced himself as Peter gestured that she should raise her glass, and the others seized theirs greedily. As they reached to clink glasses with her, she looked from one to the next and noticed a family trait—they all had crooked teeth spaced wide apart, the children as well as the adults.

At last, the mother of the family reappeared—warmly dressed in a baggy, holey sweater—and came to the table. It was she who opened the conversation.

"So you've come to ask about the Mahdals, have you?" She was straightaway given a glass, which was filled to the brim. She emptied it in a single gulp, wiped her mouth on her sleeve, then turned back to Dora. "They haven't lived here for ages. Mahdalka died in the early '80s, and her son and daughter-in-law died a few years ago. And the grandkids found something better. Who would want to live at the end of the world if they had a choice, eh?"

"Do you know where they moved to?"

"I don't. We never had much to do with them. They were an odd bunch, that's for sure. It's best to keep out of the way of people like that."

"I should think they went somewhere far, far away, where no one'd know them," said Peter. "They had a lot to be ashamed of."

"Why do you say that?" Dora asked, not wanting to let on what she already knew.

"Some of the things they did weren't honest. Old Mahdalka was a witch, and people used to call her one. The witch. They say she collaborated with the Germans and got away with it. Later, too, she got away with all kinds of things. The police would come for her, take her away for a couple of days, then dump her back here as if nothing had happened. But it goes without saying that she did harm to a lot of people. People said she had a powerful protector somewhere in Hradiště. She must have; otherwise, she'd never have gotten away with all her roguery. Maybe they let her off because she was a snitch—she knew lots of things about people here that they'd rather have kept quiet. Either way, it was only after the revolution, when she'd been dead for years, that folk stopped being frightened, and boy did they pay that family back! It's no wonder her grandkids made themselves scarce."

Miloš had moved his chair next to Dora's. Now he refilled her glass.

"No more for me, thanks," she said.

"She'll get used to it," sneered the woman who had introduced herself as Marie, Peter's wife.

"Why are you looking for them?" The old woman's suddenly suspicious expression was reflected in the faces of both daughters-in-law. "It never meant anything good when folk came looking for Mahdalka."

"Because of my aunt. They had a falling-out. My aunt's name was Surmenová, and like me, she was from Žítková. Does the name mean anything to you?"

The woman closed her eyes; Dora could tell that she was thinking hard.

"Wasn't she the cursed one? She was, wasn't she? The word was that Mahdalka had put a curse on her family in Žítková and then run away from them. All the women who might be goddesses like her. Rid herself of the competition." She cackled, then nodded at Peter to pour her another drink. After she drained it, she continued: "If she was the one, then the curse is still in force, isn't it? It applies to all women in the family. So if that's the reason you were looking for her, I don't envy you, my girl. If I were you, I'd have a good long drink."

She gestured encouragement to Dora to down the contents of the glass she was clutching. Dora was so taken aback by the old woman's having hit the bull's-eye that she did as she was told. The sharp, bitter taste traveled down her throat and spread slowly to her stomach. Peter refilled her glass immediately.

"But don't you worry your head about that. It's probably just talk, you know. In the end, what's supposed to happen, happens anyway, so there's no point in fretting. If you did, you'd worry your life away."

The room filled with noise as other members of the family argued about the effectiveness of curses and ways of lifting them.

"At full moon, recite the curse backward and then say the Lord's Prayer from back to front. That returns the curse to the one who made it."

"But she's dead!"

"Then it passes to her children and to their children after that."

"If their blood spatters Mahdalka's grave, the curse can be overturned!"

"Shut up! You think someone would have himself cut open over it?"

"It is enough to bathe in sage."

In the meantime, the shot glasses had been emptied and refilled to a regular rhythm, their bottoms clacking against the tabletop ever more quickly and loudly. Dora sipped at her own glass pensively.

From behind, through the exposed slats of the chair's back, she felt a hand slip under her blouse. It was Miloš's. The shock caused her to spill the remainder of her brandy. The women, who were watching her every move, hooted with delight. The infectious laughter spread to the others, and soon everyone was laughing—the old woman, the men, the dopey-faced children playing on the dusty floor.

Dora was increasingly uneasy among these people. Notwithstanding their protests, she got up to leave, saying her goodbyes as she headed to the door, and practically tore her coat from its peg. Relief broke over her with the first breath of fresh air.

As she reached the gate, Miloš came sprinting up behind her, visibly boosted by another glass of brandy, a residue of which glinted on his upper lip.

"Would you like to marry me?" he asked breathlessly.

In the short time since her departure, the family had obviously convinced him that a curse was not a plague, plied him with brandy for courage, and sent him out to try his luck.

"Not really, but thanks for asking," she said, embarrassed.

From inside the house, the disturbing laughter rang out again. She thought it best not to look in its direction. She needed to be out of reach of this peculiar family as soon as possible. She was aware of something perverse and odd in their behavior and in how everyone—the men, the women, the children—looked alike. In her haste, she slammed the gate behind her. Then she ran down the hill, back to the Czech side.

Janigena

*H*er trips to Žítková that winter were sad ones. Without Jakoubek, who was still in the hospital, there wasn't even much point in her making them.

Today, as usual, she left his bedside at the end of visiting hours. Less than twenty minutes later, she again had the feeling that she was neglecting him. Although she could do nothing for him at the hospital, she felt that her place was next to him, next to his bed, and nowhere else. What if he came around and started looking for her? So from Friday to Sunday, she spent her afternoons at his bedside, celebrating Christmas Eve sitting next to a rickety table with a vase containing a tuft of conifer branches.

The bus pulled up at the Uherské Hradiště station. All those who, a moment earlier, had been leaning against the railings rushed to the doors. It was bitingly cold. The last to board the bus, Dora made her way along the narrow aisle to the vacant double seat at the back. As always, the bus proceeded through the villages up to Uherský Brod at a brisk pace before slowing down appreciably to take the narrow hairpin curves carved into the hills of the White Carpathians. Dora pulled out her newspaper.

She turned to the front page of the local news section. Her gaze fell on a large photograph of a sight well known to her—the interior of the church at Hrozenkov. Immediately she knew that something bad had happened. She did not even finish reading the article under the bold-print headline. Irma was dead.

When in Hrozenkov with Jakoubek, Dora liked to take her time and visit her neighbors to ask what was new. This time, however, she passed through the village at a brisk pace. She wanted to get up to the Bedová as soon as possible. She didn't even stop to exchange a few words with the neighbors she met; she didn't want to hear chatter about Irma's death from women grateful for every listener. She nodded and hurried on her way. In the morning she would go down to Baglárka's, and they would go to the cemetery together.

Now that she was out of range of the streetlights of Starý Hrozenkov, she took out her flashlight and switched it on. The climb to the Bedová was dark. The only other light came from the windows of the Hodulíks' cottage. Before, there would have been a more distant light from Irma's cottage. The woodland alternated with the open hillside. The golden disc of weak light showed only a few feet of path ahead. Dora's sturdy boots crunched through the trampled snow. She was happy to reach her own front door.

Having dropped the rucksack containing her frozen clothes, she went straight to the range. Soon a fire was crackling, and she heated up some soup. To warm herself, she sat as close to the oven door as she could. She took in the room. Since that time, she had been here often, but still, she couldn't get used to the emptiness Jakoubek had left behind.

And now Irma was dead. Dora should have realized when she saw her in the autumn that things weren't going to get any better. A wheezing, wizened old woman lost in her bedclothes. She had much for which to be grateful to Irma, and there was much she had still wanted to ask her about. For instance, had she had at least an inkling about Surmena and Fuksena's child?

Now Dora would have to get by without her. Without her memory that had reached back almost to the dawn of the last century. Without the wisdom that, albeit coarsely, had urged her onward.

The soup came to a boil. Dora removed the pan from the stove, reached into it with a spoon, and ate a little. She wasn't hungry, but she couldn't free herself of the mundane rituals she had performed every Friday for years. Realizing this, she stoked the fire and secured the iron door of the oven. Then she undressed and slipped into bed, eager to sleep through the night.

She was woken by a gentle, rhythmic tapping on the windowpane. This must have been going on for some time; she had been aware of it in her sleep. She got out of bed and walked across the dark room to the window, through which she saw the pale face of Janigena framed by a bulky fur hat with its earflaps down. Wide awake with surprise, she threw her coat over her shoulders and went to unlock the door. While Janigena was stamping her feet loudly before the threshold, Dora had time to feed the stove with more wood and so revive the dying fire. Flickering flames shone into the darkness from around the oven door.

Janigena stood awkwardly at the door, squeezing the fur hat in her hands. Her cheeks were rosy from the night frost. The golden half-light of the room made much of her rough beauty. Dora helped her out of her wet coat, which she draped over the rail above the range.

It was Janigena who broke the silence. "I waited for you on the Koprvazy."

Dora didn't speak. She was still taken aback that Janigena was here, in her house.

"I was there several times," Janigena went on, without a shadow of remorse.

Dora just nodded. To keep herself busy in this unusual situation, she started to prepare tea. Confused, Janigena sat down on the bench next to the stove. It was a while before she tried again. "They said at the shop that you'd come on your own again."

This time Dora replied. "Jakoubek's still in the hospital."

Janigena coughed and mumbled that she was sorry about that.

"So Irma died," said Dora.

"Yes," said Janigena. "The funeral's already taken place. I didn't realize she was so important to you."

"Well, she was."

Janigena shrugged and wondered what to say next. "Her time had come."

"I suppose so."

Neither one of them knew how to continue. They had never talked much; there had been nothing for them to discuss. Their meetings had had an express purpose and passed without unnecessary conversation.

But Dora knew they couldn't go on like this. Suddenly too many things had lost their original meaning, and what it was, exactly, that the two of them had together needed to be cleared up. And changed.

"I don't want to go to the Koprvazy anymore," she said.

Janigena kept a bewildered silence.

"I want to sell the place," Dora went on. "I never want to go back there. I need to get rid of it. There's no reason for me to have two cottages. It's not as if Jakoubek could be there on his own . . ."

Her voice faltered. In an effort to suppress a surge of sadness, she turned away and bit painfully into her lip.

She was surprised when she felt Janigena's embrace from behind and her brandy-soaked breath against her temple. She closed her eyes and curled up, as though she wished to be consumed by Janigena's mighty frame. This was what she needed—someone's sympathy. She was tired of managing everything on her own.

Suddenly the words were pouring out of her. "They're going to stop letting me have him on weekends; I know they are. He's not doing well."

Janigena whispered into her hair. "He'll get better. You'll see."

"But what if he doesn't?"

Dora felt cold tears on her cheeks. The first tears in weeks. Having reached the surface, they flooded out. Her body was twitching. Janigena stroked her shoulder, powerless to help her.

After a while Janigena led Dora to the table and sat her on one of the chairs before going to the range to pour tea. Then she sat opposite Dora in silence, waiting for her to calm down.

At last Dora spoke. "How's your husband?"

She didn't know why she had said this. Perhaps the gratitude she felt to Janigena for spending these moments with her had spilled over into bitterness at the thought of being without her again in a few hours' time. There was something insidious in her broaching a topic that had never before been raised between them.

Janigena paused before whispering with reluctance, "Still the same."

"Will he get better?"

"No."

"Is he doing rehabilitation?"

"Not anymore. He doesn't want to. His spine was broken in two, and there's nothing to be done. All hope is in vain."

"How are the kids taking it?"

Visibly dismayed, Janigena pushed back in her chair and crossed her arms over her chest. Her nervous blinking suggested that her short, brushlike eyelashes were trying to scare away the question. But Dora wouldn't be put off—she wanted this to be spoken between them. She stared at Janigena and waited for her answer.

"Worse than I am. At least, at first they took it worse. They missed a man about the place more than I did. Now it's better—they've practically flown the nest, thankfully."

For a moment it seemed that Janigena had brought the conversation to an end. She was obviously struggling. Instead she took a deep breath and blurted out, "They'd never forgive me if they found out . . . I'd never get over that!"

Dora would never have expected such a fierce reaction from quiet, reticent Janigena, but now that it had come, she would seize the opportunity it gave her.

"It can't go on like this," she said energetically. "I can't take it like this any longer. The constant fear, the secrecy, the bad conscience . . . And I'm scared too. How long can we keep this secret? How long can we keep meeting every now and then in a hut?"

A few moments earlier, Dora had had no idea that what they were doing weighed so heavily on Janigena. Everything else had been dwarfed by her concern for Jakoubek. It had rushed out at her, and in the flood of words, she had sensed the shape of what she wanted. What would it be like not to have to hide? What would it be like not to live a pretense? To live together?

But then Janigena exclaimed in a voice shaking with agitation, "You know very well that no one must find out! You know that, don't you?"

"So what do we do now? Do you want to live like this forever? To wipe up the piss of a man who can't move and who's never mattered to you anyway? All for the sake of what other people think?"

Janigena struck the tabletop with her open hand. "Stop! That's enough, do you hear? *You* can talk—you who'll leave again on Sunday, you with your other home! But what about me? Where can I hide? It's *me* they'll look at here like I'm some kind of animal! It's *me* they'll spit at! My own kids'll turn their backs on me."

The thought of this was so real to her that her voice broke as she uttered it. Dora realized that she had gone too far, and suddenly she was afraid. Why she was afraid and what she was afraid of, she didn't know. All she did know was that something had risen inside her that she wouldn't be able to keep down, that would make it impossible for her to live as before.

They sat opposite each other in silence—Janigena with her head in her hands, Dora staring at the tabletop—and the minutes went by. Had the fire not started to die, they might have sat like that till morning. Dora stood up and threw more woodchips into the stove. As she returned to the table, Janigena seized her hand and pulled her onto her lap.

Janigena spoke quietly, with her head buried in Dora's blouse. "I can't leave him; it's impossible. I'd feel like a rat if I did, after all these years. Sometimes I can hardly bear to be at home, but I can't walk away from it all. Besides, I can't just please myself—unlike him . . . unlike the kids."

Dora said nothing. Her throat felt as though a butterfly were fluttering about inside it, tickling her with the soft bristles of its colorful wings, preventing her from swallowing, let alone responding.

"But I can't imagine what I would do if what . . . what we have together came to an end. I used to wish so much that I didn't have these feelings for you, even to wish that you didn't exist." Janigena paused and then added in a quiet voice, "But lately it's been different."

Dora felt a surge of happiness carry her to a deep, calm, soundless place; she felt like a fetus in the womb, hidden and safe amid the bends of her innards. She snuggled closer to Janigena before taking her lover's head in her hands and turning it toward her.

"Life sucks," muttered Janigena, her eyes shut tight to hold back the tears.

Dora could feel Janigena's heart pounding. She comforted her by stroking her temples and gently ruffling the thick, gray-streaked hair that fell over her face and wouldn't hold behind her ears. On her forehead, which was usually covered by a carelessly cut fringe, Dora fingers brushed against the rough, raised skin of a birthmark.

As Janigena found Dora's mouth, Dora remembered.

Part V

Jindřich Švanc

*D*ora had waited for this moment for years and had been burning with impatience in the past few months while bargaining went on at the government level. She followed the reports with a sense of suspense. Then it came into force. The clause on access to files kept on collaborators with and members of the State Security Police was expanded; now anyone could take a look at them.

She could have sworn that she was the first to submit an application: the day after the law was passed, she sent her request to view the file of the agent Jindřich Švanc.

It was not processed within ninety days, as promised. It was five months before she received an email granting her permission to visit the archive in Kanice.

The archive was deep in the woods beyond Brno. At first she and her colleague Lenka Pavlíková failed to spot the small sign that showed the way, and they drove past the turn.

Many years had passed since she had learned of the existence of Švanc. And in all those years, she had not really gotten behind the mask of the man who had done so much damage to Surmena's life and, as a result, to hers and Jakoubek's. The fragments of information she had gathered on Švanc were still not enough to form a full picture of his life and understand him.

She didn't know what to expect from that full picture. Perhaps she was hoping for relief once nothing stood between her and her festering curiosity.

On that July day, she would find out.

His file was not half as thick as Surmena's. It comprised barely a hundred pages of copied documents in which the real names of others had been carefully blacked out. Dora was surprised. She had been expecting more—stack after stack of sheets, dozens of names, the exposure of a plot, fireworks. Ready for battle, she was faced not by a whole army but by a handful of embarrassed troops.

She sat at a desk in the reading room. There was no air-conditioning, and the sweat ran down her cheeks and along her spine. Her light summer dress clung to her body.

At lunchtime they asked her to leave the building and carefully locked the door behind her, as if she were the one they should fear. She was tempted to tap her forehead at the archive staff, including the small woman with an old-fashioned perm whose task it was to watch over her, and exclaim, "I'm not the one you should be afraid of! What about those names you are still keeping secret eighteen years after the revolution? What about those names you are protecting from members of the public like me?"

She got through the midday break on a shaded bench beyond the fence that surrounded the grounds. She looked askance at the lens of the camera above the gate as it slowly took in the whole site. With a disposable fork, she ate a salad she had prepared that morning, even though she hadn't known there would be no refreshments available in this back-of-beyond place.

Why had they chosen this location? So that those with a desire to acquaint themselves with the demons of their past found it impossible to get to the damn files? It was a forty-five-minute bus ride out here, and the stop was a walk of a mile and a half from the archive. Having learned this from the website, she had decided to ask Lenka Pavlíková for a lift.

"I wish you luck," Lenka had said to her as she dropped her off.

In a way, it was Lenka's doing, Dora told herself. Had it not been for her, it never would have crossed Dora's mind to go in search of Surmena. And certainly not in the archives of the State Security Police.

"Call me when you're getting ready to leave. I'll pick you up," Lenka had added as she started the car.

Dora had nodded. Then she had headed for the unsightly concrete building of the Security Services Archive.

A little later, the gate made a clicking sound, her signal to return to the building and reimmerse herself in the file. Impatient to resume, she stuffed what remained of her lunch into her bag and went back. The camera eye followed her slight figure.

At the end of that day, she felt she knew him at last. He stood naked before her: she had the dates of all the important milestones in his life, from his birth to his death. That morning the evil he represented had been cast in gloom; now it had firm lines and bright colors. He had been a man without scruples who had pursued his goals relentlessly.

In the beginning, however, there had been nothing to suggest that he would develop into a man so ruthless. He had grown up in an ordinary family, his father self-employed, his mother a housewife. There was a large age gap between him and his younger sister. They had a house with a garden and livestock. They also had a respectable position in the Czech-German community of their small village, where, according to the form he had completed on being accepted in the Sicherheitsdienst, several of their ancestors had been mayor. So where had things gone wrong?

Did he have higher ambitions than to be a painter and decorator? Was he or the beautiful wife he brought home when barely out of short pants put off by the smell of paint? Probably both of them were. There was a child on the way, and the imminent economic crisis was about to deprive him of the home he dreamed of.

If Ingeborg Pitínová was to be believed, he must have felt trapped by the wails of his wife on one side and the complaints of his mother on the other; both surely took their grievances out on him, and it is unlikely that they minced their words. When he and his wife were alone in the evenings, she probably called him a miserable cripple. The leg that had been shattered by his fall from a ladder was not healing well: for six months he was unable to work, and he would live with the consequences forever.

Maybe he got the idea after one of their arguments. Words may have been spoken that caused the cup of patience to run over and long-suppressed anger to seek a target. Maybe this anger had taken him to the unlocked door on the veranda of the villa of Leo Weissmann, a Jew with wealth enough to share. But what did he use this wealth for? Nothing—it was just for show; he would boast about his garden, the wicker furniture on his veranda, and the servant who kept his house. Doubtless, young Schwannze believed himself to be in far greater need, with a wife to care for and a child on the way.

To get into Weissmann's house in the early hours must have been pretty easy for him, but finding where the money was kept was surely a trickier proposition. In her mind's eye, Dora saw him searching through dressers, rummaging through the contents of shelves ever more frantically, desperate to get the whole thing over with. But then Weissmann caught him at it, which was a mistake on his part because by this time, Schwannze was so mad that he turned all his rage on him in a fit of hysteria, stabbing Weissmann several times with a knife.

Surely he wondered how Weissmann survived the attack. When he left the house, the man was evidently grunting his last. The servant must have found him in time because the next morning, news of the burglary, and the fact that he had barely survived the assault, was all over the village. For several days the constabulary combed the village. How Schwannze must have struggled for sleep, thought Dora. At night he would wake up in terror, reliving the awful sensation of sticking a knife right up to the hilt in human flesh, again and again, and sweating at the thought of the punishment for such a deed. He must have lost weight. A figure of skin and bones who dragged his left leg. Some strands of his hair suddenly turned white. So as not to draw attention to himself, he sold none of what he had managed to steal from the villa. So that six months later, they found the whole hoard, right down to the last coin—even the gold menorah.

Weissmann's return from the hospital must have shattered all his remaining calm. Would Weissmann recognize him? The uncertainty would have been agonizing. One day he saw Weissmann sitting in his garden, and he could hold back no longer. He had to rid himself of the tension, even at the cost of betraying himself to his victim. Dora imagined him leaving his house and heading for that fence, his steps slowing incrementally as he approached. Weissmann's convalescence was a demanding one; overwhelmed by fatigue and the afternoon sun, he was dozing. He had a plaster cast around his neck, and his arm was in a sling. Perhaps even then, the first time, they struck up a friendly conversation. Schwannze must have been mightily relieved. His joy at Weissmann's failure to recognize him would surely have been incentive enough for him to leap over the fence and plant a kiss on Weissmann's cheek. The enthusiasm apparent in his greeting was hardly surprising, his earlier indifference notwithstanding; after the incident he would have bent over backward to please Weissmann. And it stayed that way until they came for him.

Weissmann went to the constabulary to denounce him. Most likely Schwannze believed that the befuddled old man had bribed the cops to interrogate him and raid his home. They didn't have a single shred of evidence that pointed directly at him. As Dora imagined it, he never would get the horrified faces of his parents and his wife's expression of disgust out of his mind. He would have fallen asleep with them before his eyes; she was sure of that.

Among the statement forms, there was a clipping from a local newspaper.

A Sensational Revelation

In the middle of last year, a violent robbery occurred in the village of Horní Němčí that almost cost local citizen Leo Weissmann his life. After a long and complicated program of care, Mr. Weissmann was able to continue his treatment at home, but this was not the end of the story: still the perpetrator of this terrible act had not been apprehended. Mr. Weissmann learned from his housemaid that in cases such as his, the celebrated goddesses of Žítková might be able to help. Herself a native of Hrozenkov, the girl had a close understanding of the arts of the local oracles. So the old man went to Žítková, where he visited the well-known goddess Surmenová. In addition to a pouch of herbs that would aid his recovery from the injuries that still pained him, he brought back a prophecy stating that the culprit would prove to be someone in his immediate proximity, most likely a neighbor who himself was in less-than-perfect health and whose behavior toward Mr. Weissmann had become unusually sweet; this behavior was not a demonstration of sympathy with the old man but of his own bad conscience. Mr. Weissmann took this story to the local constabulary. Although at first it was not believed, its truth would eventually become apparent. The stolen items were found at the home of Heinrich Schwannze, a neighbor of Mr. Weissmann's. This sensational revelation had its sequel in a courtroom in Uherské Hradiště, where a verdict of guilty was passed on the accused. We undertake to keep our readers informed of further developments in the case.

Prison couldn't have been easy for Schwannze. A failed thief, a cripple, a man whose wife had left him for a better life with someone else. Apparently, she had been picked up by some guy in a car. His sister, Ina, wrote to him in prison that the car had surely been borrowed because it had a Vienna license plate; still, the man's Czech was damn good. Who could say where the little tart had chatted him up? But in any case, he should be glad to be rid of that dreadful person. It was just a shame that she hadn't left the child behind with them.

It was as though Schwannze had materialized before Dora's eyes, in a tight little cell, as his three cellmates saw him, shaking with boundless impotence and rage. She heard their derisive remarks quite distinctly: *"His wife takes off and he calls himself a man?"*; *"Maybe he doesn't even know how to do it"*; *"A cuckold, that's what he is!"*

After five years of his ten-year sentence, they let him out of prison on probation. He was skinny, grizzled, full of hate. He no longer took the slightest pleasure from life. And he wasn't yet thirty.

After that he probably lay about at home for a few months. He was unemployed because with his reputation, no one would give him a job; besides, there were no jobs to be had. Closed up within four walls, exposed to the accusing gaze of his parents and sister, as he was too ashamed to go out. Maybe he would shut himself up in an outhouse with a bottle of brandy; maybe toward dawn he would be drunk, overwhelmed by self-pity and desperation over his ruined life and prepared to do something to himself.

But his homecoming was in 1939, a year of sudden and widespread change. And the new time offered opportunities to the likes of him too. As soon as he got wind of the fact that the new boat and the new captain could change his life, he applied for German citizenship, which he was soon granted on the basis of nothing more than documents testifying to the German origins of his parents, who had registered as German nationals throughout the years of the First Republic. Schwannze became a true German; the blot on his reputation shrank to the size of a minor unpleasantness that officials of the occupying power were quite prepared to overlook. From one day to the next, he was no longer convicted scum. Hardly had his regulation prisoner's haircut grown out than he became a person with social privileges, as if by the wave of a magic wand. When the time came, he would never forget to stress that all the woes of his life were down to Jews, as represented by Horní Němčí businessman Leo Weissmann, and Czechoslovakian justice.

In recognition of the second chance he had been given, Heinrich Schwannze gave loyalty and tireless endeavor in pursuit of the suffocation of the remnants of the First Republic. And the new masters took notice of his heartfelt commitment and his desire for a decent post within the attractive structure of the new apparatus. His rise was vertiginous.

Dora read all about it in Schwannze's file. He began with a few well-directed denunciations and a little gossipmongering. His claims reached the ears of a superior officer and were pursued by an officer more senior still, with the result that this keen local man was drawn into the Sicherheitsdienst in Zlín. The short report in Dora's hands had been penned at SS headquarters in Zlín by a junior officer, SS-Obersturmführer Graz, who referred to Schwannze as a careerist who was well acquainted with local circumstances. Schwannze had been a *Gewährsmann* and a *Zubringer*; now Graz was recommending his employment as a *Vertrauensmann*. In the "Evaluation" column, Graz wrote the following: *"He is a promising fellow who always obeys orders and has a firm belief in the victory of the swastika and the Führer's program."* In January 1940 Schwannze was given the gloriously low registration number B-7. Dora could imagine his having quickly to appropriate attributes of Germanness, how he became ever more German as his superiors looked on; in greeting he would always raise his right arm and click his heels so that the sound echoed off the surrounding walls. Back among Czechs, he would again be silent and unobtrusive, never letting on that his ears were primed to pick up on whatever might be going on. A year or two later, he had risen so high that they were giving him exceptional assignments; the one concerning the Communist leaflets was a case in point.

According to an informant, a cell of the Communist resistance had met in Svárov in autumn 1943. A brief report on the action made clear that Schwannze was deployed as a provocateur. He headed to the pub, where he sought to make contact with the ringleaders. He spoke in the dialect of Moravian Slovakia, ordered himself one brandy after another, hinted at and then openly prophesied the fall of the Reich and the victory of communism. *"The Soviets won't leave us in the soup!"* he declaimed. Bothered by this strange customer, the landlord was of a mind to call the constable. By slyly distributing Communist leaflets to the other customers, the strange man was committing a criminal act; by failing to report this, the rest of them would be committing a criminal act too. Let the cops deal with him, the landlord decided. He closed the pub and waited. In addition to the leaflets, the Czech police found on him a loaded gun and a Communist Party membership card; they passed the case to their German superiors. This was not a happy development for Schwannze, and he must have feared the failure of his mission. Dora could think of no other explanation for what she read in the record of his interrogation, conducted by constables Dobrovský and Cígler. *"He wept uncontrollably, pleaded and tried emotional blackmail by insisting he had a family to care for. [. . .] He would shoot himself in front of them; he was absolutely desperate. He calmed down only once the pistol had been thrown in the pond and the leaflets burned.*" Then he was released. A fortnight later the Gestapo apprehended the two Czech traitors and delivered them for interrogation to Brno headquarters, where after a brief trial, they were executed in winter 1943. Schwannze was given a pay raise.

The thin section of the file devoted to Schwannze's Nazi past ended here. There was nothing about his obsession with the goddesses or his role in the search for the American airmen. By the end of '44, perhaps no one was interested in reports on the activities of a V-Mann, or perhaps further information on his deployments had been lost. *Or had the reports been taken out?* Dora wondered, the suspicion gnawing away at her. *Surely not,* she answered herself. If they'd wanted to keep such documents secret, they would have shredded the whole file. The action with the Communist leaflets had cast the comrade of Líček's eulogy in a completely new light. Later it would be a means of keeping him in check.

Dora couldn't imagine what he had promised them. What could he do to make them interested in him? What could he give that others couldn't? He had found a way. In the end it wasn't such a big problem that he had failed to get his documents through and so disappear, together with his imperial masters, who, it seemed, had had no qualms about leaving him to the multitudes he had informed on. He was taken right at the beginning of May 1945. Five months later he was convicted by a people's court for having *"supported the National Socialist movement by submitting to the Sicherheitsdienst in Zlín reports on the activities of various people at a time of increased threat to the republic, thereby committing the criminal act of intriguing against the republic as formulated in §1 of Criminal Code 50/1923."*

Schwannze denied his guilt. At the end of the hearing, he declared: *"I do not recognize the validity of statements extorted by blows and beatings during the performance of an investigation. I assert that all such statements are fabrications and were dictated to me."*

He might have expected a heavier sentence than five years behind bars. But after his earlier stretch, the prospect of another prison term would have been all but unbearable for him. He must have been so convincing in his protestations that they heard him out. To the judgment handed down on October 3, 1945, was appended a note written lightly in pencil: *"Prison? Or better to make good use of him?"*

The second option was chosen. Schwannze was thrown a lifeline, and he grabbed it. He behaved exactly as instructed. The following statement, lavish in its praise, was entered in his prison file in late January 1948: *"In performance of his punishment the convicted has shown himself to be a supporter of the people's democratic republic. In minor cases of work-related indiscipline on the part of other prisoners, he has acted repeatedly in the interests of order and obedience to prison authorities. We appreciate his readiness to keep us informed as regards the prevalent mood among the prisoner collective. His behavior is good; it is clear that his punishment is fulfilling its educational purpose. In terms of politics, he expresses regret for his misguided attitude to the Nazi occupiers; he is studying Marxism by his own initiative. He speaks of a people's democracy as the only way forward. For these reasons, we are inclined to accept the proposal of the Regional Committee of the National Security Corps that Heinrich Schwannze should be granted a pardon."*

The pardon was granted in March 1948. Less than a month later, the Uherské Hradiště District Office of the State Security Police opened a personnel file for an employee named Jindřich Švanc.

Dora asked herself again what exactly it was about this man that could have impressed them so much. What did he provide them with? Amid documentation testifying to his accepting an offer of cooperation, taking up his new employment, becoming a member of the party, several promotions, salary assessments, and leave of absence for participation in activities of the Revolutionary Trade Union Movement, there was nothing that offered an explanation. Or was there? Among papers of little importance, she found a commendation from a Lieutenant Kužela, Švanc's managing authority, *"For excellence in performance of an action with his former people."* Former people? This was the early 1950s. Could paranoia about plots against the state led by malcontents who had been hangers-on in Protectorate times have broken out even here, in the fields and vineyards of South Moravia, where people's thoughts were on their next tipple rather than coups d'état?

Maybe someone had let off his big mouth in the pub; maybe someone had offered the careless opinion that things had been better under Hitler; maybe that person had been an erstwhile sympathizer with the Germans whom Švanc, with his local knowledge, had recognized. That person would then disappear behind bars for many years, convicted of spying for an information service in the West, even for Gehlen himself. How many such people had been dragged from the pub table straight to the interrogation room, with its dull-green, blood-and-spittle-spattered tiles?

Naturally they denied it. But the information had to be wrested from them somehow.

This was one of Švanc's roles—and judging by the commendations he gathered, he was one of the best at it. He was the one who tested out the gimmicks they thought up in his department, such as the inserting of metal plates and a supply of electricity in the shoes of a person under interrogation, who would then squirm like a rag doll, eyes bulging and popping and producing drops of blood at the corners. They always tried to switch off the power before the treatment left too much of a mark.

"Thanks to the collective of Karel Kahrda, Antonín Líček, and Jindřich Švanc for its exemplary work." Then soon afterward a farewell to *"exemplary operative Jindřich Švanc,"* who was moving a few floors up, to the administrative department of the District Office of the State Security Police. After all, he was almost fifty and had a troublesome leg.

He was no longer in such good shape that he could take care, behind closed doors, of enemies of the young Socialist republic.

He held on to one case only—the one he had worked on since the beginning of his career. He had to give up the "GODDESSES" file: no connection between the goddesses and "his former people" had been established. But his pursuit of the goddesses did not end there. As it soon turned out, he had good reason to keep it up: one of them was exposed as an enemy of the state who caused economic losses by private enterprise and was reluctant to involve herself with the cooperative. The kind of person who wrought far-reaching and irreversible damage on the health of ill-informed Socialist citizens.

Surmena's case was concluded successfully in 1979.

A month later he put in for retirement. He had served longer than his allotted time.

Dora imagined the women in his office arranging a little party for him. They would have ordered open sandwiches and a few chocolate cones; after three o'clock they would have gone through to the conference room and opened a bottle of wine. In the early evening, when the hens had returned to their broods and the men, too, had tired of the office environment, Švanc would have left the building in possession of a stiff folder containing a piece of paper bearing the trite message "A heartfelt farewell to an outstanding operative" and the signatures of all his comrade colleagues. Dora was tangibly aware of how he must have felt. Good. He would have felt good, too, throughout his last seven years, walking his dog in the park near his Jarošov home, spending summers of well-earned rest at his new hillside cottage. A cottage with a splendid view of the Bedová, the Koprvazy, and the Černá.

So now she knew. There was nothing left to reveal. She had reached the end of the marked path; her own and Surmena's past was spread out before her. All she needed to do now was write up her study.

The Bedová

*I*t was the last day of July. Dora left and locked her office shortly after midday before going down one flight of stairs and knocking on the door of Lenka Pavlíková's office. Then they went together to the canteen in the basement.

Dora was in the mood to celebrate.

It was her last day at work prior to a month's leave, which she had been granted in order to complete her study. Four long weeks spent on the Bedová, near Jakoubek, whom she'd be able to visit nearly every day.

"Only a month? Is that long enough to get it done?" Lenka asked doubtfully.

They were facing one another over lunch trays with a floral pattern. Valerian, Dora realized; Surmena had made Jakoubek drink a tincture from its roots to calm his seizures.

Dora nodded and smiled. The details from Švanc's file were the last piece of the jigsaw of materials on Surmena she had collected eight years ago. She was confident she would complete her first draft of the study in the next month.

"Klímová took six months," Lenka continued.

"Yes, but she was still collecting materials. Fortunately, I already have everything I need."

"Even all of the appraisals?"

"Yes. I'm really pleased with those. The consultant at the Center for the Treatment of Somatoform Disorders just happened to be working on a paper on folk medicine practices. He's so interested in the goddesses that we even went to Žítková together to meet some old folk who had been treated by them."

Lenka's eyes sparkled with encouragement. "That's amazing! It looks like you're about to vindicate the goddesses."

"It does, doesn't it?" said Dora, smiling. She pulled a dish of thick tomato soup toward her. "And to clear them of having collaborated with the Germans. Well, not all of them, but Surmena and a few others."

Steam rose from the hot soup.

"Did I tell you about the conclusions of the German team?"

Lenka shook her head.

"They were convinced they'd found remnants of Old Germanic gnosis in the practices of the goddesses. Apparently, their magic rituals resembled rituals of Old Germanic priestesses. It seems that such relics have survived in very few places—in enclaves of populations that were driven to the hills, where they remained cut off from civilization. The people of these close communities preserved the teachings of their ancestors, albeit in a form that was necessarily contaminated to some degree by Christianity."

Lenka thought for a moment. "I don't think that's a completely unknown theory. I've heard something about it before. It would be wonderful if it could be proven in the case of the goddesses! Do you think it will be?"

Dora shook her head. "I think it might be better than that."

"Better? How?"

"All indications suggest that what the Germans considered evidence of Old Germanic gnosis—types of incantations, the divination process, ways of treating and healing a client's subconscious and psyche in general, a respect for the mysteries of nature—has a great deal in common with the gnosis of the Slavs."

"Do you mean to say that they were wrong? That they misinterpreted the practices of the goddesses?"

"Not necessarily. Probably they were right. It's just that their hypothesis is consistent with what we know about the practices of the Old Slavic priestesses later known to scholars of Latin as *incantatorae*, meaning chanters of magical spells, mediators of magical practices and rituals, including the art of healing. Think of the mythical figures of Kazi, Teta, and Libuše, parts of a tradition that is surely much longer, and who had many successors. It is my belief that the goddesses of Žítková drew on the same knowledge as they did."

Lenka's surprise was apparent. She pushed away her empty soup dish. "So what are the goddesses a relic of, Germanic or Slavic gnosis?"

"That's just it. With so many features in common, I think the only logical explanation is a shared Indo-European basis. If my study can prove as much, the phenomenon of the goddesses of Žítková will take its place among the oldest cultural heritage of Central Europe."

Lenka's bright enthusiasm was a striking contrast to the dull risotto in front of them. But then she shook her head in disgust. "It's terrible, isn't it? Dozens of generations of bearers of ancient learning survive the advent of Christianity, the witch trials of early modern times, the carryings-on of local priests and justice, and the scholarly inquiries of the SS. And then they're eliminated by the Bolsheviks."

Dora nodded in sad agreement. "I'm afraid you're right. But I'm going to try one more thing. When I finish my study, I'm going to send it to Irma Gabrhelová's daughters, the last Kopanice goddesses. They're the only ones who can revive the tradition. Even if they do, though, I doubt they'll be able to remember much—they left their mother when they were very young."

They went on with their meal in silence until Dora asked, "How did things work out with your uncle? The one you found on the lists."

Lenka sighed. "I let it go. He's nearly eighty, and my father is seventy-five. I didn't have the heart to have him exposed and dragged through the dirt. Although he did some pretty rotten things, according to his file. Informed on anyone he could."

"I'm sorry to hear that," said Dora.

Lenka made a grim smile and shrugged. Dora was struck by the compassion in this gesture.

A few minutes later they left the canteen. Lenka clapped Dora on the shoulder, gave her a cheery smile, and wished her luck with the writing. Then she headed off in the direction of the stairs.

After that, Dora stayed on the Bedová.

In the mornings, she wrote. In the afternoons, she made short visits to the hospital in Uherské Hradiště, where Jakoubek was receiving intensive care. By now she knew all the patients, nurses, and doctors, who had helped her accept that Jakoubek would forever be dependent on others for care she could not provide.

Now that she had come to terms with this, her life was spread between her work, visits to the hospital, and evenings in Žítková that more and more were enlivened by the presence of Janigena.

Dora pulled away from her computer and leaned back in the wooden seat.

Things had come to a head between them in the past few weeks. How were they to go on? For years hardly a word had passed between them; now they were swimming in words, like the aftermath of a tsunami. On their Saturday evenings together, they debated their future wildly and passionately. How should they live, now that they could spend more than just Saturday nights together? Dora would be here for a whole month. A week earlier Janigena had buried her husband; now she was free.

Dora stretched, got up from her desk, and crossed to the window. From the cottage on the Koprvazy opposite, lights shone into the night. She smiled in its direction. Her new neighbors had been there several months now. They were strange people, but that was perhaps to be expected. No local people would live under that service tree.

She wondered if anyone had told the newcomers about it. She supposed not; if the couple had known, she doubted they would have taken to the half-dilapidated cottage and its cursed tree with such enthusiasm. Each carrying a child in a sling, they pranced about their yard in flowing tie-dye clothing. A few months ago she had heard that they intended to turn the place into an eco-farm. Dora didn't mind what name they gave to working a field.

In recent weeks a number of sheep and a goat had appeared on the hillside opposite, and the field had been seeded. Although it all ran like clockwork, when the strange couple made their occasional appearances down in Hrozenkov, the locals tapped their foreheads. Dora couldn't really blame them. The couple had come to Moravské Kopanice with an obviously positive attitude about the hills, the soil, and village life, but they didn't fit in with the locals. It was as if they were from a different century; they were naive to the point of childishness, and the benevolent smiles never left their faces. Everything that is natural is pure, they seemed to be saying. But the folk up here drank spirits, very few of them still toiled in the fields, and they drove up to Žítková in cars—mostly only on weekends, as all but the oldest of them worked elsewhere.

Dora continued to look out of the window until the lights opposite were extinguished. She checked her watch: it was after midnight—time to switch off the computer and go to bed.

She turned back to her laptop with a sense of satisfaction. The draft of her book was nearly two hundred pages long, and it was almost complete. She took care to save the file. A few more movements of the mouse, and the screen went black.

She had just switched off the light when she heard the creak of the gate and footsteps on the front path. Her body felt a surge of excitement, as though her blood were suddenly awash with adrenaline.

It could only be Janigena. So she *had* come! She felt a rush of hope that today things would turn out differently—that Janigena would not leave. Dora hurried to the double-bottomed chest, her laptop in her hands. In this chest Surmena had stored her few valuables; now Dora placed things in here she would hate to lose. For the event that someone other than Janigena would force entry to her home, she told herself, before she heard the familiar staccato knock.

I was on my way from the office for the municipality of Žítková, where they had let me use the landline to telephone Alžběta Baglárová's cottage. Also, they had shown me on an aerial map and pointed out the path I should take—down the hill, through the woods, into a neighboring valley, then back up again, toward the Rokytová hill. It sounded pretty straightforward, but I'd been walking for more than an hour and was starting to worry. At the office they had told me that I'd be there in no time.

I pulled my mobile out of my bag, intending to call to make sure that I was heading in the right direction. Not a chance: zero signal. I was lost in the hills, heading into the woods, looking for a woman who had perhaps forgotten that I was coming to see her. But they had told me that her memory was excellent, even though she was eighty-seven.

I put the phone back in my bag and walked onward and upward. The woods were pleasantly cooling; had it not been for the eerie silence, I might even have begun to enjoy myself. But amid the endlessly monotonous murmur of leaves and the confusion of greens and browns, my thoughts became ever darker. Mugging. Rape. Murder. Fortunately, the woodland became less dense, and the trees gave way to an apple orchard. This had to be the place. Rokytová began where apple trees appeared among the spruces, they had told me down at the office. This was where Alžběta Baglárová—the locality's oldest resident, who had known the last goddesses—would be waiting for me.

"Welcome," said a voice as I approached the little house. At first it was not clear to me where the voice was coming from. Then I spotted her face at the narrow, curtained window. "Bring some water from the spring over there, will you? You'll be needing a refreshing drink."

A hand holding a glass pitcher reached out of the window and gestured toward a spreading oak. Next to this a small roof had been built to protect the spring.

On handing over the filled jug, I was admitted into the cottage. The room—apparently the only one the cottage contained, with the exception of the vestibule—was sparsely furnished. Mrs. Baglárová waved me onto a chair. Then she went to the kitchen cupboard next to the oven and produced two small glasses. As she shuffled up to the table, I looked into the jug of spring water; there were small translucent shapes swimming about in it.

On getting to the table, she, too, looked into the pitcher.

"Impatient, aren't you? Couldn't wait for the trickle to fill it, could you? Well, you'll just have to go again."

She grabbed the jug and, with a flick of the wrist, emptied its contents out of the window. She was right: I'd had no patience with the thin trickle; besides, the water beneath it had appeared just as clean.

When I returned, the glasses had been joined on the table by a dish containing sliced apple.

"From the orchard here. Nice and sweet. Help yourself."

"Thank you."

"You're here about the goddesses, then?"

I nodded. She poured out the miraculous spring water. Good for the eyes, apparently. Good for one's health altogether.

"They send your type to me quite often. Journalists and students. If they'd published everything I told them, there'd be no need for any more of your visits. You could've read all about it. But the few newspaper articles I got to see were worse than useless. No one has ever written about them properly. What do you need to know about them for?"

"A book," I said.

"Which university?"

"It won't be an academic study," I replied, not without embarrassment. Perhaps she would think the whole idea a little undignified. "It'll be a novel."

"I see," said Mrs. Baglárová thoughtfully. "That needn't be a bad thing. At least it'll be easier for folk to understand."

I smiled.

"So what do you know already?"

I thought about how I should answer. Where should I start? Studies in Czech and European social anthropology and ethnology and the ethnography of magical practices across the world, from Inuits to shamans? A master's dissertation on the Kopanice region written at universities in Prague and Brno? Books on esoteric, magical, and religious themes and the history of witch trials and inquisitions? Archives of the Czech and Slovak Republics?

"I've read Hofer and other ethnographers of the nineteenth and twentieth centuries. And I've read Jilík, a lot of newspaper articles and academic studies, and the chronicles of Žítková, Hrozenkov, Vyškovec, and Vápenice."

"Have you come across anything by a woman called Idesová? Dora Idesová?"

This question caught me unawares. It hadn't crossed my mind that this old woman might know a researcher from the Department of Ethnology at the Academy of Sciences in Brno.

"Well, yes, I have. Several studies in academic journals, and most of all the dissertation she wrote on the history of the goddesses of Žítková. She found materials going right back to the seventeenth century and bringing her up to Hofer's time. I read the dissertation not long ago. It covers a lot of ground, but to tell the truth, I don't think it . . . makes the most of its potential."

"And that's all?"

"What do you mean?"

"Have you found anything else by Dora Idesová?"

"No. That's all she published, at least under that name. How come you know her? She's not exactly an authority in the field . . . Sorry, what I meant to say was . . . I didn't realize her work had such a broad readership."

"She came from these parts."

"Really?"

"Yes, she lived a few fields from here, on the Bedová. You might take a look at it—you can get back to Hrozenkov over the Bedová. And then you can give me a ring and let me know whether the place is still empty or there's already someone living there. After the trouble, you know, no one wanted to live there. But it's a few years ago now, and maybe folk have forgotten."

I didn't know what she was talking about. I didn't wish to pry, but I couldn't stop myself from asking, "What trouble?"

Mrs. Baglárová cleared her throat. "They found her there dead."

I gasped. "She's dead? But she was still young!"

"Someone attacked her and broke her neck. That's all I know. I don't suppose the police know any more than I do. They didn't have a lot to go on. Not many clues, I mean. It happened in the summertime, and it was a few weeks before they found her. She didn't come here all that often, you know. Sometimes she stayed in Brno, sometimes with her brother in Hradiště. So no one here thought to look for her. They started looking only after she hadn't turned up at work for a while. And they found her on the Bedová. What was left of her, I mean. Since then they've had telephone lines installed in these out-of-the-way cottages."

I was speechless.

"Don't you fancy the apple?"

I thanked her and shook my head. She placed a slice in her own mouth and said between chews, "No one here was much surprised by it."

"By what?"

"That she died like that. You're researching the goddesses, you say? Well, then, write this down, young lady. We can talk about it now. Now that it's all over. D'you know what they say?"

I shook my head again.

"That Dora Idesová's family was cursed. She was the daughter and niece of goddesses, you know. Surmena, her aunt, and Justýna Ruchárka, her grandmother, were well-known goddesses. Maybe it was in Dora too. But if it was, she never made any use of it. She was of her generation: times had changed, and young women didn't want to be goddesses anymore—it wasn't modern, and the normalizers looked down on it. But it didn't help her that she didn't practice, just like it didn't help Surmena that she did. D'you know how Surmena died? In the madhouse. And Dora's mother, Irena? Her own husband killed her with an ax. And Dora? My old man used to tell me how the lads in the pub would put bets on how she would meet her end. But even they couldn't have thought up what actually happened."

"Did you say cursed?"

"So you don't believe me? Dora didn't believe it either. She wasn't even supposed to know about it. Surmena did all she could to keep it from her. But Dora came to it by herself. She went on about it for so long that Irma told her about what Mahdalka had done to them."

"But wasn't she a goddess too?"

"Of course."

"I thought goddesses were—how should I put it?—supposed to help people."

"That's right, they are. But not all of them do. Josifčena Mahdalová was a different kind of goddess. She'd stop at nothing. She put a curse on her own mother, sisters, and niece, and she watched as one after the other died. I'm sure Surmena's end gave her the greatest pleasure.

Surmena spent her whole life trying to break that curse, you know. But how to go about it? She could have tried to destroy Mahdalka and all her kin, but she was hardly likely to do that, was she? But maybe she did. From what Surmena told me, a few days after the liberation, when people were fleeing to the wood, she found Fuksena's body. Mahdalka was Fuksena's guardian; Fuksena was Mahdalka's successor. Was she really dead already, or did Surmena help her on her way? We'll never know. Fuksena had a sharp tongue. She and Surmena surely exchanged words about Mahdalka's curse. Who can say what happened after that? The times were wild, and Surmena could have come by her injury in all kinds of ways. Maybe she really did have a fall, as she said. All I know for sure is what I saw for myself. She came hobbling to me with a child, a girl just a few months old, whom she couldn't bring herself to kill. I had to get the child out of here, she told me, as far away as I could. Fuksena's child was Fuksena's successor, and Mahdalka's too. It was associated with the curse, so if I didn't get it out of here, something bad was bound to happen to it. I tried to convince her that it was surely enough for the child to grow up in ignorance of where she was from and what was inside her. Surmena was unconvinced until I pointed out that old Josifčena would go easier on her if there was a danger of harming the child.

"With my sister's help, we got in touch with a childless couple over Brod way, and that's where we sent her. Mahdalka prowled the village like a wild-woman, pouncing on anyone she suspected of knowing something. Everyone just shrugged. The word got around that the child had been taken by a beast of the forest. But no one would have spoken up, even if they had known something: people didn't like Mahdalka. Surmena and Mahdalka never went anywhere near each other, so I don't know how Surmena got Mahdalka to understand that something would happen to her only remaining successor if she didn't keep clear of her own kin. Anyway, Mahdalka did as she was told.

"After the girl grew up and learned that she wasn't the natural child of the couple in Brod, everything changed. They had all kinds of problems with her, and in the end, she ran away from home. I knew this from my sister, who sometimes talked about her when she came to visit me. So I told Surmena—no one but Surmena, I swear to God. I've no idea how Mahdalka found out that Surmena no longer had any power over her successor, but find out she surely did, because after that, things started to happen. Within the year, Irena was dead. Not many years later, Surmena, too, was gone. Just before Surmena's trial, the trial she never returned from, my sister wrote that the girl—by now a woman—had come to her senses and got in touch. Apparently, she was settled here in Kopanice. Can you believe that? My heart almost stopped when I found out. So she had found her way back to her own people.

"I broke the news to Surmena, and it knocked her sideways. She muttered over and over about what a misfortune it was. But she wasn't given the time to do anything about it—a few days later, they put her away. So she couldn't stop the evil from reaching Dora. Thank God Dora didn't have children! At least this way, there's an end to it."

I sat there breathless, taking in the old woman's words. Even in my wildest dreams, I never would have come up with a story like this.

"It's such a pity that Dora died before she could publish her work on the goddesses. She gathered material on them her whole life long. No one knew more about the goddesses than she did. From both sides: she lived among them, and she studied them for years. There'd have been nothing left for you to do—you'd have found it all in Dora's work. Has the cat got your tongue? Is there nothing you want to ask me? You should take the chance while I'm still all right. Some afternoons when the pressure's low, I feel so rotten that I have to lie down. So ask away."

My throat was tight as I took out my Dictaphone and the notepad in which I'd prepared two pages of questions in dense handwriting. I stared at the questions and didn't know where to begin.

It was almost five o'clock when I left. Mrs. Baglárová was keen for me to get going; if I lost my way, I'd still have time to find my way out of the woods before nightfall.

As I slowly descended the Rokytová, the sun was already behind the ridge, the small settlement engulfed in the shadows of the trees. So the ethnographer Dora Idesová was the last descendant of the goddesses, and now she was dead, murdered.

A coincidence?

Or a curse?

The thought of it made me shudder.

The woods received me by the murmur of its leaves. The long branches of the first spruces swayed and rocked in my direction. *Come on in.* I caught myself wondering why they were moving when there was no wind. The meadow I'd just crossed had been perfectly still. The trees were not to be trusted.

A kestrel flew over the ridge and called out in alarm, a sound that was carried far into the distance. I was overwhelmed by an indescribable anxiety.

AUTHOR'S NOTE

Although this book is based on the life stories of real Žítková women, it does not concur with reality in every detail. Out of respect for these women and, above all, for members of their families who still live in Žítková, Starý Hrozenkov, and Drietoma, I decided to use real names in some cases only. Many of the stories and episodes here are ascribed to other goddesses, and some of them are fictitious.

Some Žítková families will surely recognize themselves in the novel. In certain cases, names have been changed (e.g., the "Mahdal" family); with older characters (e.g., from the time of the goddesses' disputes with Josef Hofer, i.e., 1900–1947), real names have been used. The novel's Surmena is a fictitious character; there was no real-life Terézie Surmenová. There was a goddess who went by the name of Surmena, but her surname was not Surmenová. The story of the Surmena of the novel is not that of the real-life Surmena; any resemblances are entirely coincidental. It is said that the real-life Surmena collaborated with the Germans. I wasn't able to discover much about her, but I liked the name, so I used it. The real-life Surmena's actual name may or may not have been Surmová or something similar. The novel's character Irma Gabrhelová is inspired by the real-life Irma Gabrhelová, the last goddess of Žítková. The words spoken by Irma in the book are not identical with words spoken by the real-life Irma. I used the name "Irma Gabrhelová" out of respect for the last bearer of Žítková's goddess tradition and the wish that her name would not sink into oblivion.

The documents used in this book are fictional, albeit based on materials in existence; there are many such materials in the archives of the Czech Republic and Slovakia.

The dead man's speech (pp. 230–231) quotes loosely from Josef Hofer's *Kopaničářské povídky* (Olomouc, 1923). The stories of Kateřina Shánělka and Kateřina Divoká (pp. 66–76) have been taken from *Krevní kniha městečka Bojkovic*, edited by Antonín Verbík (Uherské Hradiště, 1971); the text has been modified. The materials of the witches' files (pp. 274–280) draw on *Himmlers Hexenkartothek. Das Interesse des Nationalsozialismus an der Hexenverfolgung*, edited by Sönke Lorenz (Bielefeld, 2000). I found materials on the case of Magdaléna Mlkva (pp. 246–255) in the State District Archive in Uherské Hradiště; names and places have been changed. I cited an article from a 1938 issue of the magazine *Pražský ilustrovaný zpravodaj* (year 19, no. 34), also from the State District Archive in Uherské Hradiště (archive for municipality of Žítková). MAFRA, a.s. provided an article from the eastern Moravia edition of the newspaper *Mladá fronta DNES* (vol. 12, no. 10) on January 12, 2001. The National Archive of Slovakia in Bratislava provided an official document.

I am grateful to Jiří Jilík for the wealth of information in his books *Žítkovské bohyně* (Alcor Puzzle, 2005) and *Žítkovské čarování* (Alcor Puzzle, 2006). I owe a debt of thanks, too, to many contemporary witnesses and staff of museums and archives. For their special help, I wish to thank Mr. Ivan Bergmann of the State District Archive in Uherské Hradiště, Mrs. Anna Borová of the Wallachian Open Air Museum, Mrs. Dana Klempová of the National Archive of Slovakia in Bratislava, and Mr. Stefan Olejniczak of the Department of Witchcraft Trial Files of Archiwum Państwowego w Poznaniu. I wish to thank David Kovařák, PhD, for the idea behind the work, for his role as a specialist consultant in history, and for providing me with much important information in the course of my research. I thank Dr. Libor Gronský and Dr. Norbert Holub for specialist advice on matters of psychiatry and Mgr. Vlaďka Jabůrková for specialist advice on legal matters.

ABOUT THE AUTHOR

Photo © 2012 Vojtěch Vlk

Kateřina Tučková is a Czech playwright, publicist, biographer, art historian, exhibition curator, and bestselling author of *The Last Goddess* and *Gerta*. She has won several literary awards, including the Magnesia Litera Award (for both *Gerta* and *The Last Goddess*), the Brno City Prize for literature, the Josef Škvorecký Award, and the Czech Bestseller Award. Kateřina is also the recipient of the Freedom, Democracy, and Human Rights Award from the Institute for the Study of Totalitarian Regimes, and of the Premio Salerno Libro d'Europa at the book fair in Salerno, Italy. Between 2015 and 2018, she was a founder and first president of the Meeting Brno festival, focusing on international and intercultural dialogue. Kateřina currently lives in Prague and Brno, Czech Republic. Her books have been translated into nineteen languages, and her latest novel in Czech is *Bílá Voda*. For more information, visit www.katerina-tuckova.cz/en/.

ABOUT THE TRANSLATOR

Andrew Oakland was born in Nottingham in the Midlands of England in 1966. He is a graduate in German from the Universities of Southampton and Nottingham. From 1994 he taught for ten years at Masaryk University in the Czech city of Brno, where he still lives. He has been a freelance translator from the Czech and the German since 2005. Novels in his translation include Michal Ajvaz's *The Golden Age* and *Empty Streets* (both published by Dalkey Archive Press; the former was a Fiction Finalist at the 2011 Best Translated Book Awards), Radka Denemarková's *Money from Hitler* (Women's Press, Toronto), Martin Fahrner's *The Invincible Seven* (Pálava Publishing, Brno), and a new rendering of *Mikeš*, Josef Lada's classic Czech work for children (published as *Nico* by Albatros, Prague).